Mortal Shield

A Novel

Mortal Shield

A Novel

by Thomas A. Taylor

Tom Taylor
6 | 6 | 08

Southeast Missouri State University Press • 2008

Mortal Shield
A novel by Thomas A. Taylor

Paper: $19
ISBN: 978-0-9798714-1-2

Cloth: $35
ISBN: 978-0-9798714-0-5

Copyright: Thomas A. Taylor
First published in 2008 in the United States of America
by Southeast Missouri State University Press

Southeast Missouri State University Press
MS 2650, One University Plaza
Cape Girardeau, MO 63701

http://www6.semo.edu/universitypress

Cover photograph by John Michael Flynn
Cover design by Liz Lester

The cover depicts a real, world-class protector whose identity is secret because he continues to protect at-risk VIPs all over the world.

Dedication

To GDE, MLA, JMA, JDS, JGA, GTH, MSL, FAL,
JBU, REA, EML, BNI, GTO, DFA, EPR, and RMA:

You continue to set the bar for public-figure protection operations.

To former Governor Christopher "Kit" Bond, who formed the original
seven-member security detail of troopers within the Missouri State
Highway Patrol in 1973:

No detail ever had a finer protectee.

Acknowledgment

There are five men who have contributed greatly to this book.

My good friend and mentor, Gavin de Becker, is—without any doubt whatsoever—the world's top security expert. When I first met Gavin, he was delivering a presentation on "advanced threat-assessment and management" at the Central Intelligence Agency. His audience included the top experts from the Secret Service, FBI, and CIA. At the conclusion of his program, I instinctively knew that if I wanted to run the most effective security detail for any governor in America, I had to learn everything Gavin could teach me about the threat-assessment business. And he has, never failing to be available, answering any question, and stirring up more innovative and provocative thoughts than my brain could easily manage. Many of our exchanges and conversations have been woven into the dialogue of this book. Gavin reviewed *Mortal Shield* and greatly improved one of the key scenes.

Another good friend and mentor, Lt. Col. Dave Grossman, was also kind enough to review *Mortal Shield* and offered many constructive comments, which greatly improved my work. I can think of no man who knows more about combat and the impact it has, physically and psychologically, on human beings. His books *On Killing* and *On Combat* are must-reads for every warrior in America. I am forever grateful for his continuous work with the law-enforcement and military community. God only knows how many lives he has saved with his heart-wrenching and mind-stretching presentations to police officers and soldiers all over the world. As Dave quotes from an ancient Greek philosopher, "Of every one hundred men, ten shouldn't even be on the battlefield, eighty are nothing but targets, and nine are real fighters. We are lucky to have them. They the battle make. Ah, but the one, one of them is a warrior. And he will bring the others back alive!" Dave is the warrior the philosopher was talking about!

My agent, Richard Curtis, has made the transition of this book—from an idea in my head in 1985, to the final product in your hands today—a reality. Thanks to Richard for his critical eye, aggressive style, and unerring judgment. Thanks to Dave for introducing my work to Richard!

My editor, Daniel Zitin, helped me turn a 600-page manuscript into a 300-page finished product. He has a keen eye for what makes a great story.

Author and friend Morley Swingle took time out of his busy schedule as Cape Girardeau County Prosecutor to scrub the manuscript and offered an extraordinary number of ideas to improve my work. If Morley ever gets tired of chasing bad guys, he would make any author an outstanding editor! His historical novel, *The Gold of Cape Girardeau*, puts his writing talents on display.

I also want to thank Dr. Susan Swartwout and the professionals at Southeast Missouri State University Press. They've made the effort worthwhile.

Thanks also to my good friend Dr. James P. McGee for his medical expertise. Few men have packed more thrills into a lifetime of adventure. Doc is a licensed pilot, SCUBA diver, psychologist, paratrooper, Marine Force Recon vet, FBI hostage negotiator, and wears a World Series ring for his work as team psychologist to the Baltimore Orioles. He makes Indiana Jones look like he's standing still.

Foreword

In this novel, you're going to find more truth about protecting public figures than you have read in any other book, or seen in a movie, or in any supposedly factual news account. That's because Tom Taylor knows the landscape of protection—he's one of the pioneers who mapped it.

Tom has been part of the protective operations for Mikhail Gorbachev, Margaret Thatcher, Henry Kissinger, and every U.S. President since Gerald Ford. When you saw television coverage of the Pope visiting America, you might not have seen Tom Taylor, but he was there. He has handled protective assignments in Russia, Japan, Korea, China, Ireland, India, Italy, Turkey, and Puerto Rico.

Tom served two terms as president of the National Governors Security Association—and I'll interrupt my recitation of his bio to make my main point: He is the ideal person to take you into the reality of protectors.

I met Tom at Central Intelligence Agency Headquarters in 1994. We were both there to participate in the Government's first Threat Management Conference, a gathering of experts committed to improving the science and art of threat assessment.

At CIA, Tom and I talked about Arthur Bremer, the man who shot Alabama Governor and presidential candidate, George Wallace. Bremer had written in his diary: "I want a big shot and not a little fat noise. I am tired of writing about it, about what I was going to do, about what I failed to do, about what I failed to do again and again."

Most assassins, you see, do not fear they are going to jail—they fear they are going to fail. While stalking Richard Nixon, Bremer wrote, "I'm as important as the start of WWI. I just need the little opening, and a second of time."

To see how right Bremer was about needing just a second of time, think of every assassination you've ever heard about. For most people, a few major ones come to mind: Julius Caesar, Abraham Lincoln, John F. Kennedy, Martin Luther King Jr., Mahatma Gandhi, Indira Gandhi, Anwar Sadat, John Lennon, Israel's Prime Minister Rabin.

When measured from start to finish, all the attacks just mentioned—combined—took place in less than one minute. Since most attacks have begun and ended in less than five seconds, time is a central character in these pages, just as it is in the real world of high-risk protection.

You're about to board the precarious rollercoaster protectors ride every day—sometimes smooth as you climb up high, sometimes getting to take in the impressive view for a moment, and sometimes diving into a steep freefall, with turns you learn about only after they've spun you around a few times.

Many novelists have to artificially create a world in which danger might be around any corner; in Tom's world, danger is a constant fact of the matter. Protectors at his level get a front-row seat to world events, and in *Mortal Shield*, you too get an intimate view of power, fame, politics, risk, fear, and heroism. The next time you see the real counterparts of the characters in this book, you'll know their essence much better.

Thanks, Tom, for a terrific novel, and for keeping your keen eyes open years before you knew you'd be writing one at all.

—Gavin de Becker, bestselling author of *The Gift of Fear*

Author's Note

Executive protection is one of the most misunderstood occupations on the planet. This is evidenced by Hollywood's portrayal of bodyguards as being huge, mindless brutes with barely enough intelligence to change their socks. And this hackneyed portrayal is largely responsible for the public's inability to appreciate the position. Certainly, those Neanderthals exist, but to be successful, executive protection requires intelligent, highly trained professionals, utilizing the best tactics and equipment available.

Bodyguards—especially the really good ones—stand on the brink of chaos and stare intently into the pit of an unknowable future, attempting to foresee coming events and, in some cases, change them. Defending against an attack is as much a mental occupation as physical, and every bit as challenging as defending against a lawsuit or disease. I know. I was a bodyguard for four Missouri governors over nearly a quarter century. I have worked and trained with world-class security personnel for presidents, governors, mayors, CEOs, and heads of state all over the world. For the most part, these professionals quietly carry out their assignments every day without incident.

Mortal Shield is a realistic portrayal of protection work, which captures the everyday challenge of guarding high-level VIPs. *Mortal Shield* delves into the hearts and minds of bodyguards, the dignitaries they protect, and the opponents they attempt to foil. Every situation, every person, and each piece of equipment described in this book is a truthful depiction of the real world. It was my goal to write a book that would enable the reader to experience real-life protective operations, so realistic that they would find themselves in harm's way. The reader will never look at public figures or their bodyguards the same way again!

In the real world, attacks against public figures in the U.S. are most likely to be undertaken by lone assailants. Firearms are the most likely weapons of attack, and handguns are far more likely to be used than long guns. Attacks are most likely to be at close range (less than 25 feet), and no major public figure has been harmed from greater than 263 feet (President Kennedy). Attacks are slightly more likely to be indoors than outdoors. Over half of the attacks have occurred at the public figure's home or office, and a little less than half while they were in or around their cars. The most striking statistic is this: nearly all public-figure attack incidents are over *in less than five seconds*. In other words, within just a few seconds, all the damage that will be done has been done. That is the ultimate challenge that bodyguards face, and it takes a special individual to do it well.

Any reference to actual locations or to real public figures is to lend authenticity to the story. For security reasons, I have changed certain protective procedures and operational secrets used to protect specific VIPs, conduct undercover investigations, and render explosive devices safe. Any resemblance to actual groups or persons (living or dead), or events, is entirely coincidental and purely the invention of my fertile imagination. The public figures depicted in this book are not intended to portray any of the VIPs I protected during my career. The views expressed in this book—while shared by many of those involved in the protection business—are those of the author, and do not reflect the official policy or position of the Missouri State Highway Patrol, the Governor's Security Division, or the National Governors Security Association.

—Thomas A. Taylor

Book One: Changing of the Guard

Stratagems are like invisible knives, which are hidden in the mind of man and flash out only when they are put to use. . . . He who is versed in the application of stratagems can plunge an orderly world into chaos or bring order to a chaotic world; he can produce thunder and lightning from a clear sky.
> —Harro von Senger, foreword, *Tricks in Combat: The 36 Stratagems*

Politics and protection don't mix.
> —Kenneth O'Donnell, aide to President John F. Kennedy

Prologue

Bible-thumpers, thought Missouri Conservation Agent Dwayne Stoddard. *Two men, two women, and a kid. No, two kids*, he realized, as one of the women shifted around, exposing an infant balanced on her hip. The group was gathered around a cheap card table in the center of their crude campsite. The two men held open Bibles. The group appeared to be discussing the meaning of a particular verse. A corkscrew of smoke drifted off their small fire pit.

Stoddard shifted the small Tasco 8 x 25mm binoculars and surveyed the rest of the campsite. Two large camouflaged tents were set up under a small stand of cottonwood trees. A gray Ford van and a blue Dodge Durango were parked next to the tents. Both vehicles bore Texas plates. He smiled. *Bet there's not a Missouri hunting license in the bunch.* It was time to go welcome them to the Show-Me State. *Ha! Show me your hunting license, Sparky!*

Stoddard keyed the mike clipped to the shoulder of his uniform and said quietly, "Ten-seventy-seven, Ripley County."

Five seconds later, the twangy drawl of Ripley County's dispatcher, Martha Sue Greene, came back in response, "Ripley County. Go ahead, ten-seventy-seven." Her thick Arkansas accent was the source for constant harassment, but she enjoyed the attention and did nothing to tone it down.

"I'm going to be out of my vehicle for a while checking on some campers down by the river," Stoddard reported. "Just off the road near Turkey Bend." It wasn't an exact location, but if he needed help, they'd be able to find him.

His radio crackled, "Ten-four, ten-seventy-seven."

Stoddard always tried to be fair, but he was also aggressive in enforcing the wildlife conservation laws; he usually led his district in arrests, and he had no intention of letting this one get away. Wilfred Hopkins, the Ripley County Circuit Court judge, often dismissed

Stoddard's cases for incomprehensible reasons incoherently explained from the bench. It didn't help Stoddard's success rate in the local courtroom that he had arrested the judge's son twice for poaching deer. Old Hopkins's obstructionism only stoked a bigger fire in Stoddard to bring in more cases to force the old jurist into making a fool of himself.

His fifteen-minute, long-range surveillance had provided him a lot of information about the group below. He had watched enough people living in the woods to instinctively know who they were and what was important to them. This was a group low on money, poorly educated, dependent on one another, peace-loving, and harmless.

Stoddard broke cover on the ridge above the campsite and walked down the grassy logging road leading to the Bible-thumpers' camp. As he came into their view, the group stopped talking and turned in his direction. They all stood at the same time. For an instant, Stoddard thought they were going to run off into the woods. He held up a hand in greeting.

One of the men offered a friendly smile. He took a few steps toward Stoddard. "Greetings, my brother. Welcome to our humble camp." The man was about thirty-five. A five-day growth of beard covered his narrow, hatchet-shaped face. He looked fit enough to throw Stoddard over his shoulder and run around the campsite without too much trouble. Despite the crisp cool air, the man wore a green sleeveless sweatshirt and blue jeans that hadn't been washed in weeks. Stoddard noticed a ten-inch knife hanging in a black nylon sheath on his right side.

"Thanks," Stoddard said in a pleasant voice. "I don't see many campers around here this early in the year."

"We like to camp under God's clear, blue skies year-round," the man said, waving a hand in the fifty-degree air. "Winter's running late this year. I think they call it an Indian summer."

"Indian summer's in the autumn," Stoddard said with a pleasant smile. "This is global warming, but there's an arctic cold front coming. In the next few days, it'll drop thirty degrees." He nodded toward the animal carcasses near their fire pit. "Looks like you caught some lunch."

The man again smiled. "Yes, God blessed us today with three fat squirrels. You're welcome to stay and help us eat them."

15

"No, thanks," Stoddard replied. "You just made it under the wire. Squirrel season ends day after tomorrow. I just need to check your hunting permit and I'll be on my way."

The group stared at him in silence. "Hunting permit?" the man finally asked.

"Yes. Whoever shot the game needs a nonresident hunting permit."

"And if we don't have one. . . ?" the man asked carefully.

"No big deal. You'll pay a fine, that's all. About one hundred twenty-five bucks in this county." It was roughly twice what the permit would have cost them.

The man again smiled. "I suppose we could do that. We don't have much cash, though."

"You'll just have to follow me to jail," Stoddard stated matter-of-factly.

"Jail?" His smile had gone stiff.

Something in the man's voice struck Stoddard as odd. He wondered what they were trying to hide. He looked at the others. None had spoken a word since he'd arrived. They stood there frozen. *They've never been confronted by an officer in uniform*, Stoddard thought.

Stoddard explained, "Since you're from out of state, you'll have to post an appearance bond on the charges. Then you can go. No big deal."

The man's demeanor suddenly changed. A fire came alive in his dull brown eyes. "This isn't right, officer. We aren't hurting anyone, yet you come into our camp and threaten to take us to jail. You have no right to do this! We just want to be left alone." He reached up and plucked at the shoulders of his sweatshirt, as though adjusting the collar. The other man casually took three steps to his right, where the table no longer separated him from Stoddard.

Stoddard noticed the movement and held up his hand. "Don't freak out on me, guys. I'm afraid you have no choice." His firm tone was intended to leave no room for negotiations. Stoddard prided himself on his ability to control people with his voice.

The group spokesman relaxed. "Oh, we all have choices, Agent Stoddard. Even you. You could turn around right now and walk away, like none of this ever happened. No one would be the wiser."

Stoddard was surprised the man had noticed his nametag. A chill ran through him. "No, I don't have a choice, Mister . . . what's your name?"

The spokesman took a step forward, and Stoddard put his hand on the grip of his holstered .40 Glock weapon. The man held out his hand to introduce himself. "You can call me Phineas," he said. Stoddard relaxed and accepted the steely handshake. The small man was strong. Stoddard noticed that Phineas had a blue tattoo of the letter "P" with a bar through it on his right biceps and the number "25" below it. The tattoo seemed vaguely familiar, but Stoddard couldn't immediately place where he'd seen it before.

In a blinding motion, the man used his left hand to lock Stoddard's beefy right arm, and drove him to the ground in an arm-bar takedown. Stoddard tried to throw the man off, but his locked elbow was painfully twisted to the point of becoming dislocated, pinning him to the ground. Stoddard felt the razor-sharp edge of the man's knife at his neck. He stopped resisting for fear of getting his throat cut.

"Agent Stoddard," the man scolded gently, "I tried to tell you to leave us alone. Now look what you've made me do."

The second man ran forward, knelt on Stoddard's back, and pulled the Glock out of the agent's holster. He used Stoddard's handcuffs to secure his hands behind his back. Only then did Phineas move the knife and roll Stoddard over. They stripped him of his car keys, pager, cell phone, radio, wallet, pocketknife, and two 13-round magazines.

"He's wearing a vest," Phineas warned his partner, referring to Stoddard's body armor. "If he tries anything funny, shoot him in the face."

Stoddard closely examined his two attackers, committing their faces to memory. The second was in his mid-thirties, taller than the first, but with a stocky build and lumberjack arms. His wavy brown hair and short beard covered a square head. His deep-set blue eyes were shifting nervously between Stoddard and Phineas, as though he was unsure what would happen next. The women and children had moved out of Stoddard's view. He would be hard put to describe them in detail, since he had been focused on the men. Stoddard silently vowed that when . . . if . . . he escaped this situation, he would see these men put away for a long time.

"Who the hell are you guys?" rasped Stoddard, twisting his hands and testing the grip his handcuffs held on his wrists. They were so tight he had no hope of pulling out of them. If given the chance, he would use the handcuff key hidden in his left boot to get loose.

Phineas leaned in close to Stoddard. His eyes were dull and lifeless, like two tarnished copper pennies. His body odor was as sharp as his hunting knife. "Hell? Wrong direction, Agent Stoddard. It would be more accurate to ask, 'Who in Heaven's name are you?'" He then whispered, as though imparting some dark secret, "Me? I'm Beowulf. Robin Hood. Saint George. William Wallace. I'm all these great men. We belong to the same order of priests."

Priests? Now it all came together. The tattoo! He had seen it once in a law-enforcement intelligence meeting. The "P" with the cross through it was the mark of the Phineas Priests. Stoddard remembered an FBI agent explaining that men did not "join" the Phineas Priesthood. It was not a group to which you pledged allegiance, paid dues, or had secret meetings. It was a *calling*. A man *became* a Phineas Priest, just as someone might become a jihadist in the Middle East. Stoddard tried to remember everything the agent had said. The "25" tattoo referred to a Biblical verse in the Book of Numbers, Chapter 25, in which Phineas found an Israelite man having sex with a Midianite woman, and killed the race-mixing couple by driving his spear through them. According to the passage, God then pledged an everlasting priesthood to Phineas and his descendants. Modern-day Phineas Priests carried out sanctions against those who violated God's laws, especially when it came to abortion and race mixing. They generally committed bank robberies, bombed abortion clinics, and assassinated homosexuals, but they were capable of carrying out acts of violence against anyone who violated their interpretation of God's word. According to FBI assessments, Phineas Priests were among the most violent and deadly terrorists in America.

Stoddard and Phineas eyed one another. "You're going to kill me, aren't you?" Stoddard asked quietly.

Phineas shrugged. "If it's God's will that you die today, you will die. If not, you will live. Your fate is out of my hands. I am merely a tool of God." He studied the agent for a moment. "We have a dilemma here. If we let you live, you and your government forces will pursue us."

Stoddard considered his response. "What if I promise to keep this between you and me? Man to man?" He had no intention of letting these criminals get away with assaulting him, but he couldn't get the vision out of his head that he was about to die an excruciating death. A frantic voice in the back of his head kept whispering, *This is it! This is it! This is it!*

"Swear to me before God that you will not pursue us if we let you live," demanded Phineas. He stared directly into Stoddard's eyes.

Stoddard stared back at his captor without blinking. "I swear! I swear to God!"

Phineas looked around the campsite, as though searching for something. "Here's the deal," he announced finally. "God has given me no sign to kill you, so you must be speaking the truth. We will secure you to that tree over there and call in your location later when we're safely out of the area. You can tell your bosses whatever you want, but you will not describe us in any way. You will blame this on 'Mud People.'"

Stoddard knew that Phineas was referring to nonwhites: blacks, Hispanics, Asians, any race other than Caucasian. Phineas Priests believed that only whites were God's chosen people.

Phineas shook his head, "If you're lying, we'll kill you and your family for the crime of blasphemy." He looked at his partner. "Give me his wallet." Phineas took out Stoddard's driver's license and examined his address. "I know where you live!" he stated forcefully, shaking the license in front of Stoddard's widening eyes. He slipped the license into his pants pocket.

"I won't tell," Stoddard swore. He felt a tremendous sense of relief. At this point, he would have said anything to get home alive and see Tamiko and Joey again.

Suddenly, Phineas's eyes narrowed. He stared in mounting rage at the open wallet and then back to Stoddard. He held out the wallet and pointed to a picture of Stoddard and his family. "What race is your wife?" he demanded.

Stoddard felt a sense of impending doom. His eyes moved to the picture of his beautiful Japanese wife. They had met when he was in the Navy, stationed in Hawaii. He refused to answer the question or look at Phineas. He could only stare at Tamiko's flawless olive skin and almond-shaped eyes; even now he felt the desire to run his fingers through her short, coal-black hair. In the picture, his six-year-old Joey, clearly a mix of both their races, sat with a huge grin, flashing his newly applied braces. Stoddard felt his face growing red. It was a sign from God.

With his right boot, the zealot pinned Stoddard's face to the cold earth. He drove the razor-sharp blade of his knife through the side of Stoddard's neck, unleashing a frantic scream through clenched teeth and a spurt of bright red blood as carotid arteries were severed. Stoddard's powerful body arched, trying to get away, but Phineas used his full weight to hold the agent down. He sawed through Stoddard's throat, nearly cutting off his head. He stepped back to watch the agent's death throes. Blood poured onto the ground, forming a steamy blackish pool. The others gathered around the still squirming body and joined hands, as Phineas led them in a quiet prayer of thanks to God for revealing the agent's immorality.

Phineas looked at his partner. "You wanted us to drive through the night to Gunner's place, but I thought we should stop here for the night. I should have listened to you."

His partner shook his head. "No one would have expected them to find us here. We had to drive off-road to get here. It was an unlucky break for us." He eyed the dying agent. "More unlucky for him."

When Stoddard's body finally succumbed, Phineas bent down and examined the dead agent. He felt no more emotion than if he had just brushed a harmless insect off his arm and squashed it beneath his boot. He ran his finger along the jagged crevice that marked Stoddard's throat and drew the symbol of the Phineas Priesthood on the agent's forehead in blood. This would mark Stoddard as an enemy of God and prevent him from entering Heaven. He carefully cut the triangular Department of Conservation shoulder patches off Stoddard's uniform. They were trophies, signifying the defeat of an adversary. They would be added to the patches of six other law-enforcement officers, who had made the fatal mistake of getting in the way of the servants of God.

Chapter 1

January 15, 1200 hours
State Capitol Building
Jefferson City, Missouri

The man stood poised on the dais, dressed in tails and top hat, his left hand resting on his family Bible and his right hand raised in the air. His handsome features were set in a proud and confident expression, and the furthest thought from his mind was that someone might show up to kill him.

Across from the man, Missouri Supreme Court Justice Louis R. Trombino stated solemnly, "I, William Ulysses Stovall, do solemnly swear . . ."

The man repeated the words. The heat from their breaths billowed out into the twenty-degree air in white, brittle clouds. They looked like two firebreathing dragons, preparing for battle.

Next to Governor-elect Stovall stood his attractive blonde wife, Patricia, and their two beaming children, nineteen-year-old Lance and twenty-year-old Heather. Mrs. Stovall, dressed in a peacock-blue outfit with a matching pillbox hat, laced her hand through the governor-elect's left arm. They presented the portrait of the ideal American family, and the public had agreed, electing him with an overwhelming 61 percent of the vote.

Trombino continued, " . . .that I will support the Constitution of the United States and of the State of Missouri. . . "

Again Stovall echoed the words, meaning every syllable with all his heart.

Standing fifteen feet behind Governor-elect Stovall was a man in a black, camel-hair topcoat, unbuttoned despite the cold. His hands were not shoved into the pockets to stave off the freezing temperatures, but rather held out in front of him at waist level, fingertips touching. It was a position of readiness. He was relaxed, yet poised for action. His solid frame appeared stocky, since he wore a thick layer of Kevlar under his white dress shirt. He wore thin, black gloves. Even with them on, he could draw and fire his weapon, if necessary. He would have preferred to wear sunglasses on this bright and clear day, but he knew it would make him stand out, since none of the other VIPs on the inaugural platform were wearing them. A close examination would have revealed a clear plastic tube extending out the back of his shirt, running to a flesh-colored earpiece in his right ear. The man was not focused on the ceremony. Lieutenant Simon Godwin, director of the Governor's Security Division (GSD) for the Missouri State Highway Patrol, was focused instead on the five thousand people who had come to the ceremony, alert for that one individual who might show up to do more than watch the new governor be sworn into office. Of the 170 law-enforcement officers assigned to the inaugural security detail, none had a more vital role in preserving the safety of the new governor.

Godwin was a no-nonsense manager who took the protection of Missouri's chief executive very seriously. He knew that most assassins throughout history simply walked up to VIPs, shoved a pistol into their chests, and pulled the trigger. That was not likely to happen here. Access to the platform was strictly controlled and the crowd had been screened for weapons. Those assassins who preferred a little more distance between them and their targets normally utilized a bomb, but the platform had been carefully swept with bomb dogs. Only a few assassins relied on the more unsure means of a knife or a sniper's rifle. Except for the attacks on President Kennedy, Martin Luther King Jr., Medgar Evers, and a few others, snipers thrived only in Hollywood. For some unknown reason, nearly all such attacks in the U.S. had taken place in the South. But there was an increased threat level for Godwin's new protectee today, and the risk that a sniper would be tempted by the huge, outdoor ceremony was increased. So Godwin was relying on his elite Special Emergency Response Team (SERT) countersnipers, perched atop the Capitol Building, to reduce the risk that a sniper would succeed.

Godwin now heard the voice of Corporal Philip Barr, the SERT spotter, over his earpiece. "TOP to all units: I've got a white male on the roof of the Broadway Building! He's carrying a black nylon case." Godwin looked up toward the white granite building, but he couldn't yet see anything on the roof. From their higher elevation, Barr and his sniper, Trooper Rocky McWilliams, watched the man from their Tactical Observation Post or TOP. Barr was looking through powerful binoculars and McWilliams through the 3 x 9 power scope on his H&K sniper rifle. "He's about thirty-five years old," Barr continued. "He just put his case down . . . I can't see it . . . he's watching the inaugural platform . . . now he's taking something out of the case."

Godwin did some calculations. The average distance for a shot by a police sniper was seventy-five yards. Based on the position of McWilliams and the man on the roof of the Broadway Building, this shot would be roughly twice that distance, still well within McWilliams's range. A piece of cake.

Trombino continued the oath, " . . .and I will faithfully demean myself. . . "

With a puff of white steam, Stovall pledged, " . . .and I will faithfully demean myself. . . "

To his right, Godwin saw Sergeant David Armstrong moving toward him. Armstrong was assigned to the First Lady, and he would respond to protect her and the children in the event of an emergency. While Godwin considered Armstrong a little overzealous at times, he had to admit that the governor's wife was in good hands. Armstrong left no stone unturned when it came to making security arrangements. Other detail members often teased Armstrong by referring to him as "Mr. Secret Service." Armstrong took it as a compliment and only smiled. Godwin motioned for Armstrong to hold his position, as he waited for the assessment of his countersnipers. It wouldn't look good if they ran and tackled the governor, only to find that the man was out feeding the pigeons on the roof.

Trombino quoted, " . . .in the office of Governor of Missouri. . . "

Stovall responded, " . . .in the office of Governor of Missouri. . . "

Godwin's eyes shifted across the open plaza to the roofline of the white granite building. Now he could see the man's head and shoulders, facing in the direction of the platform. As the man again bent down to his case, Godwin shifted his weight to the balls of his feet, ready to move. He mentally rehearsed his options. If the man indeed had a weapon, he and Armstrong would quickly move to the governor-elect and his family, push them down behind the bulletproof lectern, and wait for Trooper McWilliams to take the man out. All they had to do now was wait, knowing officers were responding to the perceived threat on the building. Godwin heard the command post dispatching a reaction team.

" . . .so help me God," Trombino concluded.

Stovall repeated forcefully, stressing each word, " . . . so . . . help . . . me . . . God!"

Now was the ideal moment for a sniper to strike, with the governor-elect standing in the open. Following the oath of office, Godwin knew the National Guard cannons on the other side of the Capitol Building would fire a nineteen-gun salute, which would cover the blast of a sniper's weapon. If that opportunity were missed, the governor would remain in the open for another fifteen minutes, while he delivered his inaugural address.

As the man stood up, Godwin already knew what Corporal Barr's voice was saying in his ear. "He's only got a camera."

An instant later, the command post responded, "We have the Capitol Police on the line. The guy is an assistant attorney-general who works in the building."

Godwin heard the commanding voice of his boss, Major Stuart Moss, immediately respond, "Moss to Command Post. I want that reaction team to contact the suspect and verify his identity." Moss was in charge of security around the inaugural platform, and he certainly didn't want anything to happen to their new leader.

"Ten-four, Major," replied the radio operator.

Godwin relaxed slightly and continued to scan the crowd. *Dummy!* he thought. *The jackass should have known better. He's going to feel really stupid when he finds out he was within a three-pound trigger pull of dying today.*

Governor Stovall was kissing his wife. The cannons from Battery D, First Battalion, 129th Field Artillery opened fire. Godwin knew it was coming, but he still felt a shock of adrenaline at the sound. This was still an ideal time for someone to strike, so he couldn't let the noise distract him. As the last cannon shot echoed across the open plaza, he heard the thundering approach of four military F-16 fighter jets from the 131st Fighter Wing of the Missouri Air National Guard, screeching overhead in their fly-over of the ceremony. As the faces of the crowd turned skyward to witness the impressive sight, Godwin's eyes continued to rake the crowd. The fatal attack on Egyptian President Anwar Sadat in 1981 had begun when everyone was distracted by a military fly-over. As the roar of the jets dissipated, Governor Stovall took the podium and began his inaugural address.

Godwin tuned it out. It was nothing but a distraction from the job he had to do. He had been protecting the Stovalls since election day—only about one hundred days—and still felt he had a lot to learn about the family.

William Stovall had exploded onto the political scene unexpectedly. As a popular and aggressive U.S. Attorney for the Eastern District of Missouri in St. Louis, Stovall had made a name for himself after 9/11 by relentlessly pursuing every lead his Joint Terrorism Task Force (JTTF) developed. He swept up an Al-Qaeda terrorist cell plotting to carry out multiple suicide bombings during a Rams football game, dismantled an Islamic terrorist fundraising organization in a wealthy suburb in northwest St. Louis County, and broke the back of a radical neo-Nazi group plotting to attack a synagogue. After the leading Republican and Democratic Party gubernatorial candidates eviscerated one another with attack ads for six months, the public was disgusted with them both. Stovall surprised everyone when he quietly threw his hat into the Democratic ring, but he did little campaigning outside the St. Louis area. Mere months before the election, the Democratic frontrunner went into the party's state convention haunted by rumors of infidelity and misuse of campaign funds. Stovall brought the splintered party factions together and captured the spotlight, along with his party's nomination. He seized the momentum with a series of high-profile campaign events that propelled him ahead of his Republican opponent, and he never looked back. The public saw him as fresh, dynamic, honest, aggressive, and sexy. He was everything the other candidate—an intelligent but boring career politician—was not. And he was an expert in homeland security.

Since the election, Stovall's transition team had been typically frantic and unorganized—too many things to accomplish, in too little time, with too many inexperienced people. Governor Stovall seemed to be a likable guy, although he could fly unexpectedly into a tirade at seemingly insignificant problems. Team-member Don Romanowski had noticed the tirades were preceded by a noticeable reddening of Stovall's face. He dubbed it "the crimson tide." Godwin was hopeful he would be easier to protect than the outgoing governor, who delighted in throwing the security detail knuckleballs. His tricks included everything from hiding from the officers who followed him during his daily walks to waiting until the last minute to tell them his plans. Godwin eyed Governor Landham in the front row of VIPs. His former boss seemed to be zoned out, not listening to Stovall's words any more closely than Godwin was. *He's probably thinking, "I'll finally be rid of these damned bodyguards,"* Godwin thought with a slight smile.

He returned his attention to the crowd. Before he knew it, the ceremony had ended. The benediction was pronounced at 1225 hours, exactly as planned, and everyone remained standing while Governor Stovall was escorted off the platform toward his new office.

Godwin fell in beside the governor and whispered into his wrist mike. "Ringmaster is leaving the stage, en route to Octagon," referring to the codename for the Governor's Office.

Godwin heard his second-in-command, Sergeant Romanowski, respond, "Copy your traffic. The route is secure." Godwin knew his team had examined every foot of the walking route back to the Governor's Office. Every spectator had been scrutinized, every trash can removed, and every possible threat considered. He began to relax for the first time this day.

As the long line of VIPs approached the building entrance, Sergeant Romanowski took the point and Sergeant Armstrong fell in behind the First Lady. From this day forward, for as long as they held the office, the Stovalls would be shadowed by their bodyguards.

"Governor Stovall! Governor Stovall!" came the excited cry of two college-aged girls, standing behind a row of metal racks holding back the overflow crowd. The governor looked over, giving them a flawless smile and waving his right hand. Fifty more feet and he'd be inside the safety of the building.

"Can we shake your hand, sir?" one girl cried, jumping up and down. "We came all the way from Poplar Bluff."

Stovall suddenly changed course and headed in their direction, unable to resist the Siren's call of enthusiastic supporters. Patricia Stovall smiled patiently and followed him. Godwin had seen the governor-elect do the same many times on the campaign trail. He always responded to the wishes of crowds, despite the fact that Godwin had cautioned against this dangerous habit.

"Ringmaster is going to the crowd!" Godwin whispered into his wrist mike. *Damn, I hate rope-lines,* he thought.

"Rosebush is following." It was Armstrong's voice, referring to the First Lady. "Has this crowd been screened?" Godwin already knew the answer.

"No," Romanowski said. "They're outside the screened area."

The crowd saw them coming and began to surge against the barrier, hopeful of shaking the new governor's hand. The officers were confronted with dozens of waving hands and shouted greetings.

Perched high on the press platform behind the crowd, camera crews for the many news organizations in attendance zoomed in on the action. The governor's staff liked them to be close, security liked for them to be far away, and the governor didn't like them at all. Nonetheless, the press was a necessary part of the political system.

Positioned at the governor's right shoulder, Godwin arrived at the rope-line just as Stovall shook the first girl's hand. Mrs. Stovall squeezed in next to her husband's left side, and Sergeant Armstrong hovered behind her with his left hand up at shoulder height, as though he were about to scratch his ear. His right hand was positioned just behind her right shoulder, not quite touching her. His eyes searched the crowd for any hazard.

Both girls were grinning and bouncing up and down. Godwin could see that both were wearing backpacks over their coats. He decided the girls were harmless and scanned the tightly packed crowd around them. Their boyfriends stood behind them, also smiling. Godwin couldn't see their hands, but they looked harmless, too. He returned his gaze to the girls. They were both holding the governor's hands, thanking him for his strong support of higher education. Governor Stovall promised to do all he could in these tight-budget times, then tried to pull out of their grasp. Godwin saw that they were not letting go, and he reached in to gently break their hold.

"Watch the green coat at nine o'clock!" SERT spotter Philip Barr warned over their earpieces. From his high-ground position, Barr was looking almost directly down into the crowd and could see movement and behaviors hidden from the officers on the ground. Godwin spotted the young, unshaven man in blue jeans and an army fatigue jacket several feet left of their position. He didn't look like he belonged at this event. The man had pushed his way to the front of the crowd and was digging into his coat. His eyes burned with intensity.

Romanowski moved in on the man and said, "Let me see those hands, sir." Godwin saw the hand emerge with a copy of the inaugural program and a Sharpie pen, as though he wanted the governor's autograph. Godwin thought, *He'll be selling it on Ebay within the hour.*

Suddenly Godwin heard Armstrong shout, "Pie!" just as an arm flashed past his face. It belonged to one of the boyfriends. The hand shoved a cream pie into the face of the governor, who grunted in surprise. Godwin froze for an instant; he heard Mrs. Stovall say, "Oh, my God!"

At the same instant, the arm of the second boyfriend shot forward with another cream pie aimed at Mrs. Stovall's face. Sergeant Armstrong grabbed Mrs. Stovall's shoulder and was pulling her out of the way when her pie came flying over the second girl's shoulder. Armstrong easily blocked the shot with his raised left hand, smashing it instead into the side of the girlfriend's face. Armstrong then spun the First Lady around and scooted her toward the safety of the Capitol Building.

Lieutenant Godwin was not responding as quickly. He lunged after the first pie-thrower, but the boy pulled out of his grasp and was swallowed by the crowd. The girls continued to hold the governor's arms, refusing to let him escape. They were now chanting, "Shame on you, Governor Stovall. Stop supporting animal experimentation!" Godwin shoved himself in between the girls and the governor, who stood in stunned silence, a white mask of custard obstructing his vision. Godwin tried to move Stovall toward the door and safety, just as Romanowski arrived to help from his point position.

"Son of a bitch!" Stovall suddenly shouted, slapping at his face and sending a spray of animal-activist pie into the crowd. The crowd around them gasped in shock. The governor was oblivious to the fact that a dozen news crews were capturing every second of the spectacle on videotape. Stovall shoved Godwin away from him and angrily wiped the mess from his face. As his face was revealed, Godwin saw the crimson tide was at flood stage. When his eyes were clear, Stovall fixed Godwin with the murderous glare he'd previously used on defendants in the federal courtroom and barked, "You moron! Get away from me!"

Chapter 2

Simon Godwin sat in the waiting room outside the office of the Superintendent of the Missouri State Highway Patrol. Few people realized that part of the mission of the Highway Patrol was to provide security for Missouri's governor and First Family. After the well-publicized inaugural pie-tossing, however, the number of people realizing the governor's safety and well-being rested with the Patrol had dramatically increased.

The silver Cross pen in Godwin's hand was poised to make a note in his planner, but the thought had escaped him. He twisted the pen closed and secured it on the inside pocket of his dark business suit. He glanced at the digital readout of his Casio watch. It was 5:08. Past quitting time. The building was emptying out and shutting down. Soon it would be just him and the bosses.

The waiting room outside Colonel Andrew DeWitt's office reminded Godwin of the one outside his dentist's office, but this one made him even more uncomfortable. He sensed that he was about to get more than his teeth drilled. On the other side of this door, in the next several minutes, words would be exchanged that could forever affect his career with the Patrol, but Godwin vowed to keep his cool. He might end up looking like a gazelle after a fracas with a pride of lions, but they wouldn't fire him. He was too hard to replace. Nobody else would put up with the shit he endured every single day.

Colonel Andrew DeWitt greeted him at the door with a forced smile, and Godwin took a seat facing the colonel's windows and the panoramic view across the manicured grounds of the GHQ complex. A quarter mile away, light traffic skimmed over Highway 50. The U.S. and Missouri flags flapped in a gentle breeze outside the windows. On the horizon Godwin could see a white plume of steam, rising from the cooling tower of the Callaway County Nuclear Plant, twenty miles away.

DeWitt was the perfect picture of a Patrol commander. At forty-one, he was young for a superintendent. Erect, handsome, and smart. You could carve wood with the crease in his pants. He seldom let anyone leave his office without mentioning his service as an Army Ranger, wounded in the 1993 firefight in Somalia—the famous "Blackhawk Down" battle. The wall behind his large oak desk—what DeWitt referred to as his "I-Love-Me" wall—was covered with pictures and plaques celebrating his successful career. He had only been head of the Highway Patrol for two months, having previously served as Major in command of the Field Operations Bureau. Following Stovall's election victory, the previous colonel had retired unexpectedly for a second career in the Department of Homeland Security. He and Stovall had clashed swords too many times in the past for there to be any hope the new governor would ask him to continue as the Patrol's superintendent. Governor Jonathan Landham had selected DeWitt from a short list of five applicants to serve as interim commander, until Governor-elect Stovall took office and selected his own superintendent. DeWitt was anxious to convince the new governor that he was the right man to hold the permanent position. That made him dangerous and unpredictable. The winds of change were blowing at gale force through the GHQ complex.

Seated across from Godwin, Major Stuart Moss gazed at him steadily. His expression said, *I didn't know this was coming*, which worried Godwin further. Godwin considered Moss to be one of the best commanders he had worked for during his twenty-five-year career. Moss was politically savvy, but rumor had it that he was on the outs with DeWitt and was not an influential member of DeWitt's inner circle.

To Godwin's right sat Lieutenant Colonel Hal Looney, a likable man who had been promoted far above his abilities. He was now little more than DeWitt's "yes-man," but they had been classmates and longtime friends. To the more cynical members of the Patrol, they were known as "Da-Wit" and "Da-Half-Wit." Looney's eyes dropped to his legal pad when Godwin looked at him. Tension filled the room. All these men carried weapons. An outsider might have predicted a gunfight was about to break out.

This wasn't going to be good. They seldom called him in for good news. Godwin lifted his collarbone two inches to present a professional, confident appearance, but under the large oak table his right leg was pumping up and down. It felt like he had snakes slithering around in his gut. He leaned forward slightly, placed his hands together on the table with his fingers lightly touching, and shifted his poker face in the direction of Colonel DeWitt. The room was silent.

"We didn't come out looking very good yesterday," DeWitt said. He tapped the front-page picture of the *Jefferson City News Tribune*, which showed a close-up of Governor Stovall's pie-covered face, shouting at his shocked detail leader. It looked like he was getting ready to bite Godwin's face off. The headline mocked: *Let Him Eat Cake!* "Anyone who missed the paper," DeWitt continued, "can just turn on Fox, CNN, or any of the broadcast channels. It's a slow news day. No truck bombs exploding in the Middle East. Your detail is a laughingstock."

Godwin had seen the footage that morning as he got ready for work. The local station had played the loop over and over, in agonizing slow motion. The single second that separated their reactions now became three or four seconds. It clearly showed him reacting too slowly, while on the other side of the governor, Sergeant Armstrong responded quickly and effectively, blocking the attack on the First Lady and whisking her away from the threat. It was a classic "what to do" and "what not to do" captured in the same piece of footage. Protective details all over the world would be studying it in training classes and pointing out the stark contrasts. Godwin was only slightly relieved that DeWitt had not mentioned that Leno and Letterman had both joked about the attack in their monologues the night before. Godwin's face reddened. What DeWitt really meant was, *You are a laughingstock!* When Godwin said nothing, DeWitt added, "Why don't you tell us about it?"

It wouldn't matter what he said, but he said it anyway. He described how the girls concealed the pies in their backpacks; how their boyfriends pulled them out when a fifth member of their animal-rights group—clad in an army jacket—had rushed forward, drawing the attention of the detail; all except Armstrong. A sixth member of the group, who stood to their right, had captured the attack on video. The group had since uploaded the footage to YouTube, along with their communiqué of why Governor Stovall had been targeted. Now it was all over the Internet. Godwin complained that he had personally briefed Stovall and his staff on how to react to such incidents on the second day the detail had begun protecting him; that he should not overreact and make the incident worse; that he should be a good sport and make a joke, such as *I ordered this pie last week*. Godwin strongly stated, "It was Governor Stovall's reaction that made the incident 'a laughingstock.'"

When Godwin was finished describing what happened, and the inherent risk involved when a protectee went to an unscreened rope-line, DeWitt answered quietly, "I've been on the phone with Governor Stovall's chief of staff five times today." Godwin had used the same technique many times in his career. He knew how the rest of the conversation would go. DeWitt had a bitter message and he was feeding it to Godwin with a big silver spoon. "Yesterday was Governor Stovall's big day. He threw a victory celebration that cost nearly one million dollars, but this"—DeWitt tapped the paper again—"is all that's being covered today."

Godwin looked down at his hands. *Twenty-five years of stellar service*, he thought. *Two seconds of inattention and the rest is all forgotten.*

It was a bad deal and everyone knew it. The stink of it hung in the air, as sharp as exhaust fumes from a city bus. The only sound was the scratching of Looney's pen on his legal pad, as he dutifully recorded the words that would be used to justify their handling of Godwin . . . whatever that turned out to be.

DeWitt jutted his chin out. Those close to him knew it was a movement that always preceded bad news. He wanted to get this problem resolved. "The governor isn't happy and I can't say I am either. We've both lost confidence in you and—in your position—trust is everything."

Moss offered his last-minute plea. "Colonel, Simon and his people are under constant stress. When the governor comes out, they have to be smiling and focused, even when they have a sick child at home. Simon has faithfully served the Patrol and the Governor's Office for many years. He gets tested every single day. It isn't fair for him to get burned on something like this. He's one of the best detail leaders in America. Hell, when any of the other governor's details have a problem, they call Simon for advice. He's the best we've got."

It was a passionate argument, but DeWitt was looking at Moss as if from a great distance. He looked back at Godwin and said quietly, "We think it's best that you move on to another assignment."

The words landed heavily on Godwin. He looked out the colonel's windows—anything to get away, even for just an instant from this place and these men. What was happening to him felt almost unbearable.

"I've decided to transfer you into the Division of Drug and Crime Control."

Godwin looked at Moss and then back to the colonel. He flinched at the statement and his face burned, as though DeWitt had reached across the table and slapped him. He resisted the impulse to bring his hands to his face; it would be an obvious sign of how defeated he felt. He had expected an ass-chewing or even a written reprimand, but not this. It suddenly struck Godwin that his dedication to the governor's protection had become his whole life, costing him everything that was meaningful. The long hours, constant phone calls, and frequent travel assignments had destroyed his marriage of twenty-one years. One day he returned home from a five-day trip to Washington DC, only to find that his wife and children had left him. Now, with the loss of his position, he felt totally empty. It was like he had lost his purpose in life. His fingers squeezed into fists.

"I'm sorry," DeWitt said. "If you want to bust up the furniture, I'll understand."

Godwin slammed his fists on the table. It sounded like a shotgun going off. The commanders around him flinched. He corralled his rage. This wasn't their fault; they were just following Stovall's orders. "I'm sorry, Colonel," he said quickly, embarrassed by his outburst. He had just given them a peek at what was going on inside him—something you were never supposed to do in protection work. You always had to guard yourself, as well as the protectee. "I'll go wherever you want me to go, and I'll do a good job." He frowned. "I hope I haven't caused you or the Patrol any problems." He was a team player and they knew it. It was one reason why they had chosen him in the first place. "When do you want me to start at DDCC?"

"Tomorrow, Simon," DeWitt said. "You've done a great job for us. I hope you understand. Major Moss has arranged for you to take over the Intelligence Unit and Organized Crime. With your experience in security operations, he thinks you'll really be an asset. You're to report to Captain Douglas at eight in the morning." He added, "It wouldn't be a good idea for you to call the governor on this."

"No problem, sir," Godwin replied. The warning had been unnecessary. Godwin knew it would violate departmental policy to seek influence in any matter of promotion or transfer. He'd be jumping out of the frying pan into the fire. At the door, he turned to them and asked, "Who's taking over the detail?" When DeWitt hesitated, Godwin said, "Romanowski has worked his heart out for years. He deserves a shot. He's more experienced and dedicated. The detail won't accept anyone else."

Colonel DeWitt glanced around the table at the others. Then he cleared his throat, jutted out his chin, and said, "We have someone else in mind."

Chapter 3

"Why me?"

Sergeant David Armstrong was both confused and excited by the news. He knew he was qualified to run the Governor's Security Division, but he only had four years on the detail, one-third the experience of the assistant director, Sergeant Don Romanowski. The detail members would be upset at the unfair ouster of Lieutenant Godwin, who was viewed as a competent and fair leader, but Romanowski was even more popular. His stylish haircut and immaculate collection of business suits had earned him the same nickname as former mob boss John Gotti: "Dapper Don." He wore the title as proudly as he did the clothes. He had a dry wit that kept everyone—including the governor's staff—in a good mood. He was the most experienced and respected veteran of the detail. The GSD members would be outraged at his being passed over. This smacked of politics.

Colonel DeWitt gave him a serious look. "We—and that includes Governor and Mrs. Stovall—think the detail has gotten sloppy. We want someone who can shape things up. Bring the expertise and capability of the detail to a higher level than any other governor's detail in America. We think that man is you."

Armstrong thought his quick reaction during the pie attack hadn't hurt his standing with the Governor and First Lady either. He had prevented her from receiving a face full of banana cream. He knew that only a second or two had separated his reaction from Godwin's. One second had forever changed the destinies of both men. In protection work, "spending time" was an apt expression. Had Godwin not spent a few too many seconds of attention on the man in the army jacket, perhaps he would have seen the pie attack coming and stopped it in time. If Godwin had responded fast enough, this conversation wouldn't be happening. Time and distance. They were the two things security people fought to control. Too much of one or too little of the other could determine whether one lived or died. And they had to negotiate every second of time their principal spent in the kill zone and every foot of distance within which he was allowed to approach the general public.

Across the table, Major Moss was looking at him with his stony gaze. Armstrong could hardly believe that they were offering him the job. It looked like Moss was still trying to make up his mind.

DeWitt was saying, "Governor Landham was a low-key public official, and he demanded low-key protection. Governor Stovall was a U.S. attorney and an acclaimed terrorist hunter. He loves the spotlight and has a much higher profile than any other governor in Missouri history. He's taken strong stands on some of the most controversial issues in the state. His gun-control position has every militia group in the Midwest screaming about their Constitutional rights. As you know, he drew larger campaign crowds than any previous governor and more than his share of protesters, too. We can't get away with the same low level of protection we gave Landham. Whatever level of protection you were providing yesterday, we need you to double that today."

"I'll need more people," Armstrong said. Without Simon Godwin, there were only seven officers in the division, and they were authorized for twelve. "The detail is operating at nearly half-staff. The overtime is killing us. Everyone is exhausted and it's no wonder mistakes are being made."

DeWitt waved a hand. "I'm not talking quantity of protection. I'm talking quality. No mistakes. You need to delight your protectee, every day. I don't want any more middle-of-the-night phone calls from the chief of staff."

Armstrong shook his head. "I still need more people."

DeWitt squirmed in his chair. "Everyone's shorthanded, David. We're over eighty officers short on the road, and eight more just got activated for military duty. DDCC is thirteen investigators short. The only group close to full capacity is the Gaming Division." Armstrong knew casinos paid the salaries and expenses for officers in Gaming, so manpower shortages in that division were rare. In other words, DeWitt was saying, *We have plenty of officers to weigh dice, but can't afford more to help protect the highest elected official in the state.* "I can't give you more people. I can't even let you fill Godwin's position, at least not until the next recruit class graduates. Just make it through the next six months with what you have, then we'll reassess. The good news is we have plenty of money to pay overtime. Your people can work the extra hours. And field personnel in each troop will support you with backup when you travel around the state."

Major Moss grumbled, "The troop commanders will scream bloody murder."

"You let me handle them," DeWitt replied.

Armstrong considered his response. This was a rare opportunity for some hard-nosed negotiating. He had to make some tough decisions, but the situation left him with no other choice. "Then I need you to promote two of my people. Underwood and Davenport are at the top of the promotion list and both are long overdue."

DeWitt looked at Moss, who nodded. "You write them up and I'll sign them," DeWitt advised. "They'll be effective on the first of February, along with yours."

Moss smiled and gave Armstrong a nod of encouragement. He seemed to be impressed that Armstrong's first official act was to take care of his best people.

Armstrong decided to go for broke. "I also need to replace two of my people. One is burned out and the other doesn't have what it takes. If I'm going to operate at half-strength, everyone has to be the best in the business."

DeWitt and Moss again exchanged glances. Moss nodded again. "Who do you want to get rid of?" DeWitt asked cautiously.

At that moment, Armstrong's BlackBerry vibrated, and he read the digital message. "Hmm," he said. "Looks like the new governor wants to see me."

Chapter 4

"Have a seat, David," Governor Stovall said as Armstrong entered his executive office. "Octagon" was an impressive, oblong chamber, fifty feet long and thirty-five feet wide. To Armstrong's left, large windows commanded a panoramic view of the Missouri River and the bluffs beyond. The thickness of the bulletproof glass in the windows distorted the view slightly. To his right, four large panels bore life-sized paintings of famous Missourians: Major James Rollins, Susan Blow, Eugene Field, and Mark Twain. The walls were carved oak with the seals of the fifty states and their territories carved in a frieze. A set of double doors at the far end of the office led into the office of Chief of Staff Bradley Naylor, who now sat in an overstuffed chair next to Stovall's broad oak desk. He looked like the governor's guard dog, although he most closely resembled a Yorkie. Naylor's spindly arms lacked the strength to do two chin-ups, but he was arguably the second most powerful man in state government. Armstrong registered his curious gaze; he felt like an odd insect under a microscope.

"Good morning," Armstrong said politely, as he sat down in an ornate chair across from Naylor.

"Well, David," Stovall began with a smile, "how do you feel about your new assignment?"

"Quite a surprise, Governor. In fact, it kind of took everyone by surprise."

Stovall nodded, as though the matter had been out of his hands. "Yes, Colonel DeWitt thought we needed to make a change. I told him I thought you'd do a great job."

Armstrong nodded. "Thank you, sir. I'll do my best."

"I've gotten to know you a little since the election. I know you were born and raised right here in Jefferson City. You're the son of a circuit judge—a good Democrat—who's been a strong leader in the party for many years."

Armstrong gave him a stiff smile. *So . . . this was about politics!* He wondered if he should inform the governor that he—in fact—was a staunch Republican and would rather have someone slam a car door on his testicles than vote for a liberal Democrat. He decided to keep that piece of news to himself. Let Ringmaster assume that he had followed his father's political leanings. And that wasn't his father's only disappointment. Clarence Armstrong had always wanted his son to be a lawyer, and when David chose the Patrol as his profession, his father all but disowned him. David Armstrong hated lawyers almost as much as he did liberal Democrats. And seated before him was one of the most liberal Democratic lawyers he had ever met. Yet the idea of risking his life for Stovall didn't bother him in the least. This was his business, his mission, his calling. It was far above partisan politics. But Armstrong also knew that one reason he had volunteered for the Governor's Security Division in the beginning was to seek his father's approval, although their relationship remained cool to this day.

"Your father helped secure my nomination last summer." Stovall paused, then leaned forward. "David, I'll be honest with you, I'd like to air some concerns I have about the detail. The officers are doing a fine job, very professional and all that. But if Pat had her way, you people would all be gone by tomorrow. She hates security. It suffocates her. I want you to keep her happy. If she wants something changed, see to it."

"Yes, sir," Armstrong said.

Patricia Moody Stovall was jokingly referred to by outsiders as PMS. The detail members were very closemouthed to anyone outside the division about her temper. They referred to her privately as "F.L." for First Lady or by her codename "Rosebush," an appropriate moniker that described her outer beauty protected by her deadly thorns. The members were professional enough that the term "PMS" was never spoken. When asked about her disposition, Romanowski would simply shrug and say, "Hey, her middle name's Moody," as though she were genetically predetermined to behave that way. Armstrong would sit down with the volatile Mrs. Stovall today and get her side of things. He had heard rumors of her tirades, particularly from FBI agents who had worked in the St. Louis office. Her hatred of security personnel came from the contract security guards who protected the FBI building and the federal courthouse. When she attempted to hunt down her husband at those locations, she was constantly stopped at security checkpoints and asked to sign in, or empty her purse, or remove her shoes and jewelry. Her usual response to that indignity was to fly into fits of rage, describing in great detail the low level on the evolutionary chain from which all security personnel obviously came, which was somewhere between orangutans and wild boars.

Governor Stovall continued. "Personally, I like having you guys around. I never have to worry about parking the car, or gassing it up, or getting a speeding ticket."

The primary goal of any protective detail was to avoid encounters with inappropriate or dangerous pursuers. Armstrong wondered, *What about keeping you alive?*

A Highway Patrol investigator assigned to the JTTF team had told Armstrong that Stovall was a control freak, hampering agents with specific instructions on how to do their investigations. The FBI agents hated him. They said he was impossible to please, always finding fault with their work. When he got elected governor, the entire office breathed a sigh of relief that he was leaving. They threw a wild party at a cop bar to celebrate. *He's a real prick. Don't ever get on his bad side. Good luck trying to protect the guy. He'll micromanage your entire operation!*

"The detail is very convenient to have around," Stovall continued. "They take care of my luggage and tips. Actually, your detail saves me a lot of money in those areas. They get me bumped up to first class on commercial flights. All very handy, but they're always underfoot. I like for them to walk alongside me, not behind. But when I'm walking with the First Lady, I want them to stay way, way back. You can't let security control your life. A governor has to show the public that he trusts them."

Armstrong nodded. "I understand, sir, and I can assure you that it won't always be necessary for us to be close. But poor positioning of bodyguards is one of the primary reasons many attacks succeed. We should never be further than the closest member of the general public."

Stovall and Naylor exchanged irritated looks. "Bullshit! I chased terrorists for three years as the U.S. Attorney. Nobody's tried to kill me yet. Godwin and I went around and around over this issue. He briefed me on every threat that came in, but he was just trying to scare me. I'm not going to tell you how to run my detail, but I expect you to be there when we need you and gone when we don't."

This was going to be a little more difficult than Armstrong had expected. It was a common misconception among VIPs that their bodyguards could flit in and out of sight, like ghosts hopping from one dimension to another. Most assassins waited for the ideal time to launch their attacks, usually when the bodyguards were absent or out of position. In 1986, Swedish Prime Minister Olaf Palme dismissed his bodyguards for the evening and took his wife to see a movie. As they were walking home on the peaceful streets of Stockholm, an assassin shot him in the back and killed him.

"Besides," Stovall continued, "if someone wants to kill you and is willing to trade his life for yours, there's nothing you can do to stop him."

Armstrong cringed at hearing those words. It was one of the biggest myths about public-figure protection. When President John F. Kennedy stated those prophetic words shortly before his assassination, the myth was born. The theory was parroted as fact by the general public, the news media, protected VIPs, their staff, and, unfortunately, even some security personnel. In the popular movie *The Bodyguard*, actor Kevin Costner played former Secret Service Agent Frank Farmer, hired to protect rock star Rachel Marron, played by singer Whitney Houston. In one scene Frank admitted to Rachel, *If someone is willing to swap his life for a kill, nothing can stop him.* When Armstrong saw the movie, he scoffed at the scene. Farmer was supposed to represent a highly trained security agent and yet the character stumbled from one blunder to another. It was something Armstrong would never tell a protectee.

But while the words sounded profound, they were, in fact, ridiculous. If they had been true, Presidential assassination would have been the norm rather than the exception. In reality, assassins had to penetrate incredible obstacles to carry out an attack. They had—literally and figuratively—only one shot at success. Assassinations failed far more often than they succeeded. Kennedy was a brilliant politician, but he knew little about VIP protection, and it cost him his life. His premature death in Dallas was absolutely unrelated to his being an effective and successful politician.

Before Armstrong could dispel the myth, Ringmaster charged on to another topic. "I'd also like to see you promote Trooper Boatright as soon as possible. It'll score some points for me with the black caucus." Cameron Boatright was the only black officer on the detail.

This was a surprise. Armstrong had to scramble for an acceptable answer. "Governor, I'd have to see where he is on the promotion list. If we have other officers higher than Boatright, it wouldn't be fair to promote him over someone else."

"I asked Godwin to do it, but he said the same thing," Stovall muttered with a wave of his hand. "I'm just telling you it would help me out. If I need to call Colonel DeWitt to get it done, I will." He paused, then mumbled, "Maybe I shouldn't be dealing with a third-level manager in these matters." Armstrong's reply clearly hadn't pleased him. He was beginning to see a side of Stovall he hadn't seen before. The governor wasn't used to being told "no."

Stovall was already moving on to the next subject on his agenda. "We don't see the children much anymore," he said. "Lance is in his first year at Yale, and Heather is working for Lewis, Bolton, Benson, and Freed, in St. Louis. I think she'll get married this year or next. When they come home, you may need to assign someone to run them around, but otherwise, we've always wanted them to lead normal lives." Armstrong had heard that both were heavy drinkers. Lance's resumé already included one DUI arrest, and Heather could polish off a bottle of wine in nothing flat, just like her mother. He was glad they were no longer underfoot—at least most of the time.

Stovall had apparently run out of instructions. He glanced up at the large clock on his wall. "I think I have an appointment coming up."

Armstrong took his cue and stood up to leave the room. "Governor, I'll do my best to make things pleasant for you and Mrs. Stovall, but I want to maintain an effective operation. The best way to achieve that is for us to have a frank and honest relationship. If there's a problem with the operation, I'd appreciate it if you would let me know, so I can fix it."

"Don't worry about that, David," the governor assured him. "You'll be the first to know."

Armstrong was already wondering what he'd gotten himself into. He couldn't help thinking of a story he'd heard about a world-class security expert hired by the CEO of a large corporation. The expert quickly implemented a security plan designed to protect the CEO from kidnapping or assassination. Two years later, the CEO summoned the security expert to break the news that they were going to let him go, as a cost-saving measure. *Besides*, he was told, *there hasn't been one security problem since we hired you!*

"By the way," Stovall called after him, "if Scheduling hasn't told you already, I'm flying to Cape Girardeau tomorrow to attend that conservation agent's funeral. What's his name, Stockwell?"

"Stoddard," said Naylor. "The wife's name is Tamiko."

"Tamiko? What kind of name is that? Is she African-American?"

"Japanese."

"Well, remind me again before I get on the plane tomorrow."

Chapter 5

The sleek Cessna Citation jet dropped out of the clouds, tested the air rising off the runway, and gently touched down, as though it weighed less than a pound. The aircraft, codenamed "Crossbow," had been purchased by the State in 1998, at a cost to the taxpayers of $3.3 million. Stovall had fallen in love with the aircraft as soon as he laid eyes on it, but his travel budget was meager, so he applied bureaucratic creativity. The cost of his excursion today, to attend the funeral of Dwayne Stoddard, would be billed to the Department of Conservation.

As they taxied toward a line of distant hangars, Armstrong whispered into his wrist mike, "Crossbow is wheels down."

Trooper Bobby Davenport responded, "I copy your arrival. The Dock is secure." In protection parlance, "the Dock" referred to any place where Governor Stovall's vehicle—whether a car, boat, or airplane—would arrive or depart from a site.

Armstrong smiled when he thought of Davenport. The guy lived for one purpose and that was protective ops. The detail was lucky to have him. Davenport was perhaps the most intriguing member of the detail. Raised in St. Louis by an Irish father and Puerto Rican mother, his fluent Spanish and adventurous spirit landed him a job as a DEA agent in Bogotá, Colombia, at the tender age of twenty-three. He was given an M16, an armored vehicle, two bodyguards, and a driver, and told to go after the drug cartels. He fired his two bodyguards after his first week, because they marked him as a target worthy of assassination. He dismissed his driver after three weeks, once he learned the city himself, because the driver marked Davenport as a target worthy of kidnapping. For the next two-and-a-half years, he drove himself in the armored vehicle and worked cases deep inside Colombia, where most agents feared to go. He took down countless drug labs. After several cases against high-level drug figures, the cartel put a $100,000 price on his head, and he survived three assassination attempts in as many months. The last was a roadside bomb that blew his armored vehicle thirty feet off the road and flipped it over on its top. The DEA finally sent the young agent—against his profane objections—to a desk job in Washington, where he could cool his heels until the heat was off. After nine months fighting his bureaucratic bosses, Davenport—at the age of twenty-six—suffered a nearly fatal heart attack. He was put on medical leave and finally quit the agency the following year. Out of money, longing for his Missouri roots, and knowing nothing but law enforcement, he applied to the Patrol and was accepted after passing a stringent medical exam. He had been on the Patrol six years, with three in the division.

As Crossbow taxied to a polished stop, Armstrong peered out his window and saw a black Lincoln Navigator pull away from a nearby hangar, followed by a dark blue Ford Crown Victoria. Both vehicles stopped next to the aircraft. While the pilot opened the door and dropped the stairs, both drivers jumped out of their cars, opened the right-side car doors, and scanned the area for unusual activity.

The Navigator was a strategically armored vehicle, codenamed "Monitor." It was the primary vehicle used to carry the governor each day. Its armor was state-of-the-art—completely invisible inside and out. The fact that it was armored was one of the division's most closely guarded secrets. It could stand up to a fierce storm of small-arms fire, and even a small explosion, and remain mobile on its run-flat tires. It had all the amenities of a luxury vehicle: separate cell-phone lines in front and back, power outlets for computers, and GPS navigation. The armored windows even rolled up and down. In the back of Monitor was a First Aid Trauma (FAT) kit, which included a small oxygen tank and an Automatic External Defibrillator (AED). It was the same equipment used by the United States Secret Service for medical emergencies involving the President and Vice President. The division had one other armored vehicle, a more traditionally armored black Chevrolet Suburban, codenamed "Merrimac." It was older than Monitor, with thick Lexan windows that wouldn't roll down. It was most often used as a backup vehicle. The vehicles were named after the first ironclad sea vessels used in combat during the Civil War.

Their Crown Vic was an unmarked vehicle assigned to the sergeant in the local zone, borrowed today to provide follow-up protection.

Armstrong pulled on his dark suit coat as he strode down the stairway. He paused at the foot of the steps and looked toward Davenport, who nodded. The coast was clear. Davenport had driven down the night before with Trooper Cameron Boatright. Since 0530 hours, they'd been busy arranging the governor's attendance at the funeral. They had advanced the funeral home, washed and fueled Monitor, briefed the follow-up driver—a corporal assigned to the Cape zone—and drove both the primary and alternate routes that would get Governor Stovall to the funeral home as quickly as possible.

Governor Stovall was next off the plane. He stretched, shouted, "Thanks, Ron," to the pilot, strode to the lead vehicle, and took the right front seat, as usual. Without waiting for the others to deplane, Davenport got behind the wheel and prepared to depart. Armstrong stood post alongside Stovall's door, waiting for the other members of the party to load up.

Normally, protective details preferred their principals to ride in the right rear seat. Immediately after being elected, Stovall had informed Lieutenant Godwin, "I always ride shotgun, unless my wife is along." Armstrong didn't like it, but Ringmaster would not be swayed. It was typical of the many concessions protective details are compelled to make to gain the acceptance of the protectee. As long as the "body man" occupied the seat behind the boss, they could push the governor down if they came under attack and could also get out of the car on the same side as their protectee, once they reached their destination. Besides, up front Stovall had an airbag. In the horrific car crash that killed Princess Diana in 1997, the bodyguard in the right front seat was the only one to survive.

Once they were on the outer road leading to I-55, Davenport spoke into his radio mike. "Davenport to Boatright." The signal was transmitted through the vehicle's extender unit to an extender unit five miles away at their destination.

Boatright had remained at the funeral home to coordinate and secure their arrival. His voice responded, "Go ahead, Bobby."

"We're en route from Crossbow," Davenport advised him. "ETA in ten."

Armstrong looked at his watch. "We're going to be late," he predicted.

"Late!" exclaimed Stovall, swiveling around in his seat. "We can't be late for this funeral!"

It was Governor Stovall's fault. They had been scheduled to leave the Capitol at 0900, but they were "wheels up" twenty minutes late. Armstrong didn't say anything.

Stovall glared at Davenport, as though the lateness had been his fault. "We can't be late, Trooper."

Davenport roared down the on-ramp to I-55 and accelerated to eighty-five. "I'll do my best, sir," he said. Armstrong figured they would make it as long as they didn't get behind a school bus or slow-moving truck. He was learning that Stovall always ran behind schedule and expected the drivers to speed to make up for lost time.

Davenport was the best driver on the detail, perhaps the best on the Patrol. When the detail could spare him, he assisted the Training Academy as a pursuit-driving instructor at the Patrol's Emergency Vehicle Operations Course (EVOC). Periodically, he took the detail members to the track and put them through the paces. Backing, parking, skid pan, ramming, high-speed evasives, chokes, J-turns, and bootlegs. He set up some wicked ambushes and everyone loved it.

Stovall turned and looked at his Cabinet members. "I taught these guys how to drive," he informed them, as though the officers were not present.

In the backseat, Kyle Wright, Director of the Conservation Department, looked surprised. Troopers were supposed to be expert drivers without the governor's guidance. "Really?" he asked. "How so, Governor?"

"Right after I won the election, these guys drove me around at the speed limit everywhere I went. It drove me nuts. When they work the road, they drive over a hundred miles an hour on emergency blood relays. You know, when they take blood from one hospital to another for some emergency. So finally I told them, since they're hauling my blood, they should drive me the same way." It was such a bizarre suggestion that Wright laughed. So did Public Safety Director Lawrence Frisbie. Only Colonel DeWitt failed to smile.

Stovall twisted around in his seat and said, "I'm serious!" When Wright and Frisbie stopped laughing, Stovall said, "Tell me about this dead agent of yours."

Wright leaned forward in his seat. "The agent's name is Dwayne Stoddard," he said. "He's originally from Cape and had been an agent with us for six years. His wife is named Tamiko. They have a son, Joey, age six."

"Damn," Stovall grimaced. "Do we have any leads on these terrorists yet?"

"Nothing new, sir," Wright responded. "They're probably halfway across the country by now, in some Christian Identity compound or something. There's a nationwide broadcast. Maybe the FBI will turn up something."

"Will we catch them?" Stovall asked.

Before Wright could respond, DeWitt said, "Yes, sir. We'll get them."

"What's the drill?" Stovall asked no one in particular.

Normally a staff person accompanied him wherever he traveled, but there wasn't room on the plane this time. That left the staff duties to Davenport, who explained all the details of what would happen at the funeral home and what the governor would have to do. He concluded with, "After you pass the casket and speak to the family, we can either go to the burial site with the funeral procession or return to the plane."

"I need to get back to the office," said Stovall brusquely. "We'll skip the cemetery, but I'd like to stop at a Starbucks on the way to the airport." Davenport was used to the drill. After Governor-elect Stovall's first week with his new protective detail, he had issued what he called his "rules of professional conduct" to Lieutenant Godwin. It was a long list of "do's and don'ts" to keep him happy. The list included tuning the radio to smooth jazz or classical music and keeping the volume low, keeping an eye out for Starbucks coffee shops or Barnes & Noble bookstores, and stocking his vehicle with Evian drinking water. Stovall paused, then asked, "Any media there?"

Davenport answered, "A busload. From as far away as St. Louis, Illinois, Kentucky, even Arkansas. There wasn't enough room on the parking lot for all the police cars, so they've parked a lot of them at a nearby school and shuttled officers to the funeral home. They're estimating about a thousand officers attending from all over the country. I saw two Florida wildlife officers when I was there earlier. There's even a four-man honor guard from the Washington Metropolitan Police."

"You're kidding!" Stovall exclaimed. "What was so special about Stoddard?"

Armstrong was stunned and, it seemed from the silence, so was everyone else in the car. DeWitt finally broke the silence. "Governor, any time a law-enforcement officer is killed in the line of duty, it's traditional that agencies from all over the country send a representative to pay their respects. When a cop is killed, it wounds the entire country."

Stovall considered the idea, then declared, "I can understand sending flowers or something, but for officers to come so far seems like a waste of resources. I can see if it was a funeral for a governor or a federal judge, but for just a conservation agent . . . seems like a waste." He looked out his window at a passing gas station. "Hmm, gas is ten cents cheaper here."

Armstrong glanced at Wright to gauge how the young director was handling the slight of his dead employee. Wright's face was nearly as red as his Givenchy tie, his jaw was clenched, and he was staring intently out his own window. Armstrong wondered if Stovall was always this insensitive. Maybe he was just in a bad mood. After all, his governorship had started with a pie in the face.

Chapter 6

Davenport silently keyed his wrist mike several times as they neared the funeral home.

"I copy your arrival," called Cameron Boatright. "Dock is secure." Like a pit boss at the Indy 500, he stood with his right arm in the air at the precise spot where Monitor's front bumper needed to rest when they stopped. Boatright was average in size, but his shaved head, fierce brown eyes, and square jaw gave him a no-nonsense appearance most people found intimidating. His broad shoulders and trim waist under his immaculate black suit exuded the essence of a confident, fearless protector.

Davenport had successfully negotiated the light traffic, and they pulled into the reserved parking space outside the funeral home with two minutes to spare. He was shocked and gratified to see the parking lot jammed with police cars, and an overflow crowd of officers standing in formation, unable to get into the building. Boatright led the group quickly up the steps and into the building, also packed with uniforms. He had never seen so many officers in one place at the same time. The follow-up driver stayed with the vehicles to keep their Dock secure, per Davenport's instructions.

As they entered the building, Stovall turned to Armstrong and muttered, "I'll say one thing for you cops, you really know how to bury your people." The comment went through Armstrong like a knife, but he remained expressionless. Surely, Stovall had attended police funerals as U.S. Attorney, but had he always regarded law-enforcement officers with such disdain?

Armstrong stayed just off the governor's right shoulder as they were escorted down the aisle to their seats. An organ was playing "The Old Rugged Cross," which continued until the family entered and was seated. Then a Baptist minister took the podium and the service began. The forest of flowers surrounding Stoddard's casket filled the building with a sickly sweet aroma.

Armstrong gazed at Stoddard's coffin and remembered a line from Homer's *The Iliad*: "No riches can compare with being alive." Armstrong was overwhelmed by the service, but he struggled to keep his emotions in check. Deeply religious, he had strong feelings about death. He had certainly attended his share of funerals. But with the widow of a slain officer sitting across from him, sobbing and being comforted by her young son—who kept whispering, "Don't worry, Mom; it'll be okay"—it was almost more than Armstrong could bear. He imagined what his own funeral would be like, with people comforting his wife, Chelle. His brother's death in Afghanistan five years earlier in the war on terror; his mother's death from breast cancer three years ago; it hit him like a tidal wave. Armstrong nearly gasped, then corralled his emotions. In less than ten seconds—it was gone.

For a bodyguard to dwell on his own mortality was not a productive exercise. It would only produce another hurdle over which he would have to leap when the chips were down and the governor was dancing with hot metal. He focused on the back of Stovall's head and mentally rehearsed his movements once the service was over.

Fearing for the governor's safety in this setting would seem, in a way, a bit ridiculous to most people. There were nearly a thousand guns in the building. But to Armstrong, the situation was ripe with risks. This was a high-profile event, and the governor's attendance was being advertised in the media, which increased the odds that someone might show up to do more than just observe the ceremony. The funeral was open to the public, and there was no screening for weapons, so the fact they were surrounded by the cavalry did little to relieve Armstrong's anxiety. Throughout history, assassins often strolled through layers of armed men to reach their prey.

As though reading his mind, Boatright's voice came over his earpiece, "If there's any trouble, the Bunker is through that door behind the minister. Hold Ringmaster in that room until I come for you." Armstrong pushed the transmit button on his wrist mike twice in response.

Halfway through the service, Boatright—who was standing post in the back of the room, watching the crowd—advised Armstrong and Davenport, "There's a man walking up the center aisle, ap-

51

proaching your position." Both men turned their heads to the left and watched the man squeeze into a pew a few rows behind them. It was typical of how the detail operated, with each member filling in the holes and watching the others' backs. Armstrong and Davenport couldn't see what was going on behind them, so it was Boatright's job to be the eyes in the back of their heads.

After the service, the funeral director came forward. With an elegant wave of his hand, he motioned for the governor to view the casket. Stovall approached the altar and paused, looking down at Stoddard's picture atop the gunmetal gray box. He was a nice-looking guy. *What a shame*, he thought, *the State probably had several thousand dollars in training tied up in this guy. It would take a year and several thousand more dollars to replace him.* Then he turned, set his features in an appropriate expression of grief, and went to comfort Tamiko Stoddard. From the eerie silence, they might have been completely alone in the building, but Stovall knew they were being watched. Every ear was tuned toward him and every eye was focused on him. He bent over and quietly spoke, "Tamiko, I'm so sorry for your loss. Dwayne was a fine officer and we are forever in his debt. The fact that officers have come from all over the country to pay their respects is a measure of how much we'll all miss him." Tamiko again broke down. Stovall squatted in front of her, cupping her hands in his. A tear trickled down his cheek and he made no effort to wipe it away.

Young Joey stood next to the governor, patted his shoulder, and said loud enough for everyone to hear, "Don't worry, mister. We'll be okay." There was hardly a dry eye in the house.

"I know, son," Stovall replied, placing a comforting hand on the boy's back. "Your dad's with God now, so you have to take good care of your mom for me. We're proud of you both. Again, I'm very sorry." With that, he stood and strode down the aisle, past the throngs of officers who formed a protective gauntlet through the building and out to the back of an open hearse. His face bore the mask of determination. He was disappointed that no press cameras were present to film his performance. The footage would have looked great in a future campaign ad. He'd even remembered their names.

Wright and the others paused to pay their respects and scurried to catch up to Stovall. Armstrong muttered into his wrist mike, "Ringmaster is coming out," alerting Boatright to check the area. He responded with two clicks. Even though their radios contained encryption chips, and it was unlikely the press or anyone else could intercept and unscramble their transmissions, they always spoke in terse phrases. They never referred to Stovall by name but used his radio code. The Secret Service used POTUS to refer to the President of the United States and FLOTUS to refer to the First Lady of the United States, as well as giving each principal a codename. But GOTSOM for Governor of the State of Missouri and FLOTSOM for First Lady of the State of Missouri just didn't sound very dignified.

As they reached the exit, Boatright met them and whispered to the governor that the press wanted a comment, motioning toward a cluster of cameras out by the street. Stovall nodded and moved in their direction. Boatright walked point, Armstrong followed off the governor's right shoulder, and Davenport went to ready Monitor for departure.

Several reporters shouted questions as the governor neared them, and he stopped, roughly in the middle of their group. As microphones were shoved toward his face, he considered his response. He was bracketed between Boatright on his left and Armstrong on his right. Both officers were scanning the faces and hands of the reporters surrounding them. Public-figure attackers—like John Hinckley and Jack Ruby—often gained close proximity to their targets by blending in with the bustling activity of the press. The hands of both officers were up at chest level, poised to sweep any threat down and away from their principal. When a long boom microphone nearly punched the governor in the nose, Boatright quickly pushed it aside and reprimanded the technician, "Careful!"

One female reporter now blurted, "Do you have a response for those who killed Agent Stoddard?"

Stovall looked at the lady and forcefully stated, "You better believe I do!"

Chapter 7

January 18, 1603 hours
Safe House
Deepwater, Missouri

The rustic log home squatted on a small hilltop in the center of eighty-five thickly wooded acres. Its backyard sloped gently down one hundred yards to a small creek, then climbed steeply to a collapsed limestone bluff. Three steel outbuildings were scattered between the house and stream. The largest building, capable of holding ten vehicles, served as a garage and workshop. A long and narrow building served as an armory, shooting range, and training center. A small shed near the log home held a heavy-duty generator and a pump for the well. The only route in or out consisted of a well-kept gravel road, which twisted for nearly a half mile from Route 52. Two gates barred anyone from driving unimpeded from the highway to the house. Each gate was bugged to ring an alarm in the home when it was opened. A large white cross was mounted on the roof of the garage. On the roof of the log home perched a satellite dish. A tattered American flag, flying upside down, was mounted on the roof of the armory. It was intended as a sign of a country in distress.

Inside the armory, a flat, blue-gray layer of smoke hung just below the rafters, and the cool air held the sharp tang of freshly fired rounds.

"Praise God!" Ezekiel Leech whispered, as he lowered the muzzle of his weapon and squinted downrange at the damaged targets. The weapon was an FN Herstal P90 STD assault weapon, a sophisticated, fully automatic, Belgian-made rifle with a bull-pup design. It fired a 5.7 x 28mm round that would penetrate Level III body armor at 200 yards, a Kevlar helmet at 150 yards, and even armor with K-30 rigid ceramic inserts at close range. It had a fifty-round magazine and could be field-stripped in five seconds. A sound suppressor snapped onto the end of the barrel, adding several inches to its length, and it had a laser target designator below the muzzle.

Leech nodded to Bobby "Gunner" Wykoff and pretended not to watch the big man swell with pride. Wykoff was an intimidating figure—6 feet, 210 pounds, huge arms and a trim waist, a neatly trimmed beard, and a tattoo of a flaming skull on his right shoulder— but he was as eager for praise and approval as a ten-year-old child. He went to church every Sunday and always paid his bills on time. He was known to his neighbors as a quiet, gentle, deeply religious man who liked to keep to himself. Leech knew those neighbors would shit themselves if they saw the 55-gallon plastic drum, buried near the tree line, which contained three duffel bags. Each bag contained a .45 Glock 21 pistol, 5 magazines loaded with 13 rounds of Winchester Black Talon ammo each, false IDs for each of the members of the group, and $10,000 in cash—their "bug out kits" lovingly prepared and maintained by ol' Gunner, the Priests' quartermaster.

Wykoff snorted. "You didn't even have to dirty your knife, if you'd used this rifle. It woulda cut through that cop's body armor like it was cardboard."

Ross Draeger let out a barking laugh. "It was something, Gunner. One minute, they were shaking hands. The next, wham! The cop was totally helpless on the ground. Slickest move I ever saw." Draeger was a former bank security guard who had served as technical advisor for their eight bank robberies committed in the Midwest over the past two years.

Leech smiled, savoring the memory, but he didn't comment. God had given him the speed and strength to defeat the bigger warrior and, with the backing of the Almighty, he feared no man alive. He put down the weapon next to another P90, two H&K UMP45 submachine guns, and the weapon he normally carried, a Colt Model 639, fully automatic, 9mm submachine gun with a laser sight under the barrel. It had an odd-looking barrel that ended abruptly, encased with an integral sound suppressor. Leech had no military or law-enforcement experience. But he had learned engineering at McDonnell-Douglas, before he lost his job there in '97, and he knew how to construct a powerful bomb that would be nearly impossible to detect. His improvised explosive devices (IEDs) had destroyed nearly a dozen abortion clinics over the past five years, killing seven doctors and three nurses, not to mention two careless Memphis PD bomb techs.

"Hey, guys, in here! There's a story about us coming on the TV." It was Spider, calling from the armory door.

The men all ran into the house. As they tailed Spider, Leech was almost mesmerized by the Black Widow in its web that was tattooed on the small of her back. It seemed to undulate as she hustled her slender frame. It was almost a shame that only men could be Phineas Priests—Leech was well aware that Spider could wield a weapon as well as any of them.

So-So was turning up the volume of the 42" Sony plasma TV. The smell coming from the kitchen reminded Leech of how she got her nickname—she was such a bad cook, she even burned water. Her sixteen-month-old son, Peter, sat in his high chair, pounding the plastic tray with his tiny fists. Seth, Spider's thirteen-year-old son by a former marriage, was sitting on the sofa, quietly watching the TV.

"What is it, Seed?" Leech demanded, using the boy's nickname. Seth was the "seed" from which another cell of Priests would grow.

He shrugged. "There's going to be something about us on the news."

They had to endure three other stories before the anchor got to the conservation agent's funeral. There was a clip of Governor Stovall outside the funeral home, surrounded by newspeople.

A female voice asked him, "Do you have a response for those who killed Agent Stoddard?"

"Yes, I do!" Stovall said fiercely. "If the terrorists who did this can hear my voice, I want you to know that you will be caught, and I hope you're given the death penalty, and that your execution comes during my term. Because I will drop the handle on you myself!"

"Be careful what you wish for," Leech growled at the set. "I may just drop the handle on you, Guv." To the rest of the group, he said, "You know . . . we've been dropping baby butchers, fags, and cops, but maybe it's time we moved up to bigger game." Imagine the damage they could inflict on the Zionist Occupational Government by taking out a governor.

There it was. The fuse was lit. Leech knew an Arab proverb that said, "It is not the bullet that kills you; it is fate." This blowhard governor had just pronounced his own fate. Leech chuckled. This guy had just sentenced himself to the death penalty.

Leech eyed his fellow Priests. They looked like they were ready for some action. "Let's check this guy out. See how vulnerable he is. One more baby-murdering asshole—God will want us to take him out."

Chapter 8

Armstrong rubbed his eyes and looked down at the blue score sheet. Incredibly, the posting for the two GSD vacancies had only drawn five applicants. So far, the board had interviewed three.

The first was a forty-nine-year-old sergeant from Troop C, who was burned-out on the road and clearly looking for a place to "retire." He'd be about as useful to the security detail as a worn-out cell-phone battery. His answers were often hesitant and filled with nonverbal cues that indicated he was being less than honest. When asked tough questions, he either nervously changed his posture or chuckled before answering. On questions requiring recall—such as, *How many years have you been on the Patrol?*—his eyes moved up and to the left, accessing his memory. On questions involving integrity—such as, *Is there anything in your past that might be used to blackmail or corrupt you?*—his eyes moved up and to the right, accessing his imagination, suggesting he was editing his answer. Neuro-linguistic Programming (NLP) was not an exact science, but Armstrong knew from his training in interview techniques that 55 percent of communication comes from nonverbal behaviors and such behaviors are more reliable than verbal behaviors. Interviewees liked to emphasize their strengths, but seldom volunteered negative information. Armstrong had given him a generous eighteen out of twenty-five points.

The second applicant was a four-year trooper out of Troop A, who had already wrecked four patrol cars and had nine physical-force reports in his file. The kid had more complaints than Dirty Harry. His NLP behaviors indicated deception on several key questions that were strong enough to be used in a training video. Many believe that protection work is a young man's game, but this kid acted like he was fresh out of high school and clearly had the maturity of a fifteen-year-old. That sounded like a good number to Armstrong, who gave him fifteen points. The kiss of death.

The third applicant was a sharp-looking female trooper from Troop E. She had a good record, a pleasant personality, and a southern accent that made Armstrong's knees weak. Her NLP behaviors indicated no deception on any of her answers. She seemed honest and straightforward. Unfortunately, when the board got to the question, "Why do you want to serve in the Governor's Security Division?" she let it drop that she was two months pregnant and was looking for somewhere that she could do some light duty. Armstrong almost came across the table at her. *Light duty?!?!* She was obviously clueless about their responsibilities and the demands of the assignment. It steamed Armstrong that so many of the Patrol's own officers looked down on such specialty assignments. Armstrong hammered her into the ground with a thirteen.

Thus far, it had been slim pickings. Romanowski had complained that the low number of "Class A" applicants was probably due to the reputation the Stovalls had as being "very difficult people to protect." This was especially true of Patricia Stovall, whose temper was said to make Hillary Rodham Clinton look like Mother Teresa. While some said that Hillary threw lamps, Patricia Moody Stovall was rumored to throw punches. Romanowski had put it to Armstrong this way: "Why should an officer with a promising career come in here, get treated like dirt, and spin his wheels for a few years while his classmates are out on the road busting bank robbers, chasing people around at a hundred miles per hour, and getting promoted?" It was an argument that Armstrong couldn't counter. He had felt the same way toward specialists when he was on the road.

Just when Armstrong was contemplating leaving the Patrol to be an insurance salesman, the fourth candidate entered the room. Trooper Marko Maximus Vanhala was an impressive sight. Nicknamed "Mount Viking" by his fellow officers, the huge Nordic trooper stood 6 feet 6 inches, weighed in at 225, and had a quiet manner about him that was refreshing. He had that rare gift of towering over people but being able to disappear in a room when he so desired. He was mature at thirty-four years of age, but had only been on the Patrol for three years. Armstrong was intrigued to learn that Vanhala had been a policeman for six years in Helsinki, Finland, where he had served on the prime minister's protective detail. During his compulsory military service with the Finnish army, Vanhala had been trained as an explosive ordnance expert. He married a stunning blonde, whom he had met at a reception for the prime minister at the American embassy. She happened to have a high-level position with Monsanto, and when she was transferred to the corporate headquarters in St. Louis, he didn't hesitate to resign and come with her. As soon as he got his citizenship papers, he immediately applied to the Patrol, was selected, and began training three months later. The other recruits in his class had elected him class president, which said a lot for his leadership abilities. He spoke excellent English with just a slight accent, as well as Finnish, German, and Swedish. Under the section for "hobbies," his resumé listed "chess" and "aikido martial arts." *The perfect combination*, thought Armstrong, *brains* and *brawn.*

When Vanhala had answered all of the board's questions, Armstrong couldn't help grinning. "When can you start?"

Vanhala gave them a polite smile. "I am free after lunch, sir."

Armstrong studied him for moment and then asked him a question that wasn't on their forms. "What kind of childhood did you have?" When Vanhala looked confused, Armstrong added, "You were a caretaker, weren't you? Never complained. Always did what everyone else wanted to do. Placed the comfort of those around you above your own."

Marko thought about his answer. He had never even considered it. That reaction confirmed Armstrong's suspicions. Finally, he shrugged and said, "I suppose."

When Vanhala had left, Armstrong looked at his two sergeants, Don Romanowski and Kacey Underwood. "What do you guys think?" he asked with mock seriousness. They weren't supposed to discuss the candidates before filling out their score sheets. John Gregory, the facilitator from the Human Resources Division, sat at the end of table, closely watching the officers for any violations of the selective process. Armstrong's eyes were dancing in a silent signal to Underwood and Romanowski for them to give Vanhala their highest score.

Romanowski shook his head. "He's a Sagittarius, L.T., and Sagittarians make terrible bodyguards." He looked up from Vanhala's resumé and saw the panicked look that Armstrong was wearing. "Their sign is a half-man and half-horse, signifying man trying to rise out of his lower nature. They're clumsy, always saying the wrong thing, and they exaggerate everything! You can hardly believe a word they say. Worst of all, they're careless!" Armstrong looked like he was about to empty his Glock in Romanowski's direction. "I'm a Taurus, so I can be counted on. Taureans have common sense and keep promises. And best of all, we have a need for security, so we are natural bodyguards. Gary Cooper was a Taurus."

Kacey Underwood couldn't resist the comeback. "So was Hitler," she muttered just loud enough for everyone to hear.

Armstrong chuckled. "'O tiger's heart wrapped in a woman's hide.'" He felt that Underwood, the detail's only female officer, was one of the best advance people they had. She had done an outstanding job as lead advance on Governor Landham's whirlwind two-week trade mission to Italy and Greece the year before. She also handled all of the threat mail and intelligence for the division. As an amateur bodybuilder before she joined the Patrol, her small stature concealed a fierce and intelligent warrior. She held the record for the fastest time for a female officer in the one-and-a-half mile run on the Patrol's annual PT test.

"Sounds a little like Shakespeare, boss," Romanowski observed, as Underwood beamed at the compliment.

"*Henry the Sixth* . . . benefits of a college education."

Romanowski turned to Underwood. "The boss is quoting Shakespeare, again. He's starting to freak me out with these quotes."

Armstrong realized that they were just pulling his leg and shook his head. They each recorded a perfect score on Vanhala's sheet and passed them to Gregory, who placed them in a neat pile with the other score sheets.

"Are you ready for the last candidate or do you want to take a break?" he asked.

Armstrong looked at the others and shrugged. "Let's knock it out now and then go to lunch."

Trooper Alex Wiedemann strode through the door like a four-star general. He leaned across the table, shaking each board member's hand with a crushing handshake. "Pleased to meet you," he stated in an enthusiastic voice. He took the chair across from their table and sat with an erect posture.

Armstrong had looked over his resumé: 28-years-old, 6 feet 3 inches tall, 195 pounds, 5 years with the Patrol, glowing evaluations, excellent ratings on his annual PT test, excellent range scores, graduated from SMSU in Springfield with a Bachelor's degree in Criminal Justice, ranked at the top of his recruit class, single, one of the top five drug interdiction officers in Troop D, only one patrol-car accident and it had been "not chargeable," three commendations, and no complaints. At least he looked good on paper.

Gregory introduced the board members. Then Armstrong began by giving him a brief rundown on division operations and what would be expected of him if he was accepted. Finally, he gave Wiedemann his standard opening line. "Trooper Wiedemann, the board recognizes that no one is perfect. However, you're expected to be honest; everything we talk about will be verified, any inconsistencies may result in your not being selected, and whatever you tell us is confidential. Understand?"

Wiedemann had leaned forward slightly, looking Armstrong straight in the eye. "Absolutely!" he responded.

Armstrong nodded. "Good. Tell us about yourself and your current assignment."

Wiedemann smiled. "Well, sir, since graduation from the Academy, I've worked the interstate zone at Springfield. It's a fast pace and I love it, but it's mostly traffic work, and I'm looking for a new challenge. I've always been fascinated with protection work."

"Have you ever worked protection?"

"Yes, sir, I've been assigned to several presidential and vice presidential visits, and on two occasions I was assigned to help the governor's detail when he was campaigning in Springfield."

Armstrong hadn't been along on those trips. He'd ask whichever one of his officers had handled that assignment how Wiedemann had performed. "So you've met the Stovalls?"

"Yes, sir. They were both on one of the trips and I found them to be very warm people."

Armstrong nearly laughed. *You've got a lot to learn, kid. You couldn't warm these people up in a microwave oven. You've only seen the happy side of their faces. Tiptoe over to the dark side and tell me what you see.* "Trooper Wiedemann, we often have to travel with the First Family, sometimes even to foreign countries. The job calls for long hours, often working double shifts for several days in a row. It isn't always glamorous, either. You may have to sit in the governor's waiting room for an entire eight-hour shift. Do you have a problem with that?"

"Not at all, sir. My record will show that I willingly work overtime projects whenever they become available. I'm not scared to put in a long day. Also, I'm single and have no ties. My family lives in Colorado. And the idea of travel intrigues me."

"Our job requires that we may have to lay down our lives for the governor, if he comes under attack. Is that something you could do, if it became necessary?" On this question, Sergeant Chuckles and Ms. Expecting had answered, "I don't know." Dirty Harry had shrugged and given them an unconvincing, "I suppose so."

Wiedemann's chin jutted up. "Absolutely! My main objective would be to keep him out of those situations, but if I failed at that, I wouldn't hesitate to risk my life. One of my commendations is for pulling an injured driver out of a car that was fully engulfed in flames."

Armstrong nodded. So far so good. This was sounding too good to be true. He was tempted to ask, "Are you pregnant?" Instead, he went on to the next question: "If we talked to your supervisors, what would they tell us about you?"

A flicker of humility flashed across Wiedemann's face, then the confidence returned. "I am certain that they would give me a glowing recommendation. I do what I'm told, and I give everything my best shot."

"One of the most important aspects of our job is to maintain confidentiality," Armstrong stated. "You will be in a position to see and hear things that could make headlines, if the information got out. If you saw the governor do something that was illegal, how would you handle it?"

Wiedemann paused, pondering the question. "That's a tough one," he admitted. "I would not talk about anything I saw or heard to my friends or family, but if I saw him do something *illegal* . . . I'd tell you or Sergeant Romanowski about that."

Armstrong threw Wiedemann another hypothetical situation. "As a law-enforcement officer, you're sworn to enforce the law and arrest violators. If you were escorting the governor into an event, and a protestor struck him in the face with a cream pie and then ran away, how would you react?"

Wiedemann smiled, knowing about the inaugural incident. He pondered the premise of the question. "That would probably qualify as a simple misdemeanor assault, and I'd like to see the idiot arrested for it," he said, thinking it through out loud, "but my chief responsibility would be the governor's safety and well-being. If I chased after the pie thrower, I'd be leaving the governor open to further assault from others who might be in the crowd." He fixed Armstrong with a confident look. "I would stay with the governor and get him away from the scene, and let others chase the bad guy."

Kacey Underwood asked the next set of questions: What are your greatest strengths and weaknesses? When was the last time you got really angry about something, and how did you handle it? What kind of people do you like to work with, and what kind do you not like to work with? What are your goals, and where would you like your career to be five years from now?

Wiedemann fielded each question, giving complete and well-thought-out answers. He was on a roll.

Romanowski asked the final set of questions: Tell us about the last time you made a serious mistake. Have you ever had a dispute with another officer or supervisor? Have you ever been disciplined, reprimanded, or suspended from duty? Is there anything in your past that might be used to blackmail or corrupt you? Why should we pick you over the other applicants for this assignment?

Again, Wiedemann gave textbook answers. Armstrong felt like vaulting the table and giving the young warrior a sloppy kiss on the forehead.

Gregory faced the board members. "Do you have any other questions for Trooper Wiedemann?" They shook their heads. Gregory eyed the applicant. "Do you have any questions for the board?"

Wiedemann grinned and held up his hands. "When do I start?"

"We have this on a fast track," Armstrong replied. "If selected, you'll start next week."

"Wow!" Wiedemann was impressed. "I promise I won't let you down."

They all shook hands and Wiedemann left, thanking them for the opportunity to apply for the position. The board members pulled out their blue sheets and began to record their notes and scores. Wiedemann's NLP behaviors had not indicated any deception, but Armstrong was certain that Wiedemann had not been a caretaker as a child. He would have been the one who was always the center of attention, a hard charger, who always did things his way. Those who loved being in the spotlight seldom liked standing in someone else's shadow. Yet, Armstrong saw promise in the young officer and gave him twenty-four points, one below Vanhala's score.

Chapter 9

February 5, 0830 hours
MSHP General Headquarters
Jefferson City, Missouri

"Sorry I'm late," said Wiedemann, rushing into Armstrong's office.

Armstrong looked up from his paperwork and gave Wiedemann a tight smile. *Great!* he thought. *His first day on the detail and he's thirty minutes late.*

Newly promoted Corporal Boatright stood and shook Wiedemann's hand. "Hi, I'm Cameron Boatright. Looks like I'm your training officer for the first few days."

Boatright had been born and raised in London, England, until he immigrated with his parents to the U.S. in 1991. He had enlisted in the Marine Corps and served six years in the elite Marine Security Guard Battalion, protecting U.S. embassies in Saudi Arabia, Algeria, and Spain. He knew enough Farsi and Spanish to get by on the streets there. His distinguished military service earned him what he wanted more than anything: U.S. citizenship. The Patrol recruited him after his discharge, and he jumped at the chance to become a state trooper. He was Armstrong's newest officer with only five months on the detail. Since he was a former road officer from Kansas City, he caught most of Ringmaster's trips over there. He knew the city like the back of his hand.

Boatright had been a star on the Troop A's SERT team, first as a countersniper, then on their entry team. He was a martial artist and served as the detail's expert in hand-to-hand combat, as well as weapons and tactics. He had made a name for himself when he once got involved in a wild car chase with two bank robbers. The bad guys crashed their getaway car and bailed out on foot. Boatright was the first officer on the scene, and he grabbed the H&K Model 93 rifle out of his trunk before taking up chase. What followed was a wild, running-gun battle through a wooded area, headed in the direction of an elementary school. Boatright knew that the gunmen wouldn't hesitate to take hostages, so he took up a position behind a tree, aimed, and dropped both gunmen with one shot each. Neither survived their headshots, and Boatright was proclaimed a hero, saving hundreds of nearby children. His .223 rounds turned the gunmen's brains to jelly. His good looks and athletic build had the same effect on the hearts of the governor's female staff members and—Armstrong secretly believed—a few of the male ones, as well.

Wiedemann gave him a skeptical look. "Sounds good. I doubt that I'll need much training, though. I'm already housebroken." He held up a copy of an executive-protection manual he had ordered over the Internet. "I've been studying up."

Boatright's eyebrows went up, and he looked in the direction of Armstrong. *You really hired us a hot dog, boss*, the look said.

"Have a seat, Alex," Armstrong instructed him. He pushed his papers aside, put his elbows on the desk, and studied his new man for several seconds. Wiedemann was dressed in a blue blazer, tan slacks, and a black golf shirt opened at the collar. Armstrong could see that Wiedemann carried his service weapon in a nice Bianchi shoulder rig that held the gun with the barrel pointed up and to the rear. *Probably cost the kid a hundred bucks*, he thought. Armstrong's eyes slid down the outfit and paused at Wiedemann's highly polished cowboy boots with pointed toes. Finally, he spoke in a patient tone. "Look, when we ask you to meet us here at eight o'clock, that doesn't mean eight-thirty. Okay?"

Wiedemann shrugged, "Sorry, it won't happen again. I was in Major Shaw's office. We were discussing my career. He thinks I'm making a mistake transferring to your detail. He says I'm on the short-list for corporal in Troop D, and it'll be harder to get promoted from your division." Shaw was in charge of the Field Operations Bureau and held the belief that if you didn't have a radar gun in one hand and a ticket book in the other, you were of little value to the organization.

Armstrong ignored the bait. "That's your decision. As far as being late, it's no big deal with me, but if you pull this with the boss, you'll throw him off schedule. It shows disrespect for others. By showing up late, you're telling them that your time is more important than theirs, and around here, no one's time is more important than the governor's.

It also shows poor planning skills, and thorough planning is what sets us apart from some minimum-wage security guard. Understand?"

"Yep," Wiedemann said lightheartedly, but his face had a shadow of irritation in it. He didn't like being corrected.

Armstrong nodded. "Good. Also, that outfit is okay for your first day, but you'll be expected to wear a business suit and dress shoes when you're around the governor. Do you have a suit?" Wiedemann looked pretty sharp . . . if he was taking a date out for popcorn and a movie.

"Does Angelina Jolie have big lips?" Wiedemann sniffed, as though Armstrong was accusing him of being some hayseed from the sticks. "Yeah, I've got a couple of suits."

"Excellent. And no golf shirts. Wear a dress shirt and tie, preferably a white long-sleeved shirt. And don't get carried away on the ties. No Mickey Mouse or Bugs Bunny stuff. Okay?"

Wiedemann's eyes hardened. "I'll be sure to leave my Snoopy tie at home," he said with some degree of sarcasm. He leaned over to Boatright and whispered, "Geez, we're working for the clothes Nazi!"

Armstrong allowed the spear of sarcasm to fly harmlessly past. "The general rule is to dress the same as the boss, even if he wears a business suit to visit a hog farm. You want to blend in, not stick out. We are representatives of the governor's office. A sharp appearance is itself a force. And leave the cop jewelry at home. No handcuff tie tacks."

Wiedemann rolled his eyes. "I get the fucking picture, L.T."

"I just don't want to see you get embarrassed," Armstrong said. "When you leave here, Cameron is going to give you a quick tour of the Mansion and assign your gear to you. You'll get a division badge, a pager and radio, a Surefire flashlight, a Fobus paddleback holster, and a smaller ASP baton. You'll want to trade your Glock 22 in for a Model 23. It's smaller and easier to conceal." The road troopers on the Patrol were issued a 21-inch ASP expandable baton. The governor's detail carried a 16-inch baton. Like the smaller Glock pistol, it was a little lighter and easier to conceal.

Wiedemann shook his head. "If it's all the same to you, Lieutenant, I'd rather carry my regular gear. The Model 22 has two extra rounds in the magazine, and the extra five inches in the blade of the

ASP adds a lot more power than your smaller version. Also, I paid an arm and a leg for this fucking holster."

Armstrong frowned. "That's the second time you've dropped the 'F-bomb' in the last thirty seconds. We're around the governor and his family every day. If you can't control your profanity, maybe you should be trying to get into one of the narcotics task forces or going back to the road. Just remember your recruit training from the Academy. We are 'gentlemen, who enforce the law.'" Armstrong was a patient and understanding leader, but he had little tolerance for crude behavior.

Wiedemann's face reddened. "Sorry."

Boatright jumped in, "If you're worried about those two extra rounds saving you, the Glock 23 accepts the Model 22 magazine. It just sticks out of the grip a little. And you'll find that you spend most of your time in crowds. The longer ASP will be difficult or impossible to swing in close quarters."

Wiedemann had made up his mind. He patted his weapon. "You guys can carry those toys if you want. I'm sticking with these."

The rookie's looking to get into a fight, not avoid one, Armstrong thought. *He's got a lot to learn about protection work.* The mistake most bodyguards made was that they approached protection work with the notion that "bigger is better." More bodyguards are better than fewer bodyguards. A bigger caliber is better than a smaller caliber. A longer baton is better than a shorter baton. This holster is better than that holster. The fact of the matter was that in nearly all attacks on public figures, the caliber of the bodyguard's weapon, his style of holster, the length of his baton, the number of rounds he carried, the availability of heavy firepower, and his expertise in the martial arts would have almost no effect on the outcome of the attack. The secret to world-class executive protection was proactive risk-reducing strategies, manipulation of the environment, and conflict-avoidance tactics, which would keep the protectee out of harm's way.

Armstrong shrugged, "Suit yourself, but the shoulder rig is out. You'll laser the boss every time you walk in front of him." He turned around and pulled a hardback copy of Gavin de Becker's book, *Just Two Seconds: Using Time and Space to Defeat Assassins*, off his credenza and slid it across the desk to Wiedemann. "Here. When you're

finished reading what you have, study this one, then we'll talk again."
There was a lot Wiedemann had to learn about protection and de
Becker's book was the best one ever written on public-figure attacks.
It was required reading for every member of the detail, and Arm-
strong's copy had highlighted passages on nearly every page.

Armstrong continued, "Cameron will take you over to the
Governor's Office. He'll show you the complex of offices there and
introduce you to the staff. After that, you've got a meeting with the
Scheduling Office to discuss the governor's trip to St. Joseph tomorrow. Once you guys have his itinerary, you'll take off and drive to St.
Joe this afternoon. You'll have all morning and part of the afternoon
to advance the visit, before we fly in at about three o'clock. He's doing
three events there and then we fly out. Pretty simple."

Wiedemann nodded, "No problem."

"Alex, advance work is the basis of what we do every day. The
governor should never arrive at any location that hasn't been checked
by one of us first." Armstrong glanced at Boatright. "Cameron will
lead you through it, and I want you to follow his instructions to
the letter. He's one of our best advance people. Okay?" Actually,
Boatright's advance work had been getting increasingly sloppy. Before
Wiedemann's arrival, Armstrong had discussed his concern with
Boatright and told him he was capable of better work. Boatright had
confessed to getting worn down by the long hours and had promised
to do better. His assignment as Wiedemann's trainer would be a test
of that promise.

"Sounds like a piece of cake," Wiedemann said with conviction.
He brushed at a piece of lint on his pants cuff.

You don't have a clue, Armstrong thought, but said, "Good." He
stood up and shook Wiedemann's hand. "Welcome aboard, Alex. I
hope you enjoy your time with us."

As they left his office, Armstrong wondered if he had made a
mistake. The staff's first impression when they met Wiedemann today
would be that he was a "cowboy," considering his outfit. And Armstrong knew that first impressions were hard to overcome. Wiedemann would have to work hard to gain their respect. On the other
hand, Trooper Marko Vanhala had started two days ago, showing up
on time, dressed in a sharp suit, and the staff was already bragging

about him. *Oh well*, he thought. Armstrong was confident that he had picked the best applicant in Vanhala, but he wasn't so sure about Wiedemann. The lanky trooper seemed to have a streak of arrogance in him wider than the wingspan of Stovall's private jet. Armstrong hoped he could train Wiedemann to become an effective protector. If not, Armstrong would have to cut him loose.

Chapter 10

"'Fourteen-thirty-five hours, Ringmaster, P.O.F., and Security depart Octagon for Jefferson City Airport, State Aviation,'" Alex Wiedemann read off the governor's itinerary. He looked over at Cameron Boatright. "How the hell do you leave somewhere at fourteen-thirty-five? Does he really do that?"

Boatright had one eye on the road ahead, and the other on the giant tractor-trailer unit that was dogging his tail. The truck had been passing everything in sight, until he caught up with Boatright's unmarked vehicle. Then the truck driver hit his brakes and veered in behind them, like Boatright didn't have a rearview mirror and might have simply failed to notice forty tons of steel screaming down on top of them. Boatright had decided to take Merrimac on the trip, and the black armored Suburban was bristling with antennae. *Damn*, he thought, *this unmarked vehicle sure doesn't fool the truckers. How the hell are we supposed to fool the terrorists?*

Boatright glanced over at his trainee. "No, he usually runs late. But the scheduler, who bases those times on what we tell her, prepares that itinerary. They just start when the boss needs to be at the event— in this case, we're shooting for a fifteen-twenty-five arrival at the first event—then allow fifteen minutes to get there from the airport. That gives us a 'wheels-down' time of fifteen-ten. It's a twenty-minute flight from Jefferson City, so that means a fourteen-fifty 'wheels-up.' We need fifteen minutes to walk out of the Governor's Office, drive to the airport, and taxi out in the jet. Voilà! Fourteen-thirty-five, we need to head for the door." Boatright grinned. "His whole day is set up that way. From the time he leaves the Mansion in the morning, until he returns in the evening, every meeting and event on his schedule is timed down to the minute."

Wiedemann shook his head in amazement. "I wouldn't want to live like that. I don't even know what I'm going to be doing two hours from now. What happens if he gets off schedule?"

"That's not good," Boatright said seriously. He pointed to the itinerary. "P.O.F. stands for Paul Oliver Fleming, the governor's press secretary. It's his job to keep the boss moving on schedule, but we're the ones who'll get pressured to make up for lost time, if we do get sidetracked. So always give the staff guy a heads-up. Five minutes before the boss really needs to depart, go to Fleming and say, 'If you want to stay on schedule, we need to leave in five minutes.' Then the monkey's on his back."

Wiedemann nodded. He hadn't realized that security work entailed something as mundane as guarding the governor's *time*. "So what's the drill for tomorrow?"

Boatright had grown tired of seeing only a shiny chrome grill in his rearview mirror and picked up his speed a little. "The Secret Service usually gets six or seven days to advance a presidential visit. We're sometimes lucky to get six or seven hours. So we've got our work cut out for us. Today, we'll start at the airport and work our way through the schedule, until we end up back at the airport. We'll have to verify the routes and drive times, as well as advance each of the three sites. I know St. Joe pretty well, so it shouldn't take too long. In the morning, we'll swing by Troop H Headquarters and borrow an unmarked car from one of the troop lieutenants for you to use. Then we'll go through the schedule again, and again, and again, until everything's set." He smiled at Wiedemann. "By the time you get back home, you'll know the city as well as I do."

Wiedemann grunted. "Be still my heart," he muttered, "I'm going to know the big city! Just tell me this: When does this job start to get interesting?"

Chapter 11

Governor Stovall's white Citation jet dropped out of the low ceiling, landed easily despite a brisk crosswind, and taxied to Cameron Boatright's vehicle. Within a few minutes, he wheeled Merrimac out of the airport property and accelerated toward their first of three events. Governor Stovall occupied the right front seat, Press Secretary Paul Fleming sat in the left captain's chair, and Armstrong held the right, directly behind the boss. An unmarked Crown Victoria patrol car, driven by a local trooper, followed them as their "Shadow" follow-up protection.

Their first stop was a groundbreaking ceremony under a large heated tent on the north side of town. It was to be the site of an auto-parts supply plant, employing nearly one hundred people. The Landham administration had lured the plant owner away from a planned move to Tennessee, but Stovall was all too happy to take credit for the work. It would be a high-profile event, having been advertised on the local radio, television, and newspaper outlets for nearly a week. They expected a crowd of about three hundred to attend.

Armstrong thumbed through the detail book that Boatright and Wiedemann had prepared for the three sites to be visited. The book included the location of the nearest hospital and police station, and listed the primary and alternate driving routes, as well as important contact numbers, the governor's medical profile, and local intelligence. They had used the division's computer in the Mansion command center to prepare much of the book. Once they were on-site, they took digital pictures of the airport and each of the three sites, and inserted the images into the Word document on Boatright's laptop. Detailed maps showing all of their routes and alternate routes, including those to the hospital, were downloaded using Microsoft's Streets and Trips program. Satellite images of each site were downloaded using Google

Earth. The document was then printed out in landscape and folded in half to create a book small enough to fit into a suit pocket. Boatright had insisted that Alex fill it out, and Armstrong was pleased to see Wiedemann had covered all their bases. He examined the layout for their first event and saw their "holding room" was a pipe-and-drape area just inside the tent. A holding room or "Bunker" was a safe place in which the protectee could relax, rest up before or after a function, or be taken to in the event of a problem. Bodyguards must know a defendable position where they can take their protectee at all times.

Governor Stovall clapped his hands twice like a magician trying to make a rabbit appear. "Okay, who has my briefing book?"

"Right here, sir," Fleming said, digging a one-inch binder out of his thick briefcase. Armstrong guessed the bag must weigh over fifty pounds with all the supplies Fleming had stuffed into it. The leather bag contained everything from press releases to the governor's hairbrush.

"What's the drill?" Stovall demanded, paging through the binder and scanning a list of attendees.

Fleming consulted an e-mail on his BlackBerry, sent from the scheduling office. "Mayor Joan Schultz and several VIPs will meet you on arrival. City Administrator Mark Monroe is the emcee. Once the program begins, he'll welcome the group and then introduce you. You'll give five-minute remarks. Just remember the three Be's: Be Brilliant, Be Brief, and Be Gone. Then Representative Russell will do five minutes, and Senator Lewis will do five. Then Mayor Schultz will do two minutes and introduce Mr. Chin, the CEO. He'll do five to seven minutes and then we'll do the official groundbreaking. After that, you can spend some time with the crowd until we leave for your next event, which is a meeting with the editorial staff of the newspaper."

Stovall nodded his head. "I need to call the office," he told Boatright.

Cameron hit the speed-dial number for the Governor's Office on the dash-mounted cellular phone, and, within seconds, Bradley Naylor was briefing the governor on developments back home.

As they crossed the Missouri River Bridge, Boatright keyed the microphone for the high-band radio, "Boatright to Wiedemann." There was no response. Perhaps Wiedemann had his radio turned down. He waited thirty seconds and then tried again. Again there was no response. Boatright's eyes flickered to Armstrong's image in the rearview mirror. Armstrong shook his head sadly, hearing another nail being driven into Wiedemann's brand-new coffin. The kid was going down the tubes faster than a ball of spit.

As they neared the site, the large circus tent came into view, and a tangle of vehicles and people clogged the entrance to the site. Boatright again called Wiedemann but received no response. He was growing concerned. It was their policy not to enter a site until the advance man gave the "all clear." There could be anything going on in there: a violent group of protesters, ripping up the tent ropes; a lone gunman, mowing down attendees; or a pipe bomb, discovered under the dais.

The plan was for Boatright to pull into an entrance past the site and circle back to the Dock, which was located behind the dais. The route avoided the flow of the crowd. Armstrong quickly used his BlackBerry to dial up Wiedemann's cell phone, but the call was forwarded to Wiedemann's voice mail. Boatright glanced at him in the mirror, and Armstrong whispered into his wrist mike, "Pull over."

As Boatright stopped, Governor Stovall looked up from his papers. "Why are we stopping?"

"They're not ready for us, sir," Armstrong responded. "It'll be just a minute." Then to their backup driver, he radioed, "Armstrong to Shadow, proceed to the Dock and confirm that they're secure."

The follow-up car swerved around them and turned into the entrance. A moment later, Wiedemann's panicked voice came over the radio, "Sorry about that. I missed your call. The Dock is secure."

As Boatright turned off the street, they saw a small group of VIPs gathered at the arrival point, and Wiedemann was standing among them. The group was laughing at something that Wiedemann was saying.

Boatright pulled up to the arrival point and noticed a news camera crew at the corner of the tent, zeroing in on his vehicle. "Looks like we've got some paperboys over here, Paul," he said. In fact, the Dock was *not* clear!

"Thanks for the notice," Fleming said sarcastically. "I can see them for myself."

When Boatright exited his car, it was all he could do to keep from choking Wiedemann. As the site man, it was Wiedemann's job to ensure that the site was safe and ready to go, that the welcoming group was in position and aware of the governor's arrival time, and also to alert Boatright to any potential problems, including news crews waiting in ambush. The fact that the greeting committee was at the Dock—rather than in the "pipe-and-drape" area inside the tent—violated another division policy: not to hold meetings at the Dock, where the governor would be exposed to the potential of sniper fire. In an attempt to correct the blunder, Boatright parked so that Merrimac shielded the group from any unwelcome eyes. Thus far, Wiedemann was proving to be more of a hindrance than a help.

Armstrong got out of the Suburban with Stovall and followed him over to the waiting VIPs—a bipartisan group of state and local officials, and company representatives—where the governor greeted them. The follow-up driver would remain with the vehicles and keep the Dock secure until they departed.

Armstrong looked at Boatright, then his eyes moved toward Wiedemann. His look said, *Get him squared away!* Wiedemann was standing there with a big grin like he was waiting to get the governor's autograph. Even worse, he was watching the governor and not those in the immediate area, a common error made by untrained security personnel. Unless Governor Stovall was getting ready to commit suicide, Wiedemann was of no value to the operation. There could have been a squad of Islamic terrorists standing behind him, and he wouldn't have been aware of it.

Boatright pulled Wiedemann aside. "Eyes on the crowd. And get your hand out of your pocket. You look like a guard at the mall. We've been calling you on the radio."

He shrugged. "I guess I couldn't hear it for the crowd noise. What's the big deal? The crowd looks okay."

Boatright couldn't believe his ears. "What's the big deal? The big deal is that the L.T. is gonna have your balls in a blender. You're on probation, man. Unless you want to end up guarding a casino boat, you'd better get your act together. Where's your earpiece?" He had helped Wiedemann put the rig on over two hours ago. Now it was gone.

"It made my ear sore, so I took it off," Wiedemann responded, rubbing his ear to indicate that it still hurt.

"Alex, we wear earpieces to keep our transmissions confidential, and so we can hear the radios in crowd situations." He had explained this earlier. "Go put your rig back on and be quick. It's game time."

Wiedemann gave him a pained look and trudged off in the direction of his car.

Boatright joined up with Armstrong, who was screening those around Stovall from behind the governor's right shoulder. Boatright took up a position off Stovall's left front, walking point in a formation referred to as the "slash." They worked their way through the VIPs and into the holding area.

Fleming went out to the dais to check the setup. Six bright silver shovels stood propped against a table with six yellow hard hats. There was an area of tilled soil in front of a sea of metal folding chairs which were rapidly filling up. A microphone and speakers were set up in front of the crowd. Fleming went over and tapped the mike to ensure that it was working. The speakers issued a crisp tapping sound in response. *Sounds good*, he thought. He spotted several members of the media and headed in their direction to make contact. They would want an opportunity to throw a few questions at the boss when this was over. Fleming wanted to feel them out and plant some ideas in their heads.

Wiedemann caught up with them as the ceremony began several minutes later. Armstrong was at stage right, and Boatright had taken stage left. Wiedemann moved next to Boatright, and Armstrong saw Boatright whisper something to him. Boatright left Wiedemann to take over stage left, while he circled the crowd, looking for troublemakers. *A smart move*, thought Armstrong. *He wants to see what else Wiedemann may have missed.* Boatright scanned every face as he walked down along the crowd, which was focused on the opening speakers. He was in his "Hunter-Killer" mode. Boatright paused at the rear of the crowd and spoke to two uniformed St. Joseph police officers, who had been screening the crowd as they arrived. Armstrong saw them shake their heads. *No problems.*

Boatright took up a position at the center aisle, where he could watch the crowd from the rear and respond to any problem. If anyone so much as broke wind, Boatright would be on top of them. Armstrong knew he was not looking for assassins. If Boatright waited until he saw an assassin, then he had waited too long. The trick was to watch for assassin-like behaviors: people who were alone, dressed inappropriately, reaching for something under their coat, seeking to get closer to the governor, paying more attention to security than to the VIPs. All of these were pre-incident indicators or PINs to public-figure attacks. It was a process they referred to as "SEE"—Suspects Exist Everywhere, learned at de Becker's Academy For Protectors. Adversaries often separate themselves from others by their dress, their mannerisms, and their behavior. It was the detail's job to pick out any suspects, take up a strong defensive position, and monitor their behaviors. In the event of trouble, Armstrong and Wiedemann would cover and evacuate the governor, moving him to Merrimac, while Boatright neutralized the threat.

Having finished his survey of the crowd, Boatright keyed his wrist mike and advised his colleagues, "We've got two oddballs on your right side, six rows from the back. One has purple hair and a white jacket with a World Wrestling Federation logo on it. The other has an ankle-length, black leather coat, shaved sidewalls, and several earrings. Don't look much like your corporate types." Armstrong picked them out and clicked his mike twice. He looked over at Wiedemann, who nodded in return. It was another missed task for Wiedemann. He should have spotted the boys before Stovall's arrival, and perhaps even engaged them in conversation to see what interest they had in the event. Armstrong would bet money they were representatives from some local protest group, Save the Spotted Owl or something.

Boatright's warning was an unnecessary precaution. The event went smoothly, and the crowd gave the governor a warm welcome and politely listened to his remarks, even the two oddballs. The crowd patiently endured the speeches by all of the VIPs, then watched as the VIPs geared up in their hard hats and shovels, and broke up ground which had already been broken. The crowd applauded their performance as it concluded, then most of them began to head for their vehicles. Several came forward for autographs and pictures with their newly elected governor, and the officers carefully screened each constituent.

Since they were several minutes from departure, Boatright sent Wiedemann ahead to scout the next site, telling him, "I'll call when we leave here. Make sure you hear us this time, and I want to see a secure Dock when I get there." Boatright then radioed the officer at the Dock to start both vehicles and prepare for departure.

One individual had moved forward and was waiting for a picture. He was a slender man in a nice-looking business suit. He patiently waited his turn, then approached Stovall and said, "Hello, Governor. Can I get a picture with you?"

"Certainly," the governor said, receiving the man's firm handshake. To the governor's right, Armstrong watched the man closely, prepared to move in if the handshake wasn't broken. The man released Stovall's hand, put his arm around the governor's shoulders, and smiled in the direction of the photographer for the event. Their photo was snapped.

"Thanks, Governor," the man said and stepped away as another person took his place. He moved several yards away and then turned to watch the activities. After a few more photos, the governor spent a few minutes talking to the press, then his entourage moved to their vehicles and headed out to their next stop.

As the man turned to leave, the photographer's assistant caught up with him.

"I need to get your name so we can send you a copy of the picture," she said.

The man looked at her for a moment, then smiled. It hadn't been his intention to get a picture of himself with Governor Stovall, but merely to check out the governor's bodyguards up close. "Sure," he said. "Why not? My name is Ezekiel Leech. L-E-E-C-H," he said, as she recorded the information. "And I'm staying at my buddy's place over in Deepwater, Missouri," giving her Wykoff's mailing address.

Leech left the tent and walked out to a blue Dodge Durango. He crawled into the passenger side and closed the door. "Did you get everything?" he asked the driver.

Ross Draeger responded, "Caught it all on tape." He nodded toward the small, digital video camera lying next to his seat. They would study the video to learn the faces and habits of the bodyguards. "How many bodyguards did you see?"

"Three," Leech said. "One didn't know what he was doing, but the other two were pretty sharp."

Bobby "Gunner" Wykoff leaned forward from the backseat. "Who was that other guy with them?"

Leech turned in his seat. "Looked like some staffer. He was handing out press releases or something. We'll have to do some more surveillance, but I think I know how we can take this guy down."

Chapter 12

Jefferson City holds the distinction of being one of the smallest state capitals in America. At less than 36,000 people—mostly state-government employees—the Missouri capital was a bustling hive of activity during the day, but the sidewalks retracted after five.

Armstrong circled the Capitol Building in his unmarked patrol car, pondering the increasing number of threats and hate mail that had recently arrived. The latest was a letter from a man in Kansas, who had threatened to "strike dead" Governor Stovall if he didn't help get the man's children back. The man had been convicted in Missouri of child molestation, the Division of Family Services had taken his children away, and he was holding Stovall personally responsible for their return. Security officers with the Kansas Bureau of Investigation were assisting in the investigation. Their governor had also been threatened by the man the year before, for vetoing a concealed-weapons bill that the Kansas legislature had passed.

Armstrong parked in front of the Capitol in a spot reserved for his detail. Walking toward the entrance, he looked up at the limestone exterior of the building that had served as Capitol since 1918. It had taken six years to build, at a cost of four million dollars—about forty cents a cubic foot—and covered three acres. Perched atop the dome, 260 feet above the ground, stood the bronze statue of Ceres, the goddess of grain. Armstrong smiled, because Romanowski had been quick to point out that when the topless lady was viewed from the east, her right hand extended from the waist made her look more like a guy with a foot-long erection. Romanowski said that it was perhaps a more fitting symbol of the legislators who worked and played inside.

Armstrong entered through the lobby doors and walked across the rotunda. His footsteps echoed on the marble floor. He couldn't help looking up at the 3,000-pound brass chandelier, hanging from the ceiling of the dome, 171 feet above him. It was the most impressive light fixture he had ever seen, and he always got a dizzy feeling looking up at it.

With less than one month under his belt as commander of the Governor's Security Division, Armstrong was quickly developing a deeper appreciation of the hazards faced by the state's chief executive. On his first tour of the Capitol Building, Romanowski had taken him into the west wing of the museum, located on the first floor. They had stopped in front of a display case, and Romanowski had pointed to a silver Smith & Wesson .44 caliber revolver behind the glass. "That's why we're here," he stated. Armstrong examined the display and read that the weapon had once belonged to Governor Thomas Crittenden. In 1881, Crittenden had offered a $5,000 reward for the "arrest and delivery" of Jesse James and his gang, who were carrying out robberies in western Missouri. Governor Crittenden kept the weapon in his desk drawer to guard against retaliation by the gang. Romanowski explained that the governor acted in the best interest of the citizens, and his actions increased the risk that he would be killed. Governors today are involved in society's most emotional issues: abortion, the death penalty, gun control, taxation, and so on. By virtue of that hazard, they deserve the best protective effort possible from the available resources. Until then, Armstrong had never considered it from that perspective.

After jogging up the stairs to the second floor, Armstrong found himself at the entrance to the Governor's Office. The reception room was crowded with members of the press, waiting for the governor's news conference to begin. Armstrong pushed his way through them to the security desk, occupied by Corporal Bobby Davenport. As Armstrong approached the desk, Davenport stood and motioned him into the office of the governor's secretary, Christine Soloman, for more privacy.

"Welcome to the zoo," Davenport said dryly.

"What's up?" Armstrong murmured. He could see a beehive of activity in Stovall's office as Christine and Paul Fleming, the governor's press secretary, prepared for the media event about to take place. Fleming's job was not only to deal with the press but also to serve as Stovall's image consultant, to create a positive environment at every stop on the governor's schedule.

"I thought you might want to sit in on this one, L.T. I just found out that the boss is going to declare war on that terrorist group that killed the conservation agent last week." Davenport glanced around to make sure no one was near. "He wants to get all the governors together in Kansas City next month to talk about it. Fleming says he doesn't know where, but I found out that the scheduler is blocking off rooms at the Grand Plaza."

Armstrong rolled his eyes toward the ceiling and looked through the doors into Stovall's office. Fleming was setting a small lectern atop the large oval table, from behind which the governor would make his announcement. Stovall was not in sight, and Armstrong guessed he was in Naylor's office, preparing his statement.

"Great! That's all we need," Armstrong groaned. "Stir up every extremist in the country and then bring in a group of governors for them to shoot at. We'll be neck deep in bomb threats by the end of the week."

Davenport grinned. "You know the George Carlin line: 'You can't fight City Hall, but you can goddamn sure blow it up.'"

Fleming walked into Christine's office, consulted his watch, and said, "Looks like it's time to feed the sharks." He eyed the two officers. "Ready, guys?"

Davenport shrugged. "You're in charge of this circus. We're just a couple of clowns."

Fleming chuckled. "Couldn't have said it better myself." He opened the door and allowed the flood of reporters to spill into Christine's office. They filed through into the Governor's Office, dragging enough electronic equipment to bug the entire capital city.

Davenport eyed each one as they walked past, looking for a strange face or someone who didn't belong. Armstrong preceded the group into Stovall's office and took a position next to the governor's desk. His eyes swept the area for anything the press didn't need to see. He noticed a handwritten memo lying next to Stovall's phone. It was from Naylor to the governor and concerned a budgetary problem with the Department of Education. Armstrong turned the memo upside down and then supervised as the reporters set up their cameras, lights, and tape recorders.

Ten minutes later, Governor Stovall strode out from Naylor's office into the spotlights and frowned into the cameras. "I thank you for coming," he began. It was his standard opening line. "I will read a prepared statement and then answer any questions." He looked down at the lectern and began his remarks.

Chapter 13

Leech slapped Seed on the back, as he led him into the armory for some training in tactics. "Let's pop some caps." Leech went over to a stack of targets. Most were a life-sized replica of a state trooper. He had given them evil expressions and five-pointed badges on their chests. One target had no hat. It depicted a rotund man with his hands in his pockets. The word "GUV" was scrawled across his chest.

"Go outside, so I can set these up," he told the boy.

"Okay," Seed replied and holstered his .380 Browning. He picked up a silenced Beretta 93R from the workbench and walked out, putting an extra magazine in the pocket of his blue coveralls.

He knew the course of fire. It would be an assault course, where he would move through the armory, eliminating "trooper" targets, until he reached the prized "GUV" target. The tricky part was that he wouldn't know exactly where Leech was placing the targets, and if he overlooked one . . . he didn't even want to think about it. Leech had once used the stun gun on him, until Seed's mother had intervened.

"Remember," said Leech, as he came out of the armory, "second best in a gunfight is dead. Use cover, don't forget to reload, and put at least two rounds into each target." He handed the boy an inert hand grenade. "Start anytime you're ready."

Seed took two rubber earplugs from a plastic case in his pocket and screwed them into his ears. He drew a deep breath, pulled the pin from the hand grenade, and tossed it into the armory. He waited for Leech's signal to indicate the explosion.

Three seconds later, Leech screamed, "GO!" into his ear, and pushed the stopwatch button on his digital watch to time him. The boy went through the door in "wrap-around" fashion, occupying the deadly opening for only a fraction of a second. He found cover behind a hay bale and scanned the interior for "hostiles," waiting for his eyes to adjust to the dark.

Two troopers watched him from fifteen feet away. He leaned around the bale with the shoulder stock of the 93R planted firmly against his arm and stroked the trigger twice. The weapon was set to fire three-round bursts with each pull of the trigger. Six 9mm rounds punched holes in the officers.

"MOVE!" The command was roared into his ear and accentuated by a poke in the back with a two-foot piece of broomstick. He was up and moving past the two targets when he saw two more to his right. He took cover behind a support beam and fired the machine pistol from a barricade position. Two more trigger pulls.

"MOVE!" This time the broomstick struck him between the shoulder blades. He gasped, then scurried to a cabinet next to the workbench for cover. Up ahead, three troopers glared at him, each five feet from the one next closest. He pulled the trigger three more times and started to leave his cover, when he realized that the slide was locked open. He had fired the weapon dry, a cardinal sin in Leech's book of survival.

"NOOO!" Leech bellowed behind the boy and struck Seed's upper arm a smart blow with the stick.

Seed regained his cover and felt in his coverall pocket for the extra magazine. It wasn't there, apparently having fallen out during his movement through the course. He dropped the weapon and pulled out the Browning pistol.

The stick buried itself in his right kidney. "You're hit, Stupid!" The blow knocked the breath out of him, and he dropped the pistol. As he bent over to retrieve it, a vicious blow landed on the side of his thigh. "You're hit again, Dummy!"

He fell on the dirt floor and clutched his leg. "Nooo!" he screamed, his vision clouded with pain.

Leech bent down and grabbed the boy's chin. "You're dead!" he hissed, glaring with disgust into Seed's eyes until the boy looked away in shame. "How many times do I have to tell you? Reload when you want to, not when you have to." Leech whirled, grabbed his Colt 639 off the workbench, and stalked out of the armory, leaving the boy by himself in the dirt.

Seed turned and looked downrange. The only target beyond the last three troopers was that of the "GUV," leering at him with pompous amusement. Safe, seemingly untouchable. Seed wondered if the real-life governor would be as unreachable and if they would all die in the attempt to kill him.

*   *   *

"How did he do?" asked Spider, as Leech entered the house. Draeger, Wykoff, and So-So were at the kitchen table, eating sandwiches.

"Not worth a damn," Leech growled, taking a can of Coke out of the refrigerator.

The group's attention was suddenly drawn to their TV set, as the noon newscast came on. An announcer on the local news station stared intently at them and said, "Today in the state capital, Governor William Stovall announced that he will spearhead a conference of the Nation's governors next month in Kansas City to fight domestic terrorism. Jon Carreon has the story from Jefferson City."

Carreon's handsome face appeared on screen with the Capitol Building in the background. He wore an expression of deep concern, as though this was the most important story he had ever covered. "An angry Governor Stovall held a press conference this morning and announced that he will chair a special Governor's Summit on Terrorism next month at an undisclosed location in Kansas City. The announcement comes nearly one month after Missouri Conservation Agent Dwayne Stoddard was brutally murdered in Ripley County, near the Arkansas line. Members of a group calling itself the Phineas Priesthood are believed to be responsible and are still at large."

A videotaped shot of Stovall came up on the screen. "Three weeks ago, I attended the funeral of Conservation Agent Dwayne Stoddard, who was murdered while carrying out his duties as a Missouri law-enforcement officer. He leaves behind a wife and a six-year-old son. The group responsible for this heinous act remains at large, despite a massive manhunt by over five hundred federal, state, and local law-enforcement officers. But the capture of these terrorists is not enough. The majority of the members in the Militia and Patriot movements are good people who abide by the rule of law. They simply have strong feelings about domestic policies. But there are many others who—like the Phineas Priesthood—espouse hatred and violence against those who are different from themselves, and we cannot allow these renegades to bully society."

Stovall paused and looked up from his notes. "I have contacted all of the governors in America, and they have agreed this is a vital issue that must be addressed. There are estimated to be over 750 hate groups in America, and every state has had similar experiences. We will meet and propose new, tough legislation to fight these terrorists and outlaw their paramilitary tactics. We will be joined by FBI Director M. Blair Novotny, who will support a joint federal and statewide effort to bring these terrorist dogs to ground."

The camera slowly zoomed in to a full-face shot of the governor. "I will not rest until the murderers of Agent Stoddard are brought to justice and given the death penalty!"

Leech raised the muzzle of his Colt submachine gun until it was inches from Stovall's face. "You just signed your own death warrant, Guv." He pulled the trigger and a dry, metallic snap sounded as the firing pin fell on the empty chamber. "You're history, pal."

The reporter returned to the screen. "The legislature has enacted antiterrorism laws in the past, but they are considered by many to be too weak. However, Governor Stovall thinks that his task force will be able to toughen the existing laws and bring some much-needed federal support to the state. He pointed out that there are currently over twenty extremist groups located in Missouri alone, many of whom run their own survival camps, but he is placing the terrorists of the Phineas Priesthood at the top of his hit-list. This is Jon Carreon in Jefferson City."

Leech switched off the set and fought to hold down his rage. "How can they call us terrorists?" he demanded. "They're the terrorists! We're holy freedom fighters. If it weren't for groups like ours, people would be like sheep against the ZOG wolves, with their FBI storm troopers kicking in every door and listening to every conversation. When someone has the courage to stand their ground, they slaughter them like they did at Ruby Ridge and Waco. It's time someone stood up to this fascist governor."

They had heard it all before. Leech could rant for hours on end about the Jews being the "spawn of Satan and Eve," and that Cain and Abel were their first offspring. The "Mongrels" referred to the "Mud People" of mixed races, which had to be eliminated. "Man" was the white descendants of Adam and Eve, the Chosen People. The

United States was their Promised Land. The "Nation" referred not to a piece of ground with definable borders but to a race of people with a common bloodline and a shared history. Man had to prepare for the second coming of Christ by cleansing the land of Jews and Mud People. And the entire xenophobic ideology was based on the Christian Identity beliefs and values, which were taken from literal interpretations of the Bible. It was a man-made, devised theology, manipulating Biblical passages to justify bigotry, racism, and murder. Rational thought, logic, and reason were abandoned in many of the perceived conspiracy theories. Leech had told them that the ZOG government maintained seven hundred concentration camps around the U.S., located at military bases, and, if captured, this is where they would be taken. He claimed that over 800,000 foreign troops were being hidden in Yellowstone National Park, awaiting orders from the New World Order to march on American citizens, killing them or sending them to camps. He often spoke of how the attacks on September 11 were actually perpetrated by the Jews and "dark forces" within the American government to justify passage of the Patriot Act, which would be used to attack freedom fighters like the Phineas Priesthood.

Draeger said quietly, "Dusting a governor might be easy, man, but are you sure you want that kind of heat?"

Leech scoffed, quoting Proverbs 8:11, "'The rich man thinks of his wealth as an impregnable defense, a high wall of safety.' What a dreamer!" He glared at Draeger. "Could it get any hotter than it is now?" He stood there for a moment, thinking, then quietly said, "We're not going to dust 'a governor.' They're all going to be in Kansas City next month, plotting our destruction. Let's make an example out of them. We'll find out where they're meeting, wire up a little surprise, and BOOM! Fifty less ZOG-ites to worry about. Even better, we can take out the head of the ZOG FBI!"

"All right!" whispered Spider, the logic suddenly falling into place for her. It seemed only right to strike here in the Heartland.

"They'll have a ton of security there, man," Draeger warned. He believed in their crusade and loved the constant action, but he didn't want to commit suicide in the process. It is a common misconception that all terrorists are suicidal. In fact, terrorists go to great lengths to plan their escapes. The 9/11 hijackers, crashing their fuel-laden planes into buildings, are a rarity, usually found only in the Middle East.

Leech paused and studied the eager faces of his warriors. "There's an old Middle East proverb that says, 'When your enemies attack, bathe in their blood. If someone is coming to kill you, get up early and kill him first.'"

With that he turned and walked outside, his mind plotting the fate of fifty governors. He had a good idea how they could infiltrate the site, but they would need to pick up some specialized equipment to pull it off. Leech wondered idly what symbol he could sew on his jacket to represent killing a chief of state. Perhaps an upside-down patch of an American flag. But a nagging voice of doubt tugged at him. This operation would carry great risk for the group, and he had to consider their long-term mission of ridding the country of all the heathen population.

Leech looked toward the sky for guidance. "Give me a sign," he whispered. "War or peace?"

For a moment, all was quiet, as though God were pondering the situation. Then a passing cloud moved across the sun, pulling a blanket of shade across their compound, and God's deep voice rode in on a brisk, cold breeze through the surrounding trees. "*C'est la guerre,*" He ordered. *It is war!*

Chapter 14

Marko Vanhala went into the downward-sweeping "S" curve fast, running about seventy-five miles per hour. He stabbed the brake pedal and felt the weight of the vehicle shift to the left front tire. Lightly touching the steering wheel at the three and nine o'clock positions, he could feel every imperfection in the pavement, transmitted through the rubber in the tires. The car was talking to him. He was—as Bobby Davenport would say—"at one with the vehicle."

"You call this driving? Pick it up a little," Davenport the protectee ordered from the right front seat.

Vanhala depressed the accelerator slightly, picking up speed as the wide blacktop curved first to the right, then back to the left. The Goodyear tires sang out in protest. He drove at a speed that he knew was almost to the point of losing control, pushing the protesting machine to its full capabilities. Vanhala attacked the curves aggressively, making a proper entry, negotiating through the apex with precision, and exiting smoothly, setting himself up for the next maneuver. Davenport was impressed, as was David Armstrong, who occupied the right rear seat.

As the road unwound into a long straightaway, Vanhala's vision extended out, evaluating and assessing, searching for obstacles ahead. He could see two cars ahead on the right shoulder. They both had the hoods up, as though one were jumpstarting the other. Both cars had their emergency flashers on. A woman stood in Vanhala's right lane, waving her arm, as if to slow them down. Vanhala glanced up in his mirror and noted that Alex Wiedemann was hot on his tail, driving the follow-up car three car lengths behind him and astraddle the lane divider.

"Left one," Vanhala muttered into his wrist mike.

Wiedemann moved into the passing lane, blocking it for Vanhala. He backed off slightly, expecting trouble, as Marko changed lanes.

To anyone it would appear to be a female motorist in distress. Just about any decent motorist would pull over to give advice, offer a lift or at least the use of their cellular phone to call for help. But these men expected something entirely different. They'd seen what men could do to other men, and they knew—deep within themselves—that this was not what it appeared to be. You could no more fool these young warriors than you could sell an oceanfront lot in Missouri to Donald Trump.

The woman in the road—Vanhala could see that it was Kacey Underwood—walked toward the passing lane, waving a red rag. She was determined to stop the motorcade. Vanhala weighed the situation as it played out in front of him. He knew that it was an attack—that was the point of the training, wasn't it? He had basically two options: zoom out into the oncoming lanes and blow through the ambush, or do an emergency turnaround and escape the way they had come. If the lanes were completely blocked, he could also ram the blocking vehicle, but that wasn't an option with the track cars they were using today. To stop and shoot it out in the kill zone was never an option. The cardinal rule was: ALWAYS KEEP MOVING!

Suddenly, his decision was made for him. The car facing him on the shoulder swerved out and blocked both of Vanhala's lanes. Cameron Boatright jumped out of the driver's seat with a strange-looking weapon. Underwood dove behind Boatright's car and produced a weapon of her own. At the same instant, Armstrong shouted, "Ambush front!" They could not drive around the right, because of the second car on the shoulder. To drive past the ambush would put the shooters on the protectee's side of the car. Vanhala could radio Wiedemann to pull alongside his right to shield them as they drove past the ambush, but the best option now was to turn around. This decision was arrived at in less than one second.

"SWITCH!" shouted "Mount Viking" into his wrist mike and stood on the brakes. The computer-controlled antilock brake system allowed him to utilize maximum braking without the fear of brake lockup, and this enabled him to maintain steering control. Wiedemann, expecting the maneuver, veered around Vanhala, then shot in front of him and hit his brakes. They came to a stop about fifty feet from the ambush vehicle with Wiedemann now the front car. Vanhala shifted to reverse and hit the gas, shooting backward. As soon as he hit twenty-five miles per hour, he released the gas and spun the steering wheel so hard to the left that it looked like he was trying to throw it out the driver's window. The car spun around, he steered into the skid, and then slammed the gear-shift lever into drive and hit the gas. Within seconds of the attack, he was accelerating away from the ambush site. He glanced up and found that Wiedemann, who had also performed the maneuver, was right on his tail.

"Great job! Great job!" Davenport cheered. "Let's go back."

Vanhala slowed and went into a wide U-turn, letting his breath out. He realized that he had been holding his breath through the entire maneuver.

They pulled up to the ambush car to find Boatright and Underwood with sour expressions on their faces. "What the hell was that?" Boatright groused.

Davenport unbuckled his five-point harness and climbed out of the car, removing his crash helmet. "Took you by surprise, huh?"

"What kind of hotdog driving crap was that?" Boatright demanded again. "Did you make that up, or is that something I haven't heard about?"

Armstrong walked up laughing. "It worked, didn't it? You guys expected us to do a standard Tandem J-turn, but Davenport suggested they do that little switch, putting Alex between you guys and our car, before the Tandem J. Worked pretty slick, huh?" The Tandem J-turn was performed when both cars stopped, and the follow-up car initiated a J-turn, followed by the lead car. When both vehicles had completed the maneuver, they then switched places. But Davenport felt that for several seconds the lead car was stopped in the kill zone with nothing between them and the bad guys. His variation of this maneuver was hard on the bodyguards in the follow-up car, but it provided maximum protection to the protectee.

Davenport walked around Vanhala's car, inspecting it. "You guys didn't hit us with one round," he chided them. "I thought you two were supposed to be the most bad-ass terrorists since the Red Army Faction." He walked around Wiedemann's car and found eight paint-ball hits on the front windshield, hood, and fenders, and three more on the back glass and trunk. "You shot the shit out of the follow-up, though." If the vehicle had been armored and the rounds had been standard small-arms ammo, the armor would have stopped them all.

Wiedemann crawled out of the car and removed his helmet. He tossed it onto the driver's seat. His hair was matted down with sweat. "Whoa!" he exclaimed. "That's a rush!" He was exhausted, and walked on rubbery legs over to the terrorists. "I thought I knew how to handle a car as a road officer, but you guys can drive circles around anybody I know."

Davenport had worked the new officers hard, since early that morning. They had practiced everything from parallel parking to evasives, including one- and two-car chokes. Davenport had taught them his "C.Y.M." turnaround, short for "Coordinated Y-turn Maneuver." It was used when there was a perceived threat or hazardous situation spotted ahead of the motorcade. The follow-up car pulled in front of the protectee's car, both came to stop, and both performed a standard Y-turn. It enabled the follow-up car to shield the protectee's car from the threat, but was tricky to do without running into one another. They had spent over an hour in the skidpan. The track cars smelled hot, like they were getting ready to catch on fire, and the engines of both were ticking loudly.

Davenport joined them. "That maneuver worked out better than I thought. I'll have to ask my Secret Service counterpart if they've ever tried that." Secret Service motorcades tended to be long parades of armored vehicles. He doubted if they had ever trained on this variation of the Tandem-J. "I think I'll call it the 'DSTJ maneuver.' The 'Davenport Switch-Tandem-J.' I'll be more famous than Tony Scotti," he said, referring to the world-class, counter-ambush driving instructor. He admitted to himself that he'd be surprised if he found that Scotti wasn't already teaching the maneuver. He looked at Wiedemann. "Well, I'm glad you got something out of this, Alex. We try to do this three or four times a year, just to keep everyone sharp."

Boatright grinned. "Yeah, we go through more paint than Sherwin-Williams."

"Okay, gather around," Armstrong instructed the new officers. When he had their attention, he asked, "Do you believe in luck?"

Wiedemann exchanged looks with Vanhala, then shrugged. "How do you mean?"

"Every culture in the world, going back to the beginning of time, has believed in luck." When they didn't respond, Armstrong continued. "Think about it, guys. The ancient Romans worshipped Fortuna, the Goddess of Luck. Today people collect four-leaf clovers, cross their fingers, wear amulets, do things in threes and sevens, wear their lucky clothing, cross their hearts, knock on wood, and toss salt over their left shoulders. I used to work the road with a guy who carried a chestnut in his pocket. He said it kept him safe from bullets. When I got on the Patrol, my wife bought me a St. Christopher's medal. He's supposed to protect travelers from calamity. I still wear it. They say if you see his image, you won't die that day." Armstrong allowed them a moment to consider his words. "People take all these precautions to sway the odds in their favor. In essence, we still worship Fortuna."

Both officers nodded. Armstrong then asked, "Did you know that Abraham Lincoln carried a four-leaf clover most of his life?"

"Didn't do him much good, did it?" Wiedemann observed dryly.

Armstrong shook his head. "Some say he wasn't carrying it the night he was killed. But that's not what killed Lincoln. What killed him was the incompetent bodyguard assigned to protect him that night. He got bored standing guard and went next door to get a drink in a saloon, leaving Lincoln unprotected. If he had stayed on post, Booth would probably have failed."

The new officers nodded their understanding. Armstrong continued, "Luck is nothing more than opportunities. Whether luck turns good or bad depends on whether *you* capitalize on it or *your opponent* capitalizes on it." He smiled. "The ancient Chinese called that the 'stratagem of serendipity.' Using psychological readiness and constant vigilance to exploit opportunities whenever and wherever they arose."

"I believe in leaving nothing to chance," Wiedemann stated with conviction.

Armstrong shook his head. "That's not true. It's not possible to eliminate every risk. Literally every situation you'll ever handle with the boss will be loaded with risks. Unscreened crowds, no follow-up car, winging events without an advance man, not wearing body armor, flying in bad weather, failing to check some detail because there wasn't enough time. You'll probably have those situations occur every week, if not every day. Despite the rantings of the major news channels every night, there is no such thing as absolute security. They squeal every time somebody sneaks a gun or knife through airport security, but the fact is that some guns and knives have always been missed and will continue to be missed. And it's not just the low quality of the airport screeners. They could put doctors, lawyers, and Congressmen on those metal detectors and they still wouldn't detect every weapon. It's like that old saying: 'Some days you eat the bear, and some days the bear eats you.' What those of us in protective ops need to do is figure out when a hungry bear is around and then force him to eat someone else."

The officers nodded, seeming to understand the lesson. Armstrong continued, "In your first two ambushes today, your protectee was killed. In your last three, you won. This last time, you guys succeeded in getting out of the ambush." He allowed them a moment to consider that. Their training that day had been designed to defeat them in their first scenarios, but to send them home with a few victories under their belts. He gestured toward their cars. "This is where most attacks occur. Statistically, most VIPs come under attack while they are in or around their cars and often within two hundred yards of their home or office. Eight of the thirteen attacks directed at U.S. Presidents were in motorcade situations. About 60 percent of the attacks on public figures are carried out while they are in or around their cars. The secret to protection is *avoiding* ambushes, presenting a hard target, and forcing the bad guys to attack somebody else. About half of the failed attacks on public figures around the world are defeated by good intelligence work. Another 30 percent are defeated by vigilance, spotting the attack before it's launched. Advance preparations defeat another 10 percent. Do you know what causes the remaining 10 percent to fail?"

Vanhala immediately answered, "Luck?"

"That's right, Marko. Luck defeats the bad guys only about 10 percent of the time. My point is that if you rely only on luck to see you through, you'll miss 90 percent of the opportunities to defeat your enemies. As the great Chinese strategist, Sun Tzu, stated over two thousand years ago: 'True excellence is to plan secretly, to move surreptitiously, to foil the enemy's intentions and balk his schemes, so that at last the day may be won without shedding a drop of blood.'"

As the rookies nodded, Armstrong looked toward his fellow instructors. "Any other lessons to share?"

Boatright stepped forward, "Don't ever forget, gentlemen, while we were training here today, somewhere in the state others were training for a different mission: To harm or embarrass our protectee. We always have to be ready for the day they show up."

They were interrupted when Armstrong's BlackBerry phone vibrated. "Armstrong," he responded. His eyes squinted as he listened. "Yes, sir," he said finally. "I'll be right there." When he terminated the call, he looked at the others. "Major Moss wants me in DDCC. It seems the FBI has some intel that concerns our detail."

Chapter 15

Armstrong was buzzed into the protective confines of the Division of Drug and Crime Control (DDCC), the Patrol's criminal-investigation section. He was mildly curious about the purpose of the sudden meeting. DDCC investigated everything from narcotics trafficking to domestic terrorism.

"Captain Douglas and Major Moss are expecting me," he told the receptionist.

"Go right on back, Lieutenant," she replied. "They're in the conference room waiting for you."

Armstrong entered the room and was surprised to see that there were three other men present, including Simon Godwin. One man, dressed in an expensive suit, he didn't recognize.

Douglas waved him inside the small office. "Pull up a chair, David. Can we get you some coffee?"

"No, thanks," Armstrong said. "I'm okay."

"Fine," said Douglas. "Well, let me make the introductions. This is Randall Massock, he's the Special-Agent-in-Charge of the Kansas City FBI office." Armstrong shook Massock's hand. He had heard the man's name, but they had never met. Massock looked like the quintessential FBI boss. He wore a dark, expensive suit, a red silk tie, and a long-sleeved white dress shirt. The cost of his black dress shoes probably ran more than Armstrong paid for an entire outfit. He had a tanned face and graying hair. *Spends his afternoons on the golf course*, Armstrong thought.

"And this is Matt Youngblood. He's an undercover investigator in our Organized Crime Unit."

Armstrong nodded at Youngblood, "Yeah, I know Matt." Armstrong hadn't seen the undercover officer for several months, since Youngblood had infiltrated a militia group in Macon County that had threatened Governor Landham.

Youngblood's deep-set green eyes carried the wary gaze of a battle-scarred wolf. He looked like an old biker. In fact, his black sweatshirt sported a Harley-Davidson logo and bore the inscription "Sturgis Motorcycle Run," a souvenir of the famed city in South Dakota which hosted the annual event attended by thousands of bikers. Youngblood was a legendary undercover officer for the Patrol, having worked four years as a narcotics investigator, then—three years ago—moving into OCU. He now spent his waking hours investigating militant and violent groups bent on destroying the government. There was no undercover officer in the Patrol who was more at risk or more deeply undercover than Youngblood. His undercover identity included a criminal record, detailing arrests for possession of an unregistered firearm, identity theft, and failure to file income-tax reports. It was all part of Youngblood's elaborate fake identity, which had been painstakingly constructed to withstand a thorough background check. His many successful operations made Randall Massock drool with envy. Youngblood had the Midas touch when it came to undercover criminal investigations.

"Of course, you know Major Moss and Lieutenant Godwin," Douglas continued, then eyed Armstrong for a moment. "I guess you're curious about this meeting. We've come up with some information that you need to be aware of." He glanced at Youngblood. "Matt got a tip a few months back that a white supremacist named Butch Riker was amassing an arsenal of stolen weapons. Matt got close to the guy and learned that the weapons were actually going to a Phineas Priest, who owns a place near Deepwater in Henry County. In case you don't know, for the last month we've been involved in a huge manhunt for a group of Phineas Priests that killed that conservation agent."

Armstrong raised his eyebrows with interest, but had no clue where this was going or how it involved the Governor's Security Division. "Yeah, I took the boss to the funeral."

Douglas continued, "We thought this Henry County guy might be involved with our group. Matt has been surveilling his farm, attending his church, and trying to get next to the guy, but Priests are very paranoid about infiltrators. They follow a policy called 'Leaderless Resistance,' which means they pretty much operate in isolation. Matt learned there was a Henry County deputy tied to the guy, and the deputy was warning the Priests about any law-enforcement investigations in the area. There could be others, so we've been running this operation on a strict need-to-know basis. This has been a major investigation, involving DDCC, the FBI, and BATF. Yesterday, we raided the farm, looking for these Priests. Matt, you can take it from here."

Youngblood's lanky frame sat slouched in his seat, exuding an easygoing manner that was disarming. He might have been just about to doze off. You could talk to the guy for two minutes and you would totally relax in his presence, which was the secret to his success. His brushy mustache turned up at the corners as he smiled and said, "L.T., you ain't gonna believe what I'm about to tell you."

Armstrong sat forward in his chair with a look of intensity on his face. He did not like the direction this conversation was taking.

Youngblood ran a hand through his thick brown hair. "These knuckleheads are planning to hit the governor."

Armstrong blinked. "What?" he finally asked.

"These guys are planning to assassinate Governor Stovall!"

Armstrong stared at the surrounding faces to be certain this wasn't some kind of prank. "Why?" he finally asked.

Youngblood shrugged. "All the right-wing groups are screaming about Stovall's antiterrorism summit next month. It could be tied to that. They claim this will be Stovall's shot at getting a state version of the Patriot Act passed through the legislature, and they see the Patriot Act as a sneaky way for the government to take away their guns. Also, Phineas Priests are radically opposed to abortion, and the governor's legislative package included that controversial bill on late-term abortions. Add the fact that Governor Stovall basically threatened to kill them, and it's not a stretch that they'd go after him."

Armstrong straightened up. "What the hell are we going to do about it? Take them down, I hope."

Douglas jumped in. "Unfortunately, they've gone underground. We conducted some overflights of the property, but didn't see any activity. Troop A SERT and FBI HRT agents raided the farm yesterday, but the Priests were gone. We checked the cell-phone records of the deputy and found three calls to the farm within hours of the raid. We found places where the Priests had dug up a plastic drum, probably containing weapons and supplies. Simon's intel unit has identified the farm owner. He's a former Aryan Nation lieutenant, who used to belong to something called a TRT, Tyranny Response Team. They were formed after 9/11 to target courthouses and intimidate judges." He handed Armstrong a flyer they had put together on Bobby Wykoff, which had a dated photo of him. "We've circulated APBs on what we know, but the deputy has lawyered up, and we don't have much as far as the identities of the others. Even if he opens up, he may have only known Wykoff. We've had his patrol car bugged for the past few weeks, and he never visited the farm."

Armstrong eyed Massock. The SAC had remained silent through the meeting. Either he knew something and wasn't saying, or he knew nothing and was just taking it all in. Armstrong knew that you don't get to be SAC by stumbling around in a clueless stupor. He recalled a 1999 case in which federal agents failed to warn then-Governor George W. Bush of Texas about a plot by militant separatists to kill him. An FBI informant had infiltrated the antigovernment group Republic of Texas (ROT) and attended meetings two years prior, at which killing Governor Bush was discussed. The FBI did not warn Bush's protective detail about the plot, because "they did not think the threats were credible."

Armstrong asked, "So, what does the FBI think about all this?"

All eyes in the room shifted to the Fed. Massock remained silent, either for drama or because he was measuring his answer. Finally, he responded, "We believe that it's a credible threat."

Armstrong resisted rolling his eyes in contempt. What the hell did that mean? To himself, he retorted, *Gee, do ya think?* He imagined that Massock's grade-school report card must have complained, "Randall doesn't play well with others."

Massock continued. "We found a metal box, containing several sets of law-enforcement shoulder patches. Agent Stoddard's patches were there, along with patches from six other dead cops. The FBI has been chasing this group for over two years now. We call them the 'Patch Collectors,' for obvious reasons. Our profilers say the patches are collected as trophies to signify their power and defiance. We lost their trail about nine months ago in Tennessee after they robbed a bank. We estimate they must have a war chest of nearly a million dollars by now. They had a firing range set up in one of their buildings, and we found a lot of spent brass, so we know they have automatic weapons. But none of their neighbors reported hearing gunfire, so they were probably suppressed weapons. They left behind a few training manuals—*White Resistance Manual, Army of God Manual, Turner Diaries, Vigilantes of Christendom*—the usual stuff. Looks like they left in a hurry."

Armstrong grimaced, "These guys are preparing for war. I don't like the thought of them being out and about. How will we know when they're going to make their move?"

Massock shrugged. "We have all our people on the case. They've collected a ton of evidence, and everything's in the lab being processed, so we may identify the others through prints or DNA. They'll surface someplace. We should know more in a few days."

Armstrong frowned. A few days in "Fed time" were not the same as "State time." Fed years were more like dog years. "My concern, Mr. Massock, is that they may 'surface' at the governor's next meet-and-greet. I want to brief the governor on this."

The room was silent for a moment, then Douglas said, "We can't tell you not to do that. I just want to remind you that Matt is a deep-cover operative. He belongs to so many Klan groups that he can't even attend all the meetings. If the extremist community gets even the slightest whiff that he's an officer," he pointed his finger at Youngblood like a pistol, "Matt could get a bullet in the back of his head."

Armstrong glanced at Youngblood and received his stony gaze. "I understand, and I'll only tell the boss that he's at risk. No details. But I'd like a heads-up if you find out these guys are getting close."

Douglas and Youngblood exchanged looks. Douglas said quietly, "They're scoping you guys out right now."

Armstrong turned pale. "They're what?"

"Show him the picture, Matt," Douglas stated.

Youngblood slid an 8 x 10 black and white photograph out of a manila envelope and handed it to Armstrong. "We found this at their farm. Do you remember this guy?"

Armstrong's mouth fell open. The picture was of two men, and he recognized it from the "photo op" on the St. Joseph trip. One was the slender man in the suit. He had his arm around the other man: Governor William Ulysses Stovall. At the picture's edge, Armstrong's own face was visible, his wary eyes on the man standing next to his boss.

Simon Godwin spoke up for the first time. "We interviewed the photographer. The guy in the photo used the name 'Ezekiel Leech' and the address of the farm. My intel unit is trying to ID him. We've run him through everything: MOSPIN, HEAT, MULES, NCIC, FinCEN, DOR, Autotrack, VICAP, EPIC, Alert, Regis, you name it, but so far nothing. It's like he doesn't exist. If that's his real name, his record is clean." Godwin handed him another flyer. "We cropped the governor out of the photo and used Leech's face to do a wanted poster on him, but there isn't a lot of info."

Armstrong studied the flyer. "Have you had Secret Service check their database? DEA? ATF?"

Godwin nodded. "He's not in the Secret Service database. I'm waiting on callbacks from DEA and ATF."

"We also found this," Youngblood said, handing Armstrong a photocopy of a handwritten note. "It was taped to their TV screen so we'd find it." The note was entitled, "Operation Regicide," a Latin term, derived from *Regis*, meaning "king," and *cide*, meaning "to kill." The letter contained a graphic, profane warning:

Governor Faggot Stovall,

> *You are in your glory now, aren't you?*
> *You have betrayed Almighty God's laws protecting the unborn.*
> *Your life is tied to that bill. Sign it and we will abort YOU!!!*
> *We are not intimidated by your empty threats.*
> *We warn only once. After that, we will take action!*
> *The bullet that will kill you has already been fired.*
> *If a bunch of towel heads almost brought America to her knees on 9/11, imagine what a unit of commandos with Aryan blood in their veins can do!*
> *Have you built your Ship of Death, Governor Stovall? O build your ship of death, for you will need it.*

In Domini potestas esse terrae (in God's authority over the earth)
[signed] *God's Holy Hit Men*

Godwin continued, "The 'Ship of Death' reference is from a 1932 poem by D. H. Lawrence. We're sending the original letter to the Secret Service in Washington, so they can run it through their FISH System."

Armstrong knew that FISH—an acronym for Forensic Information System for Handwriting—was the largest database of handwriting samples in the world. Samples of text could be scanned and digitized into FISH, then compared to previously recorded materials, examining isolated upper- and lower-case letters, traced or line-followed characters, interactively measured features, and text independent features. They could search the entire database, specific regions of the country, types of writing instruments, or even different languages. If the person who wrote this threat had ever threatened a U.S. President, the Secret Service would have it in their system and should be able to match it up to a hit-list of possible suspects.

"I want a copy of this photo and letter," Armstrong demanded. "If the boss starts feeling bulletproof and thinks I'm just being paranoid, I'll let him read it." It was the policy of the detail not to pass along any threat information to Governor Stovall, unless it served a purpose. Armstrong knew this case would be the exception to the rule.

Major Moss had remained silent through the meeting. His deep voice now took over the room. "David, the colonel wanted me to remind your detail that we don't want anything to happen to the governor. Whatever you have to do, whatever resources you need, we expect you to run an impregnable operation until we put these guys in the ground."

Chapter 16

Chief of Staff Bradley Naylor sat behind his massive walnut desk and contemplated his response. Armstrong yawned, crossed his legs, and focused on the picturesque view out Naylor's office windows. Perhaps it was a mistake to run this by Naylor first, but Armstrong knew the only prayer he had of getting the governor to cancel his summit would be with the backing of the chief of staff.

Naylor cleared his throat to regain Armstrong's attention. "You say that a group of extremists may be planning to kill the governor?"

Armstrong gave Naylor the patient look a teacher might give to a slow student. "That's right," he said after several seconds.

Naylor clasped his hands in a prayer position and rested his chin on his fingertips. "And you want the governor to cancel his terrorism summit and keep a low profile until they can be arrested?"

"Piece of cake, huh?"

Naylor dropped his hands and leaned forward. "Look again, Lieutenant Armstrong. It looks more like a piece of crap to me! This is the governor's first year in office. We have a huge legislative agenda to complete. You might want to check the governor's block calendar. He's going to be busier than Regis Philbin at a beauty pageant between now and the end of the session."

Armstrong sat up in his chair. "Look, Brad, I hate to shove a stick in your spokes, but this isn't some angry constituent who's making an idle threat because his taxes are too high. We believe this group has already committed several murders."

Naylor leaned back and asked, "Where is this information coming from? Is it an undercover officer or informant? What is their identity? If we're going to put the governor in hiding, I have to know everything."

"Sorry," Armstrong said, holding his hands up. "I've already told you more than I should." The fact that Matt Youngblood was working a deep-cover operation on the group had to remain a secret. Armstrong knew if he told Naylor any details, the chief of staff couldn't resist passing them along to his favorite reporter.

Naylor held up the picture taken at the St. Joseph groundbreaking. "This fellow Leech doesn't look so dangerous. I don't see any scars or tattoos. You say he doesn't even have a criminal record. If he intended to harm the governor, why didn't he do it when he had his arm around him?"

Armstrong pointed toward the photo. "That's what we call 'targeted travel,' Brad. He's checking us out. Gathering intelligence. It's one of the clearest indications that they intend to do the governor harm."

Naylor had grown tired of the redundant security measures that surrounded his boss and found them over-the-top. Those around the protected figure became entangled in the security like a wall of razor wire at nearly every step. Bodyguards, armored vehicles, bulletproof glass, locked doors, keyed elevators, video cameras, alarm systems; he found it all ridiculous and overly paranoid. The only things missing were the moat of alligators and the pit of boiling oil. He recalled the words of the German poet Schiller: "He who is overcautious will accomplish little."

Naylor dismissed him with a wave of his hand. "Well, when you get more information, come back and see me. But until then, damn the terrorists and full speed ahead!"

Chapter 17

Seventy. No, seventy-five, thought Trooper Ronald Carr, visually estimating the speed of the approaching headlights. He waited until the vehicle was within a quarter mile of him before unlocking his Stalker radar unit. The "target" window of his dash unit immediately displayed the reading "76," with the speed of his patrol car displayed as "59" in the "patrol" window, which corresponded with his calibrated speedometer. It was all part of the tracking history: the visual estimation of the target vehicle and the correct "ground" speed of his patrol car, verifying the target speed. Sixteen miles per hour over the speed limit and good enough for a traffic summons in this county. Immediately, the front of the approaching van dipped down, and the speed in the target window dropped down to "63." *Ah, he's got a radar detector,* thought Carr. *Definitely a ticket!*

Radar, an acronym for "radio detection and ranging," operates on the Doppler principle and was first developed by the British shortly before World War II. Carr's radar unit actually measured two speeds: the speed of the patrol car relative to the terrain and the relative speed at which a target vehicle was closing with the patrol vehicle. It then used those two speeds to determine the target vehicle's true speed. A switchable microwave transmitter allowed the unit to remain ready without sending out a signal that could be picked up by a radar detector, warning the motorist. When he released the switch, a radio signal traveled out the antenna of the radar head at the speed of light—186,000 miles per second—bounced off the surface of the van, and returned to the radar unit at the same speed but at a different frequency, in this case a high Doppler shift. The large, flat surface of the approaching van provided an excellent reflective capability and gave Carr an instantaneous, strong reading. The reading was captured at the same instant that the violator's radar detector began to chirp, but well before the driver released the accelerator and began to brake.

"Gotcha, slick," he muttered as the van flashed by him. In that instant, there was still enough daylight that he made several observations. There was a white female driving, with a bearded, white male next to her. They were both wearing startled "Oh-no-he-got-me" expressions, and the van was still showing brake lights. He also noted that it had Texas plates.

There were no vehicles behind Trooper Carr and the next approaching vehicle was over a half mile away. He switched on the red lights of his visibar, executed a smooth U-turn, and accelerated after the van. His new Ford Crown Victoria contained a high-performance engine, and it would be futile for the van to try to get away.

"Damn! He turned around!" exclaimed Draeger, looking in the right side-mirror. "Now we've stepped in it." They had no way of knowing whether they were being stopped for speeding or for killing that conservation agent, so he assumed the worst. So-So had slowed down to fifty, but wasn't pulling over.

"Pull over, Stupid!" he barked. "Before he has a chance to call in our plate." He lifted his shirt and pulled his SIG-Sauer .45 out of his waistband. "Just distract him until Leech and I can kill him." He watched in the mirror while the officer pulled in behind them.

Further back up the road, Leech had seen the van's brake lights and watched in horror as the patrol car turned around in pursuit. He sharply reduced his own speed and barked at Wykoff, Spider, and Seed, "Get ready!"

Trooper Carr didn't like stopping vans, especially the ones you couldn't see into, like the one he now had stopped. Its back windows were covered with black shutters, and the side windows were darkly tinted. He had developed the habit of having the driver get out and come back, rather than blindly approaching the driver. He normally would have called in the plate before stopping the vehicle, but the radio was busy with a pursuit going on in another zone. He attempted to scribble the license number on his pad, but only got the first four digits, before the vehicle got stopped. There was a "Support Your Local Police" sticker on the rear bumper.

He angled his car with the hood closer to the road than the trunk, thus putting the engine block between him and the violator. Opening his door, he released his seat belt, but remained seated and motioned to the lady driver, who was watching him in her mirror, to come back to his car. She turned and said something to the passenger.

Carr switched on his P.A. and keyed the mike. "Driver of the van. Step out and come back to the patrol car." She remained seated, setting off alarm bells in Carr's head. Something was going on here. He started to radio for backup when the lady stepped out and stood next to her open door. Calling wouldn't have done much good anyhow. He knew that the next nearest officer was about twenty minutes away.

Carr, slightly perturbed with the uncooperative violator, stepped out of his car but remained behind the door. "Step back here, please," he ordered. She walked back, and he left the cover of his door, meeting her between their vehicles with her back to the van. He stood so that he could glance over her left shoulder and see the passenger inside the vehicle in the van's right mirror. "I need to see your license and registration."

Rather than comply, she reached up and began tugging at the shoulders of her blue sweater. Inside the van, Carr heard a baby begin to cry and glanced up to check on the location of the passenger. Draeger was turned around, as though attending to the child, but was actually pinching his foot to make him cry. Under the plastic baby seat, his hand rested on the grip of his SIG-Sauer. *If he comes alongside the van, I'll shoot him through the side window*, Draeger thought.

Trooper Carr had been focused on So-So's suspicious movements. He had not noticed a blue Dodge Durango pulling onto the shoulder several yards behind his car. He did not hear the silent approach of its driver, who stopped at the right rear fender of Carr's vehicle. He was also unaware of the red laser dot now playing across his back, like a flickering insect. The whirring sound of Leech's silenced Colt submachine gun was lost in the growl of Carr's idling engine. It might have been his air compressor kicking on. But the shock of three subsonic 9mm rounds unexpectedly impacting his body armor had a profound effect on him. He flinched, then wheeled to his left in an effort to get away as three more rounds chewed into the back of the van, missing So-So by inches. Carr's armor took two hits and stopped them both. But the third bullet clipped his upper shoulder, just above his vest. The round broke his left collarbone and punched through the front of his shoulder, shattering the radio microphone clipped to his epaulet. The plastic mike exploded from the impact, cutting his neck and cheek. It was a survivable wound, but it shocked Carr and left his arm unusable. He hit the ground between the vehicles, out of Leech's sight. He rolled under the back of the van, clawing at his own weapon. He sighted back toward his car and saw two feet, now positioned behind his trunk. He brought up his .40 Glock. Without using the Trijicon night sights, he fired three quick rounds under his vehicle. The bark of his weapon didn't even register on his senses.

Leech danced to his right and hit the ground behind the trooper's right rear tire. Draeger had bounded out of the van with his pistol and was bent down trying to locate the officer. So-So had disappeared back into the driver's seat of the van. The firefight paused momentarily, then the brake lights flashed on the van as So-So put it in gear, and the vehicle began to roll forward. Carr realized he would be exposed and attempted to stand up. He was halfway up, when Draeger suddenly appeared from around the van. The dazed officer and cold-blooded terrorist stared at each other for what seemed like an hour, but Carr had the drop on him. His Glock was staring at Draeger's chest, while Draeger's SIG-Sauer was off target. Then a muffled shot from the trooper's right struck Carr in the right jaw, and he went down like a lead weight.

Chapter 18

"Damn!" Draeger spat. "Is everybody okay?"

Leech had held his fire at the officer from under the patrol car, because he didn't want to hit the van tires and blow one out. When he saw the officer getting up, he popped up from behind the car, switched his weapon to semi-auto fire, and fired the headshot. He now emerged with his weapon on the downed officer. "Is he dead?" he asked.

Draeger bent over and looked at the officer's bloody features. "Head shot got him," he concluded. "Nice going. He had the drop on me." He grinned at Leech. "I don't know why the hell he didn't just shoot me. You must have stunned him pretty good."

Leech checked up and down the highway. Luckily, no vehicle had gone by since the officer had stopped them. He grabbed the trooper by the back of his collar and dragged the body down into the drainage ditch along the shoulder. He squatted over the officer's body, took out his hunting knife, and began cutting the shoulder patches off his uniform.

"Come on, man!" Draeger shouted to him. From his tone, it was obvious he couldn't believe Leech was taking souvenirs.

Leech cut one patch off, then got the other. Standing, he stuffed them in his pocket, stepped back, and sighted his weapon on the swollen and bloody face of the officer. *Another round or two, just to be sure.*

"Car coming!" Draeger shouted, causing Leech to look up. A pair of headlights had just broken the crest of a hill nearly a mile away, but was closing quickly. Leech lunged to the patrol car. Climbing behind the wheel, he shouted at Draeger, "Follow me!" The police radio was blaring excitedly, calling officers into position for the pursuit in the adjoining county. But to Leech it sounded as though the radio traffic was referring to their position.

Leech looked down at the console, covered with several toggle switches and buttons. He stabbed the button marked Red Lights, killing the swirling beacons on the roof of the car. Throwing the gearshift in drive, he gunned the vehicle, spinning its tires as he accelerated down the road. So-So pulled the van out behind him, then Wykoff followed in the Durango. As the three-vehicle caravan sped down the road, distancing itself from the headlights behind, Leech began to formulate escape and evasion plans that would get them out of the area.

Chapter 19

Trooper Ronald Carr became aware of movement and sat up. He heard the squalling of tires and tried to open his eyes, but they were nearly swollen shut. The low-powered, 158-grain, subsonic round from Leech's weapon had impacted on his jaw, one inch back from the corner of his mouth. It broke his jaw in two places and knocked him cold. Taking the path of least resistance, it ricocheted along his jawbone, knocked loose several teeth, and exited below the left corner of his mouth. The blow made a mess of his face, but the wound was far from fatal.

He reached for his radio mike, but found it destroyed. With the wound to his face, he wouldn't have been able to talk anyway.

I'm not going to die, he decided. *Not here! Not now!* Carr mentally took stock of his wounds. His face was numb and burned like hell. He touched it with his right hand and felt something wet. His fingers traced around and touched a loose flap of skin at the exit wound. *Jesus*, he thought, *I've been shot in the face!* The realization left him lightheaded. His left shoulder actually hurt more, with a dull, deep ache setting in around the wound. His left arm hung limply to his side. Carr began to feel like he might pass out, but a car suddenly zoomed by less than thirty feet from his position. He looked around quickly, causing a searing pain to stab through his neck and shoulder, and bringing bright spots to his limited vision. He had to sit there several minutes for the pain to subside. In that time, he heard two other cars go past him. *I've got to get up*, he thought, feeling himself grow weaker by the minute. Carr slowly twisted around and got to his knees. A wave of nausea swept over him, and he nearly vomited. When his head cleared, he slowly stood and staggered toward the road. He stood on the shoulder of the highway, trying to remember exactly where the nearest town was located. Carr began walking west, in the direction of a farmhouse that he knew was a few miles away.

He had only walked for a few minutes when he noticed a set of headlights coming in his direction. *I've got to stop that car*, he thought, beginning to feel weaker from the loss of blood. He walked into the roadway, hunched over, with one arm hanging and the other waving slowly.

Emery Jarvis and his seventy-three-year-old wife, Billie Jean, were frightened out of their wits when a bloody figure came staggering into their headlights like a mindless zombie. Emery veered his Buick around the hulking menace, intending to speed away, until Billie Jean ordered, "Stop and help that officer, you old fool!"

Emery pulled to the shoulder and backed slowly to the figure. He recognized the trooper's uniform. "Dear God!" he gasped. He got out to help the stricken officer.

Carr slumped in the backseat, unable to talk, as the elderly couple raced up the road to the hospital in Butler, a town of about four thousand people. The Jarvises thought the officer had been involved in a terrible wreck or was hit by another car. It would be another hour before his wounds were treated, and he slowly described to investigators, through gritted teeth, the events he had endured. Their interview was cut short when the medi-flight helicopter arrived to transport Carr to a trauma center in Kansas City.

One item stood out from the rest. It galvanized the officers into action faster than the ravaged appearance of their fellow officer. The missing shoulder patches told them that the Patch Collectors were alive and well, and willing to coldly murder any officer who got in their way. They vowed that Leech had collected his last patch.

Chapter 20

Leech knelt next to the old barn and listened. He looked back toward the gravel road and saw Draeger move across the headlights of the Durango.

Utilizing a lead car and a chase car was a cop-killing technique Leech had learned during his stay at the survivalist compound in Oklahoma. If the lead car was stopped, the occupants of the chase car came to their rescue, and vice versa. It wasn't anything new. The terrorist group FSLN and others had used a similar method for thirty years.

They quickly had to ditch the cop car, and the bullet-riddled van had now become a liability. Leech took the first blacktop road he came to after fleeing the scene of the shooting. He headed north, driving hard, but not recklessly. So-So and Wykoff followed at a respectable distance, where they could keep his taillights in sight. Eventually, he came to a gravel road running west, and his instincts told him to take it. He passed a number of farmhouses, but all showed signs of life. After a while, the hulk of an old barn floated into his headlights like a ghost ship in the fog. He slowed and stopped in the road. There were no houses or lights in sight. The other vehicles stopped behind him.

A heavy chain kept the door shut, but its links were draped over a nail, rather than padlocked. He released the chain, pulled the door open a foot, and looked inside. Nothing. Not even a scrawny cow. Just a load of hay that looked like it had been there for a while. He slid the door all the way open, returned to the patrol car, and drove it into the barn as far as he could go. Leech then took off his sweatshirt and wiped down the interior to remove his fingerprints. The console, the steering wheel, the door handles. He tried to remember if he had touched anything else. He saw a partial license number of the van on the trooper's notepad and tore off the whole pad, so that no impressions would be left.

Leech reached into his pocket and took out an M33 fragmentation grenade. He pushed it down between the driver's seat and the door, wedging it in place. He then carefully pulled the pin out. It was a little surprise for the evidence technician who would open the door, releasing the spoon. He crawled across the console and exited out the passenger's door, leaving the car unlocked. Maybe he'd take out a sloppy cop who found the car and decided to look inside before the evidence people arrived. So much the better. Satisfied, he secured the barn door and returned to the other vehicles.

"How's the van?" he asked Draeger.

"It took some hits. You can see the holes pretty easily, and the cop's blood is splattered there. Think we should abandon it in the barn, too?"

Leech thought for a moment. Many of their weapons and most of their stash of cash were concealed in the vehicle. "No," he said finally. "Let's keep going and try to make it closer to Kansas City. Tomorrow, we'll rent an old body shop or something. We have to keep these vehicles under cover, until we can get something new." They quickly changed license plates, clipping a Mississippi plate over the one from Texas. He took a roll of duct tape and put patches over the bullet holes to conceal them. It looked a little strange, but might mask them from any curious observer.

When he jumped into the Durango, Spider had a road map spread out, with her finger close to where they were. She traced out a route taking them further north and west. "If we take these roads, we'll eventually cross into Kansas and hit U.S. 69. Then head back north to Kansas City," she suggested.

"Good idea," he agreed. Getting out of Missouri had become their first priority.

They were well inside Kansas when they heard over their scanner a Missouri Highway Patrol dispatch on a blue van with Texas plates, the plate number, and accurate descriptions of Draeger and So-So. The group was stunned, particularly when it was put out as an "attempted" murder of a trooper. He had survived! Leech pounded the dash in rage. Now they would definitely have to ditch the van.

116

They did so at a large car dealership. They parked the van on the back part of the lot, where customers' vehicles were left to be serviced and used cars were parked. Draeger backed the vehicle up against a wall, so the bullet holes in back were hidden from view. They quickly transferred everything they could from the van to the Durango. Leech took a road atlas and traced a line from Missouri, through their location in Kansas, to I-70, and then west to Utah. He circled the city of Ogden and stuffed the book under the driver's seat. Before leaving, Draeger reached under the dash of the van and carefully removed a stainless-steel pin, arming an explosive charge in the back. He closed the door, leaving it unlocked, and pushed the button on what looked like a garage-door opener. He saw a red light on the dash come on. Whoever opened the door would trigger a powerful thermite explosive charge next to the gas tank. There would be little left of the vehicle—or the person who triggered it—once the fire was put out. In case the device failed or was defeated, the map might throw the cops off.

As they proceeded at a leisurely pace toward their target area, Leech thanked God for stepping in each time they faced disaster. When the police raid of their farm was poised for launch, God compelled one of their deputy friends to call and warn them. When the trooper tried to intervene, God enabled Leech to put him down and get away. When an alert was broadcast for their vehicle, God enabled them to intercept the broadcast and ditch the vehicle. Leech had no doubt that when it came to destroying a room full of baby-killing governors, God would not let this golden opportunity escape them.

Book Two: The Blood of Kings

The storms of ruin live! . . . our bloody lion lapped its fill, gorging on the blood of kings.
   —Aeschylus, 450 B.C., *Agamemnon*

Once that first bullet goes past your head, politics and all that shit just goes right out the window.
   —SFC "Hoot" Gibson, Delta Force operator, from the movie *Black Hawk Down*

Chapter 21

"I guess you know the governor likes to be driven fast," commented Corporal Bobby Davenport, glancing out the window of the car. His eyes scanned the sky for the telltale shape of the governor's jet. "Some troopers poke along, and it drives him nuts." He glanced over at his monster backup-driver. Victor Truman's eyes were concealed behind his teardrop sunglasses. The tightness of his mouth was matched only by his death grip on the steering wheel. "And for God's sake, Vic, don't stop for a yellow light. Just go through it."

Truman rotated his head toward Davenport. "I'll give the son-of-a-bitch the ride of his life," he muttered, wondering why he had ever volunteered for this assignment. *Never again*, he decided. *I'd rather wrestle a puking drunk any day than drive some candy-ass, pencil-neck, money-hungry, backslapping, whining politician around town. I'd rather kiss a federal judge's ass.* The thought sent a cold chill through him.

"Well," Davenport laughed, "don't overdo it." He pictured Truman jumping cars like a Bigfoot monster truck. He eyed the skyline again. The plane was past due.

Davenport had originally been assigned to drive the Stovalls from the airport to the hotel, with Truman driving a follow-up vehicle. But Armstrong had called him thirty minutes ago and said, "Schedule change number thirteen: Rosebush has decided she wants you to run her over to the Country Club Plaza for some shopping. Whoever your Shadow driver is will take the governor, Naylor, and me to the hotel in Monitor. I just called Kacey and told her to be waiting for you at the Plaza." That would be a big help to Davenport. He could simply drop the ladies off and stage the car until they were ready for a pickup.

Davenport spotted the white jet coming in over the downtown area, on final approach. "Here we go," he informed Truman. They readied the vehicles and drove out to the aircraft when it was stopped. There was a flurry of activity as everyone deplaned, packed the luggage into the back of Monitor, and headed for the hotel. As usual, Governor Stovall sat up front with Truman, and Armstrong and Naylor sat behind. Davenport drove Rosebush in the Crown Vic as follow-up.

They hadn't gone three blocks into the downtown area before Truman saw the traffic light they were approaching turn yellow. He started to hit the gas and go through, but then thought, *I wonder what Pencil Neck will do if I stop.* Behind him, Davenport saw brake lights and groaned.

Before Truman's SUV even came to a complete stop, Governor Stovall turned to him and said, "What's your name, Trooper?"

In the backseat, Armstrong thought, *Oh no, here it comes.*

Truman's head swiveled slowly on his thick neck, like the deck gun of a battleship, bringing its weapon to bear on an enemy vessel. He responded in a voice steeped with impending doom, "Trooper First Class Victor Truman at your service, Governor."

Unfazed by Truman's fierce posturing, Governor Stovall turned to his chief of staff in back and said lightly, "Brad, let's make sure we send a safe-driving medal to Trooper First Class Victor Truman when we get back to the office. His superior driving skills have just cost me two minutes at this red light, but—no doubt—saved my life from some reckless driver."

There was a moment of silence as Truman faced the light, waiting for it to turn green. His ears had taken on a bright red coloration. Armstrong could see that it extended down the nape of Truman's thick neck. *He's putting on his war paint,* Armstrong thought.

At the first hint of green, Truman floored the gas pedal, leaving thirty feet of black marks. He accelerated on the four-lane undivided avenue, weaving in and out of traffic like a NASCAR-pro wheeling a high-performance machine down an asphalt speedway. He alternately stabbed the brakes and the accelerator, as needed. The buildings flew past Armstrong's window in a blur, and he debated whether or not to tell Truman to slow down. Armstrong clicked his wrist mike several times, but Truman ignored the signal in his earpiece. Traffic was light, and they weren't that far from the hotel, so Armstrong decided to let

Truman dig his own grave. Within six heart-stopping minutes, they slid into the drive in front of the hotel. It would normally have taken about ten minutes to negotiate the five-mile drive through traffic.

Truman threw the SUV in park, turned to Armstrong, and said, "Lieutenant Armstrong, take a note. Remind me to send Governor Stovall a Mr. Nice Guy trophy for being such a patient passenger." He then turned and grinned at the governor, showing Stovall some teeth. *Take that, Pencil Neck!*

Bradley Naylor sat meekly in back, thinking that he might need to change his shorts when he got to his room. Armstrong was looking at the roof of the vehicle, figuring that his brief command was probably over. *They'll probably ship me to Tarkio*, he thought. *I wonder what a house trailer costs in Tarkio?* It was a joke among road troopers that if you really screwed up they'd send you to that tiny wasteland in the northwest corner of the state.

Stovall had a shocked look on his face. He was not used to being taken down a notch by anyone, much less an underling. He slowly got out of the vehicle, then turned, and examined his driver. He suddenly grinned and said, "Trooper, that's some of the best driving I've seen in a long time." He turned to Armstrong. "See that this officer is assigned as my full-time driver during the rest of the conference." As Stovall entered the hotel, he smiled. Truman was cursing and pounding the steering wheel.

Chapter 22

"What are these?" Governor Stovall demanded, looking at the two walk-through metal detectors. From his tone, the devices might have been two hookers hiding under the officers' beds.

Lieutenant Simon Godwin glanced uneasily at Lieutenant Armstrong. Godwin was not surprised when Major Moss assigned him as officer-in-charge of the security detail for the Governor's Summit on Terrorism. After all, he was an expert in providing security for governors' meetings. But he was stunned when Stovall suddenly waltzed back into his life like nothing had ever happened. He had not seen the governor since his transfer to DDCC. Godwin had a sinking feeling when the governor strolled into the command post with Armstrong in tow and informed him that he wanted a tour of the security operation.

"These are our metal detectors, Governor. We can't see into men's hearts, but we can sure look in their pockets. All meeting attendees will file through one of these, and we'll also check inside purses and briefcases. It'll ensure. . . "

"Who authorized this?" Stovall demanded of Armstrong. "No one said anything to me about strip-searching people."

Godwin responded, "Governor, we won't strip-search anyone. They'll simply walk through. . . "

Stovall didn't even look at Godwin. He said again to Armstrong, "I asked, who authorized this, David?"

Armstrong didn't like where this was going. "Governor, Lieutenant Godwin was assigned to come up with a security plan to ensure that all of the governors are safe in their meetings. There has been a lot of adverse publicity on the conference and we've had some threats. . . "

"Get Paul Fleming on the phone," Stovall demanded, holding out his hand.

Armstrong unclipped his BlackBerry from his belt and selected the office number for Fleming. His secretary answered, and Armstrong advised her that the governor was on the phone. When Fleming answered, Armstrong handed the instrument to Stovall.

"Paul? What's this about adverse publicity for my meetings?" Fleming said he didn't have a clue what the governor was talking about. "Well, I'm told by my security detail that there has been adverse publicity, and they're setting up an armed camp over here. Looks more like a bunker than a hotel. I can't have VIPs coming in here, thinking they're in danger and that we can't protect them." Fleming said he knew of no threats, and the stories in the press had not said much about security. "I thought as much," Stovall said and terminated the call. Both officers couldn't help but notice the crimson tide lapping at the governor's chin. They both knew what it meant. Ringmaster was one wrong response away from boiling over.

Stovall studied the officers for a moment. "Gentlemen," he finally addressed them quietly, "I understand you don't want to have any incidents—neither do I—but I will not have you treating my meetings like we're in Baghdad or Bosnia. Missouri is not a Third World nation controlled by warlords. I expect you to maintain a secure environment, but we will not be doing the belly crawl through the lobby or stepping over sandbags to get to our rooms. Do I make myself clear?"

"Yes, Governor," both officers responded. Godwin's face was as red as a baboon's butt, and his expression looked nearly as ugly. Armstrong looked calm and under control. He had detached himself from the confrontation, as though observing a neighbor's child throwing a fit.

Stovall continued, "You can't possibly believe terrorists would actually waltz in here with their guns blazing. I realize we'll have a troublemaker or two. If there is an incident, handle it. Otherwise, keep the hell out of my way! I do not want to read one story in the press about the hotel being turned into a foxhole! I don't want to hear about any VIPs getting hassled by security or about anyone getting bitten by your bomb dogs. Do I need to run all this by Colonel De-Witt?"

"That won't be necessary, Governor," Armstrong assured him. "We'll see to it." He could almost hear the skin on Godwin's forehead ticking from the heat like an overheated engine block. Godwin was in a mood that Romanowski would describe as "blacker than ten feet up a whale's ass."

Stovall's face suddenly lifted, as though another personality had shifted into position. Romanowski had once observed that there were six or seven different individuals lurking in Stovall's body, and you were never really sure which one would pop out of his skin. "This guy's got more personalities than Sybil," Romanowski had stated.

"Super!" Stovall exclaimed. It was one of his favorite expressions. "Now I want to see what the meeting rooms look like." As they walked in that direction, he inquired casually, "You aren't going to have any uniformed people in there, I hope."

Not anymore! Armstrong thought, and decided that after the tour he would sit down with Godwin to go over the plan. They'd have to figure out a way to squeeze the Rhino into a pink dress and blonde wig, where it didn't look quite so threatening.

Chapter 23

Governor Stovall looked up from his notes and gazed over the crowd assembled before him. Every governor was in place, watching him intently. Their seats were arranged around a table in what was referred to in the business as a "hollow square." Over two hundred spectators were already seated, with more entering through the doors in the back. A horde of media occupied a press riser in the back of the room, like a flock of hungry vultures. A contingent of serious-looking men, and a few women, were lining the walls. *Mostly security people,* thought Stovall, irritated. *Why do they need to be in here? It's insane to think that a terrorist would try to do anything with all this protection around.* On that note, he cleared his throat, leaned into the microphone, and began his opening remarks.

"Fellow governors, ladies and gentlemen. On April 19, 1995, a bomb devastated the Alfred P. Murrah Federal Building in Oklahoma City. Initial reports identified the culprit as a Middle Eastern terrorist. We could not fathom such an act being carried out by another American. The nation was shocked to later learn that it was, in fact, one of our own." Stovall allowed several seconds for the idea to sink in. "Since 9/11, law-enforcement agencies in many of our states have uncovered suspected sleeper cells, made up of international terrorists. In Missouri, our state budget has been crippled by mounting security costs." He paused again for effect.

"A recent study by the U.S. Fish and Wildlife Service indicated that assaults against wildlife officers are nine times more likely to be fatal than attacks on other law-enforcement officers. It also showed that four-out-of-five of their assailants were carrying firearms, as compared to one-in-five assailants of urban officers. These figures struck home seven weeks ago when a Missouri conservation agent was brutally murdered. This heinous act was carried out by a small group of heavily armed, highly trained terrorists, whose twisted philosophy is to bring down our form of government. Preliminary evidence indicates this same group assaulted a Missouri trooper two weeks ago, less than a hundred miles from here. The innocent owner of a farm was killed the following day by a booby trap they placed in the officer's stolen patrol car." He focused past the teleprompter to the crowd and found that they were totally absorbed in his message.

"It's been said that this is a nation of laws, not men. We as a nation, therefore, can no longer tolerate men who have gone beyond the laws of a democratic society, resorting to assassination, armed robbery, and the spreading of racial hatred and bigotry, as a means of changing the system. Here in Missouri, I plan to introduce sweeping legislation, which will help us to take our cities and towns back from these terrorists.

"These groups often hide in our national forests and state parks. The Forest Service lists 835,000 acres of our forests as 'constrained,' too dangerous to be used by the public. In the past year alone, Missouri law-enforcement officers seized over 800,000 marijuana plants, valued at over 650 million dollars, rating us among the top five marijuana-producing states in the nation. Our neighbors—Kansas, Tennessee, and Kentucky—also share that distinction.

"And marijuana isn't the only curse haunting our parks. Last year, there were over six hundred clandestine methamphetamine labs seized by the Missouri State Highway Patrol in our state. Our officers are finding weapons in a third of those labs, and it's not unusual to find pipe bombs and other explosive devices. For each pound of meth produced by these labs, they produce five pounds of hazardous waste. Campers and hikers have stumbled into booby traps set by these renegade groups to protect their illegal operations.

"There is a war raging in our states, and it's high time we did something about it! I don't have all of the answers, but hopefully at the conclusion of this conference, we will be unified in the goal to rid our states of these extremist groups.

"I believe that a two-pronged attack would be most effective. One, we must agree on ways to coordinate our statewide efforts to make them more effective; and two, as a group, we must take proposals to the White House in Washington, to present to the President and his Cabinet. I have recently spoken to the President about this problem. He agrees it is vital to address these issues together. The federal laws may have adequate strength, but I think we all agree that there needs to be better enforcement.

"Our best hope obviously lies in a team effort, rather than chasing these groups from one state to another. Together, there is no problem we can't solve. Divided, we will most likely fail. We live in an area rich with legends of outlaws, from Jesse James to Bonnie and Clyde, and—more recently—Timothy McVeigh, Eric Rudolph, and Unabomber Theodore Kaczynski. Let us restore the strong sense of law and order that our forefathers brought to the Midwest one hundred years ago. As the Greek dramatist Aristophanes explained, nearly four hundred years before Christ: 'Men of sense often learn from their enemies. Prudence is the best safeguard. This principle cannot be learned from a friend, but an enemy extorts it immediately. It is from their foes, not their friends, that cities learn the lesson of building high walls and ships of war. And this lesson saves their children, their homes, and their properties.'"

He paused and scanned the room. The silence wasn't because he had put them to sleep but was due instead to the grave realization of the problem's enormity. Terrorists had to be dealt with swiftly and harshly, and everyone knew that you don't negotiate with them. But trillions of dollars had been poured into antinarcotics and antiterrorism efforts, and it didn't appear that things were any better now than they had been in recent history. In fact, the situation looked worse. That would also make his proposed solutions more appealing.

Stovall concluded his remarks. "I hate to open this conference on such a down note, but we all face a grave problem, and the solutions will not be quick and easy. The task before us is daunting. I will first call on Governor Caine of Kansas, who will relate some new enforcement efforts taking place in his state."

As Caine began his remarks, Stovall stepped back from the podium, and his eyes swept the room. He was startled to see Simon Godwin standing in the back. Their eyes locked, and the exchange was not friendly. He decided to have Naylor inquire about why Godwin was involved in the conference. Even if he had some assignment here, he shouldn't need to be in the meeting room. *What the hell is he doing in here?* Stovall wondered.

Chapter 24

Armstrong paused in his conversation with a Tennessee trooper, hearing Romanowski's voice calling him in his earpiece. Armstrong spoke into his wrist mike, "Go ahead, Don."

"Ten-twenty?" asked Romanowski. *What's your location?*

"I'm outside the CP," answered Armstrong. "What do you need?"

"Ringmaster wants to see you ASAP. We're just outside the ballroom."

What now? Armstrong wondered. "I'll be right down." He looked at the Tennessee officer. "I've got to run, but it was nice talking to you." The trooper nodded knowingly. When the boss calls, you drop whatever you're doing and come running.

Armstrong bounded down the staircase and found the governor giving a statement to a news crew outside the ballroom. Romanowski was on one side and Marko Vanhala was on the other, both out of camera range. Crowded in close were Naylor and Fleming, listening intently to the questions and responses.

Armstrong walked over to Romanowski. "What's up?"

Romanowski shrugged. "He just asked where you were and said to get you down here."

Stovall was saying that he was "confident the governors could think outside the box and reach a consensus agreement that would have a dynamic impact on the issues at hand." Before another question could be thrown at him, Fleming jumped in like a referee between two grapplers. "Sorry, the governor has to run," he lied. Before the news crew could object, Stovall took his cue and was gone. It was as well-rehearsed a maneuver as a pro quarterback handing the ball off to his tailback.

Stovall walked over to Armstrong, and Romanowski gave them some room. "I've got a favor to ask," the governor said seriously.

"Yes, sir. What is it?"

"I need you to go pick up Lance and Heather."

"Sure. Where are they?" Armstrong was relieved. After all the mystery, he was expecting something serious like: "I need you to assassinate the lieutenant governor."

"They're coming in on the afternoon Amtrak from St. Louis, so they'll be at the station soon. Take my car and driver. I'll be tied up here all afternoon anyway."

Armstrong looked at his watch. "I'll handle it personally, Governor."

"Super!" Stovall stated. He turned and went back into the ballroom, followed by Vanhala.

Romanowski stayed with Armstrong, who walked toward the staircase and spoke into his wrist mike. "Armstrong to Davenport."

"I'm in the downroom, L.T.," Davenport responded immediately.

"Get Monitor and pick me up in front of the lobby. We need to make a pickup at the Amtrak Station."

"Be there in five mikes."

Although Governor Stovall had requested Victor Truman as his driver, Armstrong had decided against it, based on Truman's performance in the high-speed transport.

Romanowski grinned. "Gotta go get the Prince and Princess, huh?" Governor Stovall's children were not very popular with the detail members and had quickly been given nicknames that fitted their personalities. In short, they thought of themselves as royalty and expected everyone to treat them that way. The Prince had recently moved to the top of the detail's shit list when it was revealed by a St. Louis journalist that Lance Stovall had a page on MySpace.com that boasted, "The coolest thing about being a governor's kid is having my own bodyguards to carry my bags, and I don't have to give them a tip. It's like having a bunch of stupid gorillas follow you around."

Armstrong rolled his eyes. "What was all that about? Why didn't he just ask you?"

Romanowski grinned. "That's just the way he is. For anything involving the family, he'll only ask you personally. It's now your responsibility to handle the task with discretion. If the *Kansas City Sun* hammers him for misuse of state resources—using a state trooper as an errand boy—he'll know it came from you."

"Great!" grumbled Armstrong. "Where's Mark David Chapman when you need him?"

Romanowski continued, "For what it's worth, I noticed that Naylor took a call, then gave the boss a message, which means that the Prince and Princess called Naylor direct. The reason they took the train is so they wouldn't have to drive themselves, and they could drink in the saloon car all the way over, so they'll be too loaded to drive when they get here. If you haven't figured it out, they're both a couple of real boozers. The Prince could use one of those hats that holds two cans of beer with a straw that runs to his mouth. Also, they know that if they hang around dad, they'll be shuttled around in cars with their own ring of bodyguards, as part of his protective package."

They had walked up to the lobby and paused at the entrance, waiting for Davenport to arrive. Romanowski looked around. "You haven't been around the kids since you've taken over the detail. The first thing they'll do is test you. They'll be really friendly at first, but before the night is over, they'll be barking orders at you like a couple of drill instructors." He raised his voice an octave, "Go get me a bottle of wine . . . We want tickets to the theater . . . We need a ride to the restaurant." His voice went back to normal. "They'll push you to see how much they can get away with. If you want my advice, tell them up front that we're here to provide protection to the governor and First Lady, not serve as their gofers. They don't realize or don't care that it undermines the security for the boss. If it was up to me, I'd give them the phone number for Rent-A-Wreck, a map of the city, and tell them to stay out of trouble."

As part of the governor's immediate family, the children would normally fall under the umbrella of protection that covered the governor and First Lady. Armstrong would ensure that they got to the hotel and were given credentials for the meetings, but he would not allow them to turn detail members into their servants or distract them from their assigned duties.

Armstrong smiled. "Ever heard of Machiavelli?"

"Isn't he that shortstop for the Cardinals?" guessed Romanowski.

Armstrong wasn't sure if he was serious or not. You could never tell with Romanowski. "No. He was a political theorist in sixteenth-century Italy. I did a paper on him in college. Ironically, he wrote a book called *The Prince* that describes how leaders should effectively deal with the populace."

"Did he work for the Stovalls' ancestors?" ventured Romanowski.

"He must have," Armstrong admitted, as he saw Davenport wheel into the drive. "Machiavelli wrote that there are two ways of dealing with situations, by law and by force. The first was for men and the second for beasts. He noted that Achilles and other great leaders were trained by Chiron the Centaur: half-man, half-beast. Therefore, great men knew both natures, because one without the other promoted instability."

Romanowski nodded, "If I understand your point, it's to our benefit to know how to deal with VIPs, as well as assholes who only think they're VIPs."

Armstrong grinned, starting out the door. "You're not as dumb as Underwood says you are. Just don't ever forget what the Chinese said about powerful people."

Romanowski gave him a quizzical look.

Armstrong called back, "'Serving the powerful is like sleeping with a tiger.'"

Chapter 25

March 2, 1822 hours
Grand Plaza Hotel
Kansas City, Missouri

If the majority of the newspaper reporters in America are liberal Democrats, as some polls have suggested and—despite their claims of being unbiased—their stories lean to the left, as most conservatives believe, then Casper Deegan made the rest of his colleagues look like William F. Buckley. His frustrated rantings against government corruption, the lost war on drugs, and the never-ending problem of police brutality, which appeared in his daily column of the *Kansas City Sun*, were so extreme as to anger all but the most left-wing loonies.

Deegan strolled along behind Governor Sandgren of Indiana, trying to look as though he were part of Sandgren's entourage. It was a gate-crashing ploy that had worked even at Presidential events. Sandgren's lanky bodyguard—a sergeant with the Indiana State Police—trailed the governor and First Lady. He looked over at Deegan's face, then his eyes dropped to Deegan's chest. Like a screaming tornado siren, the yellow ribbon hanging under Deegan's credential announced him as a member of the press. At the lavish Governors-Only banquet that was about to begin in the ballroom, Deegan would be as welcome as a leper at an AIDS convention.

As Governor and Mrs. Sandgren reached the credential checkpoint outside the ballroom entrance, a smiling staff person welcomed them warmly. As Deegan reached the door, the smile disappeared from the staff guy, and the iron grip of Trooper Matt Schubert locked itself on Deegan's upper right arm, stopping the spindly reporter in his tracks.

"Pardon me, sir," stated Schubert with a diplomatic smile. "Are you lost?"

Deegan looked around as though confused. "Isn't this where the press party is?"

"No, sir," Schubert said patiently. "As you know very well, the press party is at Mahoney's Pub up in the Westport area."

"Westport?" Deegan asked, stalling for time. He tried to look over Schubert's shoulder for a glimpse of the governors inside.

"Yes, sir, Westport. About five blocks north of here. If you hurry, you can probably still make happy hour." Schubert shifted slightly to his right, spoiling Deegan's already limited view of the ballroom.

Deegan decided to shift from defense to offense. He pulled his pad and pen out of his coat pocket, flourishing them like a street thug with a switchblade knife. "You're very astute, Trooper. . . "

"Schubert, sir; now if you don't mind. . . " Schubert applied a subtle amount of pressure to Deegan's arm to get him going in the other direction.

Deegan dug his heels into the carpet. "Trooper Schubert," he said, with a heavy dose of indignation, "I'm here to cover the governors' conference, and you are impeding my abilities to do that." It was a tone that normally intimidated others.

"Yes, sir, I am," stated Schubert flatly. "This event is closed to the press." He exerted an increasing amount of pressure. There was another governor approaching, and he wanted to get the reporter out of the way.

Deegan appeared to give in. "Okay," he said, "I'll leave." Schubert's hand released him. Deegan gave the officer a friendly smile. "I apologize, but—like you—I have a job to do. This must be nicer duty than wrestling some drunk driver along the side of the road, though."

Schubert scanned the entourage of Governor and Mrs. Throck-morton of Ohio, as they walked past and entered the ballroom. The two Ohio state troopers escorting them nodded to him. "It's okay," he responded. "I'd rather be a lifeguard on *Baywatch*."

Deegan looked shocked. "What's not to like? Smell that food, Trooper Schubert. When this thing starts you'll be in there dining with a bunch of governors, probably having steak and lobster."

Schubert frowned. "Yeah, right. If my relief ever gets here, I'll be lucky to get a sandwich out of some vending machine."

"You mean they're not feeding you guys?" Deegan asked, shaking his head in disbelief.

"No, sir. That's probably where they came up with the name 'Governors-Only' banquet." Schubert suddenly remembered that he was talking to a reporter and decided to say no more.

134

"Well, I would think they could spare a few bites for their body-guards." When Schubert just looked at him, Deegan knew the "interview" was over. "You have a pleasant evening, Trooper Schubert," he said cheerfully and walked toward the elevators. Deegan smiled. He had his headline for tomorrow's column.

Chapter 26

March 2, 2330 hours
Grand Plaza Hotel
Kansas City, Missouri

Romanowski sat in the lobby bar of the Grand Plaza and sipped his Diet Coke. He eyed a couple who were approaching Governor Stovall's table and recognized the man as Governor Winfred H. Blair of Georgia and his wife, Joyce. Their massive bodyguard, Sergeant Leland Justice of the Georgia State Patrol, dressed in an expensive-looking blue suit, trailed them. To everyone who knew him, Justice went by the sobriquet "Quick." Justice's eyes swept the patrons in the bar and he spotted Romanowski, Armstrong, and Underwood on the other side of the room. Romanowski motioned to an empty chair at their table and Justice nodded.

Underwood groaned inwardly. She had first met Justice over three years ago, and he'd been making moves on her ever since. It was only a matter of time until Justice had his hands all over her. If she wasn't assigned to the First Lady, she'd excuse herself and go to bed. But duty called, and she knew the Stovalls would probably close down the bar. Then she'd have to contend with the persistent Justice, following her back to her room like a hound dog in heat. She watched as the Blairs joined the Stovalls at their table, and Justice made his way over to the security table.

Despite his high-pitched voice, Justice looked like he could be a noseguard for a pro football team. He was tanned and handsome, with short blond hair, eyes as clear and blue as a Caribbean lagoon, and dimples so deep that Kacey imagined he must have to clean them with a Q-tip. He would have looked perfectly at home pumping iron on some California beach or modeling a suit on the cover of *GQ*.

"Greetings, everybody," Justice twanged formally. He winked at Romanowski. "Well, if it isn't the Dapper Don. Haven't seen you since Bubba got impeached." He ran his hand across Underwood's back, and it irritated her. *He's checking to see if I'm wearing a bra*, she thought. He always caressed her back in the same place. "And how are you, Darlin'?" Justice drooled at her.

She managed a smile. "Fine, Quick. Isn't it past your bedtime?"

"Care to tuck me in?" he challenged, as he slid his bulk into the chair across from her and adjusted his position so that he had an unobstructed view of his protectees.

"Where's your driver?" Armstrong asked, looking around. The Missouri trooper assigned as Governor Blair's driver was nowhere in sight.

"I gave the boy the night off," answered Justice. "These kids today can only stand post for eight or ten hours. After that, they ain't worth a damn." A waitress floated by and Justice intercepted her, ordering a club soda with lime.

Romanowski nodded. "Not many of us old-timers left around, are there?"

Justice eyed Romanowski. "We're droppin' like flies in a cloud of Raid bug spray. How much longer are you gonna be in this business? You been doin' this for—what—nine or ten years?"

"Twelve," Romanowski responded, glancing in the direction of the Stovalls' table. He had chosen a seat that allowed him to keep his back to the wall, and face the protectees. While he talked to those at his table, he maintained an alert eye toward the Stovalls. If the governor or First Lady left for the restroom or asked for their check, he would alert the others. In fact, he had asked the waitress who was waiting on the Stovalls to alert *him* when the governor asked for his check. To a passerby, it would look like the officers were taking the night off, but—after fifteen hours of duty—they were still very much on duty and were expected to be alert for any threat.

Armstrong eyed the big Georgia officer. He guessed the level of Justice's body fat at about 5 percent. He looked like the stereotypical bodyguard, heavy on the brawn, but a little light in the old cranial cavity. Armstrong preferred them the other way around. As Justice leaned back and stretched, his suit coat fell open, and Armstrong saw that he carried a Smith & Wesson Model 645 on his right side and two extra clips in a leather pouch on his left. The stainless-steel .45 auto matched Justice perfectly, big and flashy with a loud bark. "Why did you get into the protection business, Quick?"

Justice waited while the waitress delivered his drink. He eyed her tight buttocks as she walked away, before he answered. "Well, my favorite movie of all time is *Blackjack* by director John Woo. He's the guy that always has the hero divin' through the air and shootin' two pistols. The hero always fires a couple hundred rounds out of his guns, but never hits anything, except glass vases, mirrors, and stuff. He never hits the bad guy. Anyway, this big guy—Dolph Lundgren—played a bodyguard assigned to protect this beautiful model."

Underwood saw where this was going and rolled her eyes. With Romanowski and Justice together, they'd need a backhoe to shovel the bullshit out of the bar tonight. She gave Justice a confused look. "I thought your favorite movie was *Ferris Bueller's Day Off*."

Justice ignored her. He sipped his drink and eyed the three officers to gauge their gullibility. "During the movie, his protectee gets depressed, so Lundgren dances with her to cheer her up. Then she throws her back out, so he runs his hands around her and pops it back into place. Then he saves her from about six or eight assassination attempts. I saw all that and thought, 'Man! That's the life for me.'"

Everyone was quiet for a moment and then Romanowski responded wistfully, "Yeah, I know what you mean, Quick. I love this job more than a lap dance with Jennifer Lopez. When I got on the detail, I was more excited than a busload of convention delegates. My head got so big you couldn't have covered it with a tarp."

"So," Underwood interjected, "what's the governor do while you're adjusting the First Lady's coccyx? Read a book or just flip through the cable channels?"

Justice grinned, lighting the bar with his perfectly white smile. "The boss uses me like his teaser stallion, Kacey, my dear. I'm supposed to heat the First Lady up—get her all lathered up and pantin'—then the boss steps in like the big stud and scores the touchdown." Everyone at the table groaned. Justice shrugged. "I'm not complain', mind you. Mrs. Blair's better lookin' than most First Ladies." The conversation around the table died down. Finally Justice asked, "What's the intel on this conference? Is it gonna be a quiet one or should I be wrappin' the boss in Kevlar?"

Armstrong shook his head. "If it was going to be a quiet one, we could all get drunk and go home. You'd better keep the Kevlar close.

This one's shaping up to be more trouble than you can stack on a flatbed truck."

Unfazed by the dire forecast, Justice grinned and launched into a story about the time he had accompanied his governor on vacation to Hilton Head Island. The boss had fallen asleep on the beach and Justice stretched out on his towel nearby, enjoying the sun. Justice leaned in and lowered his voice as he got into the meat of the story. "When the boss rolled over, his suit shifted around and his onions fell out. I didn't notice until about an hour later when two women were walking past him. They started laughing and took his picture. I ran over to him and saw his nuts were burned to a crisp." Everyone at the table was chuckling and shaking their heads. Justice continued, "I didn't know whether to throw my towel over him or push them back into his suit. So I shook him awake and said, 'Hey, Boss, don't look now, but your corks have bobbed to the surface!'" Kacey grimaced at the vision, wondering how she would have handled that situation.

Not to be outdone, Romanowski recounted the time Governor Landham had eaten some bad calamari and "accidentally shit himself halfway through his speech to five hundred business leaders." Landham cut the speech short and unexpectedly walked off the stage. Romanowski caught up with him as he fled through the service corridor, trying to find the service elevator to return to his room. Romanowski said, "He was wearing a tan suit, and I noticed the seat of his pants was black as pitch. When I got him in the elevator and the doors shut, the smell hit me in the face. The boss and I looked at each other and he said, 'Sorry, Don, but I ate some bad squid and now I'm squirting ink!'"

Their banter continued for over an hour on topics that included overtime pay, whether Glocks were better than Smiths, and the unending persistence of terrorists. But anytime you get a bunch of bodyguards together, the topic of conversation inevitably gets around to "who killed JFK?" Romanowski considered himself to be somewhat of an expert on the history of assassination. From the stabbing of Caesar to the shooting of Rabin, he could launch into a profound discussion of the details of the event, right down to the type of weapon, time of day, the injuries inflicted, and the fate of the assassin. Armstrong knew that Romanowski was one of the few people around who could actually give you an informed answer to the question: If Trujillo had been driving faster, would he have survived his attack?

Justice—more to stir the discussion than to explain his true beliefs—took the tack that Oswald was a patsy, set up by the government to take the fall for an assassination which was actually carried out by the Cubans and the military industrial complex.

Romanowski nearly fell out of his chair. "Jesus-on-a-Segway, Quick, you're a cop! Slap a tourniquet on your bleeding, liberal heart, and try looking at the evidence! Oswald had motive, means, and opportunity. He purchased the weapon. He worked in the kill zone. He fled the scene. He killed a cop. He hid in a theater. He resisted arrest. Not exactly the actions of an innocent man. Even Johnnie Cochran couldn't have gotten him off."

Justice shook his head, unconvinced. "I've been to the Sixth Floor Museum at Dealey Plaza. Michael Jordan in his prime couldn't have made that shot. It was the hobos on the grassy knoll. That's why several people ran up there. Stevie Wonder could see that. If Oswald did the shooting, he would have shot straight down when Kennedy was right under him, not when he was moving away."

Romanowski nearly knocked over his Diet Coke as he waved his arms. "You want to talk about shooting down? Read Gerald Posner's book *Case Closed*. He shoots down every crazy theory that was ever cooked up to sell a book. Oswald took a shot with the same rifle at General Walker in New Orleans, just seven months prior to Kennedy. And tell me this, name one other time when people ran *toward* gunfire. If a bullet had been fired over Zapruder's shoulder, he would have flinched. But his camera didn't even move."

Justice shook his head. "If you believe that, then you believe that Jeffrey Dahmer was just a nice kid with bad breath. The polls don't lie, brother. Over 80 percent of the American people can't be wrong. They believe there was a conspiracy and someone other than Oswald killed the president." Justice winked at Underwood. She was the youngest officer at the table, and her troubled expression indicated she didn't know whom to believe. "Tell him I'm right, Kacey," he told her.

She shrugged. "That happened long before I was born. All I know is from watching the Oliver Stone movie." It was clearly the wrong thing to say.

140

Romanowski gaped at her. "'Et tu, Brute?' Stone's movie? You can't be serious. Stone must have been stoned when he made that piece of garbage. He took every stupid conspiracy theory that was out there, loaded them into a gun, and fired them at the audience like buckshot, hoping one or two pellets would strike home." He pointed an accusing finger at Justice. "That silly-ass movie is the reason why your brilliant American couch potatoes believe there's a conspiracy. Most of them are like Underwood; they weren't even alive when it happened. They're too damned lazy to pick up the *Warren Commission Report* and read it. It may have missed a few details, but they basically got it right. Oswald killed Kennedy."

Justice was not swayed. "The Commission was a bunch of rich, old white guys, who had every reason to cover things up. Their report has more holes than a putt-putt golf course. And the media was in it up to their necks, too. It's all a matter of record. The House Select Committee in 1979 concluded there was a conspiracy."

Romanowski shook his head, "Nice try, O'Cave of Eternal Bullshit, but the Committee concluded that Oswald fired the shots that killed Kennedy, and it was 'probably' the result of a conspiracy. Then they ruled out the Russians, the Cubans, the mob, and the Feds as being involved. Let's see, who's left? Oh, yeah, Elvis!" Romanowski looked on the verge of stroking out. His face was as red as their waitress's tiny outfit. "They based their conclusion on a police recording that supposedly captured the sound of a fourth shot. That evidence has since been proven bogus. You want to believe in conspiracies, Quick? Fine! Here's one for you: Elvis did it on Nixon's orders. And then the mob pumped Elvis full of drugs so he wouldn't talk. But when he sobered up and threatened to come clean, President Carter had him carted off in a UFO and declared him dead."

Justice squared around on Romanowski, his blue eyes blazing, as though he was preparing to leap over the table. "You insult Carter and you insult me. He was just a good ol' Georgia boy, like yours truly. The Feds had Elvis held at Area 51 until Carter was out of office. Reagan had him carted off in the UFO, and everyone knows it!"

Finally, the waitress signaled that the VIPs were asking for their checks. The officers quickly settled their own account, putting their Dealey Plaza debate on hold. They left a generous tip on the table and moved out into the lobby to wait for their protectees to exit. Romanowski went to hold an elevator.

As sure as Betty Crocker makes good cookies, Justice informed Underwood that he was willing to give her a back rub when they got back to their rooms. Underwood paused before declining. After all, Justice—despite his crude demeanor—was a gorgeous hunk, they were both single, and her back was screaming bloody murder. "No thanks," she said finally.

"You sure, hotshot?" he asked. He opened his lids and his pale blue eyes watered with sincerity, like a blond Labrador begging to be let inside. "I'll rub a little Vicks on your chest and make you sing."

She shook her head tiredly. "Nobody touches the twins but me," she said. "I need to get up in five hours. Besides, you've never heard me sing."

*   *   *

As the group escorted their protectees to their rooms, two ladies paid their check and left the bar. Their table next to Governor Stovall's had been an ideal surveillance post, providing a wealth of valuable intelligence about the conference as they eavesdropped on Governor Stovall's grousing about the "top-heavy security detail" and how he had trimmed it back. Spider and So-So flagged a cab outside the lobby and gave the driver an address within two blocks of their nearby safe house.

Chapter 27

Bradley Naylor found Armstrong in the hotel lobby and pulled him aside. "What's this I hear about the governor being threatened?" he demanded.

Armstrong studied the arrogant chief of staff. Romanowski, in his irreverent style, had dubbed him "Brad the Impaler," or sometimes "Vlad Naylor." Both names were a tribute to the bloodthirsty Prince Vlad III Dracula. The fifteenth-century ruler was also known as Vlad Tepes, meaning "Vlad the Impaler," named for his favorite form of execution: impaling people on stakes while they were still alive. Sometimes Armstrong wanted to tell Naylor to take a flying leap off the dome of the Capitol Building, but Naylor had the political clout to "impale" his career. Armstrong suspected he'd had a hand in Godwin's reassignment.

"This morning, Romanowski found a message for the governor. It was left at the message desk and contained a conditional threat: 'If you outlaw guns, you won't leave here alive.' Conditional threats are always spoken from a position of weakness. The man is actually saying, 'I don't want to kill you; I want you to not outlaw guns.' Hotel security caught the guy on one of their video cameras. We've already located and interviewed him. He's a local nut job. KCPD thinks he's the same guy who threatened their mayor two months ago. He thinks the mayor has been replaced by an identical imposter."

Naylor gave him a look like he thought Armstrong was pulling his leg.

Armstrong continued, "It's a rare mental disorder known as Capgras Syndrome."

Naylor was a pretty smart guy, but he'd never heard of Capgras. For all he knew, Armstrong was making it up. "Do you think the threat is real or a hoax?" Vlad inquired, with all the innocence of a copperhead snake, coiled quietly on Armstrong's career footpath. Armstrong knew the scenario: Naylor would establish the line of culpability early on. If nothing happened to the governor, nothing would be said. If an incident occurred, then Naylor could claim that he had questioned Armstrong and that Armstrong had shrugged it off.

"There's no way to tell, Brad. We treat all threats as though they were real, but the fact remains that threats—whether they're conditional or direct—are not an important pre-incident indicator for public-figure attack. Real assassins are like bank robbers; they never warn you they're coming. What action would you like me to take?" There . . . the ball was back in Naylor's court.

"You're the security expert. Handle it as you see fit," Naylor snapped. Passing shot . . . the point, as usual, to the lawyer. Armstrong thought Shakespeare had it right: *First thing we do, let's kill all the lawyers.*

Naylor moved on to another topic. "I understand Corporal Boatright beat up some guy in the lobby yesterday. Was that *really* necessary?" His tone indicated that the man would have obviously surrendered, if they had only given him half a chance.

Armstrong fought to control his temper. "The guy was a member of the Klan who came to confront the governors. When they tried to get him to leave, he pulled a knife on them. He had a .357 and an assault weapon in his vehicle. He's got a rap sheet longer than Madonna's limo. Boatright used only the force necessary to neutralize the threat. It was either that or blow the top of his head off. You tell me which action would be easier for the press to tolerate," he said tightly.

"I heard three cops held one man down and tortured him," Naylor countered. "Witnesses said Boatright broke the man's arm in retribution, not self-defense. If that's true, the important work being carried out by the governors downstairs will be overshadowed by headlines screaming about another Rodney King outrage. David, when the Missouri State Highway Patrol swaggered through the doors of this hotel, the laws of this state and the rights of its citizens did not cease to exist. The governor heard it looked like they were shooting a Steven Seagal movie in the lobby."

Armstrong's face took on a red coloration. "The lobby was full of civilians who could have been killed by the guy!" He pulled out his

BlackBerry and opened an e-mail from Boatright. "Here's a picture of the guy after he was handcuffed. Boatright took it with his cell-phone camera." The picture showed a huge man with a blond crewcut. His left arm was handcuffed to his belt, his broken right arm hung limply at his side, and his face was twisted with pain. There was not a mark on his face. "He doesn't look very beaten up to me. Since Boatright is black, he let two white KCPD officers confront the guy. When the guy told them to 'go fuck themselves,' they tried to grab him. He punched one officer in the throat, putting him out of commission. The other officer grabbed him in a chokehold, but the guy flipped him and took out the knife to stab him in the chest." Armstrong pulled up another file. "The video camera behind the front desk caught the whole thing." In surprisingly clear detail, the video file played, showing the entire fight at half speed. Armstrong narrated the footage. "Here's the first officer going down. Here's the second officer getting flipped. Here's Boatright jumping in. He puts a Brazilian jiujitsu move on him, called a Kimura. Twisted the guy's arm so far behind him that it snapped his forearm before he dropped the knife." The video ended and Armstrong returned his BlackBerry to its holster. "Physical-force reports were filled out by all of the officers involved. Statements were taken from all the witnesses. A review board will take a hard look at how the incident was handled. If Boatright was out of line, he'll be disciplined for his actions. Personally, I hope they hang a medal on him. He clearly saved the officer's life."

Naylor saw his indictment of the officers' actions fly out the window. A jury would laugh him out of the courtroom, whether he was prosecuting the officers for brutality or trying to defend the suspect. He decided to drop that topic as well. He held up his newspaper so that Armstrong could see the front page. "Have you caught Deegan's column in this morning's *Sun*, yet?"

Armstrong squinted at the piece. "No. What's he complaining about now?" The angry font jumped out at him: TROOPERS GO HUNGRY WHILE GOVERNORS FEAST AT TAXPAYER'S EXPENSE! He groaned.

"Nice, huh?" Naylor replied, as Armstrong skimmed the piece. "Here's the kicker: he quotes a 'Trooper Schubert' as saying that security personnel weren't allowed to eat with the governors they were assigned to protect, and that the troopers would have to forage for food in vending machines, like a band of homeless vagrants." When Armstrong didn't respond, Naylor continued. "Paul Fleming is having a stroke right about now. We're confused. Since when do lowly troopers assigned to security duty take it on themselves to conduct interviews with the press?" His sarcastic tone supplied the obvious answer: *NEVER!*

Armstrong was embarrassed, but he wanted to reserve judgment until he could talk with Trooper Schubert. "Brad, you know how these press guys are. I doubt that Schubert even knew who Deegan was." It was a weak argument. The officers had been warned about talking to outsiders, and Deegan was probably wearing a press credential. Schubert was chosen for the post because he was a handsome and conscientious officer. After this indiscretion, Armstrong was certain that Lieutenant Godwin would let Schubert finish up his security assignment guarding the governors' cars in the garage.

Brad the Impaler folded the paper and pointed it at Armstrong like a wooden stake. "This had better be the last interview conducted by anyone, except Governor Stovall, Paul Fleming, or me!" he hissed.

"No problem," Armstrong assured him, wanting to stuff the rolled up paper down Naylor's bony throat.

Naylor glanced around to make sure no one was in earshot. When he confirmed they were alone, he changed directions again like a star runningback, veering in and out of tacklers. It was a tactic that kept people off-balance. "Why is Lieutenant Godwin here?" he asked bluntly.

This question caught Armstrong off guard. "He's in charge of the conference security detail," he answered cautiously.

"Well, he was inside the meeting room, glaring at the governor during his opening address. Whatever job Godwin has, surely he doesn't need to be in there. If there's a threat, it should be headed off before it gets to the meeting room."

Armstrong was stunned. "What do you want me to do, Brad, order him to stay away from the boss? How about if I get an order of protection, banning him from coming within one hundred feet of the governor? Technically, as a division director, I outrank him, but I'm not going to order another lieutenant to stay away." It was a cardinal rule that protectors choose their positions, not politicians.

Naylor threw up his hands in defense. "I'm just telling you. Your job is to consider the governor's well-being, and the presence of Godwin is very discomforting to him. He would be much happier if Godwin was not in the meeting room."

If the boss feels bad about how he screwed Godwin, then he deserves to be uncomfortable, thought Armstrong. He couldn't believe his ears. "Lieutenant Godwin's assignment is to maintain a secure environment for the governors' meetings. His long experience and instincts in protective operations makes him perfectly suited for that job. If you're ordering me to tie his hands and restrict him to the fringes of this operation, then you'll take the responsibility if anything happens." Since he had taken over the detail, Armstrong had bent over backwards to carry out Naylor's edicts, but this was going too far. "Brad," Armstrong continued quietly, "let me explain it this way. Imagine that you're a surgeon and I need heart surgery. I come into your office and ask you to do the operation, but I tell you to use a sharp piece of glass off the street instead of a scalpel, because I don't like scalpels. You'd refuse, and for good reason. You're asking us to do security but to do it badly, and we can't comply. We'd be negligent."

Naylor's face hardened. His arrogance prohibited him from accepting criticism from anyone who questioned his authority. His negotiation skills followed the "Pepsodent Strategy": *Treat everyone like a tube of toothpaste; the harder you squeeze them, the more you'll get out.* When he spoke, his words carried the weight of the Governor's Office, and Armstrong obviously hadn't grasped that concept. "I'll relate your comments to the governor and to Colonel DeWitt. I'm sure they'll both be disappointed in your response."

Among Armstrong's many skills was his training in Verbal Judo techniques. One of the basic rules of that approach was to allow the adversary to have the last word, as long as the officer has his way. In other words, ignore the long-haired drunk calling the officer "a stinking pig," as long as he was allowing the officer to apply the handcuffs and place him in the patrol car. It wasn't always easy to ignore provocation, but Armstrong resisted the urge to grab Naylor by the throat and choke him. Instead, he pictured the chief of staff standing in the lobby in his underwear—a big pair of SpongeBob SquarePants boxers covering his pasty white body—with long black socks up to his knees and an orange propeller cap. The vision brought a smile to

Armstrong's face, and he responded pleasantly, "Thanks, Brad. I knew you'd understand."

Naylor was livid. He spun around and stalked off toward the elevators, like a spoiled child barred from grabbing all his desires at Toys "R" Us.

Armstrong's mind returned to the threat letter, and he reconsidered the validity of it. He suddenly thought of Emma Sanders, an eighty-three-year-old retired schoolteacher and self-proclaimed prophet. She lived alone in an old house on the east side of Jefferson City. Emma had called the Governor's Mansion two months ago and talked to Kacey Underwood about a dream she had experienced the night before. Governor Stovall was walking out the glass doors of a large hotel, surrounded by four stern-looking bodyguards. He wore a white suit and a cowboy hat with a long quail feather in the band. As he reached his car, a sniper fired two shots, and two bloody holes appeared on the governor's suit. No matter how hard they tried, the bodyguards were unable to stop the bleeding or even get the car door open to take him to the hospital, and he died in their embrace. As they drew their guns to return fire, the bullets only went a few feet before dropping to the pavement like harmless pebbles. Emma was delighted when Underwood asked if she and Armstrong could come over and take her statement.

They found the inside of her small house to be very neat. They also noted there were toys scattered around the living room, but there were no children. A birdcage, but no birds. An aquarium, but no fish. The more they listened to Emma's rambling statement of conspiracies and assassinations, the more they realized she was a lonely old lady who was crying out for attention. They politely thanked her and left. She now called Underwood and talked to her every few days about her new visions.

Armstrong pictured the weathered face of the old schoolteacher. The web of wrinkles cut her face so deeply that Underwood had remarked, "You couldn't fill them with a putty knife and a gallon of latex caulk." Armstrong looked across the foyer to the glass walls of the elegant hotel lobby and muttered, "Emma, maybe you aren't so crazy after all."

Chapter 28

It was easy. Easier than Spider had imagined. She and So-So had only to present their fake, laminated press IDs, the voucher letter bearing the Houser Communications Incorporated logo, and their registration fee to the girl at the press registration desk. She then gave them colored press credentials for the conference. Leech had spent two days carefully making the fake IDs, but the girl had barely glanced at them.

So-So was nervous, her eyes darting in one direction then another. "Calm down," muttered Spider. "Nobody's going to recognize us." She was right. They had gone to a nearby mall, found a beauty salon, and each had had a complete makeover done. When they returned to the safe house, the men hardly recognized them. The trendy clothes, short haircuts, and oversized eyeglasses had transformed the scraggly biker moms into upwardly mobile, investigative journalists, hammering at the glass ceiling.

They carried their equipment cases toward the press entrance. A metal detector and two officers, one in uniform, barred their passage.

"Who are you ladies with?" asked the officer in plainclothes.

Spider responded in her official anchorwoman voice, "I'm Barbara Walters and this is my colleague, Katie Couric. We're here to interview the governor." She was flirting with him.

The officer laughed. "Yeah, right. Got any grenades in those cases?"

Not yet, cop, Spider thought. She started to say something snappy like: *We're fresh out of grenades, but we just got in a load of claymores that'll blow your ears off*, but security personnel seldom found bomb jokes funny. She smiled seductively. "There's nothing quite so exciting as a man in uniform asking to see a girl's firecrackers." Spider was actually enjoying this.

So-So bent over, her shaking hands pretending to check the latches on her case. A droplet of sweat rolled down So-So's nose and disappeared into the carpet. She fought the urge to flee.

"Okay, Xena the Warrior Princess. Let's have a look inside," he chuckled, pointing to their cases. They were thorough. She had to give them that. Every case was checked. He even pressed his fingers into the Styrofoam padding. The cases contained only legitimate equipment. He told Spider to turn on her camera, and he looked through the eyepiece to ensure that it worked. He motioned to a canine team, and a bomb dog checked out the cases. Everything passed.

"Now for you two," he said, motioning to the metal detector.

"This thing won't give me breast cancer or anything will it?" Spider asked in a serious tone.

"Not for ten or twenty years," he responded. When she gave him a dark look, he promised, "You'll be okay."

So-So, her heart pounding, followed Spider through. A sharp whistle sounded, nearly giving her a heart attack.

"You probably picked up her boot knife," Spider said dryly.

The officer looked So-So over. "Take off that bracelet and step back through," he instructed her. She removed the heavy metal trinket. This time she passed the sweep.

They collected their equipment, thanked the officers for their help, and moved into the press headquarters next to the meeting room. The room was cluttered with machines that could copy, fax, type, collate, compute, monitor, record, and transmit anything that occurred in the meeting room. Over thirty media people went about their business without giving the newcomers even the slightest glance. The women stored their equipment in a corner and moved toward the door that led into the conference room. The afternoon session was just beginning. They recognized Governor Stovall at the podium, listening intently as the governor of Iowa responded to his question.

Spider looked over the room. It was packed with VIPs, government employees, business leaders, members of the press, and law-enforcement officials. It was a target-rich environment. The surreal situation left Spider feeling dizzy. The room was orderly now, but tomorrow it would be devastated by their assault. Body parts would litter the floor like sticks of firewood. And they would become the most famous patriots in North America since Timothy McVeigh destroyed the Alfred P. Murrah Federal Building.

Chapter 29

"You guys in the press are more irritating than a cloud of dog-pecker gnats!" roared Lieutenant Godwin, glaring down at the stony face of a reporter about half his age. It was reminiscent of an old movie in which the tough-as-nails drill instructor chewed out a new recruit, except the reporter wasn't standing at attention.

Darren Rankovich—ace reporter for the *Topeka Informer*—considered himself to be fairly sophisticated. But he didn't have a clue what "dog-pecker gnats" were, although the name didn't sound very flattering. He held up his hands in surrender. "I admit, it may not have been a good idea, but the people. . . "

" . . .have a right to know," Godwin finished the age-old excuse for sloppy journalism. "You're not reporting news, son, you're creating it. Who the hell gave you the right to try to sneak this through security?" he growled, holding up the dummy hand grenade in the reporter's face. "You were lucky you weren't shot!"

Rankovich looked to his right, searching for an ally. Major Joe Fortman of the Kansas City Police Department stood with arms folded and glaring eyes. No ally there. Fortman was in charge of the twenty-five KCPD officers assigned to the conference security detail. "I apologize," Rankovich said with a smug smile. "We were just working on a story about the security measures, and we wanted to test how effective it was." He shrugged, as though it wasn't any big deal. "Apparently, it's pretty tight. You should be happy."

Godwin grew another two inches. "I'll tell you what makes me happy, Mr. Sixty Minutes, and that is throwing your sorry hide out of my conference." He held out a calloused hand. "Press pass," he demanded.

Rankovich didn't move. "You can't take my press pass," he said flatly, shoving his hands deep into the pockets of his stonewashed jeans. His blue, button-down collar shirt, narrow black tie, brown silk sport coat, and cordovan loafers with no socks, rounded off his fashion statement, violating every rule of good taste in the book. He looked like an anchorman for MTV.

Godwin took hold of the color-coded plastic ID, hanging on a cord around Rankovich's neck, and jerked it away. The snapping cord was just strong enough to bite painfully into the back of the reporter's neck. "Owww," he whined. "That hurt!"

"Sergeant Wells," Godwin ordered, "escort Wolf Blitzer here out of my command post!" Wells took hold of the reporter's elbow and pulled him toward the door. Godwin added, "And if he's seen in the hotel again, have him arrested."

Fortman watched them leave and turned back to his counterpart. "I think you were too easy on him, Simon."

Godwin broke into a grin. "I didn't think I could keep a straight face through all that," he confided. "I've got two kids older than him. I would have had him arrested, but our fearless governor said after Boatright's incident in the lobby that he doesn't want anyone arrested unless absolutely necessary. We wouldn't want to let the public know that people actually oppose his ideas!" He pitched the grenade to Fortman, who caught it neatly. It was a replica of the old MK2 fragmentation model with a serrated body, available at any Army surplus store for about five bucks. "Which one of your people caught him?"

Fortman examined the olive-green device. "Rivers and Murphy. They noticed the bulge in his coat pocket, and he was nervous as hell. He tried to sneak around the magnetometer with it while they were busy checking several other people." He set the device on a table. "We need to let this story get out. The threat of expulsion will keep the rest of those jackals in line."

"I agree. We also need to put your guys up for a commendation. That was damn good work. I'll ask Armstrong to have the governor send them a nice thank-you. Get their picture taken with him or something."

Fortman nodded. "That would be nice. It'll motivate the rest of the troops. Hopefully, that's as close as we'll come to a real terrorist incident."

Chapter 30

It took less than two hours. Bradley Naylor and Paul Fleming stalked into the command post and demanded that the shift commander immediately produce Lieutenants Godwin and Armstrong, as though he were hiding them in a secret location. Sergeant Wells yawned, took a sip from his coffee mug, and advised the radio dispatcher to page the officers. Within five minutes, both men walked through the door. Naylor waggled a finger at them to join him in a corner of the room.

"What's this we hear about you kicking out a reporter?" Naylor demanded of them both.

Godwin spoke up. "*I* had him kicked out. He tried to smuggle a grenade into the meeting room, for God's sake."

"I heard it was a toy," Naylor countered.

Fleming now joined the fray. "His editor has called me twice and they're screaming bloody murder. They've apologized and want us to reinstate the reporter's credentials."

Godwin's face moved closer to Fleming, as though he were angling for a bite at the staffer's throat. "You've got to be kidding. We should have arrested the son of a bitch! Letting him come back will send a message to the whole bunch that anything goes, and all they have to do is whine to the governor's. . . ," Godwin searched for the right word and decided against *butt boy*, ". . .staff, and they can have their way. It's like giving a drunk driver his bottle back and telling him to be careful on his way home. I was going to ask the governor to commend the officers that caught the guy."

"You've got to be kidding. The governor is livid," announced Naylor, as though the weight of his words would change the commander's mind. "He told you two not to be harassing the meeting attendees, and that includes the press. They're not the enemy. They have a job to do, too."

Godwin folded his arms. The matter was closed to further discussion. "You let him back in and you can get someone else to run this operation." It was an empty threat and they knew it. Godwin would do what he was told.

Armstrong had remained silent during the exchange, and he now spoke up. "Look, guys, this reporter technically committed a felony. His paper is hardly in a position to be demanding anything. They were out to embarrass the governor. Their story would have jeopardized the safety of every governor who's here. If I were you two, I'd let them know that the governor is livid with *them*, and that they owe *him* a big one. But getting back into this conference is out of the question for the guy who was caught. If they want to send another reporter in his place, fine. But this guy's not to come back to the hotel. Take a hard line with them and they'll respect you for it."

Naylor and Fleming exchanged glances. First the Deegan piece and now this! They were less than happy with Armstrong's performance, but they were getting nowhere at this level. If they wanted anything done, they'd have to track down Colonel DeWitt, but he was unlikely to bend on this issue, either. Fleming shrugged.

Naylor looked at Armstrong. "We'll go along with your decision for now, but I want to stress that the governor wants only good press out of this meeting. So far, the biggest headlines have been from your bungling the operation." The staffers turned and stalked out of the room, as though joined at the hip.

Godwin glared after them. "I'd like to put an armlock on those pimps and frog-march them all the way back to Jeff City."

Armstrong was thinking more along the lines of drowning them in the hotel pool. He grinned at Godwin. "I once heard a story where two Secret Service agents had a run-in with President Nixon's senior staff. One agent told the other, 'Come the revolution, be sure to save two bullets—one for Haldeman and one for Erlichman.'"

Godwin liked that idea and chuckled, "Yeah, I may save a whole clip for Naylor and Fleming."

Despite their feelings, the security operation had moved out over thin ice. They would have to walk lightly until the conference was over to avoid further confrontations.

Chapter 31

March 3, 1810 hours
Grand Plaza Hotel
Kansas City, Missouri

Iowa Trooper Kyle Spencer took a monstrous bite out of his turkey club sandwich and chased it with a gulp of iced tea. He glanced again at his watch. *Damn!* It had taken longer than he anticipated to get served in the hotel restaurant, and he was now supposed to be waiting outside the lobby. The Missouri trooper assigned as the driver for the Iowa governor had taken the First Lady shopping, and they were due back any minute. Spencer was to meet the First Lady and escort her up to her room so the driver could secure the car in the garage. The day had been hectic, and Spencer had not had an opportunity to eat since breakfast. The governor was resting up in his room, guarded by Spencer's partner, so he had taken the chance to get a quick bite. Spencer pulled the conference detail book out of his black leather portfolio to check the starting time of the next event. A moment later, he returned it to the portfolio.

"Excuse me," said an attractive lady seated at a table next to Spencer, startling him. "Are you with the security detail?"

Spencer eyed her momentarily. "Pardon me, ma'am?"

The lady smiled and extended a hand. "I'm sorry to intrude, but we're attending the conference and I noticed your security pin. I thought I saw you with one of the governors today."

Spencer shook her hand and nodded. "Yes, ma'am." He stuffed several fries into his mouth. The last thing he wanted was to get involved with a lengthy discussion on security. He was always cautious of strangers.

The lady motioned to her companions, a younger lady, not quite as attractive, and a teenaged boy. "I have a favor to ask. Would you mind taking a picture of us?" She held a small digital camera.

"Sure thing," Spencer said. He took the camera, stood, and walked several feet from their table. He turned and examined the camera to figure out its operation.

The attractive lady walked over and stood close to him. Her perfume was tantalizing. "Just look through the viewfinder," she explained, "then push this button here. When the light turns green, the flash is ready to fire. Okay?"

"No problem," he said, as she moved back to their table. "Smile big, now." The flash fired and the moment was captured. He returned to their table and held the camera out.

"Could you take one of my son and me by the window?" she asked. Without waiting for a response, they rose and walked to the windows, which offered a scenic view of the Country Club Plaza.

Why not? thought Spencer. He lined up a good shot and pushed the button.

"Thanks so much," Spider said with a flirting smile, as she and Seed returned to their table.

At that moment, Spencer's cell phone rang and he quickly answered it. "Spencer."

"Hey, man, this is Harding. The First Lady and I are about five minutes out."

"Okay," said Spencer, "I'll meet you out front." He scribbled his name and room number on the check, grabbed his portfolio, and scurried out the door, leaving a half-eaten plate of food behind. In his haste, he didn't notice that his copy of the conference detail book was missing. It contained copies of the hotel floor plans, post assignments, bomb-sweep schedules, motorcade routes, and emergency evacuation plans.

Spider, Seed, and So-So also rose from their table. They quickly paid their check and left the hotel. So-So carried the red tote bag issued to all meeting attendees, and the bag was now transporting the yield of her theft.

Chapter 32

"Here's the conference room." Spider's narration of the day's film-ing was starting to bore Leech. He had to admit, though, that they had gotten much more than he expected. They had filmed all key areas in the hotel and most of the security operation, including the command post. In addition, Spider's press packet contained a sched-ule of events, including the time that FBI Director Novotny would be addressing the group. They all agreed, that was when they should strike. They now had enough intelligence to plan a successful assault and would spend much of the night going over their plans.

But the biggest coup of all was So-So's theft of the detail book. When she and Spider produced it, Leech raised both arms and ex-claimed, "YES, JESUS!!!" He couldn't have asked for more. Its secrets would greatly increase their odds of success. He had fixed his admir-ing eyes on both women. "'I will go before you and level the moun-tains,'" he quoted, "Isaiah, chapter forty-five, verse two."

By chance, they had spotted the security officer in the restaurant. When Spencer looked through the detail book, Spider had nudged So-So and nodded in his direction. As they watched, he slid the book back into his open portfolio beside him. Spider suggested the ruse to distract him, enabling So-So to remove it while he wasn't looking. It was a bold move, but a risk that would produce high returns, if suc-cessful.

The video picture now blurred. "It's not even in focus," Leech complained and then, as if the machine heard him, the picture cleared. The room was steady for several seconds, then blurred again. "Lord God," he mumbled.

"That thing's hard to operate!" Spider exclaimed. "I bet you couldn't do any better." She was getting irritated. No one could please him.

"Even Seed could do better." He couldn't resist the opportunity to insult them both in the same breath. "Try setting it on auto focus."

Suddenly the picture cleared, showing Sergeant Kacey Underwood escorting Mrs. Stovall into the meeting room, where she took a seat behind her husband to listen.

"Who's that?" Leech asked, coming to the edge of his seat. He was obviously interested.

"That's Governor Stovall's wife," explained Spider.

His eyes lit up. Wives! He had an idea for a backup plan. This mission was going to be a lot more fun than he had even hoped!

After the video was finished, Leech slapped his knees and stood up. After a pause, he quietly told the others of a dream he'd had the night before. In it, a herd of elephants was destroying the land. They were huge and powerful and too big to be stopped. Suddenly, a pack of wolves attacked the elephants from the tall grass around them. It was a lightning-fast and vicious attack, and the wolves killed two of the elephants and wounded several others before the elephants could react. By that time, the wolves had disappeared back into the tall grass. He stated that he saw it as a sign from God that the government could be destroyed, but only through the use of "asymmetrical warfare." The story sent a chill through the others. Most of them believed that Leech received his inspiration directly from The Almighty.

"So," Leech concluded. "I think we'll go with our original plan." He laughed. The idea of transporting the components for a bomb into the meeting room and actually assembling it right under their noses left him giddy. *It's ingenious*, he thought. *Totally unexpected!* He examined the intent faces of his disciples. "Now let's discuss what we do after the initial blast."

Chapter 33

March 3, 2155 hours
Grand Plaza Hotel
Kansas City, Missouri

"What's in there, Kacey?" asked Patricia Stovall, as she and Sergeant Underwood walked past the command post on their way back to their rooms. They had been checking out the location of the First Ladies' breakfast, scheduled for the next morning. Mrs. Stovall would be hosting the event and giving a presentation, and she wanted to check out the arrangements before going to bed.

Underwood pointed to the doorway on the left, "That's the security downroom. It's where the officers can relax and take a break while the meetings are going on." She motioned to the center door. "That's the command post, which is open around-the-clock. And the door on the right is the package-screening room, where the bomb detail works."

Before Underwood could pull her away, the First Lady stated, "I want to look in the command post."

Officers assigned to command-post duty find it to be a restrictive assignment. They are trapped—unable to leave—and in a "forced waiting" mode over a period of several hours or even days. They often become territorial, guarding their small confines like a pit bull patrols his fenced yard. They can become irritable and vocal. Underwood was aware of all these factors and decided to precede Rosebush into the CP, so there weren't any surprises.

As they entered the room, Mrs. Stovall stopped inside the door and looked around smiling, marveling at all of the equipment. Several officers occupied the office and it looked like business was slow. They looked up at their visitors. The night-duty supervisor was a salty, twenty-year sergeant named Greg Lipp. He was known for working well under pressure, being organized, and running a tight ship. The fact that he was outspoken and lacked "people skills" was the primary reason he was assigned to the dogwatch. Lipp sat with his back to the door, reading the *USA Today* sports page, unaware of his visitors.

Underwood decided to check her message box to see if any schedule changes had been posted. As she moved past Lipp, he looked up from his paper. "Well, well, if it isn't Sergeant Kacey 'Look-But-Don't-Touch' Underwood. Decide to grace us with your presence?"

She growled in a low tone, "Stand back, Sarge, I'm on a mission from God."

Lipp sneered, "I heard they've got you chasing around behind the First Lady, sniffing up her skirt. Tell me something, Kacey, how's old PMS's blood pressure? Has she blown her famous cork yet and busted anyone's balls?"

It didn't dawn on Sergeant Lipp that the room had grown totally quiet. The radios were even silent. Those present would later claim that the temperature in the room even dropped twenty degrees. Nor did it register as genuine shock that Underwood had spun around and was staring at him with an astonished, mouth-wide-open look, as though she had suddenly swallowed her tongue. He took her expression to be one of mock outrage. "Don't give me that, Underwood. Nobody would want to be the putz that had to clean up after that frost bitch!" he said with a grin on his face. He looked around the room. *Why is everyone looking at me like that?* he wondered.

From behind him came the sound of high heels biting into the carpet. Lipp spun around and was aghast at the sight of the "frost bitch" bearing down on him like a rabid Rottweiler.

"What did you call me?" Patricia Stovall demanded, closing to within inches of the stocky officer. "PMS? Frost bitch? Well, I'll tell you what, Mister, I haven't busted any balls tonight, but how about we start with yours?" She cupped her hand, as if holding two eggs, then slowly closed her fist, crushing the imaginary shells. Everyone in the room winced, even Underwood.

"I-I-I'm sorry, Mrs. Stovall," he stammered. He could not have ended his career any quicker than if he had taken a dive off the roof of the hotel. "Please forgive me, ma'am!"

Without another word, Rosebush spun on her polished heels and stomped out of the room. Lipp would swear that at that moment he detected a pungent aroma, like burnt rubber . . . or perhaps scorched flesh.

Underwood stood where she was, glued to the floor. She finally broke herself free and took off in pursuit of her protectee. She caught

160

the First Lady at the elevators. Underwood said quietly, "Mrs. Stovall, he was just joking around. Don't take it seriously."

Patricia Stovall's green eyes moved to Underwood's face and held it in an icy gaze. "Welcome to the view above the glass ceiling, Kacey. You'd better learn to be strong or they'll eat you alive. This jerk won't even get to finish out his shift."

Chapter 34

Armstrong was jarred out of a deep sleep by an incessant ringing noise. He stabbed the snooze button of his alarm clock three times before realizing that the noise was coming from his phone. He picked it up, but had not yet reached the level of intelligent speech and only listened. He was still suspended between his dream—a frightful sequence in which he was swimming through a sea of venomous snakes—and reality (arguably the same sequence). In another sixty seconds he could easily be back to sleep.

"Lieutenant Armstrong? Hello?" came the voice of Randy "Boomer" Wilson, the new night-duty supervisor in the command post.

Mrs. Stovall was right. One phone call from her room to Colonel DeWitt, and Sergeant Greg Lipp had been sent packing, back to his home in Cuba, Missouri. He would have plenty of time, during the drive, to contemplate his future with the Patrol. Mrs. Stovall insisted that the Patrol's Professional Standards Division—the internal-affairs unit—initiate an official investigation against Lipp for misconduct. Colonel DeWitt assured her he'd "look into it," but felt it probably wouldn't amount to much. Lipp had not criticized her publicly. He'd made inappropriate remarks to others in an area, which was, in fact, restricted from the public. It probably wouldn't rate much more than a written reprimand or short suspension, but there would definitely be some discipline handed out over this incident.

"This better be good, Boomer," Armstrong growled into the mouthpiece.

"Sorry, sir, but we have two fire alarms sounding on the tenth floor, one floor beneath the governors' floors," stated Sergeant Wilson. "Hotel security and one of our troopers from the post on the governors' floors are responding to check it out."

Armstrong knew that the hotel fire alarms were silent, sounding only in the hotel security command center. Security people always responded. If it were an actual emergency, audible alarms would be activated on the floor of the emergency, as well as one floor below and two floors above. Hotel guests would be directed by a recorded voice over the intercom system to use the fire stairs and evacuate to the driveway in front of the lobby. Armstrong had made other arrangements for the governors. They were to be taken to a secure holding room which also served as the drivers' downroom.

It is a general rule in protective operations to never allow a protectee to stay above the sixth floor in any hotel. Even the tallest fire-department ladders cannot extend above that level. But in the real world, the top floors are often designed specifically for the visiting VIP. Suites, executive lounges, and lavish restaurants are perched on the top floors, providing the VIP with breathtaking views of the city. Governor Stovall's staff insisted on the governors' being housed on the eleventh and twelfth floors of the Grand Plaza, the top levels where the rooms were mostly suites. To compensate for that problem, Armstrong designated his room on the sixth floor as a "jump room." If any of the governors became trapped on the upper floors, their security details would bring them to Armstrong's sleeping room, where a Kansas City Fire Department ladder truck would be able to reach them.

"Have you notified Godwin?"

"Yes," Wilson responded. "He's already headed up to the governors' floors."

"I'll have my radio on in a second," Armstrong stated. "Call me when you know something more."

Armstrong jumped out of bed, pulled on a pair of jeans and a gray T-shirt which had the Highway Patrol logo on it. He stuffed his feet—sockless—into a pair of loafers, slid his Glock into his waistband, and pulled on a blue sport coat to cover the weapon. He grabbed the radio on his way out the door. A set of fire stairs was two doors away. He sprinted up four floors to where the alarms had activated. When he exited the stairwell onto the floor, everything was quiet. He sniffed the air but smelled no smoke. Suddenly a hotel security guard approached him in the corridor.

"Find anything?" Armstrong asked him.

"Someone pulled two alarm stations on this floor," he said, pointing back in the direction from which he had come, "but there's no fire. Probably just a prank." They turned and saw a trooper assigned to watch the governors' floors trotting toward them from the other direction. He shook his head, indicating that he had found nothing.

Armstrong rubbed his chin, evaluating the situation. Were they missing something? Was this a child's prank or the prelude to a terrorist attack, meant to pull them out of position? He turned to the trooper. "Get back up to your post and check every inch of the governors' floors." The trooper bounded into the stairwell without further instructions. Armstrong looked at the hotel security guard. "What do you think, Paul?"

The guard shrugged. Everything looked fine to him. They got false alarms all the time.

Armstrong had no authority over them, so he put his instructions in the form of a polite request. "If you guys don't mind, assign someone to this floor, just in case."

"No problem," the guard said. "I'll stay up here myself." His supervisor had instructed him to give the Patrol every courtesy.

"I'm going down to our command post," Armstrong said, turning toward the elevators. He picked up a house phone next to the elevator bank and called the CP. He preferred to communicate over a landline, which was more secure than the radio.

"Command Post," Wilson answered.

"This is Armstrong. We didn't find anything up here. Do a post check and alert everyone to be on their toes. Also, get hold of Godwin, and tell him I'm headed down to the CP, and ask him to meet me there."

"Sure thing," Wilson replied.

Armstrong decided to touch base with Godwin and see how the roll call went, before going back to bed. It was going to be a short night.

*   *   *

A block from the hotel, Seed slid into the Houser Communications van and shut the door. Leech put the vehicle in gear and pulled away from the curb. "How'd it go?" he asked.

"I pulled two fire alarms, like you told me, but they didn't go off."

"They're probably silent alarms," Leech responded. "Did you bump into anyone?"

"Nope, not a soul."

"Good boy," he grinned. It was a little risky—rather like poking a sleeping guard dog with a sharp stick—but Leech thought it might not be a bad idea to harass the enemy before game day. Maybe it would cost the security detail some sleep, and their fatigue would enhance the chances that Leech's raid would be successful. The stolen detail book had told them the governors were occupying the top two floors, which had a roving 24-hour shift of guards, but there were no posts on the floors below. "Let's go home and get some sleep. Hopefully, this will give them a restless night."

Chapter 35

With only three hours of sleep, Armstrong walked into the command post and looked around. A radio dispatcher sat at the console, reading the morning paper. The day-shift supervisor, Sergeant Sam O'Reilly, was on the telephone, apparently on hold. There wasn't much stirring at this early hour, but in another hour officers would be scurrying about the room as though the building were ablaze.

In the corner of the room, Lieutenant Simon Godwin was already on his second cup of coffee. He squinted at the screen of his IBM ThinkPad laptop computer, then punched a key, causing his Hewlett Packard DeskJet printer to spring into action. He glanced up as Armstrong approached. "Good morning, David. You're up awfully early."

"Not as early as you. Anything new going on?" Armstrong poured himself a cup of coffee from a large hotel flask and sat across from Godwin. Armstrong felt exhausted and vowed that he would sleep for a week once the conference was over.

Godwin slid an arrest report across the table to him. "A man in a Webber Security Guard uniform approached the KCPD checkpoint at the garage entrance late last night and asked the officers where he could find Governor Brand from Nebraska. He had a .38 revolver in his holster, a blackjack in his back pocket, and a canister of mace on his belt. They asked why he needed to see Brand, and the man said, 'Because someone needs to kill him.' Needless to say, this sparked their interest and they quickly disarmed him."

Armstrong skimmed over the report. It was written in typical police jargon: *I came, I saw, I conquered.* "Yeah, I heard about this. Was he a real security guard?"

"Believe it or not, he's been a commissioned guard with the company for three months. Kind of scary, huh? He was an antisubmarine warfare specialist in the Navy and was discharged under less than honorable circumstances several years ago. He went AWOL for four months and said his senior chief petty officer was harassing him. His file indicates behavioral and disciplinary problems. He's had a checkered work history since then. He told the officers that his house and car are booby-trapped with biological weapons and propane-tank bombs. The FBI's joined in and they're searching his house as we speak."

Armstrong nodded. "Where's this guy now?"

"KCPD has him locked up."

"What did they charge him with?"

Godwin frowned. "The guy's weapon was in plain view and he carries it as part of his job, so we didn't have much there. As it turned out, the guy has twenty-one unpaid parking tickets in the city, so they're holding him on that, at least until the governors leave town. Of course, if they turn up anything at his house, that'll change things a bit."

Armstrong shook his head in disbelief. "What's he upset at Governor Brand over?"

"He's angry about seat-belt laws. He apparently got a ticket for not wearing his seat belt in Nebraska three weeks ago. He went home, cut all the seat belts out of his car, and mailed them to Governor Brand with a threatening letter. He blames excessive government regulations for destroying his life. We called an officer from Brand's detail. He remembers the letter, but they didn't take it seriously. Turns out the man told the arresting officer in Nebraska the same thing: that 'someone needed to kill him for writing the ticket.' It's technically not a threat. We used to have a guy who always wrote Governor Landham and said, 'I pray that God kills you and your family.'"

Godwin's printer had finished spitting out a multipage report. He bundled the pages together and slid them across to Armstrong. "I just ran him on MOSAIC. On a scale of one-to-ten, this guy rated an eight. He's got more red flags than China." He definitely posed a threat to the governors.

Armstrong sipped his coffee as he skimmed over the report. Since 1995, the Governor's Security Division had utilized a state-of-the-art, computer-assisted, threat-assessment system called MOSAIC to assess all inappropriate communications directed at the governor or any other public figure. Gavin de Becker and Associates, a world-class, California-based security firm, had developed the system. MOSAIC was used by numerous local, state, and federal law-enforcement agencies, as well as many large corporations, to assess threats to their executives. Godwin, Underwood, and Armstrong were among the most capable MOSAIC assessors on any governors' detail in the country, probably second only to the California detail. All three officers were graduates of de Becker's Advanced Threat Assessment and Management Academy and his Academy For Protectors, both in California.

He slid the report back to Godwin. "Send any updates to my BlackBerry. Well, today's the last day." He looked at his watch. "In another five hours, we can fold up our tents and go home." All-in-all, the conference had gone well. All of the incidents—the threatening security guard, the death-threat letter, the rowdy Klansman, the reporter with the grenade, the protesters, the false fire alarms, and five bomb threats phoned into the hotel—had been intercepted by the security screen and quickly handled.

"Yeah. Novotny's the last big speaker today. I talked to his FBI detail to see if they've had any adverse intelligence. They said their advance guy will be here around o-nine hundred to check out the arrangements. I figured you'd want to meet him and coordinate Novotny's arrival."

Armstrong nodded. "Sure. Have you ever worked with them?"

Godwin laughed. "Yeah, they're okay, but it's funny. If a state trooper is assigned to protect a governor, it's considered to be an elite assignment, and you try to get the best officers for the job. In the FBI, being assigned to protect the director or the attorney general is considered to be a job for losers, agents who are total screw-ups. At least, that's what I've always heard." Armstrong shook his head in amazement, unable to understand that line of thinking. It clearly denoted a total ignorance of the protective function. Imagine the Secret Service assigning their most incompetent agents to the Presidential Protection Division!

Armstrong examined Godwin's face and asked him something that had been on his mind. "Simon, I'm not trying to horn in on your turf, but I'm curious about something. I suggested beefing up the security in the service corridor behind the meeting room—they only have one officer back there—and also setting up a checkpoint near the service elevators in the pre-function area. Also, there isn't any security outside the command post. I've noticed some unauthorized people in here, looking around for a few minutes before someone notices them and kicks them out. Yesterday, amid all the confusion, two ladies with the press stuck their cameras in the door and panned the room before Wells saw them and ran them off. Those three areas were the most obvious gaps in security, but I've noticed nothing was changed. In fact, all the checkpoints seem to have been scaled back. There aren't enough officers to effectively screen the number of people coming through, and they're going to miss something. What's up?"

Godwin rolled his bloodshot eyes at the ceiling. He looked like he hadn't slept in days. "You can chalk that one up to our fearless leader. After Ringmaster's little tour the other day, he must have had Naylor complain to Colonel DeWitt. The colonel more or less ordered us to scale back. I tried to make a strong case against it, but I think my credibility is shot with DeWitt. I made some adjustments, but I think we're covered. He's already suggested that we start thinking about cutting people loose early to avoid some overtime."

"O-o-okay," Armstrong said, but his tone clearly indicated, *If something happens, don't say I didn't warn you.* It seemed that Governor Stovall and Colonel DeWitt had fallen prey to the "1 + 1 = 3" syndrome. If nothing happens on day one, and nothing happens on day two, then nothing will happen on day three. It was a formula for disaster. If an individual or group was plotting an attack, their window of opportunity was rapidly closing.

Godwin read Armstrong's troubled expression. "Feeling vulnerable today, are we? Take it easy, David. Remember what I always say: If you feel vulnerable in a given situation, you should take steps to change the situation. It's like Gavin de Becker says: 'When a gazelle finds itself alone with the lion, it doesn't just wait to see how the carnivore will behave. It evaluates its options and resources all the while and, if it perceives that it's too vulnerable, puts more distance between itself and the hunter. It changes the situation.'"

Armstrong grinned. "Yeah, I won't forget." He paused for a moment. "Look, Simon, I've never had the chance to say anything, but I'm sorry how things turned out for you. You always ran a great detail."

Godwin shrugged, "Don't worry about me. It's been a good move. The hours are better." He smiled. "My wife and I are back together."

"That's great, Simon!" Armstrong had heard they had been living apart.

"We're going on a cruise next week. It's a new beginning for us." Godwin shook a finger at him. "Don't let this job do to you what it did to me. I was consumed twenty-four-seven. Every day you drive the governor where he wants to go, eat where he wants to eat, and do what he wants to do. It's like you lose your own identity. When I got home, I took it out on my family. Once, Judy had chicken fixed for dinner. I dumped it in the trash and demanded she grill some steaks. It was my way of establishing control of my life. Two weeks later, she'd moved out with the kids."

Armstrong nodded. His own marriage was already feeling the added stress of his new command responsibilities. He vowed to keep his work in perspective. He realized he hadn't called Chelle since he'd arrived in Kansas City.

Godwin continued, "David, there are no higher stakes than what we do every day. We always have to be ready if the worst happens." He leaned forward and lowered his voice. "The real tragedy is, these people we protect don't care. What happened to me can happen to anyone, even you, my friend. Watch your back. I laid my life on the line for these people, and they cut me loose without so much as a 'see ya later.'"

Armstrong nodded and glanced around the room to verify that they were still alone. He considered telling Godwin about Naylor's conversation. It was something that Godwin needed to know, he decided. "Simon, I had an interesting conversation with Brad Naylor yesterday. He complained that your presence in the meeting room upset Ringmaster during his opening address. This is the last day of the conference, and the only reason I even mention it is that he threatened to go to the colonel when I blew him off." Godwin's face was expressionless. Armstrong continued, "That's just for your info. I thought you'd want to know."

Godwin nodded. "Bizarre! Well, we wouldn't want to make the boss uncomfortable, would we?" He gathered up his folder and prepared to leave. "Thanks for the warning. I'll try to stay out of his way until this thing is over."

Chapter 36

Clad in an expensive suit and looking much like the pampered son of some visiting governor, Seed crossed the hotel lobby and descended the stairs to the ballroom level. He carried the bright-red canvas bag given to all registered attendees for the conference. It was the bag Spider had received upon check-in. He confidently approached the magnetometer, as though the governors were waiting for him to arrive.

A uniformed Kansas City police officer eyed the approaching boy and noticed he was not wearing a conference credential. But he hardly looked like a terrorist. *Probably some governor's kid,* the officer thought. He couldn't enter the ballroom without a credential, but he could enter the pre-function area.

"Hey, Chief," the officer said, "I need to check in that bag, then I need you to step through the machine." The bag contained two books, some papers, and a VHS videocassette. The officer recognized the video as one issued in everyone's gift bag. The video was a fourteen-minute address by Governor and Mrs. Stovall, welcoming the meeting attendees to Missouri and highlighting attractions in the Kansas City area. The officer had seen a hundred of them in his screenings, and he didn't even give this one a second look. The officer watched as the boy stepped through the magnetometer without setting off the alarm, then handed his bag to him and said, "Have a nice day, son."

Watching proudly from the ballroom entrance was Seed's mother. The boy looked no more nervous than if he was walking into a church or classroom. She stepped over to him and crouched down. "My, don't you look sharp!" she said, squeezing his arms. Seed smiled but said nothing. He opened his bag, and Spider took the videotape. She pecked him on the cheek and studied his face. *This may be the last time I see you*, she thought. "I'll see you later," she whispered and touched his hands. The statement was as much for her as it was for her son.

She stood and carried the videotape into the ballroom. Their exchange had generated no interest amidst the bustling activity in the pre-function area. If the officer had taken the tape out of Seed's bag, he would have found it unusually heavy. Had he flipped up the tape cover, he would have seen only a strip of videotape, secured in place to make it appear normal. But if he had taken the cassette apart, he would have found it filled not with tape but with Semtex plastic explosive. Spider's research on the security procedures revealed that the bomb dogs were used only to screen press equipment. Non-media attendees were only screened visually and through the magnetometer, the result of Governor Stovall's edict to not needlessly harass meeting attendees.

Spider stepped over to the press riser and moved to her tripod-mounted video camera. When she pressed the eject button, the tape container opened up. Bending down to cover her movements, she flipped up the tape cover on the cassette and ran her finger under the strip of tape. She felt and pulled out a black wire which ended in a small male plug. The other end terminated in a blasting cap which was buried in the explosive. The blasting cap—itself an explosive—also had to be smuggled in, since it would not have gotten by a bomb dog. Spider plugged the wire into a female connector on a black electronics box, hanging from the tripod next to the battery pack. She inserted the cassette into the camera and pushed the container closed.

Ingenious, Spider thought. Leech had referred to it as a "Trojan Horse" device, and that description struck her as perfect. She had to hand it to them. It was Leech's idea to build the bomb in the meeting room, which she had thought was a suicidal plan. But Leech's handiwork at constructing a device that could go undetected had made the task unbelievably easy. He had made only two alterations to the camera. The first was to open it up and fill every available space with stainless-steel ball bearings, glued in place for added shrapnel. Since he couldn't fit as many as he wanted into the space, the second alteration was to glue a sheet of ball bearings into a flat plastic box and affix the box to the left side of the camera, which didn't have any controls.

The box was painted the same dark gray color as the camera body and blended in perfectly. While the camera was unusually heavy, it still worked. The explosive in the cassette would simply propel the shrapnel throughout the room.

They knew it wouldn't kill everyone, but there should be widespread damage. They certainly couldn't approach the 9/11 death toll of nearly 3,000 and probably wouldn't top Tim McVeigh's bombing in Oklahoma City that had killed 169. But if they took out even half of this distinguished group, it would drive a stake in the government's heart and terrify every politician in the world. She now had only to wait until the right moment to initiate the firing mechanism, which would give the attendees an experience they would never forget and provide a story to the media that they would squawk about for years.

Chapter 37

Simon Godwin's dark sunglasses hid his eyes as he scanned the crowd. The group of over three hundred young people had been building all morning in the protest area across the street from the hotel. They were very organized; Godwin had to give them that. Though he had never met any of them, he recognized several faces from photos that his intelligence unit had gathered on the group. The police department had erected metal racks along the curb to serve as a barrier between the crowd and a squad of KCPD officers in riot gear. A KCPD officer with a video camera stood behind the line of officers and videotaped the demonstrators, while a long-haired demonstrator with a similar camera stood against the barrier and videotaped the officers. A skirmish was on the verge of breaking out, but a less experienced officer might have missed the signs. There was a subtle warning, like a wisp of smoke from under a pile of dry leaves.

As though reading his mind, Major Joe Fortman stated, "Looks like they're gearing up." He sensed it, too.

Godwin grunted in agreement, but the timetable of events was predictable. The crescendo would build, but not explode, until the arrival of FBI Director Novotny. As if on signal, a stocky woman in a white coat and blue jeans began beating a tom-tom and chanting, "Scream! Shout! Throw the bums out! Scream! Shout! Throw the bums out!" The crowd joined in, raising an impressive level of noise. Many waved banners and placards, which expressed outrage at the governors' plan to expand their police state. The tom-tom lady wore a yellow armband, marking her as a group leader, but most of those in the crowd sported red or black bandanas around their necks or heads. Armstrong knew that when things got ugly, the bandanas would be tied around their faces to obscure their identities.

Colonel Andrew DeWitt strode up behind them and eyed the demonstrators. "What group is this?" he asked.

Godwin responded, "It's a mix, actually. Part environmentalists, part animal-rights, part gay-rights, part pro-choice, as well as any other anti-establishment group. Unlike the single-issue groups from the sixties, these factions band together to pool their resources. We generally refer to them as anarchists, mainly because they've adopted many of that group's tactics." Similar groups had raised havoc at the WTO meeting in Seattle, Washington, in 1999, and the free-trade meetings in Miami, Florida, in 2003, as well as the RNC and DNC conventions, both in 2004.

They watched as Sergeant Stuart Hardwood, KCPD Intelligence Unit, broke off his negotiations with the group's leader—a bearded man about thirty years old—and trotted across the street to their position. Over the noise of the crowd, Hardwood reported, "He says they don't plan to disrupt Novotny's arrival, and they promise to be orderly."

Fortman nodded. "Yeah, and my daddy owns Microsoft." He looked over at Godwin. "Sergeant Hardwood tells me that you know a lot about this group. Can they be trusted?"

Godwin stifled a grin. "I would sooner turn my back on a pit bull." He crossed his arms to resist pointing. "That U-Haul truck parked down the street is where they keep their puppets. They'll raise a lot of noise for a while, until we get used to it and start to relax. About thirty minutes prior to Novotny's arrival—say around ten-thirty—they'll try to bring over the puppets, which are about ten feet tall. They look pretty harmless, just a couple of big, mean-looking politicians. But inside the puppets is where they keep their dragon sleeves."

DeWitt frowned. "What are dragon sleeves?"

Godwin explained, "They take a piece of PVC pipe about three feet long and install steel bolts through the middle. Then they create a human chain with a person sticking their arm in one end, and the next person sticking their arm in the other end. They hold onto the bolts, so you can't pull them apart. They'll link twenty or thirty people together, and run the human chain across the street to block it, probably when Novotny's vehicle arrives. It's pretty effective."

"How do you get them apart?" DeWitt asked, with a worried look on his face. "Can you cut the sleeve in half?"

Godwin shook his head, "They fill the middle with tar to gum up the saw blades, or nails imbedded in epoxy. No, the trick is to take them down when the puppets come out of the truck, but before they can get them into position."

Fortman anticipated DeWitt's next question. "Your SERT team on the roof is watching the truck. As soon as they open the doors, we'll move in and seize the truck and those around it. At the same time, we're going to take several of the ringleaders into custody. They're not expecting us to do that, and it should unnerve the others. We'll detain them long enough for Novotny to get in and out."

DeWitt nodded. "Sounds like everything is covered. How will we know when they're ready to move?"

Godwin responded, "Sergeant Matt Youngblood has infiltrated the crowd as a protester, plus we've been monitoring the secret traffic on their website for about a month. The St. Louis PD Intelligence Unit has a guy that corresponds with them. That's where most of this group is from. They drove over yesterday, and they've been feeling us out ever since they arrived, posing as spectators or members of the other protest groups. But we know from their e-mail traffic that their main goal is to block Novotny's motorcade from entering the hotel."

DeWitt nodded, impressed with the level of intelligence sharing that was evident. It certainly looked like the officers had everything under control. He looked at his watch. "Chief Hammond and I are getting ready to go to the airport to meet Novotny and escort him here. Page me if things get out of control."

Godwin and Fortman exchanged glances, both thinking, *Gee, I never would have thought of paging you if there was trouble!* Godwin merely responded, "Yes, sir," as DeWitt turned and ambled back into the garage.

"Command Post, Godwin," the dispatcher's voice called in Godwin's earpiece.

"Go ahead, Command Post," he responded into his wrist mike.

"The FBI advance man is up here looking for you. He said he's been calling you."

Godwin checked his BlackBerry and frowned at the "1 missed call" message. "Sorry, I missed it due to the crowd noise," he said. "Advise him that I'm down at the garage entrance."

After a pause, the dispatcher responded, "He's on his way down."

Godwin checked his watch. He wanted to hang around here to make sure that Fortman's riot troops didn't burn down the Plaza.

Godwin eyed the noisy protesters. The enthusiastic young people had no way of knowing the authorities knew their plan better than they did.

Two hundred yards across from Godwin's position, Ross Draeger focused the crosshairs of his scope on Godwin's face and whispered, "Bang!" He recognized Godwin as being the chief of Governor Stovall's Praetorian Guard when the governor was pie-struck on his inaugural day. From the sniper's nest in his van on the third level of a parking garage, Draeger could see down into the garage entrance of the hotel and the doors to the ballroom level. He watched as Godwin turned and strode back into the building. When the shooting started, Draeger would take out any officers who came into his view. And he decided that if the governor's chief bodyguard wandered back into his scope, Draeger would strike him down with one of his deadly Glaser rounds.

Chapter 38

March 4, 0950 hours
Grand Plaza Hotel
Kansas City, Missouri

"Good morning, Trooper Romanowski," announced Lance "The Prince" Stovall, unconsciously demoting the Dapper Don two ranks. He referred to all of the officers as troopers. "When is the FBI director going to be here?" The Prince was followed by a sleepy-looking "Princess" Heather.

Romanowski had stepped outside the ballroom to work some blood back into his buttocks, while Marko Vanhala stood post inside. He glanced at his watch. *Geez, they're up early this morning.* He hadn't seen much of the governor's children since they had arrived. They usually didn't show up, unless there was free food and liquor, or a celebrity around. *Put out a salt block*, he thought, *and the cattle will quickly show up.*

"In about an hour," he responded warily. Romanowski smelled a foul odor in the question.

Heather spoke next. "We'd like to meet with him when he arrives."

Romanowski eyed them patiently, like a mother whose nine-year-old had just asked for the keys to the family car. "That's not my department. I'm not assigned to Director Novotny, and if I were, it wouldn't be my place to get you a meeting. Maybe you should run that by Naylor first. Then he can run it by Novotny's staff. That's normally how these things are done."

The Prince and Princess exchanged knowing glances. "Don't give us that," Heather objected. "You bodyguards all know each other. You could get us an audience, if you wanted to. Just let us stand where his motorcade arrives, so we can walk in with him."

"I could arrange that, if I was an unprofessional *bodyguard*," he said the word as though it contained an acrid taste. "But that's not the way we operate, and you two know it. Now run along or you won't get any Pop-Tarts for lunch."

The Prince's features twisted into a sneer. "Today, you've lost a good friend to law enforcement! You guys never like it when we show up, but you're supposed to take care of us, too. I'll have your job for this."

Romanowski smiled and thought, *You wouldn't want my job, son. I have to deal with assholes like you every day.* If Romanowski had a dollar for every time some VIP threatened to fire him, he'd be sipping Blackbeard Ale on the deck of a sailboat anchored at St. Thomas right about now, but he held his tongue. One of the most important aspects of executive protection—especially for details assigned to high-level VIPs—is professionalism. The axiom in the industry was: "Never forget who's boss, and never forget to treat them that way." No matter how good he or she is, the bodyguard who violates that rule will not last very long in the business.

"Sorry," Romanowski responded, "but you'll have to get Naylor to set that up." He withstood their icy glares for several seconds until they whirled and stalked into the ballroom. Romanowski shook his head. *Geez*, he thought, *I haven't seen him that mad since I accidentally slammed the door to Monitor on his hand during the campaign.*

Chapter 39

FBI Special Agent Byron Sanders eyed the small group as they exited the doors from the ballroom level and approached his position. "Who the hell is this?" he asked Armstrong.

Armstrong muttered, "That's Governor Stovall, and his son and daughter." A straight-faced Sergeant Romanowski accompanied them, but Armstrong could tell he was steamed that the Prince and Princess had gotten their way. "They're here to officially greet Director Novotny."

Now it was Sanders's turn to be miffed. This wasn't on the director's itinerary, and the director didn't like surprises. It would be embarrassing if Novotny exited his vehicle and was unable to recall a VIP's name. As Novotny's advance man, Sanders would catch the blame for this change of plans. He sighed, pulling out his cell-phone. "What're their names?" When Armstrong told him, Sanders dialed the number for the cell phone in Novotny's vehicle.

"Temmons," answered the detail leader.

"This is Sanders. Where're you at?"

"We're about five minutes out. What's up?"

Sanders turned and walked out of earshot from the group. "Tell 'M' that Governor William Stovall and his son and daughter will greet him on arrival."

"What're the kids' names?"

"Lance and Heather," Sanders responded.

"Any other changes we need to know about?"

"No. On arrival, we'll still go to the holding room for a few minutes. Then, when they're ready for him, Governor Stovall will introduce 'M.' After his speech, he'll stay for questions, shake the governors' hands, then we depart for the airport." Even though the schedule was the same as planned, Sanders ran through it to verify the plan.

"Okay," said Temmons. "Is everything quiet?"

Sanders snorted. "It's not too bad now, but you should have been here thirty minutes ago. The cops had it out with a bunch of protesters and hauled a bunch of them off. There's still a crowd outside, but there shouldn't be any trouble."

Temmons saw they were approaching the Country Club Plaza. "We're about three blocks away. Arrival in one minute."

Sanders returned to the group. "They'll be here in one minute," he told Armstrong.

Security was tight with several KCPD officers manning the checkpoint at the garage entrance. A squad of others tended to the unruly looking group of protesters on the curb opposite the hotel. In keeping with their plan, Fortman's riot squad had swooped down on the anarchists, seizing their truck—containing the deadly puppets—and removing the protest leaders. It broke the back of the anarchists' plan, but the remaining members joined in with the small anti-gun-control crowd, and they were doing their best to mount a second offensive. One demonstrator held a sign that proclaimed: FBI STORM TROOPERS MURDERED INNOCENT WOMEN AND CHILDREN AT WACO AND RUBY RIDGE! It was a legacy that the FBI would never live down. The SERT countersnipers watched through binoculars from their lofty perch atop the hotel. Somewhere among the screaming horde, Matt Youngblood blended into the group like a camouflaged hunter in the forest, monitoring their plans.

Since the Kansas City FBI office did not have access to an armored vehicle, Sanders had asked Armstrong if they could borrow Stovall's Lincoln Navigator and driver to pick up the FBI director. A protective detail must be ready to depart at a moment's notice, so Armstrong refused to assign Davenport and Monitor to the task. Instead, he gave them Alex Wiedemann, driving the older Merrimac.

Precisely one minute later, Merrimac, followed by a Chevrolet Impala sedan, eased through the checkpoint amid hooting and screamed profanities from the crowd. The motorcade looped around in front of the greeting party and stopped at the curb. Two agents bounded out of the follow-up vehicle and positioned themselves on each side of the armored Suburban. Governor Stovall stepped off the curb and tried to open Novotny's door, but found it locked. He squinted through the smoked glass, trying to make out the occupants inside. Agent Temmons got out of the right front and said, "I'll get that." Stovall stepped back on the curb, embarrassed and irritated. Temmons waited for the detail to form up. As soon as he touched the door handle, Wiedemann triggered the automatic door locks. The Stovalls stood poised, like children awaiting a glimpse of Santa Claus.

As Temmons opened the right rear door, Novotny slid out smiling. "Governor Stovall! And this must be Lance and Heather! It's great to see you again." Highway Patrol Colonel DeWitt and Kansas City Police Chief James Hammond also unloaded from the vehicle. They had met Novotny's jet at the Downtown Airport and ridden with him to the hotel, briefing him on state and local law-enforcement issues.

The governor shook Novotny's hand. The Prince and Princess glowed, since he remembered their names—an oddity since he had never met them before. The group exchanged pleasantries, and then Armstrong and Sanders herded them inside to the Bunker.

As the Prince passed Romanowski, he smirked and said, "Gee, Trooper Romanowski, thanks for setting this up for us." The Princess cackled with delight.

Romanowski gave them a blank stare and made a mental note to forget to pick them up the next time they flew into Jefferson City and needed a ride to the Governor's Mansion. He soothed his damaged ego by recalling the old proverb: "The higher the monkey climbs, the more you see of his behind."

Chapter 40

FBI Director M. Blair Novotny laid his papers on the podium, adjusted the microphone, and scanned the packed room before him. He noticed Colonel DeWitt and Chief Hammond seated in the front row. He glanced to his left. One of his FBI bodyguards, Temmons, was stationed there, Sanders was at stage right, and another was in the back of the room. The drivers were parked outside the ballroom level entrance, staging his bulletproof Suburban and the follow-up car. There were more weapons in the room than at an NRA gun show. He felt totally safe.

The "M" stood for Michael, but Novotny had grown up a James Bond fan. When he had the opportunity to move from his position as a federal judge to FBI director, he couldn't resist. He was now addressed widely by the same title as Bond's boss, the legendary head of British Secret Service. It was in the pattern of past FBI directors, such as J. Edgar Hoover and L. Patrick Gray.

"Governor Stovall, honorable guests, ladies and gentlemen. It is an honor to be here this morning, once again in the company of this distinguished group." He knew most of the governors personally, and had addressed their conferences before. He turned to Stovall, who was seated to his right. "Governor Stovall, I appreciate the invitation to attend this summit, and the President sends his best. Thank you for leading the way and reminding us that our efforts to combat terrorism are a bipartisan effort on behalf of all Americans. I can assure you that the FBI shares in your concerns. Our mission is to help you both protect our nation from harm and safeguard our cherished freedoms."

Stovall bowed his head graciously and made a note to have Fleming get a videotape of the speech. The FBI director's remarks would go great in Stovall's future political campaigns.

Novotny looked around the table. "Dante's *Inferno* described Geryon, the Monster of Fraud, with these words: 'Now see the sharp-tailed beast that mounts the brink. He passes mountains, breaks through walls and weapons. Behold the beast that makes the whole world stink.'

"This description seems to fit the terrorist group known as Phineas Priests. Terrorists stalk the Earth like hostile armies, and this group truly makes the whole world stink. Like Geryon, they perpetrate the worst kind of fraud, decrying our way of government, while basking in its benefits. They advertise their beliefs in a free press under the First Amendment, arm themselves with weapons under the Second Amendment, flee in their vehicles across interstate highways paved with state and federal tax dollars, and invoke their rights under the Fourth and Fifth Amendments once authorities capture them. It is hard to imagine all the hatred and violence that some Americans can bring upon their fellow Americans over simple policy differences. The Greek philosopher Bias wrote 'Most men are bad.' I believe he had it wrong. While our society seems to be under constant attack by bad men—certainly, the media seems to focus all their resources to cover their acts—the overwhelming majority of Americans are good, law-abiding people.

"The world today has changed dramatically in the past several years. These changes have caused shifts in political, social, and economic conditions. Combined with advancements in technology and transportation, they have made it easier for people around the world to engage in unprecedented mobility. Unfortunately, this has also enabled fugitives and international terrorists to flit about the planet like killer bees, constantly moving and adapting to ever-changing conditions. We have found it increasingly more difficult to bring some of these individuals to justice, but they will be caught eventually. We will put Geryon back into the pit, where he belongs.

"Each year, some twenty-four thousand Americans are murdered by their fellow citizens. If we turned on our TV, and the news announced that twenty-four thousand Americans were suddenly killed in some foreign country, we would undoubtedly declare war on that country. But since the deaths are scattered out over time, and the cause is listed as crime, we shrug our shoulders in a fatalistic gesture that says 'nothing can be done.' Well, I'm not a fatalist. As Ralph Barton Perry stated: 'Fatalism, whether pious or pessimistic, stands flatly discredited. It serves as an excuse for practical inaction or mental indolence. To believe that the future is predestined by nonhuman causes saves men from the trouble of doing; to believe that conscious will is merely a mask for irrational impulses saves men from the trouble of thinking.'

"What is required? Constant vigilance! John Stuart Mill recognized eternal vigilance as the price of liberty. We have to be able to forecast what's coming around the corner and be prepared for it before it arrives. We need to do a better job of collecting and analyzing intelligence, and dispensing it to all law-enforcement agencies, not just a select few. We have to do a better job of training. I'm told that Conservation Agent Dwayne Stoddard, who was murdered in January, had not been trained in recognizing and dealing with extremist groups. If we are vigilant, if we are dedicated, and if we are proactive, we can make a significant difference for this nation. We can't allow ourselves to become complacent with one or two victories. There is an old axiom that only the strong survive.

"Adlai Stevenson once said that the burdens of office stagger the imagination. We've seen the forces of terrorism at work around our country. The attacks on the World Trade Center, the Pentagon, and in Oklahoma City, and the staggering toll reaped by two young racists in their attack on Columbine High School in Colorado, were punches in the American gut. They knocked the wind out of us, but also had the effect of waking us up. These attacks demonstrated the worst in humanity, but also the best in law enforcement. In each of these incidents, the heroes were local police officers, state troopers, firefighters, and EMTs, as well as common citizens. They are our first line of defense. They are there when tragedy strikes. They are there when the bombs go off. You governors are on the front lines, as well.

"Today our country operates under a constant Yellow terrorist threat warning level. Certain sectors like the aircraft and nuclear power-plant industry, and major cities like New York, Los Angeles, and Washington DC, operate under a constant state of Orange. And they do this without a sufficient level of monetary support from the federal government. I know you're hurting. I am pleased to report that Congress has recently allocated funds that will allow the FBI to hire an additional five hundred agents to help you fight the war against terrorism. In addition, the President's budget contains two hundred fifty million dollars to support the fight against murderous gangs like the Phineas Priests. You know your needs and resources better than we do, so we need your input in how that money can be most effectively spent. We must form stronger, more effective partnerships that will enable us to exchange threat warnings with you in a timely manner. I am confident that, working together, we can and will make a difference in the fight against terrorism. The lives of our citizens and the future of our free Republic depend on it."

Novotny paused and looked around the table. "Thank you for your time," he said and took his seat, as a round of applause rippled through the crowd and around the table. Most of the governors weren't smiling. Novotny had just told them that, on average, each state would only get ten extra FBI agents and five million dollars to help fight terrorism. It was rather like rolling a large boulder into the Grand Canyon in an attempt to fill it up.

No one had left the room during his stirring speech; no one, except a female journalist on the press riser. When Novotny compared Phineas Priests to the monster Geryon, Spider had glared at the group of VIPs, barely able to keep herself from crying out, "You are the monsters!" As he concluded his remarks, she turned the camera so the left side was facing the governors. Due to the way in which Leech had constructed the bomb, this would "fire" the shrapnel in their direction, operating like a claymore mine. Then, in a movement that would forever change people's lives, she flipped a switch on the electronics package. *Bomb's away!* she thought and quickly left the room. In a matter of moments, the atmosphere in the room would be transformed from one of decorum to one of utter chaos and destruction.

Chapter 41

As Spider left the meeting room, she turned and walked to the service elevators to meet Leech and the others. Wearing red blazers and black slacks that resembled those worn by hotel security employees, they had just gotten off the elevators and shut both of them down. Leech dropped a gear bag at their feet, and they quickly dug out their weapons and equipment.

Leech's plan of assault was simple, using speed, surprise, and overpowering firepower as the basic tactics of destruction. It avoided the security team's strongest point—the pre-function area—and focused on its biggest weakness: the service corridor behind the meeting room. During their planning session, they relied on Wykoff's combat experience to decide how best to breech the heavily guarded ballroom. He referred to this as an "indirect approach" and had quoted Frederick the Great: "Three men behind the enemy are worth more than fifty in front of him."

Forming a circle, they joined hands, and Leech examined each of their faces. They all looked ready for what was to follow. He whispered, "'Draw near, you executioners of the city, each with his destroying weapon in his hand . . . And they went forth, and slew in the city.'" They knew it was from his namesake chapter in the Bible: Ezekiel, chapter 9, verses 1 and 7. He had quoted it before.

They broke their circle. Leech, Wykoff, and So-So headed down the service corridor to the back of the meeting rooms, while Spider maintained a holding position that would prevent officers from closing in behind them. Hers was a diversionary assault to delay the reaction of those officers in the pre-function area, enabling Leech to carry out his bloody business inside the meeting room.

She pulled a ski mask down over her face, removed the pin on a hand grenade, and waited for the explosion of the camera bomb to trigger her attack.

Chapter 42

"Sir, we've got a little problem," said Trooper Jerrold Harding.

Lieutenant Godwin had just returned to the pre-function area after working the crowd of protesters during Novotny's arrival. He recognized Harding as being the driver assigned to the Iowa Governor. "What's up, Jerry?" He steeled himself, used to seeing "little problems" mushroom into overwhelming disasters.

Harding gestured toward his companion. "This is Trooper Kyle Spencer with the Iowa detail." Spencer nodded at Armstrong, wearing an embarrassed look on his face. "He can't find his copy of the detail book."

Godwin's stomach turned over. "What happened to it, Kyle?" Behind Harding, Godwin noticed an attractive lady with a press credential leave the meeting room, cross the pre-function area as though she had a purpose, and disappear into the corridor where the service elevators were located. *That's strange*, he thought. There was something familiar about her, too, like he had seen her prior to the conference. *Maybe she's a TV reporter*, he thought. As soon as he was finished with this crisis, he'd go check her out.

"Well, Lieutenant, I remember I had it in my portfolio at dinner last night, because I looked up some stuff in it. But this morning I noticed it's gone. I've already checked the restaurant and they didn't find anything." Spencer was clearly uncomfortable with the admission, but Godwin appreciated the information. Some people would not have brought it to his attention.

"Do you think you misplaced it or was it stolen?" Godwin asked calmly, as though the manual was one of many others that had disappeared. This was edging closer to the disaster category than a mere problem. He was glad the conference was almost over.

Spencer scratched his head. "I wish I could say, sir. Nothing else is missing, but I might have left it lying somewhere. I thought you guys should know."

"If you find it or can think of anywhere else we can check, please let me know, Trooper," Godwin advised him. *Colonel DeWitt will go ballistic*, he thought, and Armstrong needed to know about this as well.

"Thanks, sir," Harding said, and he and Spencer moved into the meeting room.

Godwin looked toward the entrance to the service corridor. The reporter had not yet returned. *She doesn't have any business back there*, he thought, and started in that direction.

Chapter 43

The Goddess Fortuna has a cruel sense of humor, and she was preparing to play a nasty trick on Brent Lively. She had been toying with him all day. A cameraman for a local TV station, Lively had the good fortune of walking into his station just as his editor was looking around for someone to send to the FBI director's speech. Fortuna cleverly arranged for the car driven by cameraman Hector Valendez, who was originally scheduled to handle that assignment, to be sideswiped by a city bus. As Valendez stood alongside the road, waiting for a cop to show up and cursing his bad luck at missing the assignment, Lively bolted out the door to cover the event. It was a seemingly lucky break for the rookie. Perhaps he would even land a personal interview with Director Novotny. He grinned when he saw that Fortuna had saved him a spot on the press riser, unaware that her cruel sense of humor had placed the spot next to Spider's position. He had been running late that morning, first stuck in traffic, then unable to find a legal place to park his small station wagon, and finally getting his gear through the security checkpoint outside. So he reveled in his good luck when he found an open space on the riser. Lively now operated the camera next to the deadly bomb.

Lively finished taping the FBI director's remarks and bent over to shut off the battery pack from his tripod-mounted camera. When he straightened up, he bumped Spider's tripod, and noticed her camera pointing sideways, one side facing the governors' table. *Oops*, he thought, *must have bumped it out of position.* He looked around to see if Spider was still close by, but she had stepped out of the room. He put his hand on the side of Spider's camera and swiveled it back around, pointing the lens toward the governors. At that precise instant, the bomb exploded, sending its deadly load through Lively's face and chest, and the tightly packed cadre of other cameramen on the riser. Investigators would later find Lively's head and both arms severed from his torso.

The pressure wave of the blast, accompanied by a million small but razor-sharp projectiles, shot through the room like a flash of lethal light, bringing down ceiling tiles and blowing down equipment. Part of the lighting was knocked out, plunging the room into an eerie semidarkness. A second of stillness ensued, then the sprinklers let loose with a drenching shower. Few people were left standing. The blast knocked nearly everyone in the room to the floor, including most of the governors' bodyguards. Many first thought that the blast was the attack, but they were wrong. It was only the opening wave of an attack.

Chapter 44

Leech peered around a wall and down the length of the service corridor and saw the steel folding chair, where the rear security guard normally sat. The chair was empty. *Damn! Where is he?*

When the camera bomb exploded, he sprinted down the corridor toward the rear entrance to the ballroom with So-So in hot pursuit. Wykoff maintained a firing position at the corner, so the Priests now controlled two of the four sides of the ballroom. He and Leech were carrying the suppressed FN P90s with their lethal, armor-piercing ammo.

Leech saw three KCPD officers sprinting toward them, including the officer assigned to this post. He had apparently gotten bored and stepped over to Merrimac to talk with Wiedemann.

Leech fired two 3-round bursts at them, and they scattered for cover. Leech veered into the alcove at the rear ballroom entrance while So-So took up a position to cover his back. She fired a burst from her suppressed H&K UMP45 at the officers as they peeked from behind their cover. Two additional officers responded from positions at the garage entrance. Within seconds, a storm of bullets crisscrossed the garage area. So-So fired a long burst that stitched across both doors and one of the run-flat tires on Merrimac, causing Wiedemann to duck down behind the steering wheel. While he was protected by Merrimac's armor, the sound of the .45 rounds impacting his vehicle was unnerving.

The hammering echo of the officers' weapons, firing within the confined space, felt to Leech like someone was standing behind him and slapping both sides of his head. He paused outside the ballroom doors and listened to the screams and shouts coming from inside the room. His plan was to kill any VIPs at the head table—especially Stovall and Novotny—then escape out the back, under the covering fire from Draeger's sniper position in the nearby parking garage.

The blast had started a deadly stopwatch. Although Leech and his team controlled the timing of the explosion, time now worked against them. With every passing second, security personnel would be responding and closing in around them. Those inside the room would be coming to their senses and drawing their own weapons. With each pull of the trigger on his deadly P90, his limited ration of armor-piercing ammo would rapidly shrink. At a firing rate of 900 rounds per minute, it wouldn't take long to exhaust the 500 rounds packed into his ten magazines. His time was very, very short, and he had to make every second count.

Leech cashed in five of those valuable seconds as he shut his eyes to adjust to the lower light level inside—the blast had probably knocked out some of the lights. Then he took a deep breath and darted through the door in search of his targets.

Chapter 45

As the explosion rattled the walls of the hotel, shocking everyone in the pre-function area, Spider stepped into the entrance and tossed the grenade into the midst of the gathered crowd. Godwin was halfway across the buffer zone outside the meeting rooms, headed in her direction when the camera bomb exploded. He froze, then he saw Spider's action. Instinctively, he shouted, "Grenade! Get down!" He shoved people out of the way, visually tracking the bouncing explosive.

The grenade skittered along the carpeted floor on a path toward the meeting-room doors, as people raced in every direction. Spider dove for cover back into the service corridor, but the grenade failed to explode, rolling along like a rotten piece of fruit. As it rolled past Godwin, he bent over, scooped it up, and tossed it back through the doorway into the service corridor. Then he wheeled and dashed into the meeting room to investigate the nature of the blast he had heard. The other officers would have to deal with the gunman. Godwin's deep sense of mission—honed by years of training and operational experience—drove him to save the life of the very man who had betrayed him, Governor William Ulysses Stovall.

Spider was stunned when the grenade flew past her. When she realized it would not explode, she leaned around the wall and fired a wild burst from her silenced Ruger MP9 into the ballroom lobby. Most of those in the pre-function area reacted to the explosion by ducking or diving to the floor. Her strafing burst was fired at chest level. Only three people were struck.

Patrol Trooper Mike Cumberland was assigned to drive Governor Richard Hampton of Illinois. He was standing outside the meeting-room doors, looking for one of the two Illinois troopers who had accompanied Hampton to the conference. Cumberland held a fax that had just arrived for the governor. He flinched at the explosion and looked around in surprise. Suddenly, people were diving in every direction. As Spider's fire raked the area, Cumberland felt a red-hot pain in his right biceps and knew he was hit. He rolled to the floor and curled up in ball, gripping the wound with his left hand in an attempt to stop the flow of blood. "I'm hit," he shouted.

KCPD Officer Janice Moore was standing post outside the meeting-room doors, checking credentials. The blast inside the closed doors stunned her, and she instinctively ducked, taking two steps forward. "Damn!" she exclaimed, as someone shouted something about a grenade. Then Spider opened fire. Two rounds struck Moore in the right side, one stopped by the side panel of her body armor, the other slipping through the opening under her right arm. These are often fatal injuries to officers, taking out a lung or the heart. But this round struck her at an angle, punching a hole through her right breast, before being caught inside the vest. It felt like someone had struck her in the chest with a hammer. Moore gasped and crumpled to the floor.

Roger Cassady, a press aide for Governor Romolo Coltrane of Arkansas, had just walked out the meeting-room doors when the camera bomb exploded. He jumped to one side and shouted, "Jesus!" to no one in particular. He stood transfixed as the pre-function area turned into a frenzied mob of activity. Then one of Spider's rounds punched a neat hole through his right forearm and grazed his ample stomach. Another took off the end of his right index finger. "Jesus Christ!" he shouted again and fled in the direction of the staircase, ignoring the searing pain of his wounds.

Spider ducked for cover as several officers returned fire, peppering the walls with pistol fire. She turned and ran down the corridor to circle the ballrooms and hook up with Leech, So-So, and Wykoff. She had only taken ten steps when two KCPD officers from the magnetometer checkpoint—using cover and advance movements—entered the corridor behind her. They opened fire simultaneously, striking her seven times in the back, buttocks, and legs with their 9mm rounds. With a pained howl, she crashed to the carpeted floor. Then she rolled to her side and leveled her weapon at them. Seeing her actions, the two officers pelted her with an additional six rounds, including an instantly fatal blow through her groin, torso, and into her chest.

Chapter 46

March 4, 1124 hours
Grand Plaza Hotel
Kansas City, Missouri

"How's the conference going?" Chelle Armstrong asked.

David Armstrong pressed his BlackBerry closer to his ear to block out the noise inside the command post. "Not too bad. It's almost over. Sorry I haven't called before now, but it's been pretty crazy."

"I miss you. I don't like you being gone so much."

He smiled, wishing that he could give her a hug. "I miss you, too. I'll be home tonight. Let's go out for a late dinner."

She was quiet for moment. "I worry about you. The news said there have been some bomb threats."

David rolled his eyes. The bomb threats were the least of the problems they had faced. "Bomb threats in the U.S. are 99 percent false, Chelle. In order to believe them, you'd have to believe that someone had the expertise to make a bomb, got his hands on the right materials, risked his life by putting it together, risked his freedom by sneaking it into the hotel and planting it, and then undid the whole thing by calling us and telling us about it."

"I know," she sighed, "but I also know you. If anything happens you'll be right in the middle of it. It scares me to know that you risk your life for these people."

Before he could respond, the shuddering growl of the blast slithered through the floor of the command post, located above the ballroom, like the wail of a ghostly dragon. The floor beneath his feet seemed to swell, as though the building had taken a deep breath. His first thought was that it was an earthquake.

Armstrong jumped to his feet. Over his BlackBerry, Chelle heard him shout, "What was that?"

At the same instant the radio began to blare with excited voices.

"There's been an explosion!" shouted one voice.

"We're under attack!" another warned. In this transmission, gunfire could be heard.

"We need help down here!" They recognized it as Simon Godwin's voice. "Code black, code black, code black!" It was the signal to lock down the hotel.

Armstrong lunged out the door, not realizing that his phone was still live and unable to hear Chelle screaming, "David! David! . . . " As he raced toward the staircase, he slid the BlackBerry into its holster, terminating the call.

Fortman began to bark orders at the radio operators and shift commanders, instructing them to request more assistance. Sergeant O'Reilly picked up a phone and called St. Luke's Hospital, less than a mile from the hotel, to advise that they were going to have multiple trauma injuries and to dispatch several ambulances. St. Luke's was the designated emergency facility for the conference and the finest trauma center in the Kansas City area. The KCPD dispatcher called in extra troops and alerted the fire department about the explosion. The Patrol dispatcher instructed "any available officer" on the detail to respond to the ballroom area.

A trooper with the Michigan governor's detail had been standing next to a fax machine in the corner of the command post, awaiting an expected message. He ran out the door to save his protectee. Around the hotel, the reaction was the same. While most human beings would panic and flee from the scene of such a disaster, dozens of officers ran toward the catastrophe to bravely face the unknown dangers.

Chapter 47

March 4, 1124 hours
Grand Plaza Hotel
Kansas City, Missouri

Prior to the blast, Sergeant Quick Justice sat six rows behind the Georgia governor and First Lady, dividing his attention between the room's occupants and his protectees. He had vaguely listened to Novotny's speech, but didn't find it interesting. The only red flashing light on his mental warning panel was the shapely figure of Sergeant Kacey Underwood, sitting on the other side of the room next to First Lady Stovall. He considered strolling over to tell Underwood good-bye, since he and the governor would be leaving for the airport soon.

The blast knocked Justice out of his chair, like the blindside tackle of a pro linebacker. He knocked over three chairs as he fell. But he was the first bodyguard in the room to react. He bounded to his feet, accidentally knocked some lady off her feet, and then dove over a tangle of chairs and people to his protectees' position.

Like everyone else, Governor and Mrs. Blair were stunned by the blast. They now lay huddled together on the floor between the front row of chairs and the conference table.

Justice cleared the obstruction like a pro tailback diving into the end zone for the winning score. Unfortunately, he landed on his First Lady's right leg, breaking her ankle. She shrieked in pain and terror. He scrambled over them on his hands and knees, his huge bulk towering over them as cover in case the ceiling collapsed. He tried to assess their injuries. A severed arm, belonging to cameraman Brent Lively, was lying between them, but Justice saw that their arms were intact. He picked it up by the elbow and tossed it away from them. The governor's face was twisted in pain; he was barely aware of his surroundings. Half of his right ear was missing, and the right side of his face was pitted with several bleeding puncture wounds. Blood stained his neck and the collar of his white shirt. The First Lady was biting her lip and whimpering for God's help. Suddenly a drop of blood splattered onto her forehead, and Justice realized his face was bleeding.

Ignoring his injury, Justice shouted into the governor's face, "Are you okay?" His voice sounded like it was coming from the next room. Justice could hardly hear, his ears deafened by the blast. The governor didn't respond.

He looked around the room, trying to formulate an escape strategy that would enable them to survive. The blast had come from their right, but other unknown dangers seemed to encircle the room like an invisible cloud of lethal nerve gas.

Chapter 48

After dropping off the videocassette to his mother, Seed returned to the Houser Communications van in the garage and checked on the well-being of the infant in the car seat. The drugged formula they had given the baby an hour ago still had him sound asleep. Seed started the van and eased it down into the garage, toward the bottom levels. He knew he would encounter a KCPD officer on a golf cart when he got to the bottom levels, where the VIP vehicles were secured. He stopped the van within sight of the guard and awaited the bomb's detonation.

When the device exploded, he watched the KCPD officer gun his golf cart toward the ballroom entrance, responding to the emergency. Seed put the van in gear and quickly followed him down to rendezvous with his mother and the others who would be escaping from the ballroom. The plan called for them to pile into the van and flee the hotel under the withering fire of Draeger's deadly Galil SR99 sniper rifle. They would drive into the garage where Draeger was located, switch vehicles, and disappear into the heavy midday traffic, eventually returning to the safe house.

As Seed approached the ballroom entrance, he noticed a KCPD officer sliding a heavy, metal gate closed behind the golf cart as it zoomed past his position. They were blocking off the area. He couldn't get through! The only route of escape would be for him to turn around, drive up through the garage, and exit out past the lobby entrance.

Seed stomped on the gas in an attempt to crash through the gate. The officer slammed the gate closed, then looked up in shock at the approaching van. He waved his arm twice and then fled from the inevitable crash. The van struck the mesh barrier, going twenty-five miles per hour. The gate heaved with the weight, but captured the vehicle in its steel mesh like a huge fish in a net.

Inside the van, Seed's airbag exploded in his face, dazing him. Suddenly, the infant began to scream behind him. It was an intensive, high-pitched scream that indicated not just fear but agony as well. Seed pushed the plastic out of his way and grimaced at a sharp pain that shot through his left arm. His left wrist was broken. Hearing shouts, Seed looked to see several officers advancing on him with their weapons out. One shouted, "Outta the van! Keep your hands where we can see them!"

As though he didn't hear, Seed reached down in the gear bag next to the driver's seat and extracted a hand grenade. As one officer pounded on the driver's window, Seed pulled the pin, released the spoon, and held the grenade out, as though offering them a beautiful stone found in a creek bed. A wide grin split his face. Leech had taught him well. His "never let them take you alive" mantra was as firmly implanted in the thirteen-year-old as his hatred of government. The officers scattered for cover as, seconds later, the frenzied screaming of the infant was replaced by an explosion. It split open the van like an aluminum beer can.

Chapter 49

Godwin dashed into the ballroom and was shocked at the confusion and chaos that had swept through like a deadly twister. It was a surreal vision. His ears were assaulted by deep-throated shouts of anger and surprise, as well as high-pitched screams of horror and pain. His nostrils captured the acrid stench of burnt wires mixed with burnt flesh. Body parts were scattered everywhere. People—some he recognized and some he didn't—were moving—some staggering and others running—in every direction. The most carnage seemed to be around the press riser, where a soggy pile of bodies writhed in agony and distress, like some nightmarish life-form in a science-fiction movie. His eyes swept the conference table. Most of the governors were lying or sitting on the floor. The room looked like it was coming apart.

He called for the "code black" and raced through the soaking shower of the sprinklers and in the direction of the podium. He saw Underwood kneeling next to Mrs. Stovall, comforting her and assessing her injuries. Marko Vanhala was already moving through a pile of overturned chairs and injured attendees, digging out the Prince and Princess who had been seated behind their mother. A nasty gash creased Marko's forehead and a stream of blood was running down his face and dripping off his chin, but he ignored it. They had all been seated in an area of the room least affected by the blast. Except for Marko's injury, they appeared to be only dazed. Mrs. Stovall was sobbing and wringing her hands, but it looked like Underwood had things under control.

As Godwin rounded the corner of the table, he spotted Romanowski lying on the floor, stunned by the explosion but with no visible signs of injury. Godwin resisted the urge to go to his aid. Romanowski would have to fend for himself. Governor Stovall, who had been standing at the time of the explosion, was now on his knees behind the podium. As Godwin lunged next to him, the governor looked at him with a dazed expression. "What the hell are you doing here?" Ringmaster demanded. *Hadn't Godwin been told to stay out of the room?*

"Are you alright, sir?" Godwin shouted, ignoring the question. He ran his hands over the governor's abdomen and examined his hands for blood. There was none, but he noticed a tear in the coat sleeve of the governor's right arm, which was showing a small, dark stain of blood. At this point, both men were soaked from the water sprinklers.

"Yeah, I think so," the governor responded. "What happened?"

Godwin looked around the room, scanning for further threats. This thing might not be over. "There was an explosion, sir. I need to get you out of here." At the moment, this room was the worst place to be. Godwin decided to evacuate the governor through the back and take him to the holding room off the service corridor until things got sorted out. As he pulled Stovall to his feet and tugged him in the direction of the rear door, the rattle of gunfire erupted in the service corridor. A hooded figure stepped through the doorway with an automatic weapon. Godwin instantly knew that this figure was not a member of the security element. He wore what looked like a hotel security uniform, but his features were concealed by a ski mask. The figure saw them and raised his weapon in their direction.

Instinctively, Godwin yelled, "Gun!" He simultaneously covered the governor's body with his own. He shoved Stovall to the right, moving at a right angle to the gunman and in the direction of a side exit, which Godwin knew led into the pressroom.

Leech fired a muffled, three-shot burst at the retreating pair and missed. Since nearly everyone in the room was sitting, kneeling, or lying down, the bullets impacted harmlessly in the far wall. Leech re-sighted, activating the laser designator with the pressure switch on the pistol grip. A red beam exited the weapon from beneath the muzzle. A red dot found Godwin's retreating back. Leech fired another burst. All three rounds struck Godwin in the left rear panel of his body armor, ripping through the garment and his flesh. He went down, pulling the governor with him. They crashed to the floor behind a row of chairs, partially hidden from Leech. Leech took four steps forward to get a clear field of fire.

Grimacing from the red-hot sting of his wounds, Godwin glanced back and saw the masked gunman coming after them. It was a nightmarish vision, like watching as an executioner approaches the lever that will drop the blade of a guillotine on your neck. He rolled over onto the governor's back, pinning him to the floor, and shielded his body.

Godwin clawed at his Glock 23 and brought it to bear on the gunman, as Leech brought his weapon to bear on Godwin. The Glock barked three times, as Godwin fired first. The rounds seemed to have no effect, impacting on Leech's thick body armor. Leech quickly returned fire, his three rounds stitching up the center of Godwin's chest, with the last round hitting him in the throat. Godwin died instantly, collapsing atop Governor Stovall's helpless body.

Chapter 50

Most of the governors' bodyguards were lining the walls in the back of the ballroom when the camera bomb had exploded, putting them nearer the blast. Most now sat stunned or seriously injured, unable to react to their protectees across the room. This included Novotny's FBI agents. Temmons was bleeding from both ears and Sanders lay near Romanowski, moaning loudly with a deep shrapnel wound to his face. His cell-phone was vibrating frantically. The Bureau was looking for their boss.

For Romanowski, one moment he was sitting and listening to the droning voices of the governors, and the next he was lying on his back, staring at the ceiling. The smell of smoke assaulted his nostrils, and his hearing was impaired with an incessant ringing sound. As the water from the sprinklers brought him to his senses, he rolled to his knees and shook his head to clear it. Distant shouts and other noises began to chip through his fog. There was also another sound.

The muffled stutter of Leech's weapon, firing at Godwin and Stovall, followed by the distinctive bark of Godwin's Glock, brought Romanowski's head around. A hooded figure was standing near the podium and sighting an automatic weapon at people in the room. Romanowski brought his own Glock out and sighted on the gunman as Leech fired the fatal rounds at Godwin.

The gunman's back was toward Romanowski, who fired four quick rounds into the center of the gunman's mass. Leech reacted immediately as the Hydra-Shok rounds struck his body armor. None of the 180-grain, jacketed hollow points penetrated his vest, but to Leech it felt like four hornets were stinging his back. He wheeled around, fired a wild, three-shot burst at Romanowski, which went high, and then he fled back toward the door to the service corridor.

So intent was Leech on killing Governor Stovall that he failed to notice the huddled figure of his other primary target, FBI Director

Novotny, lying curled up in a ball at his feet. Leech's dripping-wet ski mask limited his field of vision, and Novotny was covering his face with his hands, but as Leech wheeled around, his foot kicked Novotny's shoulder, nearly tripping up the terrorist.

Others in the room now returned fire at Leech, including several rounds from Underwood's and Vanhala's Glocks. Mrs. Stovall shrieked at the cacophony of their weapons as they ejected hot brass all around her. The air around the governors' table was suddenly alive with hot metal.

Romanowski hugged the floor when Leech fired at him, then he fired six more rounds at the retreating figure. One round clipped Leech's unprotected buttocks, and another punched a nasty hole in the back of his right thigh. The second round did what it was designed to do: fragment, dumping all its deadly energy into the tissue. To Leech, it felt like he had backed into the ripping blades of a chain saw. He gasped and pitched forward, tumbling through the door and landing in the service corridor.

Chapter 51

So-So was totally focused on the law-enforcement officers moving in on her position. She nearly shot Leech when he came crashing out beside her. She saw he was hit badly and had lost his weapon. She fired a burst at the officers to beat them back, then stooped to help Leech to his feet. A KCPD officer—a master-class marksman with the tactical team—sent two well-placed rounds at her. One struck her right armpit, which was not covered by her armor, and the second clipped the nape of her exposed neck, fracturing the fourth and fifth cervical vertebrae. So-So went down like a trapdoor had opened under her. She was dead within a minute, as she bled out internally. Investigators would later find seven other police bullets from the firefight imbedded in her armor.

Leech, unaware of her condition and unable to locate his assault weapon, tried to crawl down the corridor in Wykoff's direction. His right leg, broken by Romanowski's round to his femur, trailed behind him at an odd angle, bleeding badly. Part of the bullet's copper jacket had sheared off and ricocheted inside his thigh, tearing his scrotum. His right testicle hung, torn and bleeding, between his legs. The wound looked frightful, but the pain was lost in the torrid river of heat that was pulsating up his spine in its frantic message to his brain that serious problems needed immediate attention.

The officers lost sight of him, but hesitated to pursue for fear of being outgunned. This guy was invincible. He had been shot to pieces, yet still fostered the will to survive. Death seemed afraid of him.

Special Agent Nick Ciabatta, a member of Novotny's FBI detail, was frantically calling Temmons and Sanders over his radio, without response. Ciabatta decided to go to them and was nearly killed by friendly fire as he burst into the ballroom with his SIG-Sauer raised.

He was met by several pistol rounds fired from bodyguards in the room, thinking he was another terrorist. The agent dove to the floor and crawled to Novotny's side.

The remaining officers in the garage left their cover to pursue Leech, but were met with a blaze of armor-piercing fire from Wykoff's P90. They heard a clattering noise, saw a grenade skittering down the tunnel toward their position, and again dove for cover. The blast crumpled part of the service corridor roof and filled the tunnel with a thick, choking cloud of plaster dust. After a moment, the dust began to settle, and two officers cautiously entered the tunnel, following a trail of Leech's blood. They heard him coughing from the dust and closed in around him.

As Leech heard the footsteps of the officers closing in, and heard their shouts—"FREEZE! DON'T MOVE, ASSHOLE! DON'T MOVE!"—he looked up in search of Wykoff, who had now disappeared. Leech rolled to his side and ripped a hand grenade from the vest pocket of his body armor. One officer pounced on Leech, knocking the wind out of him, and the grenade rolled out of his hands with the pin intact. Overpowered by the weight of his captors and weakened from the loss of blood, Leech was handcuffed roughly. The officers quickly stripped away his armaments and armor. As they rolled him over, Leech attempted to bite an officer's hand and was rewarded with a boot toe in the face. The officers' faces exploded in a bright cloud of stars, and the white-hot burning in his buttocks and thigh mercifully faded away.

Chapter 52

March 4, 1128 hours
Grand Plaza Hotel
Kansas City, Missouri

Inside the ballroom, Romanowski executed a tactical reload, replacing the nearly empty magazine in his weapon with the extra one from his belt pouch. Since the used magazine still held three rounds, he pushed it into his waistband, rather than discard it. Those three rounds might be what it took to see him through this situation.

He lurched to his feet and ran, crouched, to the governor's position. The gunfire had stopped, but he didn't want to be hit by friendly fire. Godwin was obviously dead, and Romanowski rolled him off the governor's squirming body. Stovall was covered with Godwin's blood.

"Are you hurt?" Romanowski asked the governor.

"My chest hurts," Stovall gasped. "It feels like all my ribs are broken. Romanowski ran his hand around the back of Stovall's head and felt a lump, apparently from hitting the floor.

At that moment, Armstrong reached their position. His eyes swept the devastation, and he felt sick to his stomach. *God help us!* he thought. "Is he okay?"

"He's got a knot on the back of his head big enough for a calf to suck, and a shrapnel wound to the right shoulder, but that's all I've found so far," Romanowski responded loudly. "He's complaining of chest pains."

"Let's move over to that corner," Armstrong told him, jutting his chin toward a vacant section of the room. It was a gamble to move him, but Armstrong felt it was more dangerous to remain in the open. There were no guarantees this thing was over. They could still hear gunfire coming from the service corridor and garage. Together, they helped Stovall to his feet and took him to the area.

As Stovall sat with his back braced against the wall, Boatright came rushing up to help. He was carrying the division's new H&K

MP7 submachine gun. "Go secure the service corridor," Armstrong ordered him in a calm voice. "Then get us an ambulance and call when it's clear to come out." Boatright lunged toward the back door with his MP7 ready. At that moment, the sprinkler system shut off. Everyone and everything in the room was dripping wet.

Bobby Davenport radioed that he was standing-by at Monitor for their evacuation. Armstrong told him to stay there until their evacuation route was secure. He would prefer that Stovall ride in an ambulance, but he'd use Monitor if there wasn't one available, since the hospital was only several blocks away. If the governor took an ambulance, Davenport would drive follow-up and haul the rest of the detail.

Hearing their exchange, Wiedemann radioed, "I have Merrimac at the Dock, if you need a ride now. The gunfire has stopped and we should have the Dock secure momentarily."

Armstrong considered their situation and made a decision. "Bobby, bring Monitor to the garage and set up a transfer triangle with Alex. We'll be out when you're ready."

"Ten-four," both officers responded.

Armstrong knelt in front of the governor and ran his hands over Stovall's torso to further assess his injuries. Stovall winced and groaned when Armstrong's hand probed his rib cage. Armstrong couldn't detect anything life-threatening, but he wanted to get Stovall to the trauma center as soon as possible. It appeared that all the blood staining Stovall's white shirt and suit coat came from Simon Godwin.

Romanowski stacked a barrier of chairs around them for what protection they offered. He squatted in front of them and closely watched the room with his Glock held in a "low ready" position. He was developing a blinding headache, and blinked his eyes several times, trying to clear his vision. In the course of only a few minutes, there had been nearly one hundred rounds fired within the room. The air now carried the sharp odor of gunpowder, and a hazy cloud seem to hang just below the ceiling.

Most of the radio traffic up to now had been excited and dis-jointed, transmitted by officers outside the kill zone. Romanowski keyed his wrist mike and quickly brought the command post up to speed. "Romanowski, Command Post. There was a bomb blast in the meeting room. We have a lot of people down. A gunman fled into the service corridor, and I just heard some explosions out there. You need to secure that area immediately, so the ambulances can be brought in to the ballroom entrance. Alert St. Luke's they'll be getting casualties. Most of the governors look okay, but several are still down. Ringmaster looks okay." He paused, adding, "Notify Watchtower to locate Bullpen and get a two-man team on him immediately." In any health emergency for Governor Stovall, it was SOP for the division to locate the lieutenant governor, codenamed "Bullpen," and put him under their umbrella of protection until the situation was resolved. Romanowski's eyes moved to the body of his close friend and commander. "Lieutenant Godwin is J-four," he said, using the code for "fatally injured."

In the command post, Major Fortman and the shift leaders listened closely to Romanowski's report. It sounded like everything was nearly under control. The hospital was already alerted. Ambulances and reinforcements were already en route. Fortman suddenly realized that all the people they would normally alert—Colonel DeWitt, Police Chief Hammond, DPS Director Frisbie, and Governor Stovall— were all in the ballroom. He rubbed his face and thought, *Jesus! This is a disaster!* But the news of Godwin's death hit him like a body blow, and the color drained from his beefy face.

Slowly, chaos was replaced by order, as responding officers and EMTs moved about the room, treating the injured. Normal triage procedures would dictate that the worst injured would be the first treated. But in this situation, the worst injured were bodyguards, staff, and press people. Right or wrong, the governors came first. When President Reagan was shot in 1981, he was quickly evacuated and arrived at the hospital only three minutes after Hinckley's first round was fired, while two bodyguards and a staff person lay seriously injured and untreated on the pavement. It was the nature of the business. It was the risk of walking alongside targeted VIPs.

Governor Stovall's eyes moved past his bodyguards, and the body of Lieutenant Godwin came into his view. Godwin's eyes were open but unfocused, staring at something beyond the ceiling. "He saved my life," Stovall said to Armstrong, as though surprised at the revelation.

Chapter 53

Through the six-power scope of his weapon, Draeger watched the firefight in the area behind the ballroom. He saw Leech stagger out and fall, and then So-So getting shot down. He could tell by the way she fell that she was probably dead. Gunfire was crackling like distant fireworks. When Seed's van had exploded earlier, an ominous sounding thud had echoed across to Draeger's position, and smoke still billowed out of the area, but the wrecked van was just out of his view.

The reticle of his scope rested on the chest of a uniformed trooper, who had emerged from the lower garage entrance. Several KCPD riot officers had maintained a skirmish line between the protesters and the hotel. High above them, two SERT countersnipers had been watching with binoculars, but both now had their H&K weapons out and were searching for targets. Throughout the attack, he could have easily dropped some of the officers, but Draeger's finger refused to squeeze the trigger. Even though his Galil weapon had a suppressor, it wouldn't take the officers long to spot his position, and then he would be in a world of hurt. This plan had been crazy from the beginning, and there would be little gained by throwing himself onto Leech's sword. He was a survivalist, not a fanatical terrorist intent on dying in battle to enter the kingdom of Heaven, even if there were seventy-two virgins awaiting his arrival, as jihadists believed.

As additional officers appeared in his kill zone and the wailing sirens of reinforcements approached the hotel, Draeger withdrew his weapon from the window of the van and covered it with a blanket.

Suddenly the right side door opened and Wykoff jumped in. "Why didn't you cover us, man?" he demanded. His eyes were wild. When he realized that he was about to be trapped by the advancing officers, he stripped off his disguise and armor, ditched his P90, and fled through the kitchen and out the loading dock. Only through good fortune was he able to make a clean escape.

Draeger was stunned to see a member of their group left alive. "I thought you were all dead. I never got a clear shot."

Wykoff's eyes narrowed as he pondered whether to kill Draeger or give him a second chance. "They got So-So and Leech. I think Spider's gone, too. Let's get back to the safe house for now."

Draeger started the ignition, exited the garage, and slowly merged into the heavy noon-hour traffic.

Chapter 54

"We're ready to move!" Armstrong radioed. He had the governor, Mrs. Stovall, and their children huddled inside the ballroom doors. Romanowski and Underwood shielded them on the sides, and Vanhala was covering their backs. All the officers had their Glocks out and ready, except Armstrong.

"The Dock is secure! The Dock is secure!" responded Boatright.

Armstrong looked at his teammates. Vanhala's face and chest were covered with dried blood, giving him a frightful appearance. Romanowski seemed unsteady on his feet. They were the most seriously injured team members, and Armstrong didn't want them falling off the speeding vehicles halfway to the hospital. "Don, you're riding with me." He looked at Vanhala. "Marko, you ride in Shadow with Alex." Both officers nodded.

Armstrong's eyes swept the room and he saw Director Novotny moving among the injured governors, trailed by Agent Ciabatta. Novotny had escaped serious injury and—despite Ciabatta's pleas for him to evacuate the hotel—insisted on providing aid to the governors and his injured detail members. Wiedemann and Merrimac were assigned to the FBI detail, but Armstrong wanted the extra coverage until they cleared the hotel. "Marko, as soon as we get to the hospital, you get that head stitched up. I'm sending Alex back here for Director Novotny. We've got enough people to cover without you." Marko nodded.

"Armstrong to TOP."

The Patrol countersniper team on the roof of the hotel responded immediately. "TOP, go!"

"Is the area secure?"

There was a momentary pause while they scanned the area. "The street is clear. KCPD has the crowd under control. Exit to the right and take Wornall Road north. We'll provide covering fire, if needed!" Wornall Road ran alongside the hotel and straight up to St. Luke's Hospital.

"Coming out!" Armstrong radioed, pushing open the doors and pulling Governor Stovall by his uninjured arm. Davenport had backed Monitor over the curb and as close as he could get to the doors, so that safety was only several feet away. Wiedemann had Merrimac parked in front at a right angle, forming an armored box called a "transfer triangle." This afforded them armor on two sides of the triangle and a concrete wall on the third, and shielded them from any hostile fire. Two ambulances had just arrived, but Armstrong decided they were going to the hospital NOW. He wanted to get Stovall there before the flood of other injured victims, which could drag the emergency room into a state of chaos.

Boatright had the right side door of Monitor open. Armstrong pushed the Stovalls inside, climbing in after them and closing the door. Romanowski jumped up front and slammed the door. Armstrong reached under the rear seat and pulled out the FAT kit. He unzipped the case and pulled out a dressing to put on the governor's arm. He could now focus on assessing and treating their injuries, while his team dealt with whatever hazards they faced.

"We're on the running boards!" Underwood barked at Boatright, slapping him on the shoulder. She climbed on the right side running board, and Boatright ran around and jumped on the left side. They both held onto the roof luggage rack with one hand and their weapon in the other, in case they had to shoot their way out of the garage. Vanhala ran to Merrimac and jumped in with Wiedemann.

"Let's go!" ordered Romanowski, when he saw their team was in place. "Romanowski to Command Post, we're en route to the hospital with Ringmaster and his family."

"Ten-four," the dispatcher responded. "The hospital is expecting you."

Davenport and Wiedemann activated their sirens and wigwag headlights as the vehicles eased out of the garage, through the ranks of KCPD officers, past the stunned and now quiet crowd of protesters, and raced away in the direction of St. Luke's trauma center.

Chapter 55

The throng of press people was restless, impatient for the press briefing to begin. They were facing their deadlines, and each had questions prepared to hurl at the governor, who, they had been told, would be facing their inquisition. What happened to allow this attack? Why didn't you foresee it coming? Who is to blame here? How did the terrorists get weapons inside the meeting room? Whose head will roll for this outrage? It was what the press did best in the wake of any disaster: step up on their platform, point at the person or group they perceived to be responsible, and proclaim to the world, "Here is your culprit!"

The press conference was taking place in a meeting room on the rooftop level of the hotel, well away from the crime scene on the ballroom level. Heavy security encased the room like a steel shroud. There seemed to be four security people for each member of the press. Ironically, Governor Stovall resisted a show of force for the meetings, but now demanded it after the attack was over. It was a typical misjudgment of amateurs who inserted themselves into areas best handled by experts.

All the television news stations had been showing footage of the dramatic escape of Governor Stovall from the hotel. His armored vehicles exiting the garage, bodyguards with weapons out clinging to the sides, and the damage from So-So's bullets running down the side of Merrimac—all captured by an NBC news crew shooting an exterior shot of the protests at the time of the explosion. This was accompanied by footage shot from inside the meeting room, which terminated at the instant of the blast. An enterprising Fox reporter, who had been inside the pressroom at the time of the explosion, grabbed his personal video camera and dashed into the devastated meeting room, capturing most of the ensuing firefight. It all dominated the national news, but the press was clamoring for fresh images and new details.

A door behind the podium opened and Governor Stovall strode to the lectern, dutifully followed by DPS Director Lawrence Frisbie and Lieutenant Colonel Hal "Da-Half-Wit" Looney, who was filling in for DeWitt. Although they were seated together when the bomb exploded, Frisbie had only sustained minor injuries, while DeWitt's shrapnel wounds had been more serious, requiring hospitalization. If there were going to be anyone in the hot seat, it would be Frisbie and Looney, not the governor. Stovall had changed out of his blood-stained clothes and wore a fresh black suit. Though his legs had no wounds, Stovall limped slightly, and though he had but a cut on one arm, it was immobilized in a dark blue sling. He was mostly sore from being manhandled by Godwin. As if not to be outdone, Frisbie had a large Band-Aid on his tanned forehead. Naylor and Fleming stood to one side with Lieutenant Armstrong. Ironically, neither of Stovall's top staff people was present in the ballroom at the time of the explosion, since they were both in Naylor's room making a conference call back to the Governor's Office.

It had been Fleming's suggestion that the news conference be done from the hotel to show the public that the area was now "safe," and the crisis was past and under control. He also insisted that Stovall wear the absurd arm sling. "It will do two things," he advised the governor. "It will mark you as a victim of this attack, not associated with the cause of it, which will soften the reporters' questions. Two, it will create sympathy in the TV viewers at home. No one would lash out at a handicapped individual." Stovall thought it was good advice and speculated that maybe he should also use a cane. Fleming immediately responded, "That may be going over the top. Just limp a little on your way to the podium. It'll create more of a heroic image." Such details were bread and butter of the modern-day politician, courting an image-hungry press in order to entertain a public with the attention span of an eight-year-old.

Stovall's face bore an expression of sadness, with just a hint of outrage playing around the corners of his eyes. He squinted into the lights and said, "Ladies and gentlemen of the press. I want to make some brief remarks and then I'll take a few questions." He looked down at his notes. "At 11:24 this morning today, a violent group of terrorists known as the Phineas Priests carried out a cowardly attack on a meeting of governors, the FBI director, and many other VIPs, law-enforcement and government officials, and members of the press. I am saddened to report that one law-enforcement officer and twelve members of the press were killed in the attack. I was also just informed a few minutes ago that a member of Governor Caine's staff, who was standing near the press riser, just passed away. In addition, many others were wounded, some very seriously. I am told that three terrorists were killed, along with an infant belonging to one of the group." This was new information and the room stirred. "One terrorist was captured and is in custody, and authorities believe that another may be at large. At this time, an intensive investigation is going on to determine exactly how this attack was carried out, and I cannot comment on the security procedures that may have been breeched."

Casper Deegan, seated on the front row, spoke up, "What do you mean, 'may have been,' Governor? If a weapon got inside that room, then security was breeched, wasn't it?"

Stovall glared at the reporter. "Casper, I just said I can't comment on that. I do wish to commend the brave officers who place their lives on the line every day to protect us and the public from these terrorist groups. They are the only thing standing between us and anarchy. I thank God that their quick reaction kept this attack from turning into a bigger disaster. I hope your stories reflect the fact that not one governor was seriously wounded in the attack, so that goal of the Patrol operation was successful."

Stovall began searching the anxious faces for someone a little less aggressive, but Deegan persisted. "Governor, we know that there was gunfire inside the room, following the explosion. So the terrorists were allowed to bring a bomb and automatic weapons inside a secured area. How can you defend the police when security was so easily breeched?"

Stovall glanced back at Frisbie and Looney. "As I said, that investigation is ongoing. Director Frisbie and Lieutenant Colonel Looney will brief you in a few moments on the specifics of their findings."

Another reporter jumped in. "Governor, these Phineas Priests have been carrying out acts of violence all over the state. Why didn't anyone recognize them when they showed up here?"

Stovall shook his head. "As I said, I won't speculate on how the security ring was penetrated, but I understand these people were wearing disguises and bore little likeness to the pictures that had been circulated. Also, there was no intelligence that they intended to strike here. I can confirm that the captured terrorist was the group's leader, Ezekiel Leech, known in the extremist circles as 'Easy Kill' because of his violent nature and disregard for human life. He sustained several wounds during the attack and is currently being held at a high-security medical facility. It is our intention that he will be charged with several counts of first-degree murder, and we will seek the death penalty against him."

His refusal to directly answer the questions stirred the reporters into a frenzy. They waved their arms and shouted for his attention. He gestured for calm and continued, "Security experts will tell you that there's no such thing as perfect protection. The Patrol followed proper procedures by setting up three rings of protection around the meeting site; it's a concept called 'Defense in Depth.' Then, when the rings were penetrated, the outer rings collapsed around the attackers, neutralizing the attack and minimizing the casualties." Though technically correct, it was "security speak" and would not impress the cable talk shows. The fact remained, the rings should not have been penetrated in the beginning. The cops, as usual, would be skewered over this, like great hunks of pork on a spit.

The governor continued, "From my standpoint, you just have to do the best you can and support the security details by listening to their sound advice and going along with their suggestions. I make it a policy to allow my detail to worry about security, while I just worry about doing the people's business." He looked around the room, then launched into his closing remarks, which Naylor and Fleming had helped him draft. "I think it's obvious that the real issue here is gun control. Each one of these terrorists had illegal, fully automatic, assault weapons. My proposed assault-weapons ban would place stronger controls on the sale of these weapons and add years to the sentences of those who use these weapons to commit crimes. I believe the argument can be made that my bill would help bring an end to this madness."

It was a flawed argument. None of the weapons used by Leech's group were "purchased." They were all stolen. And there were a dozen

Class "A" felonies already on the books that would put the group away for the rest of their lives; indeed, more likely on death row. If Stovall's proposals were already in effect, they would have no more prevented the attack than could a judge's order of protection stop a demented man's bullets aimed at his estranged spouse or his fellow co-workers. Unfortunately, the governor's inane statement went unchallenged by the pro-gun-control media. In fact, their stories would all support that angle.

An attractive female anchorperson from a local TV station lobbed the governor a softball. "Governor, can you tell us anything about the officer who was killed?"

Stovall gazed over the group, as though gathering his thoughts, then smacked the slow pitch out of the park. "Some of you may know that the fallen officer was my former detail leader, Lieutenant Simon Godwin. He had recently transferred into the Criminal Bureau and was fulfilling an intelligence assignment for this conference, and frankly I felt safer with him here. His wife, Judy, survives him, and I spoke with her on the phone about an hour ago. He was a dedicated officer and a true friend. He protected my family and me since my election, and today he saved my life. He reacted in the highest traditions of protective service and laid down his life in place of mine. That is a debt that no man can ever repay." A tear appeared in Stovall's right eye, and he paused to dab a finger at it. When he resumed, his voice broke. "He was like a son to Pat and me. We will miss him dearly, and our hearts go out to his wife and family."

With that, he turned and walked out the door behind him, ignoring further shouted questions. Frisbie and Looney reluctantly took his position.

Chapter 56

The turnout for Godwin's funeral was the largest in Hannibal's history, requiring that it be held in the local high-school gymnasium. Officers from all over the country came to pay their respects, including troopers assigned to many governors' details, and members of the U.S. Secret Service. As Godwin had requested in his funeral document filed with the Human Resources Division of the Patrol, he was buried in full dress uniform and was given a Patrol honor guard. His love of the Patrol was intact to the end. He was the thirty-fourth Patrol officer to be killed in the line of duty since the agency was created in 1931.

Conspicuously absent among the attending VIPs, who were eager to be seen in support of the law-enforcement community, was Governor William Ulysses Stovall. The governor let it be known that he wanted to attend the funeral, but could not get out of an "important meeting" in Washington DC. If anyone had bothered to find out, the meeting was little more than a chance to swagger about Capitol Hill and the White House, and relate stories of his near-death experience. The governor's approval polls had shot up since the attack, and the media was already pronouncing him a "shoo-in" if he decided to run for re-election. Stovall had weighed the points he could gain by being seen in close proximity to Godwin's flag-draped casket, versus the points he might lose by the harsh and pointed questions shouted at him by a scandal-hungry press. He decided not to tempt fate and opted for the trip to Washington.

The members of the Missouri governor's detail served as pallbearers for Godwin's casket, and every officer attended but one. In order for the entire detail to participate in the funeral, Lieutenant Armstrong had taken it on himself to escort Governor and Mrs. Stovall to Washington. Armstrong knew the trip was just an excuse for the Stovalls to get out of town during an uncomfortable period.

Armstrong considered that perhaps the biggest irony of the attack was that, if Spider's grenade had exploded, Godwin would have most likely been killed in the blast. If so, he could not have run into the ballroom and saved Stovall's life. Without much doubt, Leech would have killed Stovall and Novotny, along with other governors huddled around and under the table. Godwin might have failed to react properly during a harmless pie attack, but when the chips were down and the bad guys were firing something more deadly than custard, Godwin had done it right. No one could have done it better.

During the funeral service, the remarks by the Methodist minister had dwelt on sacrifice and centered on John 15:13: "Greater love hath no man than this, that a man lay down his life for another." He described Godwin's heroic actions during the attack in Kansas City. How Godwin had picked up the grenade, not knowing that it was a dud, in an action that would have saved others if the device had exploded. In fact, his shouted warning enabled nearly everyone to seek cover before Spider's raking gunfire, saving additional lives. How he again risked his life by entering the ballroom and quickly going to the governor's aid. How—when confronted by a heavily armed terrorist—he had placed his body between the gunman and the governor, taking six rounds that were meant for Governor Stovall. In fact, one of the first three rounds to hit him clipped his heart, producing what the coroner described as a "non-survivable wound." He was, in essence, a dead man while he continued to cover the governor and fight back, by returning fire at Leech. In the vernacular of the profession, he had fulfilled the ultimate obligation and "soaked up six for the boss." The minister concluded by quoting from Milton's *Samson Agonistes*:

Samson hath quit himself
Like Samson, and heroically hath finished
A life heroic.

As the minister took his seat, Sergeant Kacey Underwood rose and strode toward the podium, looking like a young warrior in her Patrol uniform. She carried no notes. Her glistening black shoes trod silently up the carpeted steps to the dais. Her gait had just a bit of hesitation in it, like walking up on a demolished vehicle knowing that you were going to find a family member inside. Adjusting the microphone to her height, she gazed out over the packed room momentarily, as though she were surprised that so many were in attendance. The room was totally silent. Several rows from the front, she saw Leland Justice's beaming face, supporting her with a tight smile and a slight nod of his head. Then she closed her eyes, tilted her head back slightly and, in a clear and strong voice, quoted from memory Theodore O'Hara's 1847 poem, *The Bivouac of the Dead*:

> The muffled drum's sad roll has beat
> The [trooper's] last tattoo;
> No more on Life's parade shall meet
> That brave and fallen few.
> On Fame's eternal camping-ground
> Their silent tents are spread,
> And Glory guards, with solemn round,
> The bivouac of the dead.

Chapter 57

As Godwin's coffin was carried out of the gymnasium and loaded in the back of the hearse, Stovall's Citation jet was beginning its final approach into Reagan National Airport. Armstrong had arranged for a staff person from Missouri's office in Washington to meet them on arrival. The Secret Service and U.S. Capitol Police were aware of their schedule and would assist them when they arrived at the White House and Capitol.

Armstrong occupied the seat between the cockpit and the four facing seats in the main part of the cabin. The events of the previous fifty-one days played through his mind like a bad movie, leaving him numb and unable to focus. He couldn't get out of his head the prophetic conversation with Godwin, warning of the weak positions in their security operation. He felt a sense of negligence that he hadn't talked Godwin into beefing up those areas or talked the governor out of scaling back security. Armstrong could have kept the conversation to himself—presumably, Godwin had not shared their comments with anyone else—but that would be the coward's way out.

When Armstrong and the governor returned to the Capitol on the day of the attack, Armstrong told Stovall of his conversation with Godwin. The governor listened quietly, then replied, "David, what's done is done. There is nothing to be served by thinking about what might have been. Hindsight is always twenty-twenty. I'd prefer that you not say anything about this matter to anyone else. It'll just make the Patrol look worse than it already does. Let the investigation reveal what it will." It was exactly what Armstrong had predicted to himself that the governor would say: *Remember, your job is to protect me!* It was a perverted slant on Armstrong's real job responsibility and let everyone but Lieutenant Godwin and Major Fortman—the conference commanders—off the hook. There was already talk that Fortman would be demoted over this. The press needed a villain to lynch.

Twelve of their own had died in the attack, and many more were seriously injured. They were stinging from the fact that the terrorists had breached security, one posing as a fellow reporter. It wouldn't be acceptable for the press to carry any of the blame.

The investigation had just discovered the bittersweet role that cameraman Brent Lively had played, evident in the strange blast pattern of the shrapnel—actually at a ninety-degree angle to the governors' position. His moving the position of the camera bomb had certainly saved governors' lives, but focused the destruction on his colleagues in the press. Strangely, the mainstream media had so far buried this angle.

Prior to flying out of Jefferson City for Washington, Armstrong had called Major Moss and told him that he was going to request a transfer back to a road assignment. "I'm not cut out for this crap," he confessed to his superior. "I can't imagine how Simon Godwin did this for so many years. I can't protect this son of a bitch for another day—hell, not another hour!"

Moss had listened patiently, stated that he understood Armstrong's feelings, and consoled him: "David, if I thought that was true, you'd be gone before this call was over. You're hurting now, but I have no doubt that the governor is safer in your hands than in anyone else's. You're a consummate professional. Simon was good, but I think you're even better." Then he doused any ideas Armstrong had about changing assignments. "Besides, Colonel DeWitt won't allow you to leave now. We have too much invested in you."

Armstrong was trapped in a thankless job, protecting thankless people who didn't understand or care what protection work was all about. Like Godwin, the more Armstrong tried to run a professional operation, the more the Stovalls would resist, until eventually he would receive a page to come to the colonel's office for reassignment. Stovall was less than three months into his first four-year term, and he would probably be re-elected to another four years after that. Armstrong's only option was to run the best operation he could until a new governor was elected.

Armstrong was outraged that the Stovalls had the insensitivity and disrespect to blow off Godwin's funeral, and the closer they got to DC, the angrier he became. *How dare they?* he asked himself as he looked back at them. The governor was going over some correspondence and Mrs. Stovall had her face buried in a book. They didn't even appear to be remotely concerned that their former detail leader was being placed in the ground . . . AT THIS VERY MOMENT! Armstrong wanted to shout at them, *How can you do this? Where is your decency? You are alive today because of him!* But he held his tongue, for now. *Perhaps one day I'll tell them off,* he thought. His anger slowly subsided, replaced by his steely sense of mission.

The public saw the Stovalls as loving, caring, deeply religious people, who spent every waking hour thinking about how they could improve the lives of Missouri's citizens. Armstrong saw two self-absorbed, arrogant elitists, who carried around façades of the ideal couple, like an attractive billboard for some tobacco product that would kill you in the end if you used it. They were about as real as a carnival sideshow, and their agenda focused only on how they could stay in power. Armstrong realized that he had never seen the Stovalls exhibit any kind of affection for one another, except in public, playing to some crowd. They never held hands, shared a kiss, or exchanged hugs. In private, they seemed to despise one another. It was what disappointed Armstrong the most about them: they were complete and accomplished frauds with distorted values, schmoozing with the rich and powerful, while seducing the electorate. He was reminded of a Chinese proverb: "His mouth is honey, his heart a sword."

Governor Stovall glanced up and saw Armstrong staring at them. "How are we doing, David?" he asked, referring to their flight schedule.

"Super, Governor," Armstrong responded slowly. "We're doing super."

Book Three:

Once more into the breech, dear friends . . .

People have asked me whether a determined assassin can kill the president. My only answer to that is you have to have an equally determined group of men and women to try to stop it. They have to be as enthusiastic about their defense of the president as the pathology that drives the assassin to kill.
                                        —Jerry Parr, retired Secret Service Agent

He seems to me
Scarce other than my king's ideal knight . . .
Doubt not, go forward; if thou doubt, the beasts
Will tear thee piecemeal.
                        —Alfred Lord Tennyson, 1885, *Idylls of the King*

Chapter 58

Prison Guard Hermann Glassgow jolted awake when he nearly rolled out of his chair in Tower 4. He shook his head to clear it and looked out over the barren exercise yard of the state prison. He was at the end of his shift and fighting to stay awake. Glassgow checked his neighboring towers to see if anyone had seen his near-fall. Billy Tackett in Tower 5 looked like he was asleep, too, but Travis Bicardi in Tower 3 was laughing and holding up a piece of paper with the score "8.4" written on it. Glassgow gave him the finger.

During Glassgow's short nap, he had dreamed that a wrecking ball had come crashing through his tower, and the inmates poured through the hole in the wall like a swarm of fire ants. Over his thirty-six years with the Department of Corrections, he'd had that same dream probably a hundred times. His eyes moved around the complex, and he wondered how much longer it would be before they tore this old place down. The penitentiary was America's oldest prison west of the Mississippi. They had started construction in 1835, and many of the underground dungeons used to isolate the most incorrigible inmates still existed, though they hadn't been used in decades. Housing Unit 4 was the oldest structure, built in 1868, and part of the wall on which Glassgow's tower was perched dated back to 1848. After scores of escapes, riots, executions, and violence, it had gained the reputation as the "bloodiest forty-seven acres in America."

The old walls had housed more than a few infamous characters: gangster "Pretty Boy" Floyd and former heavyweight boxing champion Sonny Liston. Political anarchist Emma Goldman had been sent here in 1917, doing two years behind the limestone walls. James Earl Ray had escaped from here prior to assassinating Martin Luther King Jr. in 1968. Glassgow had heard a rumor that they were going to transfer terrorist Ezekiel Leech here in a few weeks. Leech was still healing from wounds he had received during his attack in Kansas City, which had almost killed a group of visiting governors.

Glassgow's older brother had once served on the death squad, escorting and preparing inmates for execution. Herman occasionally helped the death squad when they began using the lethal injection method in 1989. After they opened the lethal-injection room at the new Potosi maximum-security prison and moved death row, he'd had an opportunity to transfer there, but by then he'd settled into his tower. He'd probably remain perched here until that wrecking ball blasted it down for real.

Spring was early again this year, and even at this early hour, it was unseasonably warm. They said it would be in the high seventies again today. Glassgow had cranked open the rear window of his tower to let in some fresh air. He suddenly detected the distant sound of running feet and turned to look out the rear window. The early morning fog had rolled in off the Missouri River overnight and blanketed the area in a cottonlike wall of vapor.

As he focused in on the sound, he saw two men in jogging clothes running in his direction down Cherry Street. Cherry ended in a T-intersection at the foot of his tower, intersecting with Capitol Street, which ran alongside the south wall. The men looked familiar, and he recognized that they were the same two who ran past his position nearly every morning, always this early.

Must be a couple of jocks, he thought with contempt, as he hitched his uniform belt up over his forty-eight-inch waist. One man was in his thirties and looked like an athlete. Small-waisted and broad-shouldered, he might be a defensive back for some semi-pro team. The other man was older, probably forty, and looked like he wanted to be an athlete. His hair was graying, but he had a slender build and was running with an easy gait. He wore headphones and carried what looked like a CD player.

Probably listening to Deepak Chopra, thought Glassgow with a smirk. He watched them closely as they reached the intersection and turned left in the direction of the Capitol Building, eight blocks down the street. The younger one spotted Glassgow in the tower and kept an eye on him until they disappeared back into the fog.

Glassgow started to hoist himself back into his chair, when he noticed a vehicle emerge silently from the fog. It came from the same direction as the men, down Cherry Street, then turned left on Capitol. It was a new Lincoln Navigator, bristling with antennas. The SUV was obviously following the runners from a discreet distance, and Glassgow wondered about them. *Maybe they're drug dealers*, he thought. He considered calling it in to the command center, but decided against it. The shift commander ridiculed everything Glassgow did and always asked, "When are you gonna retire and open up that tower? I've got twenty guys begging for a tower job."

With a grunt, Glassgow hoisted himself up into his high chair, balanced his bulk into a stable position, and waited for his relief to show up. Life was good in his tower and he was in no big hurry to retire.

Glassgow would have been surprised had he followed the runners and their tail car down the street. As the two men reached the intersection at Madison Street, the driver in the SUV lifted a radio mike to his lips and said, "Romanowski to Watchtower, gate please."

As the men ran along the front of the Governor's Mansion, code-named "Watchtower," the drive-in gate groaned open, and the men turned into the drive without slowing. A moment later, the Lincoln pulled into the drive behind them, and the gate groaned shut. As the vehicle parked at the back door of the Mansion, both runners were stretching out their muscles in front of the garage.

The older man asked his companion, "How fast, David?"

The younger runner squinted at his runner's watch. "Forty-seven minutes, Governor."

Governor William Ulysses Stovall pulled his headphones off and stopped the Tony Robbins CD that was playing. "That's our best time, yet. I'm feeling stronger each day."

Stovall had taken up jogging only a few weeks before, after the attack in Kansas City which had nearly taken his life. At first, Armstrong had argued that it wasn't safe to jog on the street and suggested that the governor use a treadmill, and Stovall had complied, for about three days. Finally, Stovall informed David that he would begin jogging early the next morning on the streets of the city and that Armstrong could either go along or not. Before Armstrong could object, Ringmaster had concluded, "I don't know what the big deal is. All but three of the people who tried to kill me are dead, and one of them is in prison!" The manhunt continued for Bobby "Gunner" Wykoff and Ross Draeger, but they had gone underground and the leads were turning cold. The last reported sighting of the pair placed them in the area of Broken Bow, Nebraska, but Matt Youngblood was skeptical of the information. The entire episode reminded Armstrong of President Bill Clinton's insistence on jogging around the streets of Washington DC after he won the White House in 1992. Even after a would-be assassin was arrested with a weapon, staked out along Clinton's route, the President not only continued to jog on the streets, but did it wearing a T-shirt that taunted "In the Line of Fire," seeming to thumb his nose at the situation. Armstrong was reminded of a quote by Winston Churchill: "Nothing in life is so exhilarating as to be shot at without result."

Stovall now looked at his chief bodyguard and noticed that Armstrong was barely sweating. "One of these days, I'll run off and leave you."

Armstrong smiled. "That won't be long, sir. I can barely keep up now."

Stovall snorted, "Nice try. You guys are tactful; I'll give you that." He started toward the door. "What time is my first appointment?"

"Eight o'clock with Senator Maxey," Armstrong quoted from memory.

"I'll be down at seven-thirty," Stovall stated and went inside.

Romanowski got out of Monitor and approached Armstrong. "You guys were tearing it up this morning," he groused. "I was afraid we might have to use the AED on him."

Armstrong gave Romanowski a pained look and muttered, "Don't say that. The boss was gasping like a fish out of water. He's really pushing himself."

Romanowski grunted. "Yeah, I haven't heard breathing that heavy since my wife last got an obscene phone call."

Cameron Boatright exited the passenger side of Monitor and walked past them, carrying a canvas briefcase. It held the division's new H&K MP7 submachine gun, a sound suppressor, and five 40-round magazines. The weapon was ideal for public-figure protection work. It was small enough to carry concealed, had nearly no recoil, and fired a small 4.6x30mm round that would penetrate body armor.

Armstrong walked toward the back door followed by Romanowski, and they entered the security command post located in the basement of the Mansion. A bank of closed-circuit TV monitors, alarm systems, telephones, radio gear, and other devices were packed into the CP, making it look like a NASA launch facility. Cameras located around the grounds provided Capitol Police Sergeant Al Rollings with a panoramic view of the surrounding area. Anyone attempting to sneak over the fence would set off a motion alarm and be picked up by the cameras.

Six Capitol police officers were assigned to work shifts around-the-clock at the Governor's Mansion. They answered the phones, screened calls, and protected the building, while the troopers protected the people in the building. It was similar to the Secret Service, where the Uniformed Division protected the White House, and the agents protected the President and his family. The Governor's Security Division had come into existence within the Missouri State Highway Patrol in 1973, by virtue of an executive order issued by then-Governor Christopher "Kit" Bond. Its function was to protect the governor and his immediate family, as well as any visiting dignitaries to whom its members were assigned. Armstrong had never met Bond, but he had heard of the close relationship Bond had shared with his troopers. He remained to this day, the most popular governor ever protected by the detail.

"You're not even sweating," Rollings observed. "You're not supposed to make the boss look bad."

Armstrong just shook his head and continued back into the break room. He grabbed a bottle of water out of the detail's refrigerator, as Boatright stowed the weapon in their gun cabinet.

Trooper Marko Vanhala was setting up a chessboard to challenge Romanowski to a few quick matches before Ringmaster came down to leave for the office. Romanowski had been delighted to learn that Vanhala was an excellent player. No one else on the detail could give Romanowski much competition, but Mount Viking could run the board with the best of them. During their matches, Vanhala would proudly relate stories of the greatest chessmasters in Finland, especially his favorite, Tomi Nyback. Marko glanced up at his supervisor. "The least you could do is break a sweat, L.T."

"What the hell is this?" Armstrong exclaimed. "Everybody's on my case this morning. Look, I'm sweating." He pointed to a wet spot on his chest about the size of a silver dollar.

Romanowski leaned over and eyeballed the area. "That's not sweat," he decided. "It looks like you were drooling on yourself or something. Probably excited about running alongside the governor."

Armstrong's right hand stabbed the air. "You're all fired," he said in his best Donald Trump voice. "I don't have to take this abuse from you guys. I'm going home to get some." As he left, he called back, "I'll be back at about nine." Out on the drive, he broke into a run. Rollings opened the gate. Armstrong made a right and headed toward his house, one mile beyond the Capitol Building.

*   *   *

From the third level of the city parking garage adjacent to the Governor's Mansion, two men in a black Chevrolet Blazer noted the time that Governor Stovall returned from his morning run, put away their camera gear, and prepared to leave the garage. Wykoff had shaved his head, giving him a very different look. Draeger had shaved his beard and had a shorter haircut, but was otherwise unchanged. They both wore bulky coats and floppy hats to obscure their appearance.

"Just like yesterday," Wykoff muttered to his colleague.

Chapter 59

Lieutenant David Armstrong fixed himself a cup of hazelnut-flavored coffee. As a young zone sergeant in Macon, supervising six even younger state troopers, Armstrong had never heard of such extravagances. He was happy to get a stale cup of coffee at the scale house or sheriff's office. Since he had transferred to the Governor's Security Division, he had become hooked on the stuff. One thing you could say about the position, it didn't take long to develop a taste for the finer things in life. Riding around in armored vehicles, staying at five-star hotels, flying around on private jets—it made for a heady experience.

He set the steaming mug down at his desk and pulled a roster out of the drawer. The book contained the addresses and phone numbers for every governor's security detail in the nation. The National Governors Security Association (NGSA) was a small and elite law-enforcement group, numbering approximately six hundred state police officers, and was very close-knit. Lieutenant Godwin had been NGSA vice president for four years, and Armstrong was toying with the idea of running for president in the next election of officers. He thumbed over to the Georgia listing and noted the number of the security line at the Governor's Office.

"Governor Blair's Office, Sergeant Justice at your service," drawled a squeaky voice, which belied the bulk of the man to whom it belonged. Armstrong pictured the muscular giant, sitting at his desk in an expensive suit.

"This is Lee Harvey Oswald," Armstrong replied in a voice that might sound like the assassin of President Kennedy. "I'd like to speak to the greatest bodyguard in the history of Georgia."

"That would be me, Mr. Oswald," Justice responded immediately, "and might I say, it's a damn shame that I wasn't protecting our late President in 1963 when he rode past your window, sir."

Armstrong laughed, "Hey, Quick, it's David Armstrong."

"Damn, son, I thought I was speaking to the dead there for a minute. How're my Missouri buddies doin'?"

"S.O.S.," Armstrong groaned. *Same old stuff.* "I've got a big favor to ask."

"Well, I figured you weren't calling just to try out your Oswald imitation. What can we do for you?"

"Governor Stovall's scheduler just informed me that the boss is headed to Atlanta this weekend to attend a fundraiser you guys are hosting for Vice President Boering. I was hoping you might help us out."

"That's right," Justice confirmed. "The VP's Secret Service detail has been all over my ass for the past two days. I get along pretty good with PPD," he said, referring to the Presidential Protection Division, "but these guys are the B-Team and they really like to throw their weight around. The lead advance guy is a real prick."

Armstrong pulled up the trip itinerary on his BlackBerry. "I'll be flying out of St. Louis on an American Airlines flight, arriving in Atlanta at thirteen-twenty hours on Friday to do the advance. Then the boss flies in on his Citation jet on Saturday, arriving at about sixteen-hundred hours. We'll do the event at the hotel, stay overnight, and fly back the next morning. Can you assign someone to us?"

"Is anyone coming out with the governor?" Justice asked.

"Yeah, the governor's personal secretary and one other officer."

"Which officer?" Justice inquired innocently.

Armstrong rolled his eyes. "Do you have a preference, Quick?" He already knew the answer.

"If it's gonna be one Sergeant Kacey 'I'm-too-sexy-for-my-shorts' Underwood, I might consider handling you guys myself."

"Quick, you'll never give up. Kacey would just as soon dive off the dome of the Capitol as go out on a date with you."

Justice clicked his tongue. "Persistence is my middle name, son."

"Well, I don't want to get your hopes up or anything, but Kacey volunteered for this trip. She hasn't been stalked lately, so I guess she misses your attention."

Justice blurted, "Yes!" and laughed out loud. "If that's the case," he replied in an exaggeratedly bored tone, "I wouldn't want to disappoint her. Fax your schedule down to me, and I'll give you my personal attention."

"Do we need to call VPD?" Armstrong asked. The Vice Presidential Protection Division in Washington DC would want to know about any VIPs who would show up with armed escorts.

"I'll take care of that down here," Justice said. "There's a final briefing scheduled for ten on Saturday morning, followed by a walk-through. I'll introduce you to Mein Fuhrer Stylesh. I think this is his first big trip as the VP's lead advance guy, and he's really been on a tear. Yesterday I reminded him that no vice president in the history of America has ever been assassinated, and he really blew his stack. Things kind of went downhill after that."

"Maybe I should call Mike Reeves at the Liaison Division and give him a heads-up," Armstrong offered. The last thing he wanted was a rift between Justice and VPD spoiling their visit. The primary job of the Secret Service Liaison Division was to coordinate joint operations and smooth over any problems.

"'The first rule of Fight Club is you don't talk about Fight Club.' I've got it under control, dog," Justice scolded him. "I'll just have to put this kid in his place and teach him to respect his elders." Justice rang off with his favorite farewell, "A.M.F." *Adios, my friend.*

Armstrong frowned, spotting a storm cloud on the horizon of the visit. He'd heard about some real disasters that resulted from such confrontations. Romanowski had recounted a story where a trooper bodyguard for the governor of one southern state and a Secret Service agent in charge of the President's motorcade stood nose-to-nose screaming at one another, while the governor and President gawked at the confrontation from inside the protective confines of the President's armored limousine. The issue: the trooper didn't like the position in the motorcade that had been assigned to the governor's car. The trooper screamed that if the agent didn't move the governor's car closer to the front of the motorcade, he would call off the Highway Patrol helicopter that was flying cover for the motorcade. The agent was screaming that if the trooper didn't get into his car, the agent would have the trooper arrested for threatening the safety of the President.

Armstrong hung up the phone, picturing the massive Sergeant Leland "Quick" Justice punching out the lead advance agent in front of the head table. The premonition sent a cold chill through him.

236

Chapter 60

Armstrong and Justice pushed their way through the crowded room and found seats along the windows of the briefing room. Justice nudged Armstrong and jutted his dimpled chin toward the front of the room at a tall, slender agent with a mustache. "That's Mein Fuhrer," he said. The guy looked like comedian David Letterman on steroids. His stony gaze was moving around the room while a site agent mumbled information into his right ear.

He's probably scanning the room for terrorists, thought Armstrong. The guy looked as serious as a severed artery.

Stylesh muttered an answer to his aide, then waved him off and addressed the room. "Okay, people, let's get started!" He waited with an impatient look on his face while the law-enforcement personnel jockeyed for seats. Armstrong expected him to launch into the "top ten reasons why Feds are better than state and local cops."

When all was quiet, he spoke, "My name is Special Agent Steve Stylesh of the Vice Presidential Protection Division. I'm the lead advance agent for this trip, and I appreciate your assistance. We could not ensure the safety of the vice president without the help from your agencies."

His tone didn't strike Armstrong as being very sincere. Armstrong looked around the room and guessed that there were about fifty officers and agents in attendance. The group included personnel with the Atlanta Police Department, Georgia State Patrol, Fulton County Sheriff's Office, and Airport Police.

"At sixteen-fifteen hours today, *Air Force Two* will touch down at the Hartsfield International Airport, and we will motorcade Vice President Boering to the site of a fundraiser, which will take place in that building," he said, pointing out the windows to a large, stone and glass building across a narrow driveway.

Stylesh then introduced the other agents on his advance team. They were seated along the front row, and each held up a hand as they were named. "Agent McMahon is in charge of the airport arrival and departure, Agent Tandy is the motorcade agent, Agent Simkins is in charge of intelligence, Agent Robertson is TSD, and Agent Humpmeyer is the site agent for the event," he said. "After the briefing, I want you to marry up with your counterpart to finalize the plans."

Stylesh referred to his notes, then continued, "There are four Class Three threats in the Atlanta area, and three are currently confined." The Secret Service classified people who posed a threat to their protectees as Class One for the lowest threat, Class Two for a moderate threat, and Class Three for the most dangerous individuals. "One of the Class Threes is out and about, but we have him under heavy surveillance. We have no intelligence of any protest groups that plan to disrupt the event, but you should be alert for spontaneous activity from pro-life, animal-rights, or anti-gun-control groups. These groups have targeted Vice President Boering in the past. In the event of a medical emergency, the designated hospital for this visit will be the Grady Memorial trauma center, and the agent assigned to the hospital is Agent Bravo. The command post will be located in the room next door, and this room will be used as a downroom."

Stylesh paced across the front of the room and back. Every eye followed him. "Two hundred and sixty three feet, people. That's the record. It's the greatest distance anyone has been from an American President and was still able to reach out and ballistically touch him. Lee Harvey Oswald's shot holds the record. Today, our rings of security go out much further than that, but if we can control what's happening within two hundred and sixty three feet of the President and Vice President, statistically speaking, they're on relatively safe ground."

"Oswald didn't really do it!" Justice whispered to Armstrong.

Stylesh paused and glanced around to see if there were any questions. "There will be two governors, four members of Congress, the mayor, and several other VIPs attending." He scanned the room and his eyes locked on Justice. "Are there any security personnel here for those VIPs?"

Justice and Armstrong raised their hands, as well as a plainclothes officer from the mayor's detail, and two troopers from Justice's detail, who would handle Governor Blair's protection. Stylesh examined each face, as though memorizing them. "Welcome, gentlemen. Do you have any questions?"

Justice spoke up, "Agent Stylesh, I'll be bringing Governor Stovall of Missouri to this event, and I'd like to be able to park his car out on that drive when we get here." He pointed to the lane that ran between the buildings.

Agent Stylesh moved over to the window and stood there with his hands locked behind him. From his manner, he might have been studying a lunar eclipse. The room was totally silent, as though holding its breath for his answer.

After several seconds, Stylesh turned to the room and said quietly, "I want everyone to look out these windows." Fifty heads turned toward the glass and strained to get a clear view. He continued, his tone raising slightly. "At sixteen-hundred hours today, I will own that driveway!" he stated forcefully. He paused, allowing his words to sink in, then continued. "I'll own the concrete in the driveway, I'll own the dirt under the concrete, and I'll own the grass alongside the concrete." He paused again. "I plan to stage the VP's motorcade on my driveway, and no one but the Vice President of the United States can use my driveway!"

Everyone in the room sat stunned. A few, including Armstrong, glanced toward Justice to see how he had taken being dressed down in public. Justice sat there for a moment, and then stood and walked up to Agent Stylesh, stopping within inches of him. Stylesh was slightly shorter than Justice's six-feet-five-inches of height, and Justice outweighed him by about fifty pounds. But Stylesh looked fit and could probably hold his own. *Oh, God*, thought Armstrong, *here we go!*

Both men eyed each other silently, like fierce warriors from rival clans. Then Justice turned and looked out the window. He studied the terrain for a moment, then turned back to Stylesh, and a grin split his face. His high-pitched voice drawled quietly, "Agent Stylesh. I noticed in your security plan that your driveway will be secured by members of the Georgia State Patrol." Stylesh nodded. Justice continued, "Then, Agent Stylesh, I would venture to say that when I pull my squad car up to those troopers—who work for me—then *I'll* own that driveway. I'll own the concrete in the driveway, the dirt underneath, and all the grass around it." He paused, letting his words register. Stylesh's mouth had tightened and his face was turning bright red. Someone in the back of the room released a nervous cough. Justice saw blood and went for the kill, "But if you guys are real nice, and promise not to cause too much trouble, I may just let you park there, too!"

Stylesh turned and studied the grounds, as though pondering the wisdom of Justice's words. His counterpart, Special Agent Tina Ready of the Atlanta Field Office, nearly fainted. Stylesh didn't know it, but Justice played golf twice a month with Jack Hurst, the special-agent-in-charge of the Atlanta Office. Stylesh was about to lock horns with a man who could not only clean his clock but also wreck his burgeoning career. If Stylesh wasn't careful, he'd end up chasing counterfeiters through Fargo, North Dakota, for the remainder of his career.

After a moment Stylesh turned back and nodded, "Perhaps if you subjected your vehicle to a canine check before entering my driveway we could find a place for the governor's car." He didn't want an unswept vehicle coming within fifty yards of the VP's limo.

Justice immediately countered, "Agent Stylesh, it is not my habit to drive my protectee around with a bomb attached to his vehicle, but a quick sniff of the fenders shouldn't delay us too much. Maybe I could allow the VP's motorcade to stay on my driveway." He turned and glanced around the room. "And needless to say, Governor Blair and Mayor Waterford will need to park on our driveway, as well."

"Needless to say. . . ," muttered Stylesh. He returned to the front of the room. "Now, let's continue with the briefing. . ."

As Justice returned to his seat, the room seemed to release a collective sigh of relief. Armstrong relaxed slightly, but feared that this wasn't the last clashing of swords between these two warriors.

Chapter 61

March 31, 1825 hours
Ambassador Suites Hotel
Atlanta, Georgia

"Did you hear that the Governor's Mansion in Arkansas burned down this morning?" Sergeant Kacey Underwood asked.

Justice looked startled. "You're kiddin'!"

Underwood replied casually, "Yeah. The only thing left is the axles!"

Justice realized he'd been had and laughed at the punchline. Ever since the scandal-ridden Clinton administration, everyone picked on the Arkansas detail. "Kacey, my dear, I miss your sense of humor. I'll have to tell that one to B.J."

Underwood was almost afraid to ask. "Who's B.J.?"

"My mom," Justice said, giving her a strange look, like she should have known.

Underwood asked carefully, "You call your mom B.J.?"

"Everybody calls her B.J. Actually she's my stepmom."

"Everybody calls your stepmom B.J.?" Underwood studied him for a beat. This had to be a joke. "Is that her real name or her nickname?"

Justice cracked a smile. "It's her real name. Her nickname is Deep Throat."

Underwood rolled her eyes and shook her head. This man needed serious counseling. He was a walking sexual-harassment suit. "Ya got me back," she groaned.

Justice's clear blue eyes returned to the activity in the holding room, where Vice President Boering, Governor Stovall, and Governor Blair had their heads together in a serious-looking strategy discussion. Things were not going well in the Democratic Party, and the Republicans were raising record levels of campaign funds for their war chest. The DNC had recently been caught in yet another fundraising scandal, involving illegal foreign contributions. Romanowski had remarked that the Democrats had more foreign money in their coffers than the United Nations.

Governor Stovall's arrival at the site had gone smoothly, with only a slight delay while a bomb dog checked the wheel wells and trunk of Justice's vehicle. Just to be safe, Armstrong had remained at the site to ensure there were no surprises while Justice made the airport pickup. Besides, with Governor Stovall, Sergeant Underwood, and Stovall's secretary, Christine Soloman, Justice didn't have a seat for Armstrong in his car.

Justice glanced past the group of VIPs and eyed Armstrong conversing with Special Agent Stylesh, who didn't look very happy. Justice wasn't sure what was being said, but he would bet a month's wages that he knew the topic.

Stylesh muttered a response to Armstrong, who turned and trudged over to Justice and Underwood. "Well, he wants you guys to leave. He says there's too many security folks in the holding room, and we only need one for the boss." Armstrong didn't necessarily disagree with the decision, but it was Stylesh's attitude that was hard to swallow. And Justice was not in a swallowing mood. His broad forehead flushed red.

"Special Agent Stylesh needs to be reminded what state he's in," Justice muttered in a voice loud enough for Stylesh to hear. "He's a guest in the fine State of Georgia. This ain't the Beltway."

Armstrong nodded patiently. The rift between Stylesh and Justice was not an indictment of the United States Secret Service or the Georgia State Patrol. Armstrong had the utmost respect for both agencies, and, more often than not, the agents he encountered treated him with respect and cooperation. It was, instead, an indictment of two powerful personalities who were letting their egos override their professionalism. Armstrong had no authority over Justice or Stylesh, but Underwood worked for him. "Kacey," he said, "I'll stick around in here and watch the boss. You go out and check the ballroom. I'll call you when we get ready to make an entrance." She nodded agreement and strode out of the holding room. Armstrong watched, hoping that Justice would follow her out. To his chagrin, he saw Justice stroll over to Stylesh, who eyed the huge trooper with a challenging glare.

Justice smiled, flashing his perfectly white teeth at Stylesh, like the molars of a great white shark tasting the chummed waters around a fishing boat. "Special Agent Stylesh," he addressed him formally. "I just want to say that, while most people make fun of you boys for being the B-Team, I admire your ability to put on a good show."

Stylesh's lips curled in an attempted smile, but it was clear that Justice's remark had hit a vital organ. "Sergeant Justice, you are a complete and searing pain in my ass. I pray that Osama bin Laden's henchmen storm the building tonight so that I don't have to listen to that whining, hick twang of yours all night."

Justice's smile never wavered. "Special Agent Stylesh, as Grandmother Justice used to say, 'Speak and be known, for a man is hidden under his tongue.'" With that he turned and walked from the room, trailing Underwood into the ballroom.

Chapter 62

The fundraiser went surprisingly well. Justice and Stylesh only clashed swords one other time. When Vice President Boering left the head table to work the crowd, Governors Stovall and Blair scrambled after him, like rock-star groupies. Stylesh and his men swarmed around Boering, as though Islamic terrorists had the building surrounded. When Justice worked his way in close to Blair and Stovall, Stylesh told him to "keep back." He didn't want Justice in the middle of his formation, in the event that one of the wealthy campaign contributors pulled out an automatic weapon and filled the air with hot lead. He wanted a clean route to evacuate the vice president. It was obvious that Justice didn't fear for the governors' safety, he just wanted to give Stylesh a hard way to go.

Standing at one side of the room, Armstrong and Underwood watched in mounting horror as the two warriors pulled, shoved, and elbowed each other across the room behind their protectees. They looked like two brides-to-be, fighting over a discounted gown in Filene's Basement. Armstrong and Underwood were both greatly relieved when Boering gave a big wave to the crowd and headed for the airport.

Stovall lingered for another fifteen minutes, then he and Soloman strolled out of the ballroom and headed for their rooms. Underwood was holding an elevator, and the group boarded without waiting.

"Did you have a good time, Christine?" asked Stovall as they rode up. Armstrong had arrested enough drunk drivers to tell that the boss was legally intoxicated. Stovall's glassy eyes glowed like his suit was on fire.

Christine gave him a dreamy smile. "Yes, it was great. I sat with Lester Flores," she said, referring to a billionaire CEO from Chicago.

Stovall grunted. Flores had become obsessed with hot-air ballooning and had nearly been killed last year when his craft crashed into the Pacific off one of the Fijian Islands. He had become something of a media celebrity. "Why don't we go over those notes for Monday," Stovall suggested. "Are you too tired?"

"That's okay. I'm too excited to sleep." She looked at Justice's dreamy blue eyes and smiled. Justice shifted his gaze to the panel of buttons next to him. Christine was nice looking, and Justice had stolen a few peeks at her hourglass figure, but he knew better than to flirt with the boss's staff.

They exited on the fourteenth floor and Armstrong led the way down the corridor, pulling the key to Stovall's room out of his pocket. He had it unlocked and opened before the rest of the group arrived. Stovall and Christine entered the spacious suite, and Armstrong followed them inside. Underwood and Justice waited outside. Armstrong's room was on one side of the suite, and Christine's was on the other. Underwood's room was across the hall. For security reasons, Stovall was registered under the name "Kevin Patrick."

Inside the suite, Stovall asked Armstrong, "What time do I need to get up, David?"

Armstrong shrugged. "It's your call, sir. All we have to do is go to the airport for the flight back."

"Fine," Stovall decided. "I'd like to go running at seven, breakfast at eight, and we'll head for the airport at nine."

Armstrong nodded. "Yes, sir. I'll set it up and be ready at seven." He had brought his running gear on the trip, expecting to work out. "Anything else?"

"No," Stovall ordered. "You guys don't need to wait up. We'll be working late."

As they spoke, Christine had kicked off her shoes and was pouring herself a glass of white wine from the bar. Armstrong couldn't help but notice that there weren't any "notes" for them to work on. *None of my business*, he thought, and let himself out, hanging Stovall's "Do Not Disturb" sign on the doorknob.

He unlocked his own door and motioned for Justice and Underwood to follow him into his room. When the door was closed, he removed his suit coat, tuned his television to the Fox News Channel, and turned toward the other officers. He spoke quietly so their words wouldn't bleed through the walls. "He wants to run in the morning at seven, eat breakfast at eight, and head for the airport at nine."

Underwood volunteered, "I'll call the pilots and give them a heads-up." She had removed her own coat, laid it carefully across the back of a chair, and flopped into an overstuffed chair in the corner of his spacious room. The body armor under her shirt gave Kacey a stocky look. Armstrong saw that her tiny waist was literally packed with gear: her .40 caliber Glock Model 23 pistol rode in a Fobus paddleback holster on her right side, an F16 ASP expandable baton was behind the holster, and a BlackBerry was in front; on her left side was her walkie-talkie, a Surefire flashlight was clipped in front, and a pouch with an extra thirteen-round clip hung behind the radio. A black nylon case with her handcuffs was hooked at the small of her back. A tiny canister of pepper spray hung inside the pocket of her suit coat and a small, razor-sharp Gerber Applegate-Fairbairn knife was clipped to her pants pocket. All told, there was nearly ten pounds of gear there. One more piece and she'd have to carry it. Armstrong was reminded of a line from Homer's *The Iliad*. Sergeant Kacey Underwood was "harnessed up in the grim gear of war."

"Fine," said Armstrong. "I'll go running with him, and you can check us out and be ready to go when we get back." As part of his advance work, he had already mapped out a four-mile running route around the downtown Atlanta area, which was relatively safe and scenic. "I think I'll just fly back with you guys, since you'll have an empty seat." He eyed the officers momentarily, mentally checking his "to-do" list. It looked like they had everything covered. "Why don't you guys take off. I think they're going to work late."

There was something about the look on Underwood's face that sent a message to Armstrong. *Is there anything going on next door that we need to be concerned about?*

Armstrong avoided her look and addressed Justice. "Why don't you meet us here for breakfast at eight?"

Justice shook his head. "No, I'll come running with you. This is my town. I'll have a second car to help haul everybody, and it can tail us while we run." He gave Kacey a sly look. "I don't suppose you'd let me buy you a drink before you turn in? To celebrate your promotion and all."

She glanced at her supervisor for approval. Armstrong threw up his hands and laughed, "Go ahead, but don't keep her out all night."

He felt like a father watching his teenage daughter about to leave on her first date. Before Armstrong could change his mind, Justice snatched Kacey's arm and dragged her out of the room.

Armstrong slowly rotated his head, listening to the bones in his neck snapping like a fistful of dry twigs. There seemed to be a dull knife embedded between his shoulderblades, and he would swear there was ground glass in his shoes. He definitely needed to find a more comfortable pair of dress shoes for these long days.

Armstrong peeled off his gear, like a samurai warrior turning in after a long day on the battlefield. He changed into a pair of gym shorts and a T-shirt bearing the highway patrol logo. He removed his contacts, brushed his teeth, emptied his bladder, and took three Advil. He flopped into his desk chair, made a few notations for his expense account, and reviewed the governor's itineraries for the next two days. Armstrong requested a 6:30 A.M. wake-up call from the front desk, setting his alarm clock for 6:45 in case they forgot. *Always have a backup plan*, he thought.

Missouri was an hour earlier than Georgia, so he called Chelle and chatted for several minutes.

"How's Kacey doing?" she asked casually, but Armstrong could tell she was jealous he was traveling with an unattached and very attractive female.

"Quick dragged her down to the bar. He'd better keep his hands to himself or she'll tear his throat out."

Chelle couldn't help herself. "My only concern is you keeping your hands to yourself."

"Easy, my lioness, easy," he chuckled. "You're all the female I can handle. You know that."

"That better be true or I'll tear your throat out. . ."

Armstrong knew she was playing with him. "It's true, my love."

". . .then I'll tear your gonads off."

"Ouch! I get the picture," he groaned. "Looks like I need to take you down to the lake for a lobster dinner. How about next weekend?"

"We're going to my sister's next weekend."

He had forgotten. "Oh, yeah. I'd rather eat a live lobster . . . shell and all."

"You hate my sister."

"No I don't. I do, however, hate her husband and kids, not to mention her two slobbering dogs."

"You promised."

"I know. We'll do it." He'd rather spend the weekend in Osama bin Laden's cave, but he knew better than to beg out. "Look, I've got to go." She wished him good night and hung up.

Crawling into bed, he lowered the volume on his TV and flipped through the channels. He suddenly heard Christine and the governor burst out in laughter next door, then it was quiet.

HBO was showing an old Harrison Ford movie, *Air Force One*, which he had seen before. He decided to watch it again. Maybe the outlandish plot would pick up his mood, although he knew that the part with the traitorous Secret Service agent would only piss him off. For all of the bodyguards employed in Hollywood, it was obvious to Armstrong that the moviemakers had not the slightest idea of what the job actually entailed.

Armstrong dozed off halfway through the film, and his keen sense of hearing had not detected the sound of Christine Soloman leaving the governor's room.

Chapter 63

March 31, 2240 hours
Ambassador Suites Hotel
Atlanta, Georgia

Down in the lobby bar, Justice casually asked Underwood, "So, how long has the boss been screwing his secretary?"

Underwood gave him a hard look. "What makes you think there's anything going on?"

"Oh, come on, Kacey," Justice drawled. "You can hardly blame the guy. Your First Lady is demented. Even the Taliban couldn't have muzzled her. She's wilder than a Mike Tyson press conference. The boss probably had Christine bent over the couch before we caught the down elevator. It's pretty obvious."

Underwood glanced around the spacious bar. There was a good-sized crowd from the fundraiser nearly filling the room. She sipped her Sam Adams draft beer and reviewed the evidence of infidelity through her mind. "I don't buy it," she stated finally, not really believing her words.

"'There are none so blind as those who will not see,'" Justice quoted softly. He sipped his club soda and studied Kacey's face. She looked depressed. Justice decided to change the subject. "Kacey, tell me a secret about yourself that no one else on your detail knows."

She thought for a moment and then responded, "When my dad came home from serving in the Navy, he got a job with the post office as a letter carrier. He used to come home every day with that big leather mailbag, and I used to love dragging it around the house with my toys in it. I can close my eyes and still smell that leather. When I was seven, I found a bundle of steamy love letters in Mom's dresser that Dad had written her while he was overseas."

"You didn't!" Justice gasped.

Kacey giggled. "Yep, loaded them in Dad's mailbag and delivered them all over the neighborhood. When the neighbors started calling, I thought Mom would die. Dad thought it was hilarious."

"I'll bet the ladies in the neighborhood never looked at your dad the same way again."

Kacey nodded. "Now it's your turn."

Justice's blue eyes twinkled. "I haven't been laid since I was in high school."

"No, I'm serious," Kacey insisted. "Tell me something that none of your people know about you."

"Let's see," Justice drawled, rolling his eyes as though searching for a box of memories in the dusty attic of his mind. "Okay, I'll give you three choices, and you guess which one is true."

She tilted her head to one side, considering the challenge. "Okay," she agreed.

Justice squinted his eyes in concentration. "I have a Bachelor's Degree in English," he said, pronouncing it "Ainglush."

Kacey giggled. That didn't seem very likely.

"I flunked out of the Navy SEALs due to a knee injury."

She pursed her lips. Perhaps a little too obvious.

"I have a birthmark on my butt shaped like a tea kettle."

Kacey frowned. That was definitely too obvious. "I don't know," she groaned. "I'll pick the Navy SEALs."

Justice grinned. "Gotcha. Actually one and three are both true. I have a degree from GSU and a teakettle birthmark."

"I want to see it," Kacey stated.

"The birthmark?"

"No, the degree. I believe the birthmark part."

Justice leaned in close to her and she could smell his cologne. "How about we slip up to your room, and I'll give you a little back rub and show you my kettle?"

He had only asked her the "back rub" question about thirty times since they had first met, and she had always turned down the offer. Her dark brown eyes studied him momentarily. After all, they were both single, and he was gorgeous: tanned and fit with a body straight out of a muscle magazine. He also had the testosterone of a teenager and the attention span of a one-year-old Labrador pup.

"What the hell," she said finally, nearly knocking Justice out of his seat. She couldn't have stunned him more if she had cracked him over the skull with a Louisville slugger. "Let's go, ya big stud."

"Wh-wh-what?" He couldn't believe his ears. This had to be some nasty female trick. Such a devious joke would cleave his heart like a butcher's blade, if untrue. A warning klaxon sounded somewhere in his brain, but he ignored it. "Are you serious?" he managed to whisper.

She leaned across the table and took his huge hand in her own. "Who's your mama? I said, let's go. I want to see what you've got. I'll bet you're hung like a frozen well rope," she said in a southern drawl that made Justice's head swim.

Justice gulped down the remainder of his drink and frantically dug a ten out of his wallet to leave on the table. "Okay," he said, trying to sound casual. His voice sounded like someone was gripping his testicles with a pair of pliers.

He stood and looked down at her. She wasn't moving and there was a wicked smile on her face.

"I swear, Quick," she said. "You're easier than our former President. I didn't even have to snap my thong undies at you." She looked at her watch. "Well, I'd better get to bed. See you in the morning, big guy." She rose and gave him a peck on the cheek. "Thanks for the drink."

Justice nearly collapsed under the weight of her words. The vision of her standing in his doorway, wearing only a skimpy pair of black thong undies and a seductive smile, floated into his mental box of unfulfilled fantasies. As Underwood strutted out of the bar, Justice whispered, "You're enough to make my bulldog break his chain!"

Chapter 64

The last thing Armstrong's detail needed was a distraction. Until Wykoff and Draeger were captured, the detail needed to be focused on Ringmaster's safety. But in the real world, protective details seldom had that luxury, and the Governor's Security Division was about to experience a series of events that would rock it to its core.

It was a day that started as any other, routine in every way. Sergeant Kacey Underwood was on duty at the Mansion, assigned to the First Lady. Armstrong had come in early to run with the boss, and then took the rest of the day off. Romanowski and Trooper Marko Vanhala were on the office shift with the governor. Stovall's itinerary for the day had no public appearances. Since it was a Saturday, he had no staff meetings, but would spend much of the day on the phone in the protective confines of his office. But the events that would rapidly transpire in the first few hours of his day would go down in the annals of governor's security as one of the most dramatic in memory. The carnage would spread, like the pressure wave of a large explosion, engulfing the residence of the First Family. At some later date, someone—most blamed Romanowski's sharp wit—would borrow the name given to the 1991 Gulf War operation and tweak it just a bit. The events on April 14 would thereafter be referred to as "Mansion Storm." The survivors of the event would speak of it in whispered tones, as though they were lucky to still be alive.

First Lady Patricia Stovall had hardly left the Mansion since surviving the terrorist attack in Kansas City only a month before. She was under the care of her personal physician, but her ailment was not physical. She had suffered no serious injuries in the bomb blast or ensuing firefight. But the trauma of the event had damaged her mentally and emotionally. One moment, her world had been secure to the point she felt suffocated by it. The next, it was blown apart in a searing explosion, followed by the hammering beat of her bodyguards' weapons forcing back the attack. They were images she couldn't get out of her head. She had withdrawn, becoming uncommunicative. Her legendary temper grew even more volatile. Then the panic attacks set in, the first one brought on when someone dropped a tray in the kitchen. The next thing she knew, she was clawing at her throat, unable to breathe, as her heart hammered away in her chest. Before, she had been confident and commanded every appearance. Now she couldn't get through the day without Prozac.

Patricia Stovall was depressed, but she wasn't blind. She noticed the changes in her husband's habits. He suddenly took up jogging. He was more meticulous with his appearance than usual. He was going to work earlier and staying later. When she called his private line at the office, he was often "away from his desk." But all of these things had other explanations. There were no concrete signs of anything to be concerned about. It was only natural that he would be busier than usual, nearing the end of the legislative session. But when she found makeup on his collar (which wasn't her shade) and detected scents on him (that were from someone else), and when he started going to the office on weekends (which he had seldom done before), Patricia Stovall didn't need a PhD in astronomy to read the writing in the stars.

When she confronted him with the accusation that he was seeing another woman, he had scoffed at the notion. But his reaction wasn't genuine. He might get away with lying to the electorate, but she could see through him like a pane of cheap glass. Her internal lie detector was recording readings, which were off the charts. Their discussion escalated into a screaming match in which she had bounced a coffee mug off his back when he walked away from her. She had banned him from their bedroom, and he had taken up residence in a third-floor guest room. Their marriage, which could only be described as "strained" at best, teetered on the brink of collapse.

She now stood on the second-floor sunporch, watching her husband get into the Navigator with his ever-present bodyguards and pull out of the driveway. Her blood began a slow boil as she watched the vehicle turn right, drive two blocks, and enter the garage entrance at the Capitol Building. Her hand slapped the thick window glass hard enough to rattle it. Then she turned and entered her dressing room.

Twenty minutes later, Kacey Underwood heard the elevator coming down and looked up in curiosity. Perhaps the First Lady wanted to go out. As the whining machinery ground to a halt, Rosebush marched to the door of the command post, waggled a finger at Underwood, then turned and strode out the door with Underwood scrambling to catch up. Capitol Police Sergeant Al Rollings raised his eyebrows and opened the drive-in gate. *Wonder where they're going*, he thought.

Both ladies jumped into Underwood's Crown Vic, and only when they reached the street did Mrs. Stovall state, "Go right." As Underwood approached the Capitol Building, the First Lady said, "Pull in the basement, and don't call anyone on your radio."

Underwood was getting a bad feeling, like driving down a steep hill toward a sharp curve and realizing that your brakes are out. She pulled into the basement and rolled toward the reserved parking area for the governor and his staff. Since it was a Saturday, there were only a few other cars in the basement. Most notable was the governor's armored Navigator, Naylor's blue BMW, and Christine Soloman's gold Chrysler 300 sedan.

Underwood pulled in and parked next to Monitor, and they both sat silently in the vehicle. Kacey dared not say a word. Her intuition told her that the First Lady's explosive temper was primed with a mercury switch. Trying to tilt her in any direction would only set it off.

The First Lady looked over at Underwood and said, "Kacey, is my husband seeing another woman?" Her voice was raspy.

The question put Underwood in a very precarious position. It was not her job to pass judgment on or talk about the private lifestyle of a protectee. But she couldn't lie to them, either. If she said no, and the affair was later determined to be a fact, her credibility would be out the window. She grimaced, "Mrs. Stovall, I've seen no proof of that." It was the best she could do.

Finally, Mrs. Stovall seemed to gather her resolve and stated, "Let's go up and see if you're right."

Underwood followed her over to the governor's private elevator. Kacey keyed the button to access the second floor. As the doors opened, Patricia Stovall marched out as though she was on a mission.

Kacey followed several feet behind. Naylor was not in his office, and Mrs. Stovall strode toward the door to her husband's office. It was unlocked. As she stepped through, she saw that this office was also empty. She hadn't been expecting this, and she stopped in her tracks.

Then both Patricia Stovall and Kacey Underwood heard the giggling. It was coming from behind the door to their left. The door was hidden in the ornate woodwork of the office. A person could walk past it without even noticing the gold doorknob with the state seal, which opened the panel. But both women knew it was there, and they knew where it led. It was a private bathroom for the governor's personal use. And there were clearly two people laughing on the other side of the door.

Patricia Stovall grabbed the knob and tried to open it, but found the door locked. Suddenly the laughter stopped, and the governor's tentative voice called out, "Ah . . . who's there?"

Kacey Underwood stood behind the First Lady watching the drama unfold, like some horrendous disaster movie. She had once seen a film in which a huge piece of ice cracked off an iceberg and plunged into the freezing water in slow motion. A second later, a huge wave rose out of the black seawater and rolled toward the cameraman, who stood helplessly watching its advance. The wave seemed to pick up speed and then smashed into the cameraman's position like a crashing jumbo jet. Kacey now understood the fear and helplessness the cameraman must have felt.

"I'm in here!" called Governor Stovall's voice again. "Brad? Is that you?"

Patricia Stovall's right fist slammed against the thick wood, sounding like a gunshot. "No, you bastard, it's your wife! Open this door right now!" A momentary silence on the other side of the wood was followed by the sound of rustling clothing. "Right now, you son of a bitch!" Mrs. Stovall screamed, stepping back and kicking the door with her right foot.

"Okay . . . ah . . . just a minute, dear," came the governor's panic-stricken voice.

"Pat?" Bradley Naylor suddenly appeared behind the women. "What are you doing here?" His voice attempted to convey a soothing tone but failed. It sounded more like a wire garrote was wound tightly around his neck.

"Back off, Bozo!" Patricia Stovall hissed, and Naylor fled back into his office. He knew when to stand his ground and when to run like hell. This was a no-brainer. He had a dog in this fight, but Naylor could see that his dog was fixing to get his balls handed to him, and he feared that he himself just might be next.

Hearing the shouts, Romanowski and Vanhala responded from the other end of the office. They hustled into the governor's office and then screeched to a halt as Underwood held up her hand in a signal to stop.

Underwood tensed as the lock was thrown and the door opened a crack. For a moment there was silence. Governor Stovall had turned out the light and he peeked out from the darkness. "What's the matter, Pat?" he asked. "Is something wrong?"

Mrs. Stovall shoved the door open and pushed past him. She found the light switch and flipped it. Christine Soloman stood in the corner of the bathroom with her hand to her mouth. The buttons on her white blouse didn't match the holes in which they were fastened, and her expression would not have been different if someone had told her that her entire family had just died in a horrendous train wreck. "I'm sorry, Pat," was all she could think to say.

"We were just kidding around," Governor Stovall offered as his explanation.

The hand came out of nowhere. Patricia Stovall's openhanded left hook caught her husband on the temple with such speed and force that it literally knocked him off his feet. The sound resembled the home run crack of a major-league bat. The governor's arms cartwheeled, as he stumbled backward and crashed to the carpeted floor of his office. It was the nightmare of every bodyguard: When you're assigned to protect two people, what do you do when they attack each other?

Romanowski and Underwood instinctively jumped between them. Mrs. Stovall lunged at her husband to inflict more damage, but Underwood pinned her against the wall as Romanowski and Vanhala helped the boss to his feet.

Mrs. Stovall was cursing like a demented sailor, spewing four-letter words and threats that the officers had not heard since leaving uniformed road duty.

Unable to bear witness to the brawl, Christine Soloman slammed the bathroom door and locked it.

The governor put a hand to his face and examined it for blood. Then his features hardened and he glared at his wife. "Get that bitch out of my office!" he commanded. Underwood thought at first he might mean Christine Soloman. Then he screamed, "Take her back to the Mansion, now!"

Despite her resistance, Kacey managed to drag the First Lady back to the elevator. When the doors closed and they descended toward the basement garage, Mrs. Stovall sagged against the railing, and Kacey grabbed her arm to keep her from falling. Kacey helped her to the car and drove back to the Mansion.

As they pulled up to the back door, Kacey asked, "Do you want me to come up with you?"

"No!" Mrs. Stovall barked. Her eyes were still ablaze and the veins stood out on her slender neck. She was getting her second wind. Hurricane Patricia blew open the car door and stormed into the Mansion.

Chapter 65

David Armstrong's BlackBerry vibrated as soon as he walked into Wal-Mart. It displayed the security number at the Mansion, followed by "9-1-1." He clicked the scroll wheel and selected the "call the Mansion" option.

"Security, Sergeant Underwood." Kacey's voice didn't sound too excited.

"This is David," he said.

Her tone changed, rising a notch. "You have to get to Watchtower ASAP!"

"What's up?" he demanded, breaking into a run toward his car.

"We're Ringside!" It was the detail's codename for a heated domestic dispute between members of the First Family.

"Any casualties?" he asked, reaching his car and digging his keys out.

"Just bruises, so far."

Suddenly an alarm sounded. "What's that sound?" Armstrong demanded.

He heard Rollings tell Underwood, "Someone just opened a third-floor window."

Underwood barked, "We need you here now!" Then she broke the connection.

"Be there in five minutes," Armstrong told the dead line. He left rubber on the parking lot and sped in the direction of the Mansion. The Saturday morning shoppers had Missouri Boulevard clogged with traffic. Armstrong drove like his trunk was on fire, weaving in and out of traffic, and blowing through yellow lights.

As Armstrong swerved into the Mansion drive, Rollings alertly spotted his personal car and opened the gate. Armstrong pulled up to the back door, and Underwood met him outside. "Come on!" she said, "You aren't gonna believe this!" She ran around the drive to the front of the Mansion, and Armstrong chased after her.

Armstrong rounded the drive which encircled the Mansion and noticed several tourists standing out by the front gate. One had a video camera and was shooting footage of the Mansion. One of the tourists pointed at something, and a lady in the group put her hand to her mouth in shock.

The first thing Armstrong noticed was clothing. Men's clothing. It was everywhere. Expensive shirts, slacks, suit coats. It looked like a bomb had gone off in the governor's closet or perhaps a hurricane had blown through. Hurricane Patricia to be precise. As they looked around in shock, several silk ties floated down and landed in front of them, like streamers of confetti at a parade of heroes. They both looked up and saw Mrs. Stovall heaving her husband's clothes out the open third-floor window. Armstrong noticed the governor's favorite medium gray Versace Medusa tie looped around the railing outside the third-floor windows, hanging on for dear life.

"Go back inside," Armstrong ordered Kacey. "Call Romanowski and have him tell the boss what's happening. Then go up and get her inside."

Underwood turned and sprinted back to the command post.

Armstrong stood there for a moment, wondering what he should do. When a bundle of suits nearly hit him, he did the only thing he could think to do. He started to pick up the governor's clothes.

Chapter 66

"She did *what?*" Governor Stovall demanded, leaning across his desk. There was already an angry bruise around his right eye, and the swelling left his head slightly misshapen. No amount of makeup would cover it. Armstrong wondered what she had struck him with, and envisioned being ordered to storm the Mansion and arrest the First Lady for assault. The image of showering her with pepper spray and dragging her out in restraints nearly caused his heart to stop.

Romanowski had informed the governor that Mrs. Stovall was in the process of "evicting" him from the Governor's Mansion, but Stovall refused to believe it. He demanded that Armstrong report to his office immediately for a firsthand report.

Armstrong cleared his throat. "Sir, she . . . ah . . . she threw all of your clothes out the Mansion window and onto the front lawn."

"She's crazy, Brad," Stovall said, pointing an accusatory finger at his chief of staff, like it was Naylor's idea that they get married. Naylor nodded his head enthusiastically, inanely accepting blame that was not his.

"Now, Governor," press aide Paul Fleming said, trying to calm things down. "She's just upset. She'll get over this."

Stovall ignored him. "Where are my clothes now?" he asked Armstrong in a worried tone. He pictured his $1,000 suits piled on the lawn like mounds of raked leaves.

"I picked them up, sir," Armstrong reassured him.

"Where are they this moment?" Stovall demanded.

Armstrong squirmed in his chair for several seconds, then answered, "They're in garbage bags in the trunk of my car."

Stovall erupted, "My one-thousand-dollar suits are in garbage bags? Are you crazy, too, David?"

"It was all I had, Governor." This was not a good day. When he left here, he would have to page Major Moss and Colonel DeWitt and relate the day's events to them. They would not be impressed.

Paul Fleming gathered his nerve and asked a question to which he feared to hear the answer. "Did anyone see this happen?"

"There were some tourists out by the front fence," Armstrong answered.

"Oh, God," Governor Stovall muttered. Could this get any worse?

"One of them had a video camera," Armstrong added in a quiet voice.

"Oh, God!" Stovall moaned, putting his head down on his desk. "Why didn't you arrest them? Seize their film or something? What good *are* you guys?"

At that point, the governor's door opened and Don Romanowski quietly entered the room. Everyone stared at him in expectation. He glanced down at his shoes, then back up. He cleared his throat and informed them, "Governor, Kacey just called. There's a news crew out in front of the Mansion, and they're asking questions about the fight that occurred there this morning."

Paul Fleming slapped his hand on the arm of his chair. "Great!" he exclaimed. "That's super!"

Romanowski let the other shoe drop. "They told Kacey that a tourist is calling around to all of the stations, trying to sell a video of the . . . incident."

Chapter 67

Corporal Bobby Davenport sat behind the wheel of a Chrysler minivan and scanned the street. There was the usual morning rush of traffic zooming past, but no indication of anything to be concerned about. Davenport had borrowed the unmarked van from DDCC for today's assignment.

"What do you think of the new guys?" Davenport asked his supervisor, Sergeant Romanowski.

Romanowski was reading an article on the front page of the morning paper about Governor Stovall being kicked out of the Mansion. A photo taken from the tourist's video accompanied it. The picture showed Patricia Stovall in the window of the Mansion with her arms flung out, and Lieutenant Armstrong scampering around below her with an armload of suits. *At least the story's below the fold*, Romanowski thought. The headline read: "The Emperor Has No Clothes . . . Literally!" He glanced at Davenport and said, "Marko is great. Did you know the Gateway Arch in St. Louis was designed by an architect from Finland?"

"Did Marko tell you that?"

"Yeah, but I looked it up, and he's right. Guy's name was Eero Saarinen."

"Marko's really smart."

Romanowski nodded. "Get him to tell you how Finland defeated the Russians in 1918. They were led by a guy named Mannerheim. He's their national hero to this day. Fascinating stuff. They must all be smart." He shook his head sadly. "Then there's Wiedemann. I found out what 'Wiedemann' means. It's Polish for 'Thinks-He-Knows-It-All.'" Once Romanowski had learned that Wiedemann was headstrong, he had immediately begun calling him "We-Da-Man." Much to Wiedemann's chagrin, everyone on the detail adopted his new name.

"You've noticed that, too?" Davenport chuckled.

Romanowski folded the paper and slid it under the seat. *When the boss comes out, I ain't letting him see that*, he thought. *Let Fleming break the news to him and suffer the consequences, as Ringmaster—no doubt—slaughters the messenger.* "The other day I sent We-Da-Man out to advance the boss's speech at the Truman Building. Thirty minutes later, he waltzes back in the Governor's Office. I said, 'You're supposed to be advancing the speech. We're getting ready to leave.' And he says, 'I *did* advance it, and everything's ready to go.' He didn't realize that when he left the site, the security left with him. The boy just can't get it through his thick skull what it is we're supposed to do. I told him that we're only as strong as our weakest link, but he just blew me off."

Davenport shook his head in amazement. "He may have been Super Trooper down at Springfield, but I don't think he's going to make it off probation up here. I think we ought to just ship him back now. He's a loose cannon."

"Now, Bobby, he may not be the sharpest tool in the shed, but give the boy a chance," Romanowski scolded him. "I can remember when you first got here. You were greener than a truckload of zucchini. He'll catch on." While it was true that Davenport had not known much about the day-to-day operations of the detail when he first arrived, his previous life as a "runnin' and gunnin'" DEA operative had filled him with an encyclopedic knowledge of protective work. Most new officers in the division took six months to learn the ropes completely. Davenport had mastered the operation in six weeks.

Their banter was broken up by the voice of Armstrong coming over their earpieces. "Armstrong to Romanowski."

"Go ahead," Romanowski responded into his wrist mike.

"We'll head for the Closet in five mikes." The Closet referred to the hotel's service elevator.

"Copy five mikes," Romanowski answered. He told Davenport, "Let's pull around."

Davenport drove a circle around the hotel for one last look around, then pulled into the underground parking garage. He stopped next to the freight elevator and expertly backed into a parking space next to Romanowski's car.

Romanowski got out and looked around. "Romanowski to Armstrong, the Dock is secure."

"Ten-four," Armstrong responded. "We'll be down in two mikes."

Romanowski looked at Davenport. "I'll see you guys at the office." He then got into his own car and left to check out their route. If he spotted any news crews lying in ambush, he'd alert the others of the trap.

Governor Stovall was a fugitive from the press. Since the story had broken, the media had desperately tried to track him down. Fleming suggested holding an impromptu press conference, but Naylor overruled him. While the governor's head was swollen and bruised, they had to evade the media. After a few days, when things quieted down a bit and the swelling had subsided, they'd do a controlled release. Armstrong had registered the governor under a false name at the hotel and snuck him into his room without anyone spotting them. The governor had spent all day Sunday in his room, making phone calls, and watching the newscasts in horror. Armstrong stayed in the room next to him and brought in his meals.

Stovall had called Christine from his room and tried to soothe her jangled nerves. A reporter had gotten wind of the fact that she was involved and called her house, leaving a message on her recorder. The governor suggested that she take the week off and go visit her mother in Tulsa.

On Sunday evening, Stovall knocked on the door to Armstrong's adjoining room. He sheepishly asked Armstrong if he would go over and pick up Christine, and bring her to his room. Armstrong looked at his boss for a moment and then politely refused. "I can't do that, sir. It's a bad idea."

Forty-five minutes later, Christine appeared at the governor's door, and he let her in. It infuriated Armstrong. Stovall had obviously called and asked her to come over. It was like dancing around a bonfire in a straw suit. *He's out of control*, Armstrong decided, and considered calling Naylor about it. He decided against it, though. It would be a violation of the governor's privacy. Christine was in the governor's room until late. After she left, Stovall told Armstrong that he wanted to go to the office on Monday morning, and he didn't want to be seen. Armstrong called Romanowski and set up the transfer.

Armstrong now rode the service elevator down with Stovall, who was wearing a hooded sweatshirt and sunglasses. He looked more like the Unabomber than the governor of Missouri. They exited the elevator, jumped into Davenport's van, and slid the door shut. Davenport pulled smoothly out of the garage and headed for the Capitol Building, five blocks away. Armstrong keyed his mike several times as they entered the basement garage.

"I copy your arrival. The Dock is secure," Romanowski assured them.

They parked in a space assigned to one of the staff and whisked Ringmaster into the private elevator, which was being held by Romanowski. Within ten minutes of leaving his hotel room, Governor Stovall was safely settled in his office.

Chapter 68

The press wasn't the only group looking for Governor Stovall. Seated in Draeger's Blazer, Wykoff lowered his binoculars and looked at his watch. "Something's wrong," he decided. "He always leaves before now. And he hasn't been jogging for two days."

Their parking spot on the third level of the parking garage across from the Governor's Mansion gave them a perfect view of the grounds and the drive-in gate. They had been parked there for over an hour and had yet to see any sign of the governor going to work.

Draeger held up the morning paper. "According to this article, he and the missus had a big fight over the weekend. She may have kicked him out."

"Well," Wykoff stated, "if we can't find him, we can't grab him."

"I could take him out from here when he leaves for work. It's too risky to snatch him," grumbled Draeger.

Wykoff turned and glared at him. "That wouldn't get Leech out of that cage up the street," he stated. "Or maybe you don't care about that?" A newspaper article the week before had described how Leech had been transferred to the Jefferson City Correctional Center for security reasons. "We have to get him out of there before they put him to death."

Draeger looked away. "What do you want to do?" he asked finally. He had failed them once. He would not fail them again.

Wykoff tossed the binoculars into the backseat. "I guess we go with Plan B."

Chapter 69

April 16, 1725 hours
Governor's Office
Jefferson City, Missouri

The security phone next to Armstrong rang and he answered, "Security, Lieutenant Armstrong."

"David, it's Stuart Moss. Anything happening?"

"No, Major, it's been pretty quiet all day." Even though Armstrong and Davenport were the only ones in the reception room, he talked in a quiet tone. "There's been a parade of people through all day—his lawyer, his minister, a few friends—and the staff has been tiptoeing around like the floor is about to cave in."

Moss chuckled, "I don't envy you guys. Look, David, Colonel DeWitt and I know the hardships you guys are working under. You have the misfortune of trying to protect people who think they don't need protection. Try to stay out of the middle of it, if you can. I was just in the colonel's office and he wanted an update on the situation. I told him that everyone was still in a holding pattern. He's concerned that you guys will be put in a no-win situation. I assured him that you can handle anything that comes up."

"Thanks for the vote of confidence. Did the colonel have any executive-level suggestions?"

"He just shook his head," Moss responded. As a member of DeWitt's staff, Moss wouldn't say anything derogatory about DeWitt's lack of leadership in dealing with Governor Stovall, but his tone sent an obvious warning to Armstrong. *In other words, you're on your own*, was clearly communicated. "Are you guys staying in the hotel again tonight?"

"No, sir. Fleming came out after lunch and told me to clear everything out of the hotel rooms and check out. The boss will be back in the Mansion tonight. Kacey's with the First Lady. Mrs. Stovall hasn't left the Mansion since this thing blew up. She's been on the phone a lot, though."

Moss grunted. "Well, keep your head down, David, and keep me informed if there's any developments. I don't like surprises."

"Will do," Armstrong said and hung up. He was looking over to Bobby Davenport and starting to say something when the door to Stovall's office opened.

Sara Cusser, Naylor's secretary, had been filling in for the missing Christine Soloman. She looked at Armstrong and said, "The governor wants to see you for a minute."

Armstrong and Davenport exchanged glances, and then Armstrong strode into Stovall's office. The governor was sprawled behind his desk, and Naylor and Fleming occupied ornate chairs across from him. It looked suspiciously to Armstrong like an ambush.

"David," Stovall said in a friendly tone, "have a seat."

Armstrong slid into a vacant chair and studied their faces. They all looked at Armstrong like they were glad to see him, which made him very uneasy.

Stovall waved a hand. "David, I really appreciate all you've done for me the last few days. I know it's been unpleasant."

"I don't mind, sir," Armstrong responded.

"That's why I wanted you to run this detail and why I told Colonel DeWitt to promote you," Stovall stated magnanimously. "I've always liked your attitude."

He's buttering me up for something, Armstrong thought. *Drop your drawers and grab your ankles, 'cause here comes the hand of friendship.* "The Goodyear Blimp" would have been a more accurate analogy.

"We have a favor to ask," Naylor said gently. He was going to be the bearer of the bad news.

Armstrong's eyes narrowed as he studied Vlad Naylor's features. "What can I do for you?" Armstrong asked, serving his question with just a teaspoon of sarcasm.

"We want you to kick the First Lady out of the Mansion," Naylor said.

"I beg your pardon?" Armstrong couldn't believe his ears. *Whose lame-brained idea was this?*

Naylor held up his hands, as though getting ready to dodge a high-speed car that was about to run him down. "She already knows you're coming."

"She what?" *When was this decided?* he wondered, then realized it had probably been decided hours ago, when Fleming told him to check out of the hotel.

Fleming came to Naylor's rescue. "All you have to do is go over and tell her that you're there to escort her out."

"I don't believe this," Armstrong said forcefully. "This isn't my job!" He looked at the governor to gauge his expression. Stovall's cool, steady gaze told Armstrong, *Don't resist! We need you to do this!*

Naylor explained, "You're the best one for this job. She respects you, you're a law-enforcement officer, and she won't let any of us on the grounds. She's refused to take my calls today, so I called her attorney and told him to advise her that she is to leave the premises and that you'll escort her out."

"When?" Armstrong asked in a tired voice.

They all looked at him like he was nuts. Naylor pointed to his watch, "Right now! She's supposed to be getting her things together, and you need to have her out of there by six o'clock."

Armstrong rubbed his hands over his face. He felt a no-win situation slowly sucking him down, as though he were struggling in quicksand. The words of Major Moss echoed through his head: *Try to stay out of the middle of it, if you can. DeWitt's concerned that you guys will be put in a no-win situation. I assured him that you can handle anything that comes up.*

Fleming piled on, "About an hour ago we put out a controlled release to the press that Governor and Mrs. Stovall are working through some personal matters and that they appreciate the kind words of support that many citizens are extending to them. Nothing was said about her leaving, and it had better not leak out from your crew. If this turns up on the Drudge Page, you're toast!"

Armstrong glared at the staffer. "My people don't leak information and you know it." He looked at Stovall. "Where are we supposed to take her?"

Ringmaster shrugged. "I don't know and I don't care. I can't carry on the people's business with her storming around the Mansion like that nut in the movie *Psycho*."

Naylor responded, "Her attorney said she'd probably go to her daughter's place in St. Louis for a while, until things get sorted out.

We've made the Citation available to her if she wants to use it. Call us when it's done."

"Okay," Armstrong said and stood to go. *Might as well get this over with.* He looked at the floor, as though expecting to see his entrails lying there.

"There's one more thing," Naylor said. Armstrong turned and gave him a curious look. Naylor continued, "We want you to inventory anything she takes with her tonight. Paintings, furniture, anything that's state property. If she tries to carry out something that doesn't belong to her, we want to know what it is and what the inventory number is. We'll want to pursue criminal charges or at least use it for leverage."

Now it was clear to Armstrong why he had been handed the job. They wanted a cop to witness the First Lady committing a felony in order to take her down. As he left the office, Armstrong was certain that he was leaving a trail of slime in the ornate blue carpeting.

Chapter 70

April 16, 1755 hours
Governor's Mansion
Jefferson City, Missouri

Capitol Police Sergeant Chuck Hillsboro and Kacey Underwood both looked up as Armstrong walked into the command post. Everyone knew something was up. The look on Armstrong's face confirmed it.

"How ya doing, boss?" asked Underwood cautiously.

Armstrong ignored her question. "Where's Rosebush?" he demanded.

"She's on the second floor," Hillsboro responded. "She just made a call from the master bedroom."

Armstrong looked at Underwood and nodded his head toward the breakroom. She followed him back and stood silently while he poured himself a cup of stale coffee. He sipped it and eyed Kacey.

"How're you holding up?" he asked. She had been on duty since seven that morning. Everyone on the detail had been working extra overtime since Armstrong had learned of the plot to kill the governor.

Kacey tilted her head to one side. "I'm doing okay, but everybody's worried about you. You've been working double shifts."

Armstrong waved his hand, dismissing the concern. "I've got an unpleasant task to do tonight. I've got to go upstairs and kick Rosebush out of the residence."

Underwood looked at him as though he was crazy. "Says who?" she asked.

"The boss. Actually, he let Naylor and Fleming break the news, but he was sitting right there like he was watching a soap opera or something. Fascinated, but uninvolved, like he was interested how it would all turn out for the actors."

Underwood whistled. "This isn't going to be fun. Do you want me to do it?"

Armstrong had to admit he was tempted to delegate it down to Underwood, but they had ordered *him* to do it. It was his responsibility. "I really appreciate your offer, but I'll do it. What I want you to do is stand out on the second-floor landing and be a witness to whatever happens."

She nodded, "I've got your back, L.T."

Armstrong turned and pushed the intercom button on the break-room phone. By leaving the handset on the cradle, it automatically triggered the speakerphone so that Kacey could hear. He pushed the two-digit code for the master bedroom. The system was set up so that the intercom issued a loud tone and then went live, allowing the caller to hear any noise in the room that was called. The governor or First Lady would hear the tone and could simply speak without having to answer the phone.

On Armstrong's end, he heard the tone and then he heard the noise of Mrs. Stovall moving about the bedroom. "Mrs. Stovall?" he announced. The noise in the bedroom stopped, but there was no response. He waited five seconds and then repeated, "Mrs. Stovall?" Armstrong heard Mrs. Stovall continue her activity without answering. She was ignoring him. Armstrong and Kacey exchanged worried looks. "Mrs. Stovall, it's David," he said again.

"WHAAAAAAT?" Rosebush suddenly screamed at the phone. Her shrill voice echoed around the twenty-foot ceilings.

Armstrong squinted his eyes shut, but maintained a calm tone. "Mrs. Stovall, I need to come up and talk to you."

The sound of broken glass exploded through the speaker as she threw something at the phone. "Don't you speak English? What's the matter with you people? Are you deaf or just dumb? Stay away!" she shouted. "Don't you dare come up here!"

Armstrong's ears reddened, and he wondered if Patricia Stovall knew that Indira Gandhi, the Prime Minister of India, was assassinated by two of her own bodyguards in 1984. *Maybe I'll do the boss a favor*, he thought.

Armstrong looked at Kacey. She shook her head sadly. Armstrong said forcefully, "Mrs. Stovall, Kacey and I are coming up. You and I need to talk." There was no response, so he disconnected the intercom. "Let's go," he said and headed for the elevator. The ride to the second floor seemed to take several minutes. When the doors opened, Armstrong walked to the heavy oak door which led to the master bedroom. Kacey took up a post behind him on the landing.

Armstrong stood facing the door for a moment, listening. There was no noise coming from inside the room. He knocked lightly on the door. After ten seconds, he knocked again. This time he detected movement on the other side, and the door opened a crack. Mrs. Stovall's tear-swollen face peered out at him.

"May I come in, please?" he asked quietly.

She looked past him to Kacey, and then swung the door open to allow him inside. As he moved to the center of the room, she closed the door and turned to face him. Armstrong saw that she was packing to leave. There were four suitcases on the floor, two hanging bags on the closet door, and a pile of unpacked items on the bed.

Armstrong cleared his throat. "I was told that you're going to your daughter's tonight. They sent me over to help you get moved." When she didn't respond, he added, "Would you like me to assign someone to you while you're away?"

"You've got to be kidding!" she exclaimed. "You're part of the reason I'm glad to be leaving. I just want some time to myself."

He frowned. "At least let me give you the number of the troop headquarters in Kirkwood. It's just a few miles from Heather's place. If you need a driver or anything, just give them a call." It was a stop-gap measure, but he'd talk to her again when things cooled off. They were not the Secret Service. There was no law requiring her to accept protection.

The First Lady was wearing a pair of faded blue jeans and a blue St. Louis Rams jersey, bearing the numeral one. The name "Stovall" was displayed across the back of her shoulders. Armstrong recognized it as a jersey the governor had given her at Christmas. It struck him as odd that she would be wearing a personal gift from the person who had just betrayed her.

He asked, "Would you like me to carry these things down for you?"

"Do you know what I'd really like, David?" she asked, moving toward him. There was a strange look in her eyes.

Armstrong tensed. "No, ma'am," he said uneasily.

She stopped in front of him and ran her hand under his suit coat and around his waist to his gun. Armstrong jumped and put his hand on top of hers to prevent her from drawing it.

She leaned up to his face and whispered, "I'd like you to let me borrow this for about fifteen minutes."

Armstrong was horrified. *What the hell did that mean?* Use it on him? Herself? The governor? He stepped back and pulled her hand away. "Stop it, Mrs. Stovall," he said. "I'm just here to help you."

He still held her left arm by the wrist. With her free hand, she grabbed his hand and pulled it to her chest, crushing it against her left breast. "You want to help? You want to make me feel better?" Armstrong struggled to break her grip, but she held his hand tightly against her breast. "Here," she groaned. "Make me feel good!"

Armstrong shoved her backward and she nearly fell. "Stop it!" he said angrily.

She put one hand over her mouth and laughed at him. "I wish you could see the look on your face right now, David." He just stared at her, as though watching in disgusted fascination as a pride of lions devoured a live antelope, their steel claws raking its quivering flesh apart. "How do you feel?" she asked him. "Betrayed? Humiliated? Well, David, welcome to my world. Now you know what it's like to live with my husband." She turned and walked into the bathroom. Armstrong stood in the middle of the room without a clue about what to say or do. He wondered, *Should I report this or keep it to myself? Did Kacey hear the exchange?*

Mrs. Stovall came out of the bathroom carrying a makeup case in one hand and a red leather tote bag in the other. She stopped and stared at him. "Well, are you going to carry those bags downstairs or not? I've got a plane to catch."

Within an hour, Armstrong sat in Underwood's car and watched as the governor's Citation jet lifted off and headed for St. Louis. Kacey reached Heather Stovall on her car phone. "Your mom's wheels up, Heather. She should be there at the airport in about fifteen minutes." Heather said that she was only a mile from the airport and thanked them for the call.

When Kacey ended her call, Armstrong used the phone to call Naylor's private number.

"Yeah," Naylor answered.

"It's me. She's wheels up."

"Good job," Naylor said with obvious relief in his voice. They had been waiting on pins and needles. "How did it go?" he asked cautiously.

Armstrong paused, debating his response. "It went okay," he said, deciding to keep their struggle to himself.

"Did she carry off any . . . anything?" Naylor knew that Armstrong was on a cell phone.

Armstrong felt dirty even answering the question. "Not that I could tell."

To say that he shaded the truth was like saying that Niagara Falls was wet. His reasoning was that Mrs. Stovall was his protectee, and it was a cardinal rule to maintain strict confidentiality of the personal behaviors or private conversations of his protectees. He didn't feel that it would be honorable to tell even Colonel DeWitt or Major Moss. He certainly couldn't tell Chelle. She'd insist he leave the detail. The only person he would consider discussing her bizarre reaction with was Governor Stovall, but under the circumstances he decided to keep it to himself for now. He hoped it wasn't a decision that he would later regret making.

Chapter 71

Governor Stovall remained in his office all morning, conducting meetings with legislative leaders who were gearing up for the end of the session in less than a month. It was going to be one of the most contentious sessions in recent memory.

Armstrong sat at the security desk, working on the schedule for May. Alex Wiedemann had drifted down the hall to get himself another cup of coffee. Armstrong's concentration was broken when Sara Cusser opened her door and waggled a finger for him to follow. "The governor wants to see you," she said with an air of aloofness. She shared Naylor's feelings for the ever-present bodyguards.

Armstrong found Governor Stovall slouched behind his desk with a look of barely-suppressed anger painting his features. Vlad Naylor's half-lidded eyes followed Armstrong across the room, like a hungry lioness crouched in the tall grass as her prey came near. Paul Fleming squirmed in his chair like the cushion held a nest of fire ants.

As Armstrong took an over-stuffed chair within their circle, Naylor began the conversation, "Well, well, well. . . ." When Armstrong didn't respond, Naylor continued, "I thought you told me that Mrs. Stovall didn't take anything that didn't belong to her?"

Armstrong looked confused. "I believe I said, 'Not that I could tell.'"

Naylor continued unabated, "The Mansion director just called and said they finished their inventory. There are ten Mansion place settings missing, as well as several valuable books from the library."

Armstrong shrugged. "Brad, I wasn't going to search her bags before she left. And how do you know that she took them?"

Naylor bristled at the question. "They were there when they were last inventoried a month ago. Where else could they be?" He sniffed and adopted the tone of an overworked bureaucrat. "I've advised her attorney that she must return the items or be prosecuted. It classifies as a felony."

Armstrong couldn't believe his ears, but in no way did he expect what he heard next.

Governor Stovall sat forward in his chair. "That's not all, David. Her attorney surprised us with something very interesting and disturbing." He closely studied his chief bodyguard's face.

Armstrong's heart fell out of his chest. He knew what was coming, but managed to keep an unknowing expression.

Naylor dove back into the fray, driving the bayonet of fear directly through Armstrong's thick chest. "The First Lady claims you sexually assaulted her the night she left. She says you grabbed her breast and that she plans to file charges against you. Sexual assault is also a felony." The room was totally quiet for several seconds as they glared at him. "Is it true?" Naylor demanded.

Armstrong faced the governor. "Sir, Mrs. Stovall was very distraught that night. She tried to grab my gun. When I grabbed her hands, she pressed my hand against her breast." It sounded obscene and frail to everyone in the room. Armstrong envisioned himself being fired. He'd be lucky to walk away with a bust in rank and a transfer out of the detail. Major Moss would be livid that he had not been briefed. Chelle might even leave him. This job and his dedication to it would prove to be his downfall. *My God*, Armstrong realized, *this is the same thing that happened to Simon Godwin!*

Naylor looked at his boss. "I recommend that he be dismissed immediately. I'll call Colonel DeWitt."

Jesus, Armstrong thought, *the jury was out all of five seconds on that verdict.* He cleared his voice and said quietly, "Governor, I didn't say anything because it was an ugly situation, and it seemed to iron itself out. Frankly, I was embarrassed and shocked. But I should have told you. I'll voluntarily leave if you like. You don't have to have any involvement in this."

Stovall smiled sadly at Naylor, "Brad, I told you she was . . . ," he searched for the right word, " . . . unstable." He looked at Armstrong. "I believe you, David, but I'm very disappointed. I'm disappointed that you didn't tell me this sooner. But I want you to stay," he said, "for now."

Chapter 72

I'm free! thought First Lady Patricia Stovall to herself, as she wheeled her daughter's Lexus down Chesterfield Parkway. She hadn't driven herself for months, relying on her husband's ever-present bodyguards to handle her transportation. But she now felt more alive than ever, as though she was finally controlling her own destiny. She had dropped Heather at her law office and decided to take a spin on the way back to Heather's plush apartment.

She recalled reading a column written by former First Lady Hillary Rodham Clinton in which she confessed, "I had a sudden impulse to drive [by myself] . . . I jumped behind the wheel of a car and, much to the discomfort of my Secret Service detail, drove myself around town. For several hours, I enjoyed a marvelous sensation of personal freedom." She now knew precisely how Mrs. Clinton had felt.

The newsman on the NPR radio station she was listening to was talking about it being the anniversary of the Oklahoma City bombing and the shootout in Waco. The terror alert level had remained at Yellow, but authorities were warning people to stay alert. She shut the radio off and smiled contentedly. The last thing she wanted to do was worry about someone blowing up another government building. They could blow up the Capitol for all she cared, hopefully with her husband in it!

Her elation was momentarily broken by the sound of the driver behind her, honking his horn repeatedly. She slowed and looked with open irritation in her rearview mirror. Two men in suits and sunglasses tailgated her in a large white sedan. One man placed a red light on the dash and it began to flash in an angry signal to stop. Her eyes dropped to her speedometer, and she saw that even with her reduced speed, she was still five miles per hour over the limit. *Unbelievable!* she thought and pulled onto the shoulder. *My first day behind the wheel in six months and I get a ticket!*

Both men got out and approached her car. The passenger stopped at her right rear fender. The driver strode to her window and displayed a silver badge in a black leather case. "Police detective, ma'am," he said. "I need to see your driver's license."

Patricia Stovall experienced a momentary panic, wondering if she had remembered to renew her license, since she seldom drove. She dug it out of her purse and verified it was still valid. "What's wrong, officer?" she asked. "Was I speeding?"

The officer ignored her question and closely examined her license. He was stocky with a shaved head and a cheap suit. He smelled of some cheap aftershave and was probably a nasty brute, just like the troopers who had made her last few months a living hell. She pulled off her designer sunglasses so he could recognize the face of his state's First Lady and give her a break. She fixed the officer with a reproachful look. "Don't you know who I am, Officer?" she asked accusingly.

Bobby "Gunner" Wykoff grinned at her. "Yes, Mrs. Stovall. I know who you are. If you'll step back to my car for a moment, we can settle this rather quickly."

Chapter 73

"Okay, what do we know?" Governor Stovall demanded of the group gathered before him.

Armstrong glanced over at Colonel DeWitt, Major Moss, and Captain Douglas. DeWitt nodded, indicating to Armstrong that he should do the briefing. Armstrong looked at his notes and ticked off the details as they knew them.

"Governor, here's what we have so far. Mrs. Stovall dropped Heather off at work at about nine-thirty this morning. At eleven o'clock, a fax arrived at the Mansion, stating that the First Lady had been taken hostage and would be traded tomorrow for Ezekiel Leech. It gave the location of Heather's car, which we found parked at the Chesterfield Mall. The message said they would fax her location at o-nine hundred and we are to bring Leech for the swap. If there are any problems, they said they'd kill her. It appears to be from the same two fugitive Phineas Priests who got away after the attack in Kansas City."

Stovall glared at the group. "How the hell did they know that Pat was staying at our daughter's apartment?"

Paul Fleming cleared his throat and said quietly, "Most of the media have been airing those rumors for the past few days. The terrorists probably learned it from watching TV or reading the paper."

"So what's the plan?" Bradley Naylor asked, wanting to shift his boss's focus back on the cops.

Armstrong shrugged. "My concern is Mrs. Stovall's safety. I say we follow the instructions."

Naylor snorted. "This is a fine time to be concerned about her safety. Why didn't you have someone assigned to protect her? We wouldn't be having this conversation right now."

Armstrong glared at the aide. "Brad, I offered to assign someone the night she left, but she refused. I can't force protection on her. We don't have the legal authority."

"Oh, that's convenient. Now that she's been snatched, you say she refused. The fact is, your detail is responsible for her safety. Period! You should have figured out a way to do it."

"That's enough!" Governor Stovall barked, bringing silence to the room. Stovall considered whether they should call in the FBI or let the Patrol handle this situation. He decided to leave the Feds out for the moment. As a former U.S. Attorney, he knew all too well that the FBI would bring their Crisis Negotiation Team, and he would lose control of the situation once the agents arrived on the scene. He rubbed his face with both hands and then eyed his communications director. "Paul, what's the political fallout of me releasing this terrorist?"

Everyone in the room, even his loyal staff, sat in stunned silence at the question. Here was the First Lady of Missouri—his wife, for God's sake—being held hostage by terrorists, and the governor wanted to weigh the polls to decide her fate.

Colonel DeWitt looked at the floor, and it was obvious he didn't have the will to lock horns with his boss. Major Moss clenched his jaw, resisting the urge to lean across the desk and smack this blithering bureaucrat in the mouth. Captain Douglas rolled his eyes at the ceiling, suppressing the same urge.

Fleming cleared his throat. "I . . . I suppose that if he's released and he gets away or kills someone else, you'll look weak and will pay a price for dealing with terrorists. If they . . . ," his eyes darted toward the officers, shifting the onus to them, ". . . can figure a way to free the First Lady, and capture or kill all the terrorists, you'll be seen as courageous and heroic. It'll give you a bump in the polls."

Moss could not sit silent any longer. "What if she's killed in the process?" he asked no one in particular. When no one responded, he looked directly at the governor. "Don't get any false hopes, sir. There are no guarantees here. We can come up with a plan, but these people are cunning and deadly. They'll have their bases covered."

Stovall looked desperately at Armstrong. "What do I do, David?" He was looking for assurances.

"Let us arrange the swap," Armstrong said immediately. "We'll do our best to safely free Mrs. Stovall *and* capture the fugitives."

Stovall stated firmly. "Okay, but I want you to handle this personally. I want you there when she's freed to ensure her safety."

Armstrong nodded, feeling some level of responsibility for her predicament. "I wouldn't have it any other way, sir." Laying his life on the line for the First Family was what they paid him to do.

Chapter 74

The throbbing beat of the Bell JetRanger helicopter blades went through Armstrong's entire body. He had grown used to flying in the governor's Citation jet, but this was his first trip up in a chopper, and he felt as unsteady as a hog on ice. He glanced up at the Patrol pilot in front, listening to the radio traffic on his headphones. Then Armstrong looked over at his prisoner.

Ezekiel "Easy Kill" Leech sat in an orange prison jumpsuit to Armstrong's left. His left leg was still bound in a cast from Romanowski's .40 caliber round, and he had struggled to climb into the helicopter, but they weren't taking any chances. Leech was hobbled with his hands cuffed to a thick leather belt and his ankles chained with shackles. The chain ran through a metal seat support, preventing him from getting out of his seat. He had more metal on him than a punk-rock band. Leech appeared to be asleep or in deep meditation. Knowing Leech's record of cutting patches off dead or wounded officers—plus the fact that Leech had killed Simon Godwin—Armstrong fantasized about opening the chopper door to see how deep a hole Leech would make in the ground, one thousand feet below them, wearing all that steel.

Leech opened his eyes and glared at Armstrong. His hatred was apparent, and Armstrong knew, if given even half a chance, Leech would kill them all.

"Penny for your thoughts," Armstrong muttered, not expecting an answer.

"I was just wondering, how do you do it? How do you lay your life on the line for such a pathetic human being?"

"I don't think you're that pathetic," Armstrong retorted, playing dumb. He knew that Leech was referring to Governor Stovall.

"I'm talking about your boss. I know who you are. You're one of Stovall's bodyguards. I shook his hand in St. Joseph, and as soon as our hands touched, God showed me a vision. In it, I was placing Stovall's head at the altar of God."

Armstrong gave him a deadpan look. "I take it back. You are pathetic."

Leech continued, "I also saw you saving the First Lady from that pie attack. Well, you won't be saving her today, bodyguard. She's going to be dead before this day is done, and you will be too. How touching that he is sending you to your demise. The brave bodyguard charges fearlessly and obediently to his death. 'Ours is not to reason why, ours is but to do or die!' Are you ready to meet the Almighty?"

Armstrong shrugged. "'The Way of the bodyguard is resolute acceptance of death,'" he said, quoting an old Samurai maxim. "If I die today, it will be facing the enemy with an empty weapon."

"How noble! I'll savor that thought when I cut you down. The Protector of the Unborn versus the Protector of the Abortionists! It rings of an epic battle—Good versus Evil, Hector versus Achilles—one that will draw the attention of the Almighty, for sure. When He stares down at us, facing off on the field of battle, who do you think He'll side with? The Priest or the Prophylactic?"

Armstrong snorted. "You call yourself a priest? If you're a priest, I'm the Pope. Who gave you the license to decide who lives and dies?"

Leech's eyes shifted to the roof of the helicopter. "He did. We've had a pact since the dawn of time! Our battle cry is: 'We must secure the existence of our people and a future for white children.'"

Armstrong grinned. "Ah, the famed 'Fourteen Words.' But as I recall, they were coined by a white racist in prison and not by God. You need to get your holy hearing aid checked."

"God speaks through all imprisoned brothers," Leech sneered. "I'll relish cutting your throat out, bodyguard."

The pilot looked back at Armstrong and said, "We're five minutes out." Armstrong felt the helicopter begin to lose altitude, giving him an uneasy feeling in the pit of his stomach.

At exactly nine o'clock that morning, a fax had arrived at the Governor's Mansion. It gave no details of the pending exchange, but simply advised Governor Stovall to have Leech standing by in a Highway Patrol helicopter ready for take-off, and that a follow-up fax would detail the exchange. The second fax arrived exactly one hour later. It advised Stovall to have Leech flown to the parking lot of the All-America Truck Stop, located at the junction of I-70 and I-370, about twenty miles west of St. Louis. The helicopter had to be on the ground at exactly 10:45, it was to "land on the white X," and they were to leave the engine running. Armstrong was to get out and go inside, leaving the pilot and Leech in the helicopter. He was to ask the front desk if there was a "message for Freeman," which would contain the final instructions for the transfer.

The fax warned that if any other cops were spotted, they'd get the First Lady's body back in a shoebox. It clearly demanded, "No FBI, no SWAT, no uniformed cops, no plainclothes cops, no other aircraft, no exceptions, no coincidences. We are watching! If you do not follow these instructions EXACTLY, a lot of people will die!!!"

Considering the flight time from the Patrol hangar at the Jefferson City Airport to the truck stop, this gave the authorities almost no time to set up surveillance. Captain Douglas had put nearly all of the Patrol's undercover investigators on call, forming several surveillance teams in each of the Patrol's nine troop headquarters. No matter where in the state this case took them, they'd have teams to quickly respond. Armstrong knew that when the helicopter left, Captain Douglas was making a flurry of calls to arrange some level of covert surveillance and security for them at the meeting site. But it would have to be very, very low-key.

Armstrong could see the sprawling complex of the truck stop through the windshield of the helicopter, and his pulse quickened. He guessed that there must be over one hundred vehicles—cars, vans, small and large trucks—parked or moving about the huge area. It was a smart spot for the swap. Lots of collateral damage available, plenty of people for the terrorists to hide among, and multiple escape routes. The environment would provide undercover officers with a lot of cover, but there was too much to watch without being obvious about it.

A burst of static sounded in Armstrong's headphones as a radio dispatcher, located at the Patrol's Troop C Headquarters in Kirkwood, advised them that investigators on-site could not locate a "white X." The pilot leaned forward slightly, as they neared the building, and Armstrong heard him respond, "Tell them there's a crude X painted on the roof of the truck stop." To Armstrong, the mark appeared to have been freshly painted. He wondered if the flat roof of the building would support the weight of the helicopter. They could see a large step van parked close to the back of the building with a ladder attached to the back of the cargo container. It was obviously intended for him to step down off the roof of the building and onto the roof of the van, and then climb the ladder down to the pavement.

Armstrong checked his watch as the helicopter closed for its final approach. It would touch the roof at exactly 10:45. The pilot had timed their trip perfectly.

"Nice work, Tim. Good luck," he told the pilot, Sergeant Tim Hendricks.

"You, too, L.T.," Hendricks responded. When Armstrong left, Hendricks would remain in the helicopter with Leech.

Armstrong shifted around in his seat. The heavy, level-III body armor under his windbreaker was confining, yet comforting, and the leg holster securing his Model 27 Glock to his left leg was starting to chafe the skin. His Model 23 Glock felt good in the small of his back. Armstrong wondered if he and the First Lady would survive this day.

Chapter 75

As soon as Armstrong entered the truck stop, the back doors of the van parked next to the building opened. Bobby Wykoff scampered up the ladder, jumped onto the roof of the building, and ran to the waiting helicopter. His features were concealed by a black ski mask. Sergeant Tim Hendricks saw him coming and was not surprised. When he was told to remain in the helicopter with the engine wound up, he knew he was to be their getaway driver.

Wykoff jumped in front and pointed Leech's Colt 9mm submachine gun at Hendricks. "Let's go!" he barked. "Fly low and to the south." He took out a GPS device to direct them to their vehicle, which was concealed near Augusta along the Missouri River.

As Armstrong waited at the desk for the message, he heard the helicopter lift off the roof and fly away. He wasn't surprised either and hoped the pilot wouldn't be harmed.

The girl behind the counter handed him a manila envelope, and Armstrong quickly tore it open and read the contents. He ran out the side door and looked around the parking lot. About one hundred yards north of the complex was a shaded area for pets to use as a "rest station." Armstrong could see a figure seated on a bench under one of the shade trees. Armstrong said, "I'm going off the air for a minute." He then reached down to his left side and turned off the small body transmitter on his belt, which was transmitting everything he said to the nearby surveillance team. He dashed across the parking lot to the area.

Mrs. Stovall was seated quietly on the bench. She appeared to be in a daze. As Armstrong neared her, he saw that her right wrist was handcuffed to the arm of the bench, which was anchored to the ground.

"Are you alright, Mrs. Stovall?" he asked, glancing around at the activity on the parking lot.

In response, Patricia Stovall looked at him and used her free hand to open the collar of her shirt. Armstrong saw three strands of yellow cord looped snugly around her neck, like an exotic necklace. Armstrong was not an explosives expert, but he knew what detonating cord looked like. And he knew what three strands of it around a human neck would do. It would easily cut a telephone pole in half. The cord was attached to a remote-controlled device with a small antenna wire. The message in his hand stated, "Mrs. Stovall is at the doggy dump north of the parking lot. Do not touch Mrs. Stovall before noon, or we will detonate the device around her neck. We are watching you!" The group wanted time for the others to make good their escape.

Armstrong knew the surveillance team would go ballistic when he stopped transmitting, but he also knew that any transmission in the vicinity of the device might set it off.

He sat down next to her on the bench and asked again, "Are you okay?"

Her eyes moved to the farmland located west of their position, as though willing her mind to escape her predicament and imagine herself sitting peacefully in a distant wheat field. "Will you stay with me?"

Armstrong said, "Of course, you couldn't talk me out of staying with you."

She took that in for a moment, really grasping what it meant. "You know, David, I guess I was fooling myself about your detail."

"How so?" he asked gently.

She looked over at him. "I've been in public life for years and we've never had a serious threat before. At least not one we were aware of. Not that we'd have listened to any of you anyway." She paused. "I guess we were a little naive."

Armstrong nodded. "I can understand that. . . ."

Mrs. Stovall interrupted and said evenly, "No, we weren't naive—we were arrogant. We knew everything. We heard what we wanted to hear and muted every message that might get in our way."

Armstrong said, "There isn't an elected official in the world who doesn't do that sometimes."

"Kind of you, David—but we went further. We didn't just ignore you, we stopped even seeing you. We wanted to make you invisible."

"Well, we like being invisible sometimes."

"Kind again, David, and that's something you gave us a lot: kindness—and we didn't give you any back—and I am sorry."

They were both quiet for a moment, and then a single tear rolled down her cheek. Armstrong touched her face and intercepted the drop before it could reach any of the electric wires. An act of kindness and protection in one—like many before it. "Please hold the tears; we don't want any moisture shorting those wires. You can really wail later, I promise." They both smiled.

Reminded of her situation, she looked back toward the field. "What a different life I'd have led had I known in advance about this moment; this moment I have to sit here, but you don't—and yet you choose to. And God, I'm grateful to not be alone right now. How much longer do you think?" She sounded tense. The sky was overcast and the air had not lost its morning chill. She was getting cold, perhaps from fear. Or was it that Death was seated next to her on the bench, embracing her in his bony arms?

Armstrong scanned the activity of the parking lot again, knowing that both the good guys and the bad were watching them. "The note says we have to stay here until noon. I have a helicopter standing by a mile from here. At noon, we'll get the bomb guys to remove the bomb, then we'll fly you to a hospital so they can check you over." The bomb detail had a jamming device they could use to disable the transmitter around her neck, just in case the terrorists changed their minds. He debated calling it in now, but he feared they had a sniper's crosshairs on them, as well. It might be better to follow the instructions.

She gazed at him. "I knew my husband wouldn't come."

Armstrong shook his head. "I wouldn't have allowed him to come. You know that."

"But he didn't ask to, did he?" Her eyes narrowed, searching his face for a lie.

"No, ma'am," he admitted. "He didn't ask."

"Sometimes I've hated him—and it's made me a bit crazy at times. Not just a bit, I guess. It's as if we used our hearts so rarely that they just dried up," she admitted. When Armstrong didn't respond, she laughed. "I know you won't say, but you know I'm right." She paused for a moment. "So why do you do it? Why not just quit? After

Simon Godwin died to save my husband, and he didn't even attend the funeral, I thought you'd all quit. That no one would be willing, no one SHOULD be willing to protect him."

Armstrong realized it was the same question that Leech had asked him only fifteen minutes before. "Ma'am," said Armstrong, still scanning to see if he could find the sniper he felt sure was watching them, "we don't protect your husband; we protect the governor, the highest elected leader of our state. The people might deserve a better man, but I can't change that. All I can do, all any of us can do, is to do our job the best we can. If everyone tried—really tried—to do that, then things wouldn't be so bad. I can't make the governor a good person. But I CAN make myself a good man." Then he looked her straight in the eye. She was surprised by the strength of character shining out. "I'm just one man, just one vote. I can't change the will of the people any more than my one vote, but I can—by God—deny any other one man the right to veto the will of the people. If every yahoo with a gripe can undo the democratic process with a bullet, then democracy can't exist. I'm not defending your husband. I am defending the very concept of representative government. Many other men have died for that ideal, and many more will die in the years to come. All men die, but if a man's death is to mean something, then he can't do better than dying to defend liberty and the concept of representative government." His eyes moved away, and he seemed slightly embarrassed. "This probably all sounds pretty foolish and hokey in this cynical age. But just remember, when you run out of men who are willing to die for these concepts, then you can give up on our nation. I'll be damned if I let that happen on my watch."

Patricia Stovall smiled sadly, an expression that said, *You are very right.* Her green eyes teared up again, and she dutifully turned her head toward Armstrong so he could catch the tears. He caught a few as they sat there, and then they were both quiet.

Reverting back to his all-business mode, Armstrong stood and looked around. "I have to report in. I'll be right back." Then he gave her a reassuring smile. "You're going to be fine."

He casually walked around the perimeter of the parking lot, as though looking for something. As he walked, he pondered his next move. Lives—including his and the First Lady's—would clearly hang in the balance on the decisions he was about to make. *What should I do?* he asked himself. Then Armstrong remembered the words of his mentor, Simon Godwin: *If you feel vulnerable in a given situation, you should take steps to change the situation right now—no waiting. When a gazelle finds itself alone with the lion, it doesn't just wait to see how the carnivore will behave. It evaluates its options and resources all the while and, if it perceives that it's too vulnerable, puts more distance between itself and the hunter. The gazelle refuses to be an easy victim.*

When he was fifty yards from Mrs. Stovall, he turned the body mike back on. "Okay," he said, as though talking to himself, "Rosebush is okay, but she has a bomb around her neck and probably a sniper's scope on her. Is Monitor here yet?"

The voice of Bobby Davenport responded. "I'm about three miles from your position, L.T." Armstrong could hear the loud drone of Monitor's engine in the background as Davenport sped to his location. When the fax had specified the location of the exchange, Armstrong had dispatched Davenport to get the armored vehicle there as quickly as possible. Davenport was followed by two bomb techs in a van with their gear, in case another IED were to be encountered.

"Bobby, when you get here, have the bomb guys put their signal jammer in Monitor and park it next to her. Tell them to walk their dog over, like they're using the rest station. I want to know if it's a real device or a hoax. Then have them leave the vehicle and go into the truck stop. I don't want anything setting that bomb off." Armstrong imagined that the air around the truck stop must be bristling with transmitted signals from CB radios, cellular phones, and God only knew what else. Any one of them could set off the bomb.

Armstrong considered what else needed to be done. "Have the chopper ready to fly us out of here, as soon as the bomb has been removed." He wondered about the status of the helicopter escape. "Have we heard anything from Hendricks?"

The voice of one of his surveillance team members crackled over his wireless earpiece. "Sergeant Hendricks just dropped them off in a field. They didn't harm him, but they handcuffed him to his chopper and disabled it. The fugitives are currently in a four-wheel-drive vehicle, trying to escape. One-thirty-MP is overhead with a FLIR unit, and pursuit cars are boxing them in now."

Armstrong knew that Patrol aircraft 130MP was a twin-engine Beechcraft. They had been tailing Hendricks's chopper ever since he had taken off. The FLIR unit—an acronym for Forward Looking In-frared—was a device that could see heat. When FLIR was used from an aircraft, the body heat of a human would be visible even in total darkness.

Armstrong smiled, visualizing the noose slowly tightening around the terrorists' necks. Leech would either be recaptured or die resisting. *Either way*, he thought, *is okay with me.* But they wouldn't be able to take them down until the bomb was deactivated. Armstrong looked at his watch. About another hour. He wondered about the others in the group. Where were they? What were they planning?

He glanced across the parking lot and spotted the purple Peterbilt tractor. There was no one in the cab, but Armstrong knew that his surveillance team was hidden in the sleeper, watching him through the small window in the side of the truck. He wondered how Captain Douglas had commandeered the vehicle so quickly and gotten it into position. He knew that other undercover officers from DDCC were quietly descending on his position, as well as four vanloads of heavily armed SERT officers to serve as a rescue force. "I'm going back off the air again," he said. "Flash your lights if you want me to come back on."

He heard two clicks over his earpiece and turned to walk back to Mrs. Stovall's position. Armstrong wondered what other actions he could take to cut down the risks against them and reduce the odds that they would all be killed.

Chapter 76

From a motor home on the parking lot across the highway from the All-America Truck Stop, Ross Draeger watched Armstrong through a large pair of binoculars. *He's the same bodyguard we saw in St. Joseph*, he realized.

It was his intention to kill the First Lady once his fellow Priests were safe, and he would kill this meddling bodyguard as well. The government had simply extracted too large a cost from them. Spider, So-So, Seed, and Peter, all dead. He would detonate the necklace bomb and probably take them both out. If that failed, he would use his deadly Galil. Either way, it was payback time.

Draeger's Galil SR-99 sniper rifle was lying across his knees. The weapon's twenty-round magazine was loaded with 7.62mm Glaser Safety Slugs. The 125-grain frangible bullets were the ultimate in antipersonnel rounds. They would leave massive, gaping wounds, providing instant, one-shot stops. The Glasers didn't have the trajectory or accuracy of a Match bullet, but they delivered 100 percent of their energy into the target, leaving the barrel at a whopping 3,000 feet per second. One of his deadly Glasers would turn Mrs. Stovall's petite body inside out. He had a back-up magazine loaded with armor-piercing ammo, if needed.

He wondered how the escape of Leech and Wykoff was going. As if in response to his thought, his cell-phone rang. "Yeah."

Wykoff's voice was littered with static. He was in a bad location. "We're on the road. No sign of pursuit. What's the situation?"

"I'm still on-site," Draeger responded loudly. "Are you sure you're clear?"

There was a moment of static, and then Wykoff answered, "Yeah, I think so."

Draeger held the phone in one hand, while he used the other to hold the binoculars. A black Lincoln Navigator had pulled up next to Mrs. Stovall. A clean-cut young man with a German shepherd got out and approached the First Lady. He stood with his hands in the pockets of his jeans, while the dog moved around the First Lady's bench and relieved himself on the fire hydrant there. Draeger's eyes narrowed.

"Then we follow the plan," he instructed Wykoff. "I'll hook up with you tonight at the safe house in East St. Louis."

"Sounds like a plan," Wykoff agreed.

Draeger continued to watch as the dog marked a tree. Then the owner called him over. The dog moved past Mrs. Stovall, sniffed around her, then sat and looked at his owner. The man placed a leash on the dog, patted him on the head, and then walked him toward the truck stop, leaving his vehicle in place. At that point, the bodyguard returned to the bench and sat down next to the First Lady.

"Shit!" spat Draeger, throwing the glasses aside.

"What happened?" demanded Wykoff.

"They just ran a bomb dog around her and it hit on the bomb!" Draeger growled in frustration. They weren't following the plan. That meant that they were all in imminent peril.

"So?" Wykoff said. "Now they know the bomb is real."

Suddenly Leech's voice came on the phone. "Ross! Take her out! Do you hear me? Take her out now!"

"They aren't following our instructions!" Draeger whispered, his eyes wide. His paranoia was growing like a virus. "They're violating the rules!" He heard a noise outside the vehicle and jerked his head around, imagining black-clad SWAT officers closing in around him.

"Kill her," screamed Leech into the phone. "They killed my family. Now, by God, I'm going to kill theirs!"

Without a word, Draeger dropped the phone and pulled out the bomb transmitter. He held it up against the window and pushed the button, expecting to see the First Lady's head tumbling through the air like a soccer ball. Nothing happened! Mrs. Stovall and Armstrong continued to sit quietly on the bench and chat, as though on a first date.

"Dammit!" growled Draeger. He ran to the side door of the motor home, opened it, and stuck his arm outside, frantically clicking the firing button. Maybe the signal was too weak inside the vehicle. Still nothing happened! *They must be jamming it!*

He had failed Leech again. He had failed God again!

He threw the transmitter down, picked up the Galil, and put the reticle of the six-power scope on the First Lady's head. The crosshairs wavered slightly as he took up the slack of the two-stage trigger. His heart hammered in his chest, and he fought to hold the weapon still. He jerked the trigger, sending a round six inches behind Mrs. Stovall's head.

Armstrong's head snapped around at the thump of Draeger's rifle and the supersonic crack of the projectile going past them. He lunged to the other side of Mrs. Stovall, putting himself and his armor between her and the gunman. Activating his mike, he shouted, "We're under fire from across the road!" When Armstrong had seen that Mrs. Stovall was handcuffed, he had readied the handcuff key on his key ring, in case it was needed. He now quickly unlocked the manacle and jerked her off the seat; the seatback exploded an instant later from Draeger's second round. Armstrong dragged her over to the armored SUV left by the bomb tech and pushed her down onto the backseat.

Draeger saw his hostage being taken away. He fired another round, but the safety slug, true to its name, shattered harmlessly against the armored glass. Against human flesh, the Glasers were awesome. Against solid objects, they had no penetration and were almost useless. Draeger looked around for his magazine of armor-piercing ammo, but didn't see it. He dropped the Galil, pulled his SIG-Sauer .45 out of his waistband, and broke into a run in their direction, firing at them.

Armstrong lunged into the front seat, started the vehicle, and spun the wheels in reverse. When he reached twenty-five miles per hour, he performed a perfect J-turn and sped around the east side of truck stop and away from Draeger. Two .45 rounds struck the window next to Armstrong's face, and three more hit the tailgate, but all were easily stopped by the vehicle's armor.

Draeger came to a stop in the middle of the highway with the slide locked back on his gun. Several vehicles slid to a halt to avoid hitting him, but he seemed unaware of them. His mind was already critiquing the miscalculations in his plan. He had clearly underestimated his opponents. He could almost hear God's deep laughter taunting his pitiful performance.

A green Dodge minivan screeched to a stop behind him. The side door slid open, and Sergeant Matt Youngblood bounded out with a .12 gauge Remington shotgun leveled on Draeger. "Drop the gun! Drop the gun!" he bellowed.

Draeger turned and stared at the undercover officer with open shock and hatred. But he dropped the gun, much to Youngblood's astonishment. He never dreamed that these Phineas Priests would surrender. He didn't know that deep within Draeger's character was a clear understanding of the concept "live to fight another day." Besides, he was out of ammo. Without a word, Draeger slowly and carefully lay on the cold pavement and spread his arms in surrender. A protective ring of heavily armed, plainclothes SERT officers encircled them, just in case Draeger had additional help. One of the officers handcuffed Draeger and pulled him to his feet.

Youngblood looked around and put a walkie-talkie to his mouth. "All units," he barked. "We're clear. We have the suspect in custody. Tell them to take the others down." The sound of several sirens began singing from different directions, as emergency vehicles responded to his position.

Youngblood saw the bomb tech and his dog running in the direction of Armstrong's vehicle. Within minutes, they would have the necklace bomb removed. In the distance, he heard the clatter of the Troop C helicopter, approaching to evacuate Armstrong and Mrs. Stovall. He took hold of Draeger's arm and pulled him toward the van. "You're shaking like a dog shitting peach seeds, slick," he gloated. "Must be all that ice water flowing through your veins." He shoved Draeger into the vehicle.

*   *   *

The young bomb tech leaned back from examining Patricia Stovall's necklace bomb. "Doesn't look too tricky. I should have it off in nothing flat." He looked at Armstrong. "L.T., if you'll just wait over behind the perimeter, I'll get started."

Armstrong's brow furrowed, but his voice remained calm, "You've got to be kidding, Miller. I'm not going anywhere." He held both of Patricia Stovall's trembling hands in his own to calm her. He gave her a reassuring squeeze.

Miller gave him a nervous look. "Sorry, sir, I can't do this with you here. It's against regulations."

"Corporal Miller," Armstrong said quietly, "if you don't remove this device now, I will." He gave Miller a serious look. "And then I'm going to wrap it around your neck!" He turned and gave Mrs. Stovall a wink. She squeezed his hands in response.

Miller considered Armstrong's words, then shrugged and began to work on the device.

"Wait," Mrs. Stovall said. She looked at the young officer. "Do you have any children, Corporal Miller?"

Miller nodded. "I have a son. He just turned three."

"What are the names of your son and wife?" she asked.

"Randy and Jennifer," Miller stated.

"Randy and Jennifer Miller," Mrs. Stovall whispered, committing the names to memory. She then closed her eyes and tilted her head back to accept whatever fate awaited her.

Armstrong put a hand on Miller's shoulder. "Let's get this thing off and go home, son."

Epilogue

Governor William Ulysses Stovall gripped the sides of the walnut podium and gazed out over the large crowd which was gathered on the north drive and lawn of the Capitol Building. It was a picture-perfect day. A light breeze fluttered the flags that were on display. The smell of fresh carnations, roses, and other flower arrangements was thick.

Stovall was in his element. This was his forte. Communicating with the public. He always seemed to know the right words and could forge a bond even at hostile gatherings. It was all he could do to keep from laughing. *The game,* he thought. *I love this game!* Crafting words that inspire others to do . . . what? Enable him to hold this powerful position. Enable him to lead this extravagant lifestyle. Enable him to . . . be! But laughing wouldn't be appropriate for this solemn occasion—honoring those who had died in the line of duty. Stovall really didn't feel a bond with these dead officers. After all, they knew the job was dangerous when they took it. He could certainly not think of anyone for whom he would give up his life. But these officers also enabled him to be. Especially when others—like Leech, Draeger, and Wykoff—were determined that he should cease to be.

It was time to comfort and inspire his enablers.

"The great writer T. S. Eliot," he began, "once said, 'I had not thought death had undone so many.'" Stovall looked over his right shoulder and waved his hand at the memorial behind him. "He might have been writing about this sacred place. Nearly fifteen thousand police officers have been killed while performing their duties since this country was founded. Nearly six hundred of those deaths were in Missouri. Each year we add more names of fallen officers to the hallowed walls of this memorial. This year, there are twelve new names, the bloodiest year in our state's history. And two of those names are Lieutenant Simon Godwin and Conservation Agent Dwayne Stoddard." Stovall waved a hand at the front row of the crowd. "Each man left behind a wife and family. I want to acknowledge Judy Godwin and Tamiko Stoddard in attendance today. Both of these great officers' lives were cut short by the same. . . ," he paused, as though searching for the right word, " . . .well, we can only call him what he is: a monster. I am happy to announce today that terrorist Ezekiel Leech has been charged with capital murder, and prosecutors are asking for the death penalty.

"I also want to report that the trials of terrorist Ross Draeger and his henchman, Bobby Wykoff, are both on schedule and that we are aggressively pursuing the death penalty in their cases, as well. Their arrests were the result of a massive, joint FBI, BATF, and Highway Patrol investigation."

Standing at the back of the crowd, Sergeant Matt Youngblood shook his head in silent frustration. For some reason, the Feds always got top billing. With his long hair and scruffy appearance, he looked out of place at the official ceremony. His hair concealed the earpiece through which he monitored the radio traffic of Armstrong's detail. Youngblood was assigned to perform undercover countersurveillance on the crowd.

Stovall continued, "Leech's group was responsible for the deaths of several officers in other states, and I can promise you this: We will not make deals with these monsters for lighter sentences!"

The crowd broke into an enthusiastic round of applause. A video crew, working for Stovall's campaign team, recorded the scene in its entire splendor. The waving flags, the ranks of uniformed policemen from all over the state standing at attention, the crowd of several hundred grieving family and friends of fallen officers. A Hollywood producer could not assemble a more touching or patriotic gathering. The film generated from this day would be spliced into every one of Stovall's campaign spots in the future. They would show the electorate that he was strong on crime, dedicated to the rule of law, and able to maintain law and order. It would be a powerful image. It would negate the stories of the messy divorce proceedings filed against him by Patricia Stovall. There were even rumors that she was threatening to run against him in the primary election. After his conversation with Mrs. Stovall before her rescue, David Armstrong had vowed he would cross party lines to give her his vote if she ran.

The cameras carefully avoided the governor's bodyguards, stoically bracketing the stage. It wouldn't do for the public to think their governor felt threatened by his loving electorate. Armstrong stood post at stage left, Don Romanowski at stage right, and Kacey Underwood was posted behind the platform. In addition, Marko Vanhala and Alex Wiedemann were working the crowd, and two SERT counter-snipers held the high ground atop the Capitol Building.

During Stovall's stirring speech, the only radio traffic consisted of SERT spotter Philip Barr's periodic observations. "TOP to all units. I've got an organizer with a backpack in the third row of the crowd . . . green shirt and black ball cap . . . at Ringmaster's one o'clock." Armstrong couldn't see the organizer, but knew he would be digging for something in the bag.

Wiedemann radioed, "Copy the organizer." Armstrong saw Wiedemann move down the rope-line as he zeroed in on the suspect. Armstrong felt satisfied that Wiedemann had settled down and was proving to be an effective protector.

Barr called out another. "There's a traveler in a red polo at Ringmaster's eleven o'clock . . . moving along the back row . . . something in his hand . . . looks like a small video camera."

Vanhala spotted the suspect's movement. "Copy the traveler at eleven o'clock." Marko noticed Matt Youngblood turn and follow the suspect. "Our U/C picked him up."

Watching his team operate, Armstrong felt a sense of pride. They were SEEing the crowd, noting behaviors consistent with public-figure attackers, and taking strong defensive positions. He would stack them up against any other protective detail in America. He was struck by the irony that everyone on the team would likely refuse to check the box next to Governor Stovall's name on a ballot, but none would hesitate to lay down his or her life for him. It was an irony that was clearly lost on their protectee.

Governor Stovall waited for the applause to die down before continuing. "An inscription on the National Law Enforcement Officers Memorial in Washington DC states, 'It is not how these officers died that made them heroes, it is how they lived.' And that couldn't be truer than of the officers we honor today. Simon Godwin literally laid his life down for me, a debt I will never be able to repay."

To Stovall's right, Armstrong frowned and thought, *You haven't even visited his grave yet!* He needed a break from the boss. In three weeks, he and Chelle were scheduled to accompany Judy Godwin and her children on the cruise she had initially canceled after Simon's death. He couldn't wait to break out of this protective bubble. He couldn't wait to spend some quiet time with Chelle.

The cameras zoomed in on Stovall's face as a tear trickled down his left cheek. He stood silent for several seconds, as though corralling his emotions. He bit his lip, then continued on. "The nineteenth century Russian author, H.P. Blavatsky, once said,

"'Strive with thy thoughts unclean before they overpower thee. Use them as they will thee, for if thou sparest them and they take root and grow, know well, these thoughts will overpower and kill thee. Beware! Suffer not their shadow to approach. For it will grow, increase in size and power, and then this thing of darkness will absorb thy being before thou hast well realized the black foul monster's presence.'"

He paused again, allowing the crowd to absorb the message. His face took on a mask of determination. "One reason we gather here today is to prevent the black foul monster of revenge from consuming us. We must allow society's laws to deal with aberrant creatures like Leech and Draeger, even though we would rather dispense our own quick and decisive form of justice. We must allow the memories and brave deeds of these heroes," his right hand swept toward the memorial, "to carry us through these grim times. It is fitting that when our emotions are in danger of being absorbed by the darkness, these champions again answer the bugle call of distress, and the memories of their right deeds save us once again. They will forever be inspiring us to do good and saving us from becoming like the evil monsters that cut short their lives!"

Stovall hung his head for a moment and then nodded to the crowd as they broke into a thunderous ovation. He gave a grateful wave of his hand and took his seat. The rotund bureaucrat, DPS Director Lawrence Frisbie, waddled to the podium to begin the roll call of fallen officers.

When the ceremony was concluded and Governor Stovall had shaken nearly every hand in the crowd, he turned and nodded at Armstrong. *I'm ready to go*, the gesture said.

Armstrong keyed his wrist mike. "Bring Monitor around."

Bobby Davenport wheeled the armored Navigator slowly around the drive and stopped a short distance from the stage, as Stovall and his entourage moved in its direction.

Covering their backs, "Dapper" Don Romanowski watched the crowd as Armstrong, the governor, and Paul Fleming loaded up and the SUV headed away in the direction of the Mansion.

"Mister, are you a bodyguard?" asked a small boy, gazing up at Romanowski. It was a question he had been asked many times before by small children at events for the governor.

Romanowski thought about it and grinned. He squatted down in front of the youngster, whom he judged to be about seven. "Oh, I'm much more than just a bodyguard, son. I'm part warrior, magician, diplomat, historian, map-reader, scout, and strategist. I can plunge an orderly world into chaos or bring order to a chaotic world. And when my buddies and I are really clicking," he winked at the boy, "we can produce thunder and lightning from a clear sky."

The boy frowned, "I don't know what that means, sir."

Romanowski gently tapped the boy on the forehead with his index finger. "'Open the pod bay doors, Hal.'"

The famous movie line went right over the boy's head. His look grew more confused. "My name is Nate. I don't know anyone named Hal. You're weird, mister."

Romanowski squeezed the boy's shoulder and gave him a patient smile. "Yes, Nate, I'm a bodyguard." He scanned the crowd around them with a look of resignation and sighed. "Don't worry, son, most of these people don't understand us either."

Author's Afterword

According to Plutarch, Alexander the Great concluded: "It is men who endure toil and dare dangers that achieve glorious deeds, and it is a lovely thing to live with courage and to die leaving behind an everlasting renown." This book is a tribute, a tribute to the everlasting renown of people who protect public figures all over the world.

Why do bodyguards lay their lives on the line for another person? An even more intriguing question is one that Leech asks of Armstrong: "Why would bodyguards lay their lives on the line for a pathetic person, whom they distrust, differ from ideologically, and don't particularly like?" The answer, I feel, lies in the exchange between David Armstrong and Patricia Stovall in Chapter 75. They do it because it is what they believe in. Powerful but pathetic men like Governor Stovall certainly exist. The Stovall character in the book represents the worst kind of protectee: a self-absorbed, insensitive elitist with a carefully orchestrated image, who must hide his arrogance, his immorality, and his driving ambition, all of which would sink him politically.

I've always been an avid reader, and one thing I've noticed is that the selfless service and hazardous assignments carried out by security agents, often under difficult circumstances, has seldom been captured with any degree of accuracy in the literary world. This book was meant to help fill that void.

Go on . . . run down to your nearest book store and pick up any novel dealing with bodyguards or assassins. First of all, you'll find the shelves glutted with books on assassins, but few are about the people hired to stop assassins. Bodyguards are often mentioned in the storyline, but are seldom the focus of the story, and rarer still is the bodyguard who displays any degree of competence. Most are anti-heroes who break every rule in the protective book, try to do it all alone, and only manage to save the principal by wildly diving through the air at the last moment. This is not to say these books are not popular or entertaining, merely that they do not portray the real world of executive protection.

Most "assassin" novels are the same: Lone assassin stalks VIP; hero stalks assassin; hero is discredited and becomes outcast; hero figures out plot; against all odds, hero lunges in at last moment and foils assassination in front of incompetent bodyguards. You never read: Hero figures out assassination plot; hero picks up cell-phone and calls bodyguard; bodyguard lunges in and saves VIP.

In the real world, public figures are faced with hazardous situations every day. Stalkers, inappropriate or threatening communications, and unwelcome approaches are all part of public life today. Security personnel are paid to screen the environment surrounding the public figure and intercept or neutralize those hazards. Unlike the lone assassin in most popular novels, any real threat to the safety or well-being of the public figure will be masked by a thousand false alerts. One of the major frustrations of every bodyguard is that their sound security procedures are often sabotaged by the public figure him- or herself. Few authors have been able to capture the essence of an authentic protective operation. If you enjoyed this book, I'd recommend reading Tom Clancy's *Executive Orders*; J.C Pollack's *Threat Case*; Vince Flynn's *Transfer of Power*, *Memorial Day*, and *Act of Treason*; Lee Child's *Without Fail*; David Morrell's *The Fifth Profession*; or Greg Rucka's series, *Keeper*, *Finder*, *Smoker*, and *Critical Space*. These are a few of the men who nailed the protection profession.

A highly trained, professional unit of security personnel, moving their protectee smoothly and safely through a hazardous environment, is a thing of beauty. It's like watching Picasso paint, Mario Andretti drive, or Tiger Woods putt. Those readers who are professionals in the business know what I mean. This book is for you, my brothers and sisters.

—*Thomas A. Taylor*

About the Author

Thomas Taylor's involvement in protective operations began in 1974, when he was assigned to the Governor's Security Division with the Missouri State Highway Patrol. He served on the protective details of four different governors, eventually rising to Commander of the Governor's Security Division for eight years. He has been part of the protective operations for the Pope, Mikhail Gorbachev, Margaret Thatcher, Henry Kissinger, and every U.S. President since Gerald Ford, handling protective assignments in Russia, Japan, Korea, China, Ireland, India, Italy, Turkey, and Puerto Rico.

Following the September 11 attacks, Thomas Taylor was named the Patrol's Anti-Terrorism Coordinator. After leaving the Patrol, he headed a team of antiterrorism specialists that evaluated the vulnerabilities of Missouri's most critical assets.

Taylor served two terms as president of the National Governors Security Association (NGSA). In that capacity, he was Senior Security Consultant for the National Governors Association (NGA) in Washington DC and helped formulate security plans for NGA events nationwide.

Thomas Taylor has trained hundreds of people in dignitary protection and survival tactics, and is a regular instructor at the Advanced Threat Assessment and Management Academy at UCLA'S Conference Center. After a nationwide search of protection experts, Taylor was selected to serve on the Development Team for the MOSAIC Threat Assessment System currently used by the U.S. Supreme Court, the CIA, the U.S. Marshals Service, and agencies protecting governors of twelve states. Thomas Taylor currently works as Special Projects Advisor for Gavin de Becker and Associates, a firm that advises and protects high-risk public figures. He served as detail leader for the large security team protecting Arnold Schwarzenegger during his campaign for governor of California.

The Institute of Police Technology and Management (IPTM) in Florida published Taylor's book, *Dodging Bullets: A Strategic Guide to World-Class Protection*, in 2000. The book has been reviewed by top public-figure protection groups all over the world, including the

International Bodyguard Association (IBA) in Ireland, the Worldwide Federation of Bodyguards (WFB) in Great Britain, and the Close Quarters Protection Operators Association (CQPOA) in the United States. His name appears in the acknowledgments of Gavin de Becker's bestsellers *The Gift of Fear* and *Fear Less*, and also the 1998 Secret Service report, *Protective Intelligence and Threat Assessment Investigations*, for his assistance in reviewing these documents. In 2007, Taylor co-authored a groundbreaking book on public-figure protection, *Just Two Seconds: Using Time and Space to Defeat Assassins*. He is currently working on a sequel to *Mortal Shield*.